When the mo
himself to the
on one big shoulder, rolled, and managed to get out one of his
revolvers.

The weapon really wasn't necessary; one hundred ninety-three pounds of canine fury flew through the air and hit the armed man sitting on the horse. When man and dog landed, the animal gnawed on the man's arm. All the outlaw's frantic attempts to evade the deadly, insistent teeth were useless.

Culpepper rose to his feet. "Bear," he called. "Let him be, now. Come on."

The huge, dark-fawn-colored mastiff took one last, lingering taste of the man's arm, then backed off, still snarling ferociously. He stopped next to Culpepper, who patted the big beast on the head. "Good boy."

ZEBRA'S HEADING WEST!

with GILES, LEGG, PARKINSON, LAKE, KAMMEN, and MANNING

KANSAS TRAIL (3517, $3.50/$4.50)
by Hascal Giles
After the Civil War ruined his life, Bennett Kell threw in his lot with a gang of thievin' guntoughs who rode the Texas-Kansas border. But there was one thing he couldn't steal—fact was, Ada McKittridge had stolen his heart.

GUNFIGHT IN MESCALITO (3601, $3.50/$4.50)
by John Legg
Jubal Crockett was a young man with a bright future—until that Mescalito jury found him guilty of murder and sentenced him to hang. Jubal'd been railroaded good and the only writ of habeus corpus was a stolen key to the jailhouse door and a fast horse!

DRIFTER'S LUCK (3396, $3.95/$4.95)
by Dan Parkinson
Byron Stillwell was a drifter who never went lookin' for trouble, but trouble always had a way of findin' him. Like the time he set that little fire up near Kansas to head off a rogue herd owned by a cattle baron named Dawes. Now Dawes figures Stillwell owes him something . . . at the least, his life.

MOUNTAIN MAN'S VENGEANCE (3619, $3.50/$4.50)
by Robert Lake
The high, rugged mountain made John Henry Trapp happy. But then a pack of gunsels thundered across his land, burned his hut, and murdered his squaw woman. Trapp hit the vengeance trail and ended up in jail. Now he's back and how that mountain has changed!

BIG HORN HELLRIDERS (3449, $3.50/$4.50)
by Robert Kammen
Wyoming was a tough land and toughness was required to tame it. Reporter Jim Haskins knew the Wyoming tinderbox was about to explode but he didn't know he was about to be thrown smack-dab in the middle of one of the bloodiest range wars ever.

TEXAS BLOOD KILL (3577, $3.50/$4.50)
by Jason Manning
Ol' Ma Foley and her band of outlaw sons were cold killers and most folks in Shelby County, Texas knew it. But Federal Marshal Jim Gantry was no local lawman and he had his guns cocked and ready when he rode into town with one of the Foley boys as his prisoner.

Available wherever paperbacks are sold, or order direct from the Publisher. Send cover price plus 50¢ per copy for mailing and handling to Zebra Books, Dept. 4440, 475 Park Avenue South, New York, N.Y. 10016. Residents of New York and Tennessee must include sales tax. DO NOT SEND CASH. For a free Zebra/Pinnacle catalog please write to the above address.

SHERIFF'S BLOOD
John Legg

ZEBRA BOOKS
KENSINGTON PUBLISHING CORP.

*For Wally and Keira Dirmyer:
I'm privileged
to have two
such very special
friends.*

ZEBRA BOOKS are published by

Kensington Publishing Corp.
475 Park Avenue South
New York, NY 10016

Copyright © 1994 by John Legg

All rights reserved. No part of this book may be reproduced in any form or by any means without the prior written consent of the Publisher, excepting brief quotes used in reviews.

If you purchased this book without a cover you should be aware that this book is stolen property. It was reported as "unsold and destroyed" to the Publisher and neither the Author nor the Publisher has received any payment for this "stripped book."

Zebra and the Z logo Reg. U.S. Pat & TM Off.

First Printing: January, 1994

Printed in the United States of America

Chapter 1

Jonas Culpepper told his companion to stay where he was, and then he stepped into the clearing amidst the tall pines of a small flat on a windswept peak in the San Juan Mountains of Colorado. He strode through the shallow, slushy covering of snow toward the small fire with the small, thin man hunched over it.

The man at the fire suddenly realized he was not alone, and he turned, unafraid—until he saw the powerfully bulky man in the long bear-fur coat. "Sheriff Culpepper!" the small man breathed. He was sparse, frail, and ratty looking, and even in the finest store-bought suit he would have looked seedy and ill-kempt. His face was pale, with that lack of color often seen on men who spent the better part of their lives deep in a hole in the ground, pulling precious metals from the earth's bosom. Graying black stubble covered the lower half of his face, and his hair hung lankly from under his wool cap.

"Here and in person, Wiley," Culpepper said quietly. He almost always spoke quietly, though he could bellow with the best of them when necessary. Still, one look at him and no one would mistake his normally soft voice for weakness. Culpepper was perhaps five-foot-ten and weighed in at around two hundred pounds. He was in his mid-twenties. Shaggy, bright red hair capped his head under his plain, mousy Stetson. His long, thick mustache and small, neatly trimmed beard were of the same hue as his hair. Piercing blue eyes peered out over a short, slightly bulbous nose. He was dressed simply in wool pants over plain boots, a linsey-woolsey-style shirt; and suspenders. His long bear-fur coat was open, exposing the San Juan County sheriff's badge on his chest. He carried two .44-caliber Remingtons in holsters worn high on his hips. A bowie knife was stuck in his gunbelt.

"What're you gonna do with me, Sheriff?" Ferd Wiley asked, voice wobbling, as it usually did, sending out small, spit-laced clouds of mist out as he spoke.

"Take you back to Silverton, boy, what in Hades do you think?"

"They're gonna hang me," Wiley whined.

Culpepper shrugged. "You should've thought of that before you made off with a couple bags full of the Anvil Mining Company's silver."

"It wasn't my doin's, Sheriff. It was Tuck made me do it."

"Speaking of Tuck, where is that pukin' scoundrel?"

Wiley looked a little uncomfortable. "I ain't sure, Sheriff. He took off yesterday, left me settin' here all by my lonesome, with damn near no food or silver."

"You're breakin' my heart, Wiley," Culpepper said easily, not really concerned. He was here to do a job and he planned to do it, hopefully without bloodshed or trouble.

Wiley shrugged, knowing he would get no sympathy from Culpepper. "You mind I have somethin' to eat before we hit the trail? I was just figurin' to have a noon meal. You're welcome to join me, if you want."

"What's on the fire?" Culpepper asked.

"Same ol' shit—bacon, beans, and coffee," Wiley said with a self-deprecating shrug.

"Reckon it won't hurt none. But," Culpepper added dryly, "you'll have to hand over your pistol first. And any other weapons you might have on your person, Mister Wiley."

"That's understandable, Sheriff," Wiley said. "If I . . ." He paused, then suddenly shouted, "Watch it, Sheriff!" He pointed beyond Culpepper.

Culpepper did not hesitate. He might look like a fool, but that was a heap better than being dead, he figured. He shoved himself to the side and dropped into the slush. He landed on one big shoulder and rolled. It took him longer to stop than he had counted on, but when he did, he had managed to get out one of his revolvers.

The weapon wasn't really necessary, as a hundred and ninety-three pounds of dark-fawn brindle mastiff flew through the air and hit the armed man sitting on the horse. When the man and dog landed, the animal gnawed on the man's arm, while he frantically squiggled and scrambled in an attempt to evade the insistent teeth. The horse whinnied and trotted off into the trees.

As Culpepper rose to his feet, he flicked a glance at Wiley. The scrawny criminal had made no move for his pistol. Culpepper moved to where he could keep a wary eye on Wiley while focusing most of his attention on the other.

"Bear," Culpepper called, "let him be, now. Come on."

The mastiff took one last, lingering taste of the man's arm, then backed off, still snarling ferociously. He stopped next to Culpepper, who patted the big beast on the head.

"Good boy, Bear," Culpepper praised the dog. He looked at the man the mastiff had attacked. "Get up there, maggot," he commanded. When the man had, holding a bloody arm and staring fearfully at the dog, Culpepper said, "Well, if it isn't that old rascal Tucker Reynolds. Glad you could join us, Tuck." Despite the evenly spoken words, there was no friendship whatsoever in Culpepper's voice.

"Eat shit, ya stinkin' law dog," Reynolds snapped.

"Such language," Culpepper chided. "You keep it up and I'll have Bear come chew on you some more."

"You keep that goddamn shit-eatin' monster away from me, you bastard."

"Well, you got the monster part wrong, but I agree he was eatin' shit," Culpepper said dryly, using one of his very rare profanities. Then he sighed, as if overwhelmed by troubles.

"But I can see that politeness isn't going to work with you," he added, almost to himself. "Such a pity, boy." He shot Reynolds in the right ankle.

"Holy shit!" Reynolds screamed, as he fell. Clutching his shattered ankle, he half raised himself and glared at Culpepper. "You whoremongerin' asswipe," he cursed, his voice filled with vehemence.

"It'd serve you well, boy, to remember that I'm the biggest toad in this here damn puddle," Culpepper responded calmly. "And if you keep on smart-mouthin' me, boy, I'll be happy to pile on the agony for you."

"Kiss my ass, you festerin' pile of hog shit."

Culpepper shook his head. It never ceased to amaze him how foolish people could be. He briefly considered putting a bullet into Reynolds' heart, but Culpepper was a man who took no joy in killing, and he avoided it whenever possible. He also pondered momentarily shooting Reynolds in the other leg, but he decided it would be all the more work for him getting Reynolds back to Silverton. He finally settled for walking over to Reynolds and kicking him in the injured ankle. "I can do this all day, if you'd like," he said evenly.

"God damn it, you dumb son . . ." He stopped in a hurry when Culpepper kicked the ankle again. When he was able to speak again, he said, "I think I've had enough for now."

"A pleasure to hear, Mister Reynolds." He put his pistol away, then reached down, grabbed the front of Reynolds' coat, and pulled him up. "Now, what say we take your pistols and get rid of them and then mosey on over to the fire? Mister Wiley's invited us to break bread with him for the nooning hour."

Reynolds said nothing; he just concentrated on making sure he did not put his right foot down.

Culpepper swiftly pulled Reynolds' two pistols and dropped them at his feet. Then he checked Reynolds over, finding secreted in an inside pocket of his coat a derringer, a pocketknife, and a large butcher knife. All got dropped on the ground. "All right, Mister Reynolds," Culpepper said. "Let's go."

"I can't walk, Sheriff," Reynolds whined.

"Then hop, skip or jump, I don't much care which." Keeping a grip on Reynolds' coat, Culpepper turned and started off, tugging the man with him.

"Jesus, Mary, and Joseph," Reynolds gasped, as he was forced to use the smashed ankle. Then he got into a rhythm of hopping, grateful at least that Culpepper was not going too fast.

Culpepper eased him down in a relatively dry spot, and one without anything near enough to grab to use as a weapon.

"What'n the goddamn hell'd you have to go warnin' him for, Ferd?" Reynolds questioned Wiley.

Wiley was uncomfortable and would not look at Reynolds. He said nothing.

"Wouldn't have made no difference," Culpepper said. "Bear was back in the trees and would've done just what he did whether Wiley'd said anything or not."

"Damn dog," Reynolds muttered.

"Watch him, Bear," Culpepper said with a small grin in Reynolds's direction just before he turned toward Wiley.

Bear growled low and deep, his wrinkled, droopy face seemingly hopeful that Reynolds would try something.

"Your weapons, please, Mister Wiley," Culpepper said.

After watching the way Culpepper had treated Reynolds, Ferd Wiley was eager to obey.

Culpepper took the pistol, belly gun, and medium-sized knife and then gathered up Reynolds' weapons. "I'll be back momentarily, gentlemen," he said. "Bear'll keep an eye on you for me. Mister Wiley, I suggest you see to your pots and pans."

He returned minutes later with his horse. Seeing that Reynolds' horse was not there, he mounted up and rode off. He was back before long, and he tied both horses to a tree.

"Soup's on, Sheriff," Wiley said.

Culpepper nodded and headed to the fire. He sat on a log and ate quietly, quickly. He had eaten better before, but he'd eaten a lot worse, too. The food was hot and filling, which was all he could expect from it.

9

Culpepper decided while he was eating that he'd spend the night here. A fire was made, there was firewood stacked up, and they had food. Reynolds' leg would need at least minimal tending, and he himself was tired. He'd been on the trail of these two men for the better part of a week. He wasn't all that far from Silverton, but he'd gone in circles trying to track the two men.

After finishing his meal—and a last leisurely cup of coffee—Culpepper unsaddled his and Reynolds' horses and tended them both.

"We stayin' here, Sheriff?" Wiley asked, when Culpepper had returned to his seat by the fire.

Culpepper nodded. He had brought a small piece of rolled-up canvas with him. He unrolled it, revealing a haunch of deer. He pulled out his big knife, sliced off several sizable chunks, and fed one to Bear. While the dog bolted that one down, Culpepper rewrapped the meat. Then he leisurely fed the mastiff the rest of what he'd cut.

When the dog had finished wolfing it down, Culpepper gave the animal some water poured into his hat. Then Bear lay with his jaw on one of Culpepper's thighs while Culpepper stroked the massive dog's head between the ears.

Finally Culpepper roused himself and stood. He went to his saddlebags and pulled out two sets of handcuffs. He cuffed Reynolds with his hands behind his back. He knew it was a lot more uncomfortable for the outlaw, but Culpepper was not about to open himself up to getting hammered by Reynolds while he tried to do something for Reynolds' ankle.

Culpepper shackled Wiley, hands in front, and then warned him, "You make a move against me, Wiley, and you'll suffer a heap more than Reynolds has done."

"I ain't plannin' nothin'," Wiley said sullenly.

"Good. After all, you did try to warn me about your pukin' scoundrel of a pal there. Since you did that, I might be disposed toward speakin' less ill of you before Judge Pfeiffer when we get back to Silverton."

"I told you to keep your goddamn mouth shut, Ferd, you egg-suckin' little asswipe, you."

Culpepper kicked the bottom of Reynolds' right boot. "That'll be enough of that out of you, boy," he said, with an edge to his voice. He looked back at Wiley. "You just set there, Ferd, whilst I work on your old friend here." He pointed at Reynolds.

Culpepper endured Reynolds' screeching for a few minutes before he got tired of it, and he thumped the outlaw on the head with a pistol butt. It didn't quite knock Reynolds out, but it made him groggy enough that he was relatively quiet. Culpepper cursed himself silently for having shot Reynolds in the ankle. Had he just shot him in the leg, it would've been ever so much easier to fashion a splint. But he persevered, and at last sat back. He wasn't real pleased with his handiwork, but he figured it would hold Reynolds for the three days or so it would take to get back to Silverton.

He cleaned up and then washed his hands off in some of the cleaner snow crowded up against the north side of a boulder. Then he got a bottle of small bottle of whiskey. Back at the fire, he filled a mug with coffee, added a dose of whiskey, and handed it to a grateful Ferd Wiley. Then Culpepper prepared the same concoction for himself and sat back on the log.

Once Culpepper was settled in, Bear disappeared, but the mastiff came trotting back soon enough, looking pleased with himself.

Reynolds came around after a while, looking around angrily. Culpepper fixed him a whiskey-coffee and allowed Wiley to hold it for Reynolds to drink. Reynolds was surprised that Culpepper had given him some whiskey, but he was too angry and too proud to speak his thanks.

Chapter 2

Three days of traveling with a crotchety Tucker Reynolds came nearabout to driving Culpepper to do something drastic, but he managed to contain his temper. Mostly. There were a few times during the journey when Culpepper allowed just a bit of his ire to show. After several good whacks on the head, Reynolds began to realize that his smart mouth was going to get him killed. The final day heading into Silverton was the quietest.

Along the way, Ferd Wiley took a heap of abuse from Reynolds, most of it profane but very quiet. Reynolds would blister Wiley in the evenings, after dinner.

Finally Culpepper had gotten tired of that, too. "Keep spoutin' off, Tuck," he said with a little grin on the second night out, "and I'll let Ferd loose on you."

"You're fulla shit, ya dumb, badge-wearin' skunk," Reynolds snarled. He was tired after two days of sitting with his hands bound behind him, having to be helped on and off his horse, and whatnot. About the only time his hands were free was when he was eating or relieving himself. In the former instance, Culpepper was always somewhere behind him, and Reynolds knew the sheriff had a gun in hand. In the latter, Culpepper also was right nearby, nonchalantly holding a pistol.

Still with a small, hard smile on his lips, Culpepper stood quietly and uncuffed Wiley. Leaving Reynolds with his hands handcuffed behind his back, Culpepper said, "Mister Wiley, he's yours to thump, if you're of a mind."

"It's temptin', Sheriff," Wiley said. "But I don't suppose it'd shut that foolish bastard up."

"Hah!" Reynolds snorted. "See, ya damn fool sheriff? He ain't nothin' but a chickenshit asswipe is all. I told ya, damn it, but you don't never listen to me, no."

"Well, Mister Wiley," Culpepper said flatly, "perhaps you don't mind listenin' to this pukin' scoundrel's drivel, but I do." He went to the supplies, grabbed something and then walked to Reynolds.

"Don't you come near me with that gag, goddamn you," Reynolds screeched. "Don't you dare . . ."

With some joy, but more relief, Culpepper jammed the cloth into Reynolds' mouth and knotted it tightly behind Reynolds' head. Reynolds jerked his head and shoulders, trying to get away from the insistent gag, but to no avail.

Culpepper wiped his hands together in exaggerated satisfaction. "Well, Ferd, time for your cuffs again."

"You gotta, Sheriff?"

"Yep," Culpepper said with no apology. He slapped the handcuffs back on Wiley's hands. He poured himself some coffee and sat. "Have some, if you want," he said to Wiley. When the scrawny outlaw had gotten himself some, Culpepper asked, "Why didn't you thump the bejesus out of Tuck when you had the chance?"

Wiley shrugged. "I wasn't ever much of a violent man, Sheriff. Nor was I ever one to whomp on the defenseless."

Culpepper nodded. He wasn't sure whether to believe Wiley, but it could be true. Even if it wasn't, it really didn't matter any.

Culpepper finally removed the gag from Reynolds' mouth for breakfast the next morning. After eating, Reynolds made a short but exceedingly profane harangue of both Culpepper and Wiley. Less than a minute into it, Culpepper rose, gag in hand.

Reynolds shut up in a hurry, but that did not stop Culpepper. Seeing that he was going to be gagged no matter what he did,

Reynolds got in a few last foul verbal blasts at Culpepper and Wiley before the knotted piece of cloth cut him off.

The ride that day was considerably more peaceful than the previous one had been, and Culpepper was grateful for that. While he was a big, powerful man, caring for three horses and two prisoners—even including one who could do much for himself—was tiring. Doing it with a crazy man ranting and raving half the time made it all the harder.

As they had since the beginning, the men rode single-file along the narrow mountain trail. Wiley was at the head, his hands cuffed in front of him, his legs free. Reynolds came next, hands cuffed behind his back, his feet bound with rope that ran under the horse's belly. He had to control the horse's movements with his knees, something hard enough to do at the best of times. Culpepper came last so he could keep an eye on his two prisoners. He was not really worried about them trying to run—he figured Wiley was too scared, and Reynolds would have a tough time maneuvering his horse around Wiley. There was always Bear for the outlaws to contend with, too. The huge dog trotted placidly alongside Culpepper's horse.

That night, it seemed as if Reynolds had learned his lesson. When Culpepper removed the gag from the outlaw's mouth, Reynolds continued to glower at the lawman, but he kept his silence, except for requests and a small bit of conversation, all in a normal tone of voice. Because of that, Culpepper allowed Reynolds to ride without the gag the next day.

Shortly after noon, the three came around another of the seemingly interminable bends in the trail and they looked out over Silverton in the small valley below. It took them just over an hour more to make their way down into the valley.

They all stopped in front of the San Juan County Jail. It was an impressive-looking place built of granite blocks unadorned by paint, trim, or fancification. One the south side was Culpepper's office. It was made of logs, but one couldn't tell that from the front, since that was covered by a plank false front.

Culpepper dismounted, as did Wiley. Both tied their horses

to the hitching rail in front of the jail. "Wait there, Ferd," Culpepper ordered, pointing to the wood sidewalk. When Wiley had stepped up onto the boards and stood waiting, Culpepper took the reins to Reynolds' horse and led the animal away from the others a little so he had some working room.

Culpepper untied the rope from Reynolds' injured ankle. Before Culpepper could even drop the end of the rope, Reynolds kicked out with his injured leg. His boot caught Culpepper in the face. The kick had little leverage, and caused Culpepper nothing more than a split lip—and a quick burst of anger.

Culpepper yanked the rope hard. It seared across the horse's belly and jerked Reynolds off the far side of the horse. Reynolds' foot stuck in the stirrup and remained there as the horse, frightened and in pain, bolted and raced off up the alley between Blair and Mineral Streets. Reynolds screamed as he bounced along in the dirt and slush on his upper back and the back of his head. The panicked horse whirled right onto Thirteenth Street.

"Idiot," Culpepper muttered. He looked at Wiley. "Watch that old cuss, Bear," he said, as he started to run. He stopped at Thirteenth Street and looked up the thoroughfare. Two men were standing in the slush-muddy street in front of a couple of cribs rented by some of Blair Street's fallen angels. They heard the commotion and looked up. Seeing what was happening, they ran into the street and managed to stop the horse.

Coattails whipping along in the wind, Culpepper marched up the street. He pulled Reynolds' foot out of the stirrup and dropped it. Then he reached down, grabbed the front of Reynolds's coat, and hauled him to his feet. "Thanks for your help, gentlemen," he said to the two men who had stopped the animal. "I'd be obliged if you was to take that horse on up to the Exchange livery."

One of the two men looked about ready to argue, but the other nodded and said, "Sure, Sheriff." Both turned and walked away, leading the horse up the street.

"And make sure it gets to the durn livery," Culpepper added. "It don't, I'll hunt you rascals down."

Both men nodded rather glumly before heading off again.

"Jail's that way, Tuck," Culpepper said evenly, giving Reynolds a moderate shove on the shoulder. Reynolds reluctantly hobbled toward the jail.

When they got there, town Marshal Wes Hennessy was waiting, a ring of keys in his hand. Culpepper and Hennessy did not get along all that well. Culpepper considered Hennessy to be a useless dandy who was more interested in drinking at the Greene Street saloons or visiting the Blair Street whorehouses than in catching lawbreakers. He also was fond of sitting around while his six policemen did most of the work. He considered himself a truly generous man, seeing as how he allowed his deputies to keep sixty percent of the fines they were allowed to assess, while keeping only forty percent.

"Got them robbers, did ya, Jonas?" he asked in his high-pitched warble. Hennessy was only in his late thirties, not more than ten years or so Culpepper's senior, but he seemed infinitely older. He was relatively tall, and fairly thin. With the store-bought suits he always wore, his neatly trimmed, gray-speckled mustache and beard, and his faded yellow hair, he looked almost elegant. He did consider himself something of a dandy, and with the amount of fines he collected—or rather, his deputies collected for him—he could afford to dress well.

"Yep, Wes, I did," Culpepper said patiently. Though he did not get along with Hennessy, he could see no reason to be rude to the man—unless it became necessary.

"Thought you might need these," Hennessy said, holding out the ring of keys.

"Obliged," Culpepper said with a nod. He opened the heavy iron door. While the jail was sturdy and almost impossible to break out of, there were times Culpepper hated it, what with the huge lock on the front door and the four locks on each of the cells inside. When he had the door open, he stepped back. Looking at Reynolds and Wiley, he said, "Inside. Both of you."

He went inside just behind the two. He struck a match to light the lantern on the wall next to the door. It relieved the darkness, but not the gloominess. The jailhouse was a little bit wider than it was long, with a small anteroom in front that held only a stove to be used for warmth. A six-foot-wide corridor ran up the right, leading to the indoor water closet. The corridor had two locked, barred doors at right angles to each other. There were only two cells, each fairly spacious, with a small vertical window with two iron bars embedded deep into the stone walls at top and bottom. There was another similar, though rather larger, window in the wall running along the corridor to the water closet. A pump for water was situated on the left-hand stone wall, centered on the edge of each cell, within reach of the prisoners. The "walls" between the cells were nothing but bars, so that with one look inside the door, every prisoner could be seen. Each cell had an iron cot bolted to the stone wall and the stone floor. On every bunk lay a thin straw-filled tick.

Culpepper had his prisoners stand facing the cells as he unlocked the corridor doors. Hennessy followed them inside, which normally would have irritated him. It didn't now, though, since it meant an extra set of eyes on the two prisoners. As Culpepper directed Reynolds and Wiley into the corridor, he stopped and looked back. "Do me a favor, Wes," he said, "go and fetch Doc McQuiston to look at Reynolds here." He was relieved when Hennessy immediately did as he was asked.

He uncuffed Reynolds and placed him in the cell nearest the door; an uncuffed Wiley went into the one at the rear. Then Culpepper left, taking the keys with him. Outside, he grabbed the two canvas bags of stolen silver and carried them into his office. He hung the keys on a peg behind his cramped messy desk, and then put the silver in the safe against the wall. He had just sat at his desk to begin doing the paperwork related to the two arrests when Hennessy and McQuiston entered.

"You have a patient for me?" the physician asked. He was a short, plump man of about fifty. His creased, open face usually brimmed with joy, and his hazel eyes glittered with life and amusement. Culpepper liked McQuiston a considerable lot.

Culpepper nodded. "Tucker Reynolds. Cell nearest the door."

"What's wrong with him?"

"Broke ankle, to start with. I had to shoot him."

McQuiston nodded, not finding any reason to argue with that. "Anything else?"

"Well, you might give him a good lookin' over." He explained quickly about the incident with the horse.

McQuiston nodded again. "Well," he said with an exaggerated sigh of fatigue, "I'd best get to it."

"Send your bill to me, Doc," Culpepper said as he led the physician to the jail.

"Don't I always?" McQuiston said with a laugh.

Culpepper went through unlocking the corridor doors and then the cell doors, once more annoyed at all the work it was. He waited patiently, leaning against the bars, eyes watchful, as McQuiston examined Reynolds and tended to his various injuries.

When the doctor was done, Culpepper saw him out, and said goodbye. His annoyance grew when he saw that Hennessy was still waiting in the office, having made himself comfortable in a chair.

"How'd you catch them?" Hennessy asked, as Culpepper settled into the creaking chair behind his desk.

"Wasn't hard," Culpepper responded, trying to keep the irritation out of his voice. "Look, Wes," he added. "I've got to write up the arrests, then go take care of the horses and make arrangements for those two scoundrels to be fed. And all before I get to fill my own belly and go see Merry. I don't aim to be rude, but I really need to get this nonsense done."

Hennessy nodded in understanding. "Sorry, Jonas," he said, rising. "Didn't mean to take up your time."

"That's all right," Culpepper said, wondering if Hennessy

really was hurt or if was just acting the role. Then he decided he didn't much care one way or the other.

Culpepper went back to his paperwork before Hennessy was even out the door. He hated doing it, but it was necessary—or so the county officials told him. The only thing he hated worse about his job was running for office. He was a lawman, he had told people more than once, not a pencil pusher or a politician. But he doggedly persisted with the paperwork and eventually finished.

Chapter 3

Culpepper pulled on his coat and went outside. He stopped for a few moments, savoring the chilly air of this high mountain valley surrounded by towering, rugged peaks. Winter was a hellacious time in Silverton, with foot upon foot of snow piling up, and temperatures more often than not down below zero. But Culpepper liked this time of year, as winter grudgingly gave way to spring. He liked it almost as much as he liked autumn, with the aspen leaves blazing in color, and the world beginning to prepare for the winter to come.

Sighing, Culpepper mounted his horse. With Bear trotting alongside, he rode to the Exchange livery up on Silverton's main thoroughfare, Greene Street, leading Wiley's horse behind him. Rather than tend to the two horses, plus Reynolds', himself, Culpepper paid Art Cassidy's nine-year-old son, Jamie, fifty cents to do it.

Then Culpepper went to Moldovan's restaurant a couple doors down from the livery and told Eleni Moldovan about the two prisoners over at the jail.

"I'll feed them," Eleni said with a firm nod. She was a short, stout, but still pretty middle-aged woman of uncertain—to Culpepper—lineage. She seemed to have unlimited energy, and she also seemed to be at the restaurant twenty-four hours a day.

"I thought you would," Culpepper said, smiling tiredly. "I expect Jimmy'll be around the office to let you in," he said of his deputy, Jimmy Cahill. "If he ain't, you send someone over to the house and get me."

"Don't you worry none about it, Sheriff," Eleni said. "We'll make do."

Culpepper finally turned toward home. The thought of being with his Merry pushed some of the tiredness off him and his steps picked up a little speed. In the early days, he used to send someone to the house to tell Merry that he was back in town and would be home soon. But he had learned over the years that she somehow knew. He wondered how, and had finally decided that she had a network of spies who reported his every movement to her. He knew the thought was ludicrous, but he'd told it to Merry once, and she had laughed raucously at it.

As always, Merry was watching out the door for him as he crossed the small bridge over Cement Creek. When his boot hit the first of the three steps up to the porch, Merry flung open the door and rushed into his arms.

The sheriff happily engulfed her in his big, strong embrace as Bear danced around looking for attention.

"People must think I'm a shameless trollop," Merry said a few minutes later, after she had allowed Culpepper into the house.

"Ain't a one of them got the nerve," Culpepper said honestly. "Besides, I'm the only one you got to worry who's thinkin' anything of you."

"And are you?" she asked, her soft brown eyes gazing intently into his piercing blue ones.

"All the time."

She kissed him quickly on the lips. "Thank you," she said simply. "Now come, take off your coat. I've got chicken and dumplings all set. And fresh bread for soppin' up with."

"Food can wait," he growled. He wanted her, and deeply. She was as pretty to him as she had been the day they'd met almost eight years ago. She was tall for a woman, though shy of his height by several inches. She had a good, strong bone structure and a straight back. Her face was broad and pretty, but more in a plain way than in an ostentatious one. Her dark brown hair was her pride, and it grew long and silky, though she most often had it pinned up in some sort of bun. She was smaller of bosom than most women of her general size and age, but that didn't bother Culpepper any. He was perfectly satisfied with the way Merry filled out her simple calico dresses.

She giggled. From her, it was not a silly sound, but one loaded with huskiness and desire. She lusted after Jonas Culpepper as much now as she had when she had first married him seven years ago. She had been afraid then to let him know she had desires, but as she'd come to know Culpepper better in a wifely way, she knew he would not be shocked or disgusted at her letting him know she had desires. Still, over the years she had learned restraint, and now knew that if they waited just a little, their intimate time would be so much more pleasurable. "There's time for that later," she said, her voice betraying her desire just a little.

"Durn," Culpepper said in mock anger. "I should've just gone over to Mabel Pierce's place over on Blair Street."

"You can do that, if you want," Merry said with a nod, her lips curled in a small smile, certain in the love of her man. "But if you do, you'd best take all your belongin's with you and stay there, for I shan't let you in this house again."

"Lord, woman," Culpepper said, feigning peevishness, "you sure know how to spoil a man's good time."

"I want to see if you can say the same thing tomorrow morning," Merry said brassily. "Now, take off your coat and wash up for supper."

"Yes'm."

Merry allowed him another small kiss on the mouth—just enough to keep him interested—before she went back to setting the table.

It still amazed her in some ways that Culpepper loved her and desired her as much as he did. His want of her had not lessened over the years.

Merriam English and Jonas Culpepper had come a long way

in the time they had known each other. The darkest days were the times their children had died. Their first, Jonas Junior, had died in infancy of scarlet fever. Three years later, their daughter had succumbed to diphtheria just before her second birthday. She had been distraught when Junior died, but when little Cecille was taken from her, Merry was devastated, thinking herself a powerful sinner to have been punished so. She thought for sure Culpepper would leave her then, and she girded herself for that crushing blow. But he had not. He had been a strong comfort to her in those mournful days, and his love and desire for her never wavered. Soon after Cecille's death, Culpepper moved them from the flat plains of eastern Colorado up here to the high mountains, figuring the change of scenery and neighbors would do her some good. Eventually she overcame most of her grief, aided by her husband's unwavering love and support. Still, she grew melancholy at times, since there had been no other children to bless their lives, though not from lack of trying. At such times, she thought herself not much of a woman, though Culpepper didn't seem to mind.

Merry found herself standing there staring at her man, and she shook herself out of the reverie to get back to her work.

Culpepper pulled off the heavy bear-fur coat and hung it on a peg next to the door. He pulled out his bowie knife and stabbed it into the wall, then unstrapped his gunbelt and hung that on another peg. He rolled up his shirtsleeves as he headed for the washbasin. By the time he had cleaned himself off some, Merry had the table set and the food served. With increasing hunger, Culpepper sat.

When he finished, Culpepper felt good, but sleepy. He had known that would happen. It was why he wanted to take Merry into the bedroom earlier, before the exhaustion hit him.

Merry could see it, but she was not worried. She thought she could revive him, given half a chance. And she intended to make sure she got that chance. "Go and shave and clean up a little, Jonas," she said quietly. "I'll clean up here and then make myself ready." After their years of being married, she could say such things boldly, without even blushing.

Culpepper smiled and nodded. He got water in a basin, his shaving soap, and a straight razor. He brought it all back to the table and then propped up a mirror against a coffeepot. Finally he sat and began to shave. When he finished that, he cleaned his teeth and then sat back to wait.

Within moments, the bedroom door opened, and Merry stepped out. Her hair was loose and flowed over her shoulders and down to the top of her buttocks. Merry wore a short, thin chemise. She normally used a long chemise as a nightshirt, but this one was rather special. She had ordered it several years ago, to wear it just for Culpepper, after he had been joshing her about the outfits some of the fallen women over on Blair Street wore. The cotton material was so thin that it hid nothing of her charms if there was a light behind her. She always felt rather licentious—but very womanly—on those rare occasions when she put it on. She had no doubt it would revive Culpepper's flagging interest.

She was right. Culpepper's eyes sparkled with lust when he saw her. He stood and moved to her and pulled her gently into his embrace. "It ain't many a man who's got a woman like you to come home to." He couldn't help but think that perhaps if more men did, there'd be less trouble in the world.

"That's true," Merry said with a sudden wave of trepidation. "I don't think many men'd want a woman with such loose morals to come home to."

"Don't you go talkin' that way about yourself, woman," Culpepper said roughly. "You're not a woman with loose morals. You're a woman who loves her husband more than most women know how to. Or want to. And you're not afraid to show it in the privacy of our home. And I durn well like you that way."

Merry smiled as she pressed her cheek against his broad chest, and she squeezed him hard.

"Now," he said huskily, "let's go tend to business."

* * *

24

"You know, Merry," he said later, "you're pretty active for an old married woman."

"Old . . . ? Married, yes, but old . . . ?" Merry protested. She punched him on the chest, doing no more damage to him than a gnat would do to Bear.

"Not only old and married, but feisty, too," Culpepper said with a laugh.

Despite his joshing with her, Merry knew her husband was tired. "Hush, now," she said, pressing a finger to his lips. "You need your rest." She slipped out of bed, naked now, and shivering in the chill of the early spring night. She opened the bedroom door so that Bear could come in and sleep in his accustomed spot on the floor at the foot of the bed. Then she blew out the lantern and hurriedly climbed back into bed. She found warmth—and even more important, comfort—in the strong arms of her man.

As he drifted quickly toward sleep, Culpepper gave thanks again for having Merry as his wife. It was true that most men did not have such a woman. Trouble was, most men—and women even more so—were so bound by convention that they could not enjoy the intimate knowledge of each other without guilt. That, Culpepper thought, was a pity and a shame. Men and women were made to be intimate with each other. The Good Book even said so.

He smiled into the darkness. It was just like him to think about how the world would be if he were in charge of everything. But he knew he could do nothing but live his life as well as he possibly could and let God sort out the way of things.

"Go to sleep, Jonas," Merry said quietly. She could feel the tension in him, and knew he was having a little trouble falling asleep.

"Yes'm," he muttered. But he let the crazy thoughts go, and was soon fast asleep.

Culpepper woke refreshed—and alone. He patted Merry's side of the bed and smiled. She had not been up long. Bear bounced into the room and slobbered on Culpepper's face as the sheriff grinned and petted the huge dog.

A smiling Merry walked into the room, wiping her hands on a cloth. She wore a regular nightshirt, but her hair still hung loose and free. "I got coffee ready," she said.

"Coffee can wait a bit."

"Again?" Merry asked in mock surprise.

"Just get yourself over here, durn you," Culpepper growled.

Merry joyfully did as requested.

Culpepper dressed and then sat eating a leisurely breakfast with Merry. It was something he enjoyed.

Partway through, Deputy Jimmy Cahill showed up and sat for coffee. He had worked with Culpepper since Culpepper had first been appointed, and then elected as county sheriff, and he knew his boss well—including how much Culpepper enjoyed his private breakfasts with Merry. So he reported that he had checked on the prisoners last night and this morning and that there was little else to report. Then he gulped down his coffee, and left.

Finally Culpepper finished his breakfast and stood. He stretched and yawned, then grinned as Merry laughed at him in delight. "Well," he said, "I better get to work. You need me to get anything or do anything while I'm out?"

"Just come home safe," Merry said, as she came around the table to kiss him.

Culpepper nodded. He put on his gunbelt and stuck the knife in it. He slapped on his old hat and, with Bear at his side, headed out.

Chapter 4

In the morning, Culpepper made a tour around town, catching up on what had happened while he had been gone. Nothing much had gone on in Silverton, and things remained quiet. It was still rather early for the action to be too heavy in Silverton. Many of the places closed down over the winter and had not yet reopened.

One of the first things Culpepper did was to hunt out Judge Sam Pfeiffer at the county courthouse and talk to him. Since things were slow, the trial for Tucker Reynolds and Ferd Wiley was scheduled for the next day.

Afterward, Culpepper began making the rounds of the town, stopping in a fair portion of many saloons in Silverton. One reason he did so was because he liked it, but another was that he was trying to avoid Silverton Marshal Wes Hennessy. Though Hennessy spent a substantial portion of every day in the saloons, he had two or three favorites. Culpepper figured that by keeping on the move—and staying out of Hennessy's favorites—he could avoid the town marshal.

Silverton was a booming place, and more and more people were making their homes here all year round, sticking out the harsh winters. With a population of about two thousand five hundred, it had the vast majority of San Juan County's three thousand residents. The city had, at Culpepper's last count, almost thirty saloons, and at least as many brothels, not counting the many smaller cribs. Despite that, the town had numerous respectable families and businesses. Before Culpepper had even arrived in Silverton, an imaginary dividing line had been drawn between the two factions of the town. The line split Greene Street. Most of the brothels, if not the saloons, were on or below the east side of Greene Street, with the respectable places holding the west side of it.

Silverton had grown considerably since Culpepper had been here, since the Denver and Rio Grande Railroad spur had arrived a little more than a year after he had. The narrow-gauge railroad, which ran between Silverton and Durango, fifty miles to the south, had been responsible for bringing in many people, and the town had boomed ever since.

Culpepper's favorite saloon was the Arlington. It had been his favorite even before well-known lawman Wyatt Earp had spent part of last year running the gambling in the place. Culpepper had gotten along well with Earp, finding him an interesting man. Culpepper was glad, though, that Earp had not stayed on too long. Such men brought nothing but trouble, and Culpepper suspected Earp would've been out looking for his job had he stayed on much longer.

While sitting in the Arlington, he was found by Wilson Pennrose, one of the several principals of the Anvil Mining Company. The tall, dapper man in the fine suit grinned when he saw Culpepper sitting at a table, and he hurried over.

"I hear you caught the robbers, Sheriff," Pennrose said as he sat. He waved imperiously at the bartender, and a drink materialized at his elbow a moment later.

The bartender also put another beer in front of Culpepper, who nodded his thanks. "I did," Culpepper said flatly.

"That's good. Very good. When's the trial?"

"Tomorrow."

"Good. Very good." He paused, as if carefully weighing his next words. "Did you find the company's silver?"

"Yep."

"Ah, good. All of it?"

"I expect most was there. Might be a few bucks' worth missin'. I can't be sure."

"Good. Very good. When do I—the company—get the silver back?"

"Whenever the judge—or I—feel like getting it back to you," Culpepper said. He was not about to be pressured by Pennrose or anyone else.

"I'll have to speak to Judge Pfeiffer about that."

"Do so. If he goes and gives me a court order telling me to give the silver back today, you'll get it. If not, you'll wait until the trial's over and done with. But I don't expect he'll be inclined to let you have it back before the trial."

Pennrose scowled, but said nothing. He jolted back the shot of good whiskey and rose. "Well, good day, Sheriff," he said, before turning and walking out.

Culpepper grinned to himself. Pennrose was not happy, and somehow, that made Culpepper feel all the better.

When he left the Arlington an hour later, it was late in the afternoon. He went back to the jail and spent another hour or so talking with Wiley, asking details about the robbery.

"God damn it, Ferd, don't you tell that son of a bitch anything!" Reynolds shouted.

Wiley looked hesitant about speaking, especially under Reynolds' verbal assault. So Culpepper turned his baleful gaze on Reynolds. "I can dig up that old gag again, if you've got a hankerin' to wear it, Tuck," he warned.

"To hell with you, Sheriff."

"You are one fractious skunk, ain't you?" Culpepper said. "I've tried to be nice to you, but . . . well, I'm done with it. Open your mouth again, and I'll put the gag back in your mouth and the cuffs back on your hands."

"Big goddamn deal. You can't do shit to scare me, Sheriff. I'm gonna get sentenced to hang tomorrow. What more can you do to me?" He sounded almost smug.

"I can gag you now and leave you that way through the trial.

Or," Culpepper added after a moment's thought, "I could save the hangman the trouble."

"Shit, sheriff—you didn't drag me all the way back here to kill me yourself. No, sir, you want it to be all nice and legal, as if that makes you somethin' goddamn special."

"It's a fact that I want things legal. On the other hand, you could've tried to jump me while I was checkin' on your welfare, and so I was forced to beat you to death."

"Shit, you still don't scare me."

Culpepper nodded. "What a strong and brave man," he said sarcastically. "But I wonder just how long you'd be that way if I was jumpin' up and down on that stove-up leg of yours."

Reynolds knew from the look in Culpepper's cold blue eyes that the San Juan County sheriff would do what he'd just threatened. He scowled but shut up.

Culpepper leaned a shoulder against the bars and turned his gaze back to Wiley. "Look, Ferd," he said, "I don't know if there's one durn thing I can do to help you at the trial tomorrow. But with the help you've given me already, I promise I'll speak up on your behalf in court. And if you tell me what happened in stealin' that silver, well, I think Judge Pfeiffer'll be disposed to look a little more favorably on you. That's the best I can do, and I think it's going to be the best deal you can get."

Wiley nodded. "There's nothin' much to tell, Sheriff. Tuck and I knew that while the company had most of its silver in the bank's vaults—especially at this time of year—we also knew that there was generally a fair portion of it in their offices up the street there. They usually didn't guard that silver too much. So he talked me into goin' partners with him. You mind I smoke some?" he suddenly asked.

"Not if you have the fixin's. I don't indulge."

"I've got 'em." Wiley made a production of rolling and lighting a cigarette. With it going, he finally said, "We got us half-drunk over at Goode's Saloon and then we snuck up to the company's office that night. We was some surprised to see a goddamn guard. Well, not a guard, really, just one of the company's goddamn clerks, workin' late. Tuck knocked him on the side of the head with his pistol butt. I thought he'd killed him—'til I heard him moan. Then, while I kept a watch out, Tuck filled two small bags with silver."

"Those two bags I took from Tuck?"

Wiley nodded.

"That wouldn't hold you very long."

Wiley shrugged. "We couldn't carry more than that anyway. Besides, that'd be more goddamn money in hand than I've ever seen before. It'd carry me a long ways."

"You must've been more than a little drunk."

Wiley shrugged again. "We got on our horses and lit out. A couple days later, Tuck says he's goin' out to hunt. He's gone for a while, and then I start to wonder. Not bein' a normally suspicious man, it took me a while, but I finally checked our supplies, and goddamn if my share of the silver is gone. Next thing I know, you come walkin' into my camp there."

Culpepper nodded and stood. "Like I said, Ferd, I ain't sure I can do you any good, but I'll give it a try before Judge Pfeiffer tomorrow." He walked out, locking the cell door behind him. He turned back to look at Wiley. "And don't let that pukin' scoundrel over there"—he pointed at Reynolds—"bother you too much tonight. There's not a damn thing he can do to you other than make a lot of noise."

"I'll try to keep that in mind, Sheriff," Wiley said.

Culpepper looked at the pitiful excuse for a man and shook his head as he walked away.

The next morning, Culpepper and Cahill—with Bear tagging along—marched the two handcuffed prisoners the short distance up Fourteenth Street to Greene Street and then up Greene to the County Courthouse. Quite a crowd watched the procession, many of them hooting and laughing.

The courtroom was packed, mostly with men who worked for the Anvil Mining Company. It had been the company's silver that Reynolds and Wiley had taken off with, and they meant to see that justice was done. Wilson Pennrose had a prominent seat in the first row, right behind the prosecutor.

It really didn't take long to find both Tucker Reynolds and Ferd Wiley guilty. The clerk who was knocked out that night—Leroy Monteith—testified and positively identified Tucker, though he was unable to identify Wiley.

Still, Wiley confessed to his part in the robbery, and that, combined with Culpepper's testimony, sealed it. The jury deliberated only forty minutes before they pronounced both men guilty.

Judge Sam Pfeiffer nodded, then announced that he was ready to sentence the two criminals—"Unless any of you've got something to say," he offered as a matter of course. He really didn't think anyone was about to add anything.

"I've got something to say," Culpepper said. "Unless you'd rather I kept my peace."

"If you got somethin' to say, Jonas, you just speak up," Pfeiffer said.

"I know both these miscreants're guilty as all get-out, Judge, but I'd like to speak a few words in defense of Ferd Wiley." He ignored the low buzz of annoyance around the courtroom. "He gave me the details of what happened in the robbery. And he 'fessed up here today. More important, though, at least to me, is that he saved my life. If he hadn't a called out a warnin', Tuck Reynolds would've shot me square in the back."

"That all, Jonas?"

"Yessir."

Pfeiffer nodded. "I'll take that into account." He paused, making sure no one else had anything to add. "I'll be back in a few minutes with the sentences. Court's recessed," he said, trying to mask his annoyance. He had planned to just hand out two death sentences and be done with it. That was what he figured was fair, and it was what the principals of the Anvil Mining Company wanted. Now, Jonas Culpepper had to go speak up in defense of one of the men. That put him on the spot as he was about ready to render his decision. The judge knew that if he ordered Wiley hanged, Culpepper—the best sheriff San Juan County had ever had—would be disgruntled and might just slack off on the job. On the other hand, if Pfeiffer did not order Wiley hanged, then Wilson Pennrose and the other principals of the mining company would be outraged. Pfeiffer did not like being in such a position, but there was no getting out of it now.

Pfeiffer sat at his desk and poured a drink. He raised the glass in something of a salute. "Damn you, Sheriff Jonas Culpepper," he muttered with a lopsided grin before downing the shot. He sat for a while longer, but then rose. There was no putting this off.

Pfeiffer went back into the courtroom and sat. "Reynolds, Wiley, stand up," he ordered. When the prisoners had done so, Pfeiffer said, "Tucker Reynolds, I sentence you to hang by the neck until you're dead. The event'll take place two weeks from tomorrow, at eleven in the morning." He looked at Wiley. "Ferd Wiley, I sentence you to a period of twenty-five years in the state penitentiary. You'll start that sentence as soon as Sheriff Culpepper can get you there, or arrange for you to be brought there. Court's adjourned."

The smacking of the gavel sparked a little outburst of annoyance in the courtroom. Pfeiffer headed for the sanctuary of his office, a sanctuary he figured would be violated in minutes.

Culpepper and Cahill walked the prisoners back to the jail—under the watchful gaze of Silverton's citizenry—where they would be held until their sentences could be carried out.

Chapter 5

It was the biggest entertainment event in Silverton since the previous summer, when the Denver cornet band had come to town to present an evening of music for the rowdy residents of Silverton.

Culpepper and Jimmy Cahill slowly drove a small carriage with Tucker Reynolds between them toward the gallows built behind the county courthouse. As they did, Culpepper figured that everyone who lived in San Juan County must be here. For many, this was something of a festival. Though bits of winter still lurked in the air, or covered the ground, the people knew that spring was coming. It was time to kick up one's heels. And what better way to get the rite of spring off right than a proper hanging? It was because of the many people in attendance that Culpepper had opted to take a carriage. With Reynolds' broken ankle, walking to the courthouse amid the swarming throngs would be dangerous for Culpepper and Cahill, as well as for Reynolds.

Bear rode on the short, flat bed of the carriage, his floppy jowls flapping with each breath.

"You didn't realize you was such a well-noted personage, did you, Tuck?" Cahill said somewhat sarcastically.

"They're here to see how a real man meets his end," Reynolds said arrogantly.

Cahill laughed. "You'll probably shit your britches when

they drop that trap door on you, Tuck. Unless you purged yourself real well this mornin', your pants'll be full of shit before you're dead."

"Leave him alone, Jimmy," Culpepper ordered quietly. "It's bad enough the scoundrel's going to his death. There's no call to make light of him along the way."

"Ah, hell, Jonas," Cahill complained, "that's half the fun of all this."

"Since when's a hangin' supposed to be fun?"

"Look around you, Jonas," Cahill said with a wave of the hand. "Look at all these people. You'd think they were goin' to a goddamn fair or circus or somethin'. This is big stuff to them, somethin' they don't see every day." Cahill was only about a year or so younger than Culpepper, but he still seemed like a little boy in many ways. He was a short, thin, whipcord tough man who was a good deputy, as long as he kept his perspective about things. He had trouble doing that sometimes, and Culpepper found it necessary to ride herd over him at such times. Like now.

"You want to be one of them, you go right on ahead," Culpepper said evenly. "If you want to continue bein' my deputy, you'll leave Reynolds alone." He looked past Reynolds at Cahill and winked. "Besides, you'll only give him a swole-up head with all your talk."

"That's tellin' him, Sheriff," Reynolds snapped. He'd been enjoying all the attention, even knowing what he'd be facing in minutes. He didn't like being found out by Culpepper, or his deputy.

There was no wall around the rear yard of the county courthouse. The gallows sat out on the flat back there, exposed to all and sundry. People were lined up along the upper reaches of Fifteenth and Sixteenth Streets, plus along the bank of a small portion of Cement Creek, and along Reese Street between Fifteenth and Sixteenth.

Hawkers worked the crowd, selling everything from peanuts to beer to strips of beef jerky, lending a true carnival atmosphere to the entire place. Culpepper shook his head in annoyance, wondering how anyone could make a party out of such an event.

As county sheriff, Culpepper could appoint a hangman, but he did not want anyone else to be stuck with such a duty, so he would do it himself, as he had the only other time a man was hanged—legally—in Silverton.

Culpepper left Cahill at the bottom of the stairs and helped Reynolds hobble up the steps. Judge Pfeiffer and Parson Wilbert Russell stood awaiting. Culpepper positioned Reynolds over the trap door. "You want the hood, Tuck?" he asked.

Reynolds shook his head. "Hell, no, Sheriff," he snarled, nerves beginning to catch up to him. "I want to watch your face when you pull the handle."

Culpepper shrugged. While he got no joy out of this, and couldn't understand the festival-like atmosphere surrounding the event, he was willing to do his job with no qualms. He would sleep just fine tonight, unless something else disturbed him. "Have it your way. You got anything you'd like to say before we send you across the divide?"

"Reckon not, 'cept maybe to have you say goodbye to your wife for me," Reynolds said with a smirk.

Culpepper's face was blank as he then gently worked the noose down over the condemned man's head. Then he tightened the knot with a swift jerk. "Try'n die with dignity, you pukin' scoundrel," Culpepper said quietly. He stepped back, allowing Parson Russell to take his place in front of the condemned man and begin reciting Scripture.

Culpepper let it go on for twenty dull, dreary minutes before he could stand it no more. He was about to fall asleep on his feet. He edged up to Russell and said quietly into the cleric's ear, "Best wrap it up, Parson. We're here to hang the man, not preach him to death."

Russell looked at Culpepper with disgust, but then decided the look in Culpepper's eyes did not bode well for him. He nodded once, curtly, then turned to face the throng again.

"Whoso diggeth a pit," he intoned, "shall fall therein; and he that rolleth a stone, it will return upon him." He paused, then led the people in the Twenty-Third Psalm.

As the chorus of "Amen" rose up from the gathered multitude, Culpepper moved toward the lever that would operate the trap door. "Last chance to speak your peace, Tuck," he offered.

"Pull the goddamn lever," Reynolds snarled.

Culpepper did so. The trap door snapped downward and Reynolds' body fell. He dangled for more than a minute, feet jerking and twitching. Then Dr. Angus McQuiston checked Reynolds over and pronounced him dead.

As the undertaker came to take the body away, the hordes of people began drifting away. Most of them were headed toward one saloon or another, where they would drink away the day and discuss the key event. When the undertaker was gone, Culpepper clomped down the stairs and with Bear on one side of him and Cahill on the other, walked slowly toward the office.

Culpepper got the keys to the jail and a small bottle of whiskey from a drawer. A curious Jimmy Cahill followed.

"It over?" Ferd Wiley asked as Culpepper neared the cell.

"Done and done," Culpepper said with a nod. "Here." He held out the bottle of whiskey. "You might as well join the celebration." Culpepper turned and walked out, locking all the doors behind him.

"You think that was wise?" Cahill asked.

Culpepper shrugged. "What hurt can it cause?" he countered.

"None, I expect." Cahill paused. "You still plannin' on havin' me take Ferd and leave for the penitentiary tomorrow, Jonas?" he asked.

"Don't see any reason to change my mind. The sooner he's out of here, the sooner things'll get back to normal."

Cahill nodded. "Then do you mind if I take off for a while, Jonas? I'd like to go see Miss June. If I'm gonna get on the trail at first light, this'll be the last time I get to see her before leavin'."

37

Culpepper nodded, but said with a slow smile, "You and that gal ought to get hitched, boy. An old rascal like you needs a good woman."

"I ain't so sure," Cahill hedged.

"Go on, get," Culpepper said with a laugh. "But be back here in time for me to take supper."

It was almost dark when Cahill came straggling back, looking well fed and somewhat self-satisfied.

"It's about durn time, boy," Culpepper said unhappily. "I was beginnin' to size up Bear to see what kind of eatin' he'd make."

Cahill laughed, still happy from an afternoon spent with June Ladimere. "Seems to me that it'd be the other way around."

Culpepper managed a grin. "Be an interestin' contest, wouldn't it?" He rose. "Well, I'd best be gettin' home. Merry'll be thinkin' I'm over on Blair Street or somethin'."

"How long you want me to stay?" Cahill asked.

"Another hour or so is all, I guess. Until Eleni Moldovan feeds Ferd. Unless it looks like something's going on."

"Fat chance," Cahill snorted.

Culpepper was not quite finished with his supper when twelve-year-old Timmy Pinckus pounded on the door. When Merry let the boy in, he marched straight up to Culpepper.

"Deputy Cahill says you're to get your butt . . ." he flushed red and cast a nervous glance at Merry ". . . to the office right now."

"Trouble?" Culpepper asked, patting his mouth with a napkin.

"I guess so, Sheriff. There was quite a crowd assemblin' outside the office. It might have somethin' to do with that."

"Thanks, Timmy," Culpepper said, rising. He pulled a dime out of his pocket and handed it to the boy.

Timmy grinned at the largesse and ran out.

"I don't know what this's about, Merry," Culpepper said, as

he strapped on his gunbelt, "but it don't bode well." He slid his knife into his belt and pulled on his coat. He headed for the door, but a premonition stopped him. He went into his bedroom and got his old McCoy and Davis 10-gauge double-barreled shotgun. He checked to make sure it was loaded. He grabbed a handful of extra shells for the scattergun and stuffed them in the pocket of his bear-fur coat. Then he kissed Merriam quickly and left, not having to call for Bear, who was right with him, tail quivering in excitement.

Culpepper crossed the small bridge over Cement Creek and headed up the alley off Mineral Street that would bring him to the county jail. He could already hear a grumbling of voices. He slipped up along the north wall of the jail and then, almost as if by magic, he was standing next to his deputy, shotgun cradled in his left arm.

Culpepper was glad there were plenty of lanterns being used. They provided a sufficient amount of light for him to keep a reasonably close eye on the angry men gathered in front of the stone jailhouse. "What're you folks doin' here?" he bellowed.

"We want that son of a bitch you got inside!" someone in the crowd hollered.

"Come and get him them," Culpepper said, shocking Cahill.

His words apparently stunned the crowd, too, for the people in the mob fell silent for a moment.

"Of course," Culpepper added, "I'll shred the first five or six of you pukes who comes up this way."

"God damn it, Sheriff," someone yelled, "let us have him. We'll save everyone a lot of time and trouble."

"Can't do that."

"We can overrun you, Sheriff," someone else yelled. "You don't need to die for the likes of that scum."

"Neither do you." He cast his eyes around the crowd, recognizing quite a few of the men. Most of them were employees of the Anvil Mining Company. Those who weren't were toughs and gunmen, criminals all, for the most part, who spent the majority of their time in the saloons of Greene Street and the whorehouses of Blair Street, and Culpepper was certain they'd been paid for their participation.

"The hell with the sheriff, boys," still another man yelled. "Let's get that bastard in there." He moved toward the jail. A few followed him, but the others hesitated.

Culpepper didn't know the man's name, but he recognized him as a petty thief and mugger, and figured the man did not deserve to live. He would make a good example. Culpepper fired a load of buckshot into the man's chest.

The man crumpled with a weak moan. The blast of the shotgun and the man's fall brought an instant silence from the crowd.

"Any of you other pukin' rascals want a dose of the same medicine?" Culpepper asked, as he extracted the spent shell and put in a fresh one.

There were mumbles and grumbles from the crowd, but little activity, until another man bolted out of the crowd, heading for Culpepper and Cahill.

Culpepper didn't really want to kill another man, so he pointed and then snapped, "Bear, get him!"

The dark brindle mastiff charged, bounding forward with long, surefooted leaps.

The man saw the animal coming and he stopped, frozen in terror. The dog hit him high on the chest and flattened him, then began gnawing at the man's arms, leaving the neck and throat until later. The man screamed and babbled as fear caught him in its grip.

Culpepper whistled. Bear hesitated only a moment before quitting his attack and trotting back to sit at Culpepper's side. His tongue slapped around his short muzzle, licking off the traces of blood.

"I'd advise you boys to go on home, now," Culpepper said. "There's been enough killin' and troublemakin' for one day. Wiley'll be out of your hair tomorrow, and he won't be botherin' no one for twenty-five years. There's no call to lynch him."

Slowly, reluctantly, the crowd began to disperse. Soon there was no one left but Culpepper, Cahill, and Bear. Some of the men leaving had even taken the dead man with them.

"Best get yourself some sleep, Jimmy," Culpepper said quietly.

"I figured to stay here with you, Jonas."

"You've got to be on the trail at first light. You need your sleep. Me and Bear'll be all right. As long as there's coffee on the stove."

Chapter 6

Culpepper paced in his office, stopping periodically to check outside through one window or the other. He knew for dead, absolute, guaranteed certain that something was wrong; he just knew it. Since the narrow-gauge railroad between Silverton and Durango hadn't started up yet after winter, he and Cahill had figured it would take Cahill and the two men deputized especially for this—Buster Reinhardt and John Maguire—a week, maybe eight days, to get to Durango and back. In Durango, the three deputies were supposed to deliver Wiley to a deputy U. S. Marshal sent out to take Wiley to the penitentiary in Florence. The wire sent in return to Culpepper's request said the deputy's name was Ned Coakley. Figure three days out, a little time for relaxing in Durango, and three days back.

But here it was only two full days since the three officers had left with their prisoner, and Culpepper was absolutely positive that something was wrong. Worse was that, if his premonition was correct, there was nothing he could do about it. Nothing but wait and pace—and grumble at Merry, which was something he hated to do, even though she understood his reasons for it.

Because of that, he decided to stay at his office as much as possible, including overnight, until he found out of his hunch was right and he decided what to do about it.

Just about the time it got dark, Bear allowed a soft, friendly—

if any sound that came out of the massive dog's short muzzle could be considered friendly—growl. Culpepper rose and slid quietly to the side of the office, away from the door and windows. A hand rested on a pistol butt.

A moment later, Merry entered the office, her arms full with a blanket, a coffeepot, and a metal lunch bucket. Her face was flushed from the exertion and the chill temperatures of the gathering mountain night, and Culpepper thought she looked perfectly lovely.

Culpepper moved away from the wall in a smooth motion that would make it seem as if it had been natural to be standing at that spot at that time. He hurried over to his wife and grabbed everything out of her hands. "What's all this?" he asked.

Merry shrugged, almost embarrassed. "I just sensed that you were feelin' that something was wrong with Jimmy. Knowin' you as I do, I figured you'd be wantin' to stick close by the office. So I brung you some things."

"You are something, woman. Durn if you ain't," Culpepper crowed quietly. "What's in the bucket?"

"Chicken, gravy, and some biscuits."

"Sounds good. You going to stay and eat with me?"

"I brought enough, in case you wanted that," Merry said, smiling warmly.

"I do," Culpepper said firmly. He shoved papers and other junk off his desk, creating some room. Then he brought up the only chair other than the one behind his desk.

Merry opened the lunch bucket and distributed food on the plates she had packed inside the bucket. She had even thought to pack a decent pile of bones and meat scraps for Bear. Merry put those in the old gold pan that served the mastiff as a feeding bowl. He had another just like it for water. Merry poured coffee for Culpepper and herself, and then she sat, waiting a moment to catch her breath.

They ate quietly, seeing no need to fill their warm, comfortable silence with words.

Soon after he was finished eating, Culpepper began getting antsy again. He kept his seat, but Merry could see the fidgeting of his hands, the restlessness of his eyes.

Merry rose and cleared up the plates and things. "Well, I'd better be gettin' home, Jonas."

He nodded and rose. "I'll walk you," he said.

"No, Jonas—you want to stay here, maybe need to stay here. I'll be all right."

"You know I don't like you walkin' around here after dark." They had discussed this more than once. Merry's walking to and from the office brought her much too close to Blair Street for his comfort. Besides, there were far too many men walking around with a cause to hate any lawman, and possibly San Juan County Sheriff Jonas Culpepper, in particular.

"I know. But I'll be fine."

Culpepper shook his head. "Take Bear," he finally said. "Send him back once you're locked in the house."

Merry nodded. "Bear'll watch over me." She came up and kissed Culpepper long and hard, the way a happily married woman who still loved and desired her husband should do. Then she pulled the shawl around her shoulders and headed out, the big mastiff walking protectively beside her.

Ten minutes later, Bear scratched at the door. Culpepper let the animal in and petted him on the head. "Our Merry get home safe, eh?" he said quietly to the dog. "Did she? Yeah? Yeah." Then he set to pacing again.

Finally he forced himself to sit in his chair. He put his feet up on the desk and pulled the blanket around him. He fell asleep almost instantly, but it was not a deep or refreshing sleep. He woke frequently, jerking up, hand on a pistol. When he saw that no one was there, he would drift back into restless slumber again.

He felt lousy the next morning when he awoke for good. Even the coffee Merry had brought him last night tasted poor to him after his uncomfortable night spent in his chair.

Merry showed up soon after with more coffee and with a

decent breakfast. The meal—and Merry's company—went a long way to cheering him, though the premonition still lingered, particularly after Merry left.

At five minutes after ten on the small, battered cuckoo clock on the office wall, Jimmy Cahill walked in, followed by Buster Reinhardt and John Maguire. The latter two were wounded, Maguire more seriously, it seemed.

"Lord almighty!" Culpepper said. He glanced out through the still open door and saw a small crowd gathered. "Come on, John," he said, helping Maguire, "sit in my big chair here. Buster, you take that other chair. Durn, I ain't got a chair for you, Jimmy."

"That's all right, Jonas," Cahill said, sliding his back down along a wall until he was sitting on the floor. "This'll do just fine." He looked exhausted.

Culpepper nodded and stepped outside. "One of you folks, go get Doc McQuiston," he commanded. "And make it quick." Then he went back inside and kicked the door shut behind him. "Any of you rascals up for some coffee?" he asked.

Cahill shook his head. "Not me." He paused only an instant. "But a shot of bug juice wouldn't hurt none."

"Same here," Maguire and Reinhardt echoed.

Culpepper got the pint bottle of Jack Daniels No. 7 Whiskey, uncorked it, and helped Maguire take a drink. Then he helped Reinhardt, and finally Cahill.

By then, Dr. Angus McQuiston had arrived. He glanced at each of the three men as he was still walking into the room, and then gravitated to Maguire. He dropped his bag on the desk, then peeled off his coat and dropped that, too.

"It ain't as bad as I feared," McQuiston said ten minutes later, wiping his hands off on a cloth as he stepped back. "He's lost a lot of blood, but the bullet didn't injure any of his vitals, and lucky for Mister Maguire, the bullet passed clean through him. Now, let's see about Mister Reinhardt."

While Reinhardt's wound was less serious than Maguire's, the bullet was still lodged in his shoulder, so McQuiston had to root around and get the slug out. That took some time, but the doctor finally managed it. Bandaging the man up was the work of but a few minutes.

McQuiston rose and rolled down his sleeves. "Both you boys need to take it easy for a spell. Couple of weeks ought to do, though you might need a little longer. Let your bodies tell you when you're ready to hooraw the town again." The physician pulled on his coat and closed his bag. He looked at Culpepper and grinned. "And, yes, Sheriff, I'll send the bill to the county offices. As if that'll do me any damn good." He clomped out, closing the door behind him.

"You three just stay where you are a bit," Culpepper ordered. He went outside and pointed at four men. "You four come with me," he commanded. Inside, he told two to help Maguire home and the other two to help Reinhardt. The men didn't like it much, but they did as requested.

Culpepper followed the men outside and told the crowd to go home. The people who had gathered groaned and grumbled, but moved off.

It was quiet in the office when Culpepper shut the door. He helped Cahill into the chair and made sure the half-empty bottle of whiskey was close enough for Cahill to reach. Then he took his own seat behind the desk. "All right, Jimmy, what the hell happened?" Culpepper asked, using a rare profanity, as mild a one as it was.

Cahill took a slow drink of whiskey, then yawned. "We were a day and a half out, maybe a little more, when all of a sudden there were a dozen men or so in the road, tellin' us to stop. It was the damnedest thing—they went and ordered us to hand Wiley over to 'em."

"Durn, I should've know some sneaky little scoundrel like Ferd Wiley'd have confederates in these parts."

"That's what I thought at first, too. But I ain't so sure, now that I've had a little time to cogitate on it."

"Why not?" Culpepper asked, surprised.

"For one thing, Ferd looked like he was gonna crap in his

britches, he was that scared. And it wasn't until I thunk back on it a little that I thought I recognized one or two of the men who were in that road."

"Outlaws?"

Cahill shook his head. "Miners. Or some kind of employees for a mining company here in Silverton. Maybe they're even hired gunmen, but I swear at least two of 'em's linked to the Anvil Minin' Company somehow."

"Vigilantes," Culpepper said sourly. "I'm beginning to like this a lot less with every word you're tellin' me, Jimmy."

"No shit." Cahill took another swallow of whiskey.

"So what happened?" The cuckoo clock chimed for noon, annoying Culpepper.

"Well, like I said, I thought they were men come to rescue Ferd, and I wasn't about to let that happen without a fight, so I told them boys to light out. Then the shootin' started." Cahill drained the whiskey bottle, looked at it as if he'd never seen it before, and then placed it back on the desk. "It was strange then, too. Lookin' back on it, it seemed like those boys were tryin' not to kill anyone—except maybe Ferd, but I think they didn't even want to shoot him down."

"Hangin'd make them feel better about themselves," Culpepper said dryly.

"That was my thinkin', too. Anyway, me, John, and Buster winged at least a couple of 'em, as we all headed for the trees along the road there. Then they took slugs and I hustled them out of there. We rode a an hour or so before I stopped and tended to John and Buster as best I could, hopin' they'd last 'til I could get 'em back here to Doc McQuiston."

"So they got Ferd, did they?" Culpepper said, anger bubbling in his stomach.

"I don't think so," Cahill said, surprising Culpepper. "I rode back that way once I'd tended to my men. When we hit the trees durin' that fight, I lost sight of Ferd straight off. I figured they'd caught him and hanged him, so I thought I'd bring the body back here, at least give him a decent burial."

47

"But . . . ?"

"But I couldn't find him anywhere. I spent a couple hours lookin' for him. I trailed the group who stopped us, but, Christ, their tracks went all over the place. I think they were lookin' for Ferd, too."

Culpepper nodded and let the information simmer in his brain a little bit. Finally he asked, "How're you doin', Jimmy?"

"Not bad, Jonas. Tired as all hell. I ain't had much sleep in the past two days."

"Think you'll be all right after a good night's sleep?"

"I reckon so. Why?"

"I want you to stick around the office the next couple days."

"You goin' out there?"

Culpepper nodded. "I'll see if I can find anything. Now that we know a little better what we're lookin' for, I might have a little more luck than you did."

"I can ride with you, Jonas," Cahill said part angrily, part petulantly. "I ain't crippled."

"I know you ain't crippled. But you're the one knows those boys who stopped you. If, as you think, they work for Anvil, they'll show up here again sooner or later. They do, and you spot them, you deputize whoever you want and however many you need and arrest them."

Cahill nodded. The exhaustion weighed on him like one of the nearby Elephant Hills. He wasn't sure he could even make it to his room to sleep. All he wanted to do was . . .

Culpepper smiled as he came around the desk. He easily lifted Cahill over his shoulder. Accompanied by the mastiff, he walked to the boardinghouse where Cahill lived and put the man to bed. Then he went home, walking almost urgently. Though he wanted to be on the move, he knew he could not leave until morning. But there was much to be done between then and now.

Chapter 7

Culpepper wasted almost four days on the journey out and back. There was no other way to look at it. Cahill had told him he wouldn't find anything where the deputy and his two men were bushwhacked, but no, Culpepper couldn't accept that; he had to go see for himself. All he found were some muddy tracks leading every which way. There were no signs of the men who had done the ambushing, and no sign of Ferd Wiley. There was no corpse to be found, either. Even Bear couldn't find a trail worth following.

He rode back to Silverton, growing angrier the closer he got to the town. None of this sat well with him. Not the call for Wiley's blood by the mob in front of the jail; not the ambush and wounding of his deputies; not the thought that the Anvil Mining Company might be behind the attack; not the thought that Wiley might have escaped.

Culpepper was not too worried about the latter. Wiley had always struck him as a coward and a follower. He would do what other men told him because he had not the brains, the brawn, nor the guts to do much on his own. Still, Wiley was a convicted felon and should be forced to serve his time in prison. On the other hand, Culpepper was fairly certain that Wiley, if he had gotten away, would have headed for parts unknown just as fast as he could. Culpepper hoped that if Wiley was free, this episode would set him back on the straight and narrow.

Wiley was the least of Culpepper's worries, though. The other things that had made him angry were far more important and carried with them far-reaching implications, none of which boded well for anyone—except possibly Anvil Mining, and even that was highly unlikely.

He stopped at his office as soon as he rode into town, told Cahill he was back, then went up to Greene Street and the Exchange livery. He left his horse. Carrying his rifle, bedroll, and saddlebags, he trudged wearily toward home.

Merry never did tell him that the reason she generally was waiting at the door for him was because she could think of nothing better to do most times when she was waiting for him to return. She had figured he'd've been home yesterday, and so she had been standing at the door almost constantly during her waking hours since yesterday afternoon.

Merry cursed herself silently at times for missing her man so much when he was gone, but she couldn't help herself. She really couldn't. The only thing that made her not feel too bad about this quirk in her was the knowledge that Culpepper missed her as much as she did him. Oh, his expression of it—such as it was—was vastly different from hers, but the feelings were the same. And, she had told herself long ago, she would continue to wait anxiously—and eagerly—for him as long as he appreciated that she did.

Culpepper found out after he was in the house that he wasn't quite as tired as he'd believed. Something about Merry's cooking and her company often revived him considerably. Still, he went to sleep early.

Culpepper met Cahill at the office in the morning. Over mugs of hot, if poor-tasting, coffee, Culpepper told of the futility of his journey. Then he asked, "You ever see any of them boys in town here?" He didn't think so, since there were no prisoners in the jail.

"Yeah, I did," Cahill said carefully.

"And you didn't arrest him?"

"Had my hands full givin' Hennessy a hand with some rowdies the other night. I spotted the son of a bitch, but there wasn't much I could do. I've been lookin' for him ever since, every time I leave the office."

"You got any ideas where he might be holed up?"

"Not really. Other than he's probably over on Blair Street somewhere."

"We got a handbill on him?"

"Nope. I looked." Cahill did not seem happy.

"That's going to make it a little harder for me to help find him, but I'll tell you this, Jimmy—if that pukin' scoundrel's in Silverton, we'll find him." He rose. "And there's no better time to start lookin' than right now."

Blair Street ran from Fourteenth Street to Eleventh, where its character and name changed. Mostly cribs and brothels lined both sides of Blair Street—and the alleys—between Eleventh and Thirteenth Streets. Dance halls and gambling parlors were nestled between the false-fronted whorehouses.

At this time of day, it was generally pretty quiet along Blair Street—not through any sense of shame at what the denizens of such a place would be doing, but because the vast majority of the paying customers—the miners—were at work. Everything was open, but there was little going on.

Culpepper and Cahill went from saloon to crib to gambling parlor to theater. They knew most of the folks who worked or lived there, and were greeted warmly enough, if not enthusiastically. At each stop they asked about the man Cahill had seen. The deputy would give the description and then wait for the shake of the head.

They worked up the east side of Blair Street, and the alleys off it, but found no luck. Stopping, Culpepper said, "I aim to go on home to have something to eat."

"Hell, Jonas, you ain't foolin' nobody. You just want to go home and wrassle with Merry some is all."

"And if I do?" Culpepper demanded, feigning outrage at the hint.

"Then I'm jealous, damn your hide," Cahill said with a laugh.

"Well, boy, if you'd quit all your fussin' around and ask Miss June to marry you, you could be doin' the same. She ain't going to wait forever for on old cuss like you, you know."

"Yeah," Cahill muttered, suddenly embarrassed. "But I don't know, Jonas. There's a heap of married men out there using Blair Street more than many of the single ones. June sure seems willin' enough to take on the duties—*all* the duties, she tells me—of a wife, but I don't want to get snookered into marryin' her and then have her turn all cold on me."

Culpepper smiled. "It's just like anything else, Jimmy. You praise her cookin', and she'll want to cook for you. You treat her well, she'll more than likely do the same to you. You teach her what a man wants from his woman in a wifely way, and treat her kind and gentle in the doin', and you'll be surprised at what some otherwise straight-laced women'll do." He saw the look of questioning in Cahill's eyes, and he grinned again. "Don't you even think to ask, you rascal," he said with a laugh.

"Damn, Jonas," Cahill muttered. Then he smiled. "Meet you back at the office in an hour?"

Culpepper nodded as he strolled away.

Culpepper left his heavy bear coat at home after lunch. As he walked across the little bridge with Bear at his side, he enjoyed the sun and the sixty-degree warmth that cloaked the day. He met Cahill at the office and they headed straight to Blair Street, figuring to hit the west side of the street this time.

In the second place they stopped, Fatty Collins' place, Cahill spotted the man he was after. He was sitting at a table near the back, drinking. Fanciful Pearl, one of Collins' working girls, was sitting on the man's lap, helping him drink his mug of beer.

Cahill stopped just inside the door, saw the man, and sucked in an angry breath.

Looking where Cahill was staring, Culpepper said, "I take it that's the feller?"

"It sure as hell is," Cahill hissed.

"Calm down, boy. He's not going anywhere."

Cahill grimaced. "Damn it, Jonas, you know how much I hate it when you give me hell—and're right about it. Let's go talk to him."

They strolled up to the table, though the man was pretty much oblivious to them. "Hey there, Fancy," Culpepper said nicely, but with a hint of warning, "go take a walk for a while. Me and Jimmy want to talk about some things with your sweetheart."

The man grabbed Fanciful Pearl's wrist and kept her on his lap. "I got nothin' to say to you two law dogs," he said with a sneer. "Now go away."

"Dang it, Bob," Fanciful Pearl snapped, "let me go. I ain't about to cross the sheriff just for the likes of you."

"I said you stay right where you're at," the man snarled.

Culpepper shook his head in annoyance and walked around the table, pulling out a pistol as he did. He cocked the revolver and placed the muzzle lightly against the man's temple. "Let the lady go, you pukin' maggot, or I'll blow your brains out. If you got any."

The man sat staring straight ahead, defiance stamped on his face. But the small balls of sweat seeping from under his hat betrayed his fear.

"I'll count to three," Culpepper said quietly. "One . . ."

"Damn it, Bob," Fanciful Pearl said, panicking a little.

"Two . . ."

Fanciful Pearl jerked her arm as hard as she could and managed to free herself. She jumped up and ran.

"Smart move," Culpepper commented, as he uncocked the Remington. Suddenly he drew the pistol back and then lashed out with it, catching the man a sharp blow between left temple and eyebrow. "That's just to let you know I'm serious in telling you that I will have no truck with reluctance on your part in speaking to me. You got that, maggot?" Culpepper placed the Remington back in the holster.

"Yeah," the man said, wanting to feel his head where he had been hit, but afraid to.

Culpepper and Cahill sat. "What's your name, boy?" Culpepper asked.

"Bob. Bob Haggard."

"Good. Who do you work for?"

"I'm between jobs right now," Haggard said flatly. "Just sort of driftin'."

"Drifters don't join bushwhackers to ambush deputy county sheriffs in the pursuit of their duties," Culpepper said evenly.

"I don't know what the hell you're talkin' about, Sheriff," Haggard said, feigning innocence.

"Like hell . . ." Cahill snapped. He shut up when Culpepper waved a hand at him.

Culpepper was about to say something to Haggard when a large, obese man shuffled up and said, "How-do, Sheriff?"

"Keep your nose out of this business, Fatty," Culpepper said quietly.

"Hell, Jonas," Fatty Collins said with a belly laugh, "you know me better'n that. All I come to see was if you and Jimmy here wanted some snake oil."

"No," Culpepper said. "But a beer'd be nice."

"Comin' right up, Sheriff," Collins said jovially. Though Culpepper had no real jurisdiction in Silverton, Collins subscribed to the belief that it never did one any good to ruffle a lawman's feathers. "How about you, Jimmy?"

"Same for me," Cahill said distractedly.

"Now, Bob," Culpepper said easily, "you were just about to tell us who hired you to join that gang of vigilantes."

"What gang of vigilantes?" Haggard asked, his face blankly innocent.

"I'm a man of considerable patience, Bob," Culpepper said. "And if you think that by sittin' here and stonewallin' me I'll give up and go away, you're sadly mistaken, you scoundrel. For if I lose my patience, I won't just walk out. Oh, no, no, no. What'll happen is that I'll take my testiness out on you in various and guaranteed painful ways. Now . . ."

Culpepper leaned back as Collins arrived and set two full glasses of beer on the scarred table. "Those're on the house, boys," he said. "Enjoy 'em."

Culpepper nodded. "Now, Bob, where were we? Ah, yes, the attack on my deputies. Who hired you for that?"

"I still don't know what you're talkin' about, Sheriff," Haggard said, his voice sounding quite reasonable.

"Well, perhaps you don't. Let me see if I can refresh your memory just a little." Culpepper took a healthy slug of beer and wiped the foam off his red mustache with the back of a hand. "Deputy Cahill here and two special deputies were takin' a criminal to Durango, where he was going to be shipped to the penitentiary in Florence when a group of men—includin' you—stopped them and attempted to take that unfortunate soul and lynch him."

"At the risk of incurrin' your wrath, Sheriff," Haggard said, "I think you're plumb loco. I was sittin' here a week, week and a half ago, with that trollop. I wasn't out tryin' to lynch Ferd."

"That's interestin'," Culpepper commented. "I never said when the attack took place. Nor did I say who the scoundrel was that was bein' escorted to his date with the hoosegow."

Haggard laughed uneasily. "Hell, Ferd Wiley's the only prisoner you've had in some time, Sheriff," he said carefully. "And everyone in town knew when he was bein' taken out of here. I even heard there was an attempted lynchin' of Ferd the night before he left."

Culpepper nodded. "All true enough. But I still think you're full of beans." He craned his head around and bellowed, "Fatty! Get Fanciful Pearl back here!"

When the young, pasty-faced prostitute sidled nervously up to the table, Culpepper asked, "Were you here with this pukin' scoundrel a week, ten days ago?" When Fanciful Pearl hesitated, Culpepper added, "Don't you worry about this maggot. He ain't going to hurt you."

"No, Sheriff," she said in a whisper. "I sure wasn't."

Chapter 8

"Thank you, Fancy," Culpepper said, rising. "That's all we need from you." He held out a hand.

Fanciful Pearl looked confused for a moment, then shook it. Her face brightened when she felt the heavy gold coin that transferred from his big hand to her small one. "Thank you, Sheriff," she said enthusiastically, as she hurried away. As soon as she was out of sight of the sheriff, she looked down to confirm with her eyes what her hand had noted—it was indeed a half-eagle piece. It would take her a couple turns lying on her back with some stinking miner to make five dollars. And she wouldn't have to give any of this money to Fatty Collins. She felt positively rich.

"All right, maggot," Culpepper said. "On your feet."

"What the hell for?" Haggard protested.

"You're under arrest. For assaultin' a deputy who was doin' his duty, attempted murder—of Ferd Wiley—attempted murder of three county deputy sheriffs, and for bein' a vomitous maggot in general."

Haggard's face went pale, and he stared into Culpepper's hard face. "You ain't joshin' about this, are you?" he asked, almost in wonder, as if it had just dawned on him that Culpepper was serious.

"No, sir, I'm not. Now, get yourself up." Culpepper stepped

just to the side and pulled the table away from Haggard. Then he moved toward Haggard a little.

Shaking some, Haggard got up. But as he did, his hand moved for the pistol at his waist.

Cahill gasped, then shouted, "Watch it!"

But Culpepper was well aware of Haggard's desperate move. The sheriff took one step forward and then hammered Haggard with a fist in the sternum with all the strength his could get out of his short, powerful, compact body.

Haggard choked in one sudden breath, then sat. His face was ghastly white, and his mouth worked furiously, though nothing came out. He sat there, trying to breathe, or choke, or just plain die, but none of those seemed likely at the moment.

Culpepper reached over and took Haggard's pistol out of the holster, ejected the shells onto the floor, and shoved the empty revolver into his own belt. Then he waited.

It took almost two minutes before Haggard could breathe again, though to him it seemed like it took an entire lifetime. But finally some air began to trickle down into his lungs. He almost felt himself relax some, but he was still too scared. He had never faced anything so horrible as to sit unable to breathe and aware of it as each exquisitely worrisome second ticked away.

When Culpepper figured that Haggard could speak again, he said, "I'm going to ask you one more time, maggot, who paid you to attack my men?"

"Wilson Pennrose," Haggard gasped.

Culpepper could not really say he was surprised. Cahill had said all along that some of the culprits appeared to be employees of a mining company—and Anvil Mining was the biggest in the region. And because Pennrose was the main man behind Anvil, it would stand to reason that he was behind this. The only surprise for Culpepper was that Pennrose had operated so much in the open, as it were, when he could easily have stayed far behind the scenes and let his minions do the dirty work for him.

"Was he behind the ruckus at the jail the night before my deputies left with Wiley?" Culpepper asked harshly.

Haggard nodded, still not trusting himself to be able to speak too much.

"All right, Jimmy, take this skunk over to the jail and lock him up," Culpepper said. "And go easy on him. We don't need a corpse on our hands. Of course, if he was to resist goin' along, a few well-directed thumps wouldn't be out of line."

Cahill nodded. He had a fiery temper at times, and knew it. But he was proud of being a lawman, and considered himself a pretty good one. Because of that, he was generally able to keep his temper in check, even when confronted with men like Bob Haggard.

"Let's go, asswipe," Cahill growled, pulling Haggard out into the saloon. He searched Haggard for weapons, finding a pocketknife and a belly gun, both of which he tossed on the table. Then he shoved Haggard on the back. "Move," he ordered.

Culpepper followed Cahill and Haggard outside. But at Twelfth Street, Culpepper turned left, while Cahill and his prisoner continued down Blair Street. Between Reese Street and Snowden Street, on Twelfth, was the headquarters of the Anvil Mining Company.

Culpepper had been in the large, single-story building only a few times, but those were enough to give him a good working knowledge of what went on in there and where people would be.

Just inside the door of the headquarters was a wide, though not very deep, open area in which there were half a dozen desks lined up in a row across the width, and one near the center doorway at the rear. Studious-looking young men worked quietly, their nib pens clacking in bottles of ink and then scratching across paper. Only one of the men, the one nearest the rear, looked up when Culpepper entered.

Beyond the office workers, straight to the back, was the boardroom, as it was known. It was a combination meeting place, dining room, and saloon for the highest officers of the

Anvil Mining Company. Along the sides were six small offices, one each for the principals of the company—except for Pennrose, who had his own office off the rear of the boardroom.

Culpepper moved unhesitatingly toward the boardroom. The young man at the desk there rose, his arms crossed on his chest. Culpepper pointed a large index finger at the man's chair. "Sit," he said quietly.

The young man—Culpepper didn't know his name—opened his mouth to protest, but then Culpepper held a forefinger up to his lips. The young man hesitated. Then, seeing the look in Culpepper's piercing blue eyes, he closed his mouth and sat.

Culpepper nodded at the man, then grabbed the door handle and turned it. The door to the boardroom was locked. "Well, durn it all, anyway," Culpepper muttered. He lowered a big right shoulder and jerked it forward.

The door caved in with a loud crunch, and then hung there on only one hinge as Culpepper pushed inside. All seven mining officials looked up, surprised and worried. They were, by and large, a well-fed lot of men, each with a tumbler of fine sourmash in front of him and a fat cigar stuck in his lips or between his fingers. They were, each and every one, dressed in good wool suits, including vests and ties, either string or long. All but one—Pennrose, who was cleanly shaven—had a mustache and beard. And they all had expressions of bewilderment mixed with fear on their faces.

"Afternoon, gentlemen," Culpepper said. "Sorry to break up your little sewin' bee here, but I have business with Mister Pennrose. The rest of you can leave, or stay, whatever you're of a mind for." He stopped and waited a moment.

No one left as Culpepper marched toward the head of the table, where a nervous-looking Wilson Pennrose sat, hands on the tabletop, crossed, with a cigar between the fingers of the one on top. Culpepper suspected no one left because Bear had come in right after Culpepper and plunked himself down near the door. He sat quietly, panting a little.

Culpepper stopped and leaned over, placing his own hands flat on the tabletop near Pennrose's. "I don't know how much clout you have, or think you have, Mister Pennrose," Culpepper said flatly, eyes boring in on Pennrose's. "And I don't really much give a hoot. What I do care about is havin' men you hire tryin' to kill my deputies."

"I have no idea what you're talking about, Sheriff," Pennrose said calmly.

"I've got Bob Haggard in jail now."

"Who's he?" Pennrose asked without blinking.

"Mister Pennrose," Culpepper said with a sigh, "I might not be the smartest man the Good Lord ever put down here, but I ain't nowhere near as dumb as you like to think I am. I know it was you who was responsible for the lynchin' party at the jail the night before Deputy Cahill rode out of Silverton with Ferd Wiley. And I know it was you who paid them bushwhackers who wounded Buster Reinhardt and John Maguire."

"You're crazy, Sheriff," Pennrose said, trying to sound lighthearted. He did not want to anger the sheriff any more than he already did.

"No, Mister Pennrose, I'm not. Now, I can't prove any of this, of course. If I could, I'd've marched you straight off to the hoosegow already. But I know it's the truth, and you know it's the truth, and I'm going to tell you this: You try some new business like this again, and I'll make sure you pay."

"Sheriff, I still don't know what you're talking about. I really don't. However, without knowing that, I can still say that Ferd Wiley was a thief and an assailant. He's just as responsible for the attack on Leroy Monteith as Tuck Reynolds was. If Reynolds was hanged, then, by God, Wiley should've been, too."

Culpepper pushed away from the table and strolled around the table until he was standing behind Pennrose. "I can see how you'd feel that way, especially since I finally figured that you were disappointed at the trial."

"I was?" Pennrose asked flatly.

"Yep. You know, I almost didn't speak up at the trial. It took me a while to figure it out, but I think I finally did. It was obvious to anyone that Judge Pfeiffer was none too happy when I asked for leniency for Wiley. I figured he was plannin' to sentence both Wiley and Reynolds to hang. No one would've argued. I finally concluded, though, and I'd wager a month's pay on it, that you 'encouraged' the judge to lean that way. But I had to go ruinin' your plans by speakin' up."

Culpepper paused to swallow a mouthful of Pennrose's whiskey. "That's good," he said, setting the glass down. "I noticed you disappeared for a while when the jury was 'deliberating.' After a bit of cogitation, I decided that you went back and had a few words with Judge Pfeiffer."

"Oh?" Pennrose asked nonchalantly. "And just what did I have to say to him?"

"You told him to give Wiley a prison term instead of sentencing him to hang."

"Why would I do that?" Pennrose asked with a snort.

Culpepper walked back around where he could watch Pennrose's face. "To keep me happy and unsuspectin'," he said flatly. He had worked this out on the way over, and he was angry at himself for not seeing it earlier. "Then you sent that lynch mob over to the jail, figurin' that me and Jimmy'd let them have Ferd. That way, you could have everything—you keep me off your back because Ferd got the leniency I asked for, and you're satisfied because both scoundrels were hanged."

"Hell of a plan, Sheriff," Pennrose said. "But it wouldn't work. Jesus, Jonas, I know you wouldn't give up a prisoner to some damn lynch mob." He sounded sincere.

Culpepper nodded. "I thought of that, too. And there's a good chance you're tellin' the truth."

Pennrose's eyebrows raised in question.

Culpepper finished off the whiskey in Pennrose's glass, much to the mining official's annoyance. "That's why you hired some of the men in the lynch mob to hit the trail and ambush Jimmy." He paused. "Givin' you the benefit of the doubt, I figure you just told those rascals to shoot high or somethin', hopin' to drive Jimmy, John, and Buster off while your men grabbed Ferd and finished up your business."

"Nice of you to give me the benefit of the doubt, especially after two of your men were wounded, from what I hear."

Culpepper nodded. "That's a fact. But I figure those maggots you hired either got spooked, or my men put up a lot more of a fight than your scoundrels were plannin' on."

"So, Sheriff," Pennrose said evenly, "where does this leave us?"

"It leaves me with one escaped prisoner, two wounded special deputies, and one angry deputy. And I'm not in the best of humors. It leaves you with . . . well, I don't know, other than the fact that it leaves you with one angry county sheriff on your tail."

"I can deal with that," Pennrose said dryly.

"I suppose you can," Culpepper said with a nod. "But you'd better hope that I don't come up with some evidence to prove any of this, or you'll find your carcass over in the hoosegow." Culpepper bent over the table again, hands down, face only inches from Pennrose's. "You might think your money and your high position both with the minin' company and as head of the county board mean you can do anything you durn well please. Well I'm here to tell you that you can't. I don't cotton to the things I think you've done, Mister Pennrose, and I'm tellin' you here and now that if you try to cross me again, I'll forget that I'm a duly sworn peace officer and land on you hard."

"That a threat, Sheriff?" Pennrose asked tightly.

"No, sir," Culpepper responded, pushing himself back up once again. "Just a warnin'." He paused. "You said before that you knew I wouldn't give up a prisoner to a lynch mob. That's true, so I also suppose you know that I'm a man of my word. I'd heed my warnin' if I was you. Good day, gentlemen."

The next day, Culpepper told Cahill about his talk with Pennrose.

"I wish we could've done something about him," Cahill said.

"Me, too. But we can't, and there's no use frettin' over it."

"What do I do about Bob Haggard?"

Culpepper shrugged. "That's up to you. I talked to Judge Pfeiffer about him yesterday. He doesn't think we have much of a case and, truth to tell, neither do I."

"Am I just supposed to let him go?" Cahill's temper began to flare.

"If you want my advice, Jimmy, I'd say, yeah, let him go. Maybe you, John, and Buster—if those two're up to it—could give him a pretty good thumpin' before you let him go, just to kind of encourage him to leave these parts and keep his ornery hide away."

Cahill mulled that possibility for a few moments, then nodded, as a small, hard smile spread over his lips. "I think that might work."

Chapter 9

The narrow-gauge Denver and Rio Grande Company's Silverton-to-Durango train puffed backward into the station. Before it had completely halted in a swirl of hissing steam and screeching brakes, the fireman, Chester Graves, had hopped off and was hotfooting it up the street.

Graves burst into the county sheriff's office, almost out of breath. Culpepper looked up sharply, wondering what this was all about. "Train," Graves puffed. "Robbed." He stood wheezing, hands on his knees.

Culpepper jumped up. "Come on, Bear!' He shouted, as he charged out the door. Minutes later he was pulling himself onto the train that still huffed and puffed as it sat at the depot.

The engineer, Lou Barber, was in a high state of agitation, and it took a little while before Culpepper got him calmed down enough to be able to talk. In the meantime, a crowd had begun gathering, lured by the whisper of trouble in the air.

Finally Culpepper began getting a little angry, and he snapped, "Lou, quit your babblin' and tell me what happened. You keep on like you're going and we'll never find out."

Barber was a nervous-looking man even in the best of times. Now he was almost shaking with agitation. He was handsome under the grease and oil and soot, in his mid-thirties, of medium height and weight. He rubbed the back of a hand across his forehead, leaving a streak of grease.

"We were eight, maybe ten miles down when I come to a damn pile of boulders on the track," Barber said. "So naturally, I stop the damn train. A couple of damn men, with guns drawn, swung onto the damn train and told me they were stickin' us up. Who was I to argue with them? So me and Chester, we stood there coolin' our heels under the muzzles of a couple of damn Colts. Then the two damn men watchin' us said we could go, but not to chase 'em. They jumped off the train, and got on their damn horses. Then they rode off."

"How many of them were there?"

"I couldn't really tell, Sheriff. At least half a dozen, I'd say, maybe more. I ventured me a little damn look out when they rode away and saw quite a few of 'em."

"What'd you do then?"

"I made a quick check of what was took, and then backed the damn train up and sent Chester runnin' for you."

Culpepper nodded. "What's gone?"

"Best I can tell, about all the cash, some jewels, and a fair portion of the silver."

Culpepper whistled softly. "You have any idea how much was on the train?"

"No, Sheriff, I surely don't. You'd have to ask Marv Coleridge, who was responsible for loadin' all the damn stuff. Or maybe Wilson Pennrose, or one of the other big chiefs of Anvil Minin'."

"I'll do that. You know who it was robbed the train?"

"Sure as hell do. It was Mack Ellsworth."

"You sure?" Culpepper wasn't all that surprised. Now that winter was gone, Ellsworth could be expected to have his gang out raiding as much as possible.

"Of course I'm sure, damn it all. He was one of the two holding a Colt revolver in my face—him and Hugh McLeod."

Culpepper nodded. He knew of both men. McLeod was Ellsworth's right-hand man. "Which way'd they go?"

Barber shrugged. "Hell if I know. They was ridin' south

along the tracks, but that don't mean they didn't cut up into the mountains the minute they were around a damn curve."

"Anything else you can think of?" Culpepper asked.

"Nope. I just hope you catch those bastards, Sheriff. And soon. I ain't of a mood to have no one go stickin' a pistol in my face."

"I don't know of anyone who does like such treatment, Mister Barber," Culpepper said. He turned and swung down off the train to where Bear was waiting patiently, tail waggling. "Come on, boy," Culpepper said, running a hand swiftly across the dog's big head.

Culpepper stopped when he spotted Lee Bondurant, a ten-year-old who made some spending money by helping out around the train depot. "Hey, Lee," Culpepper called, "go find Jimmy Cahill for me. Tell him to get himself over to the office right off. There's a dime in it for you. Come on over to the office later and I'll pay up."

"Yessir." Lee's eyes widened. "What's goin' on, Sheriff?" he asked, eager to have privileged information.

"None of your beeswax, boy," Culpepper said, but not in an unfriendly way. "Just go on and do what I told you."

Despite a sense of urgency, Culpepper walked slowly toward his office. He needed time to think, to cover the possibilities in his mind. Not that there was all that much to think about. It was obvious he would swear in a posse and get on Ellsworth's trail. Still, by the time he reached his office, he had decided that there was nothing unforeseen in this case. What needed to be done was simple and straightforward, and he was comfortable with it.

At the office, he unlocked the drawer in which he kept his ammunition. He took out two boxes of .44-caliber cartridges. He set them on the desk, then locked the drawer. He was getting some sets of handcuffs from a box along one wall when Cahill entered.

"You wanted to see me, Jonas?" Cahill asked.

Culpepper straightened. "Yep. Mack Ellsworth and his scoundrels robbed the train."

Cahill's eyes raised. "He's gettin' an early start this year."

Culpepper nodded. "This year, though, I aim to see that he also gets an early stop." He sighed. "I'll need to rustle up a posse, which I'll do, now that you're here. I want you to stay in Silverton and keep an eye on things."

Cahill nodded. "Knowin' those bastards, they'll be pullin' robberies up in Chattanooga or Red Mountain City the minute you and the posse ride out of Silverton."

"Those scoundrels pull somethin' like that, and I'll be one angry feller."

Cahill laughed a little. "I'm sure Ellsworth and his boys'll be quakin' in their boots at the thought of that."

Culpepper grinned a little, nodding. "I suppose they will." The situation was serious, but it did have its humorous aspects. "I'm going up to see Pennrose. While I'm gone, send somebody over to the Exchange and have Art saddle my horse."

"What're you goin' to see Pennrose about?" He was still angry about the likelihood that Wilson Pennrose had been the one responsible for him, Reinhardt, and Maguire being attacked.

"Get some help. It's Anvil Mining's money that was taken; Penrose should be willin' to help. I'll be back here before I pull out," Culpepper said as he and Bear turned for the door. He swiftly strode up Thirteenth Street to Greene, down to Twelfth, and up Twelfth to the Anvil Mining Company headquarters.

Culpepper noted that the door to the boardroom had been fixed since he'd been here more than a week ago. It was unlocked this time, and he walked straight in.

"Sheriff," Pennrose said evenly. He seemed angry. "You're here about the robbery?" he asked.

"You heard, then?"

"Of course," Pennrose snapped. "What're you going to do about it?"

"Well, I thought I'd let someone else handle it," Culpepper

said dryly. Noticing the apoplectic look on Pennrose's face, he said, "I'm going after them. That's why I'm here."

"What can I do for you?"

"Get me some of your men for a posse."

"Why should I do that?"

"How much was taken from the train today?" Culpepper countered.

"More than a hundred thousand in cash," Pennrose said sourly. "Maybe a third that much in silver bullion, plus some thousands in jewelry and other things. Why?"

"How much of it belonged to Anvil Mining?"

"Damn near all of it." Pennrose paused. "I want the men who took it, and I want all of it returned."

"Then give me a couple of your men for a posse."

"Chasin' outlaws is your job, Sheriff. My men's job is minin' silver."

Culpepper shrugged. "It ain't my silver and cash that was taken," he said nonchalantly. "I reckon I don't have to worry too much about gettin' it back."

"I'll make damn sure you never win another election in Silverton, you overstuffed son of a bitch."

Culpepper shrugged. "If it means I don't have to deal with rascals like you, I might not even run in the next election. I'm curious about one thing, though. Since most of what was stolen belonged to you and Anvil Minin', why aren't you more interested in helpin' me get the pukin' scoundrels who did it?" He paused, allowing Pennrose to speak.

When nothing was forthcoming, Culpepper said, "It's not unheard of for a man like you to be involved with someone like Mack Ellsworth. You tellin' him what the train's carryin', and when it's leavin'. Ellsworth hits the train, you sit here and make noises, then the two of you split the loot."

"I've never been so goddamn insulted, Sheriff. You'll pay for that someday, I swear to God you will."

"Well, until then, why don't you help me out? It might make some others think more kindly of you."

"I don't give a good goddamn what anyone thinks of me."

"So I figured. But if you're not workin' with Ellsworth, helpin' me out here might go a long way to convincin' me and others." He grinned tightly. "And, there's always a chance you could saddle me with one of your gunmen, who might shoot me in the back, thereby allowing you to fulfill your threat."

"I wouldn't have someone shoot you in the back, Sheriff," Pennrose said seriously. "If I sent men against you, they'll come at you head-on."

"I'll take that as a compliment."

"You should." Pennrose sat in thought for a little, then nodded. "You have a point, Sheriff," he finally said. "How many men you want?"

"Five, six ought to do it. I should be able to get a few from town."

"When?"

"At the Exchange in an hour."

"They'll be there. And, Sheriff, these'll be miners. I want the few—and I emphasize that it's very few—gunmen in Anvil's employ to stay here. Just in case Ellsworth and his men decide to pay Silverton a visit."

Culpepper nodded. He would feel more comfortable without several of Pennrose's hired guns riding with him. On the other hand, neither the townsmen nor the miners would be hunters of men, and that could be trouble on the trail of a gang like Mack Ellsworth's. Well, there was nothing he could do about it now.

Culpepper headed back to the office. There he told Cahill to round up some volunteers for a posse, to make sure supplies were available and that everyone's horse was ready.

"Where're you gonna be while I'm doin' all the work?" Cahill asked a little petulantly.

"Home, tellin' Merry what's going on," Culpepper said without any shame or snideness.

Cahill nodded. "Sorry, Jonas."

"Nothin' to be sorry for, Jimmy. I appreciate your help."

"I know." Cahill smiled a little. "Well, you'd best get goin'. You've got less than an hour, which means I've got less than an hour, and I've got a hell of a lot more work than you do at the moment."

As usual, Merry was not happy to see her husband go, but she said nothing about it. Instead, she fed Culpepper well, dragged him to their well-used bed for a bit, and then helped him get ready to leave. She knew he had a job to do and that she did not need to make it any harder for him.

For his part, Culpepper knew how Merry felt, and he really appreciated the fact that she did not make a scene about the many inconveniences brought by his job. As he did nearly every time he got ready to leave town because of his work, he silently vowed that someday he would reward Merry for her devotion and quiet support. He could never figure out how, though.

Then he was heading for Greene Street and the livery stable. Cahill was there with eleven men—six of them townsmen, including John Maguire and Buster Reinhardt; the other five were miners. All had horses saddled, and Cahill had two mules packed with supplies enough to last the group several days.

"Everyone got enough ammunition? And blankets?" Culpepper asked.

The men nodded or growled a low affirmative.

"You sure you two rascals are up to this?" he asked, looking from Maguire to Reinhardt. "It's only been two weeks."

Both nodded.

"All right," Culpepper said. He put his saddlebags and bedroll on his horse and then shoved his Winchester into a saddle scabbard. With a last look around, Culpepper pulled his bulk into the saddle. "Let's ride, boys," he said.

Chapter 10

They followed the Denver and Rio Grande tracks, moving at a good pace. When they encountered the pile of boulders, Culpepper dismounted and began looking around for sign. When he found some hoofprints that he thought belonged to the outlaws, he brought Bear over and had him sniff at the tracks a little. "All right, boy, follow them," he said to the dog, before pulling himself back into the saddle.

Bear was not a tracking dog by any means, but his natural ability to smell far more than a man could meant he could follow a trail as long as its scent was fairly clear to him. And Culpepper figured that having Bear follow the track was a lot better than having to do it himself.

The trail headed south, following the railroad tracks, and after a few miles, Culpepper figured Ellsworth and his gang were heading for Durango. The outlaws often spent time there, though they spread their blight for miles in all directions.

They camped that night on the eastern shore of a small lake. Because of the lake, there was plenty of game to be had, and they dined on fresh elk that Buster Reinhardt had brought down. The place also had plenty of wood from the pines and aspens growing thickly nearby, and there was even some new grass the animals could forage on.

Culpepper had the men up before dawn the next morning, though, and on the trail after a hasty breakfast. The outlaws had a five- or six-hour head start on him, and Culpepper wanted to make up some of that time.

Bear continued to followed the scent, or at least, so it seemed to Culpepper and the others. They had no reason to doubt the animal, since he was still moving along the railroad tracks.

Culpepper was surprised when late in the afternoon Bear suddenly turned west a few miles from Durango. Culpepper called to the dog to halt, and then he stopped, thinking. Finally he nodded. "Come on, Bear, this way," he called.

Confused, the dog loped over toward his master, tail wagging furiously.

"You can follow the trail again tomorrow," Culpepper said, as if the dog would understand.

"We goin' into Durango?" one of the miners—Luke Brown—asked. He was one who'd thought that following the dog was foolish.

"For the night," Culpepper said with a nod.

"Then what?" Brown asked.

"Then we come back here tomorrow and go that way." Culpepper pointed west.

"What'n hell for?" Brown whined.

"Because that's the way I say to go," Culpepper said flatly. "You want out of the posse, turn yourself around and go back to Silverton."

No one said anything; they were all too frightened of Culpepper, especially when he got that stubborn look on his broad face.

Soon after, they were riding into Durango. Following Culpepper's lead, they stopped in front of the office of town Marshal Ed Hernandez. "Buster, you and the rest of the men take the horses down to the livery and see to them. Mine, too. Then go get us some rooms over at Peña's Hotel. I'll meet you there and we can go fill our stomachs."

"You payin' for all this, Sheriff?" another miner—Ward Graham—asked. The other men laughed.

"Good Lord, no," Culpepper said with a grin. "You boys

think I owe Anvil Minin' or something? But," he added, "the county'll pay, since you rascals're part of an official posse. Now git."

Culpepper went into the marshal's office and was a little surprised to see Hernandez himself inside. He had dealt with the man on several occasions in the years he'd been San Juan County sheriff, and had found that Hernandez was smart, witty, and a thoroughly professional lawman.

"Sheriff Culpepper," Hernandez said with a smile, rising to shake Culpepper's hand. Hernandez was tall and lanky, with a craggy face, longish pitch-black hair, a thin black mustache, and dark eyes. His skin was dark enough that some might mistake him for an Indian.

"How've you been, Ed?"

"Just fine. You?"

"The same."

Hernandez poured them each a cup of coffee, then sat. "So what brings you down to Durango, Jonas?" Hernandez asked. "You sure as hell didn't come down here just to say hello to me." Hernandez had almost no trace of an accent.

"If I had the leisure to just come down here on a visit, I'd be a lot happier feller, I can tell you. But, no, this is business. Mack Ellsworth and his men hit the train out of Silverton yesterday morning. Those pukin' scoundrels got away with one big passel of cash and silver."

"They're bad ones, all right," Hernandez agreed as he rolled a *cigarito*. "They're here in Durango often enough, but they've never done anything in town I can arrest them for. Nothing provable, anyway. Hell, even Sheriff Hammond hasn't been able to do much about them."

"So I figured," Culpepper said with an annoyed shake of the head. "They been here the last day or so?"

Hernandez shook his head. "Haven't seen hide nor hair of any of his men in a couple weeks."

"Figured that, too."

"Sorry."

Culpepper shrugged. "It ain't your fault. Has Frank said anything about them?"

"Not to me. What makes you think they're here? Other than the fact that they like to think of this as 'home' sometimes."

"Followed their tracks all the way down from where they robbed the train. A couple miles out of town, though, Bear here tried to tell us the trail turned west."

Hernandez's eyebrows raised. "That's odd."

"I thought so."

"Wonder what that old bastard is up to."

"I'll be durned if I know. But I sure aim to find out."

Hernandez nodded. "If he was in town, or even real close to the outskirts, I'd offer you some help," he said apologetically. "But my jurisdiction doesn't run too far outside of Durango."

"I know," Culpepper said with a nod. He gulped some coffee down. "I was just lookin' for information."

"You might go see Frank. Even if he hasn't seen any of Ellsworth's men, he's still got jurisdiction in La Plata County. He might want to go along with you."

Culpepper nodded again. "I'll talk to him. He around town, I suppose?"

"Somewhere."

"Thanks, Ed," Culpepper said, rising. He swallowed the rest of his coffee and left. He checked his pocketwatch. He still had a little time before his posse was at the hotel. He turned up the street, walking swiftly toward the sheriff's office. He found La Plata County Sheriff Frank Hammond inside. The two men went through the greeting and pleasantry rituals before getting to the point.

"I ain't seen 'em neither," Hammond said, after Culpepper had explained his short visit to Hernandez's a few minutes ago.

"You have any idea where they might be headed?" Culpepper asked. "It don't seem natural for them to turn west two or three miles outside of Durango."

"Maybe they've found a new hideout or somethin'," Hammond said with a shrug. "Tell you the truth, Jonas, I'm glad those sons of bitches're out of my hair. Let them pester some other poor bastard of a sheriff and let him worry about 'em. You ought to do the same."

Culpepper laughed. "Easy for you to say, Frank. You don't have to run for election on a record of not havin' been able to bring Mack Ellsworth to heel."

"Sure I do," Hammond said, joining in the laughter.

"Not when it's the Anvil Minin' Company's money that was taken."

"I see your point." Hammond paused. He didn't really want to go along with Culpepper, but he figured that as a fellow lawman, he ought to offer. "You want my help?" he finally asked.

Culpepper thought it over a few moments. He had never taken to Frank Hammond much. He liked Ed Hernandez a lot better. Hernandez was more pleasant to be around, and much better at his job than Hammond. Indeed, Hammond looked like an outlaw most of the time. He was of medium height and had a scraggly beard and mustache. His face was hard-looking and was pocked and scarred. He wore black almost exclusively—black hat, coat, wool pants, boots. The only thing relieving the blackness was his crisp white boiled shirt.

"Reckon not," Culpepper said. "You've got your own duties here. If you knew where they might be holed up, I'd have accepted your help. The way it sounds, though, you'd be just as blind out there as the rest of us are. No reason to put you through that."

"You sure?" Hammond asked solicitously.

"Yep." Culpepper rose. "Well, Sheriff, thanks for your help, such as it was."

Hammond nodded and shook Culpepper's hand again, this time without getting up. "Sorry I couldn't be of more help to you, Jonas."

Culpepper nodded and left. He headed right to Peña's. The

hotel keeper smiled wanly at him. "Upstairs, Señor," Peña said. "Rooms eleven and twelve."

"Only two rooms?" Culpepper asked, annoyed.

"*Sí*, Señor. That's all I have open."

Culpepper nodded and trudged up the stairs. He opened the door to room eleven, which he reached first. Reinhardt and all the townsmen from Silverton—except Maguire—were inside.

"John's next door with the miners," Reinhardt said. "I figured it'd be a good idea if he kept an eye on them, considerin' who they work for and all, Jonas."

Culpepper nodded. "Good thinkin', Buster." Both men were holding up quite well and seemed none the worse for their wounds. He looked around the room. "It's going to be a mite crowded in here tonight, boys," he finally said sourly.

"Nothin' we—all of us—haven't been through before, Jonas," Reinhardt said. "We'll live through it." He paused. "You can have the bed. Me and the others'll spread out on the floor."

Culpepper nodded acceptance. He did not even think of being a martyr and turning down the offer. "All right, now that that's settled, let's go line our flues. I'm hungry."

Peña's had a restaurant, and Culpepper had found in previous trips that it was one of the best in Durango. The food was plentiful, well cooked, and inexpensive.

By the time they finished eating, it was dark and, since it had been a long, hard couple of days on the trail, Culpepper urged everyone to go to sleep. It seemed as if all the men took his advice.

Culpepper slept surprisingly well, considering the cacophony of snores, belches, and flatulence that echoed around the cramped room. He felt pretty refreshed when he awoke. He and the men ate in Peña's restaurant again. While he settled the bill with Peña, making sure he got receipts so he'd be reimbursed by San Juan County, Reinhardt, Maguire, and the others went to the livery to saddle the horses and pack the mule.

Culpepper and Bear waited outside the hotel for the posse to come along, which it eventually did. Then they rode out of town the same way they'd come in. When they neared the spot where Bear had tried to turn them west yesterday, Culpepper dismounted and talked quietly to the dog. "Now you can go find them boys, Bear," he said softly. "You follow them no matter where they go. Go on now, find them."

Bear bounded off, happy to be free again, and once more reassured that he was in his master's favor. The men followed.

They traveled slowly, allowing Bear to keep on the track without much trouble. Culpepper didn't want to wear the horses down too much, either. He hoped that Ellsworth's gang had gone not much farther and then had holed up, figuring they were safe from pursuit.

They were down out of the mountainous land, where peaks rose up all over, though they were still in the high country. But it was relatively flat, and quite barren, compared with the region around Silverton. Here there were no tall, stately pines, thin, noisy aspens, or places of thick brush. The land was speckled with scrubby brush, sage and stunted, wind-twisted cedars. Not far to the north, the La Plata Mountains rose tall toward the sky. It was the only thing that even remotely resembled the Silverton area, though they were less than seventy miles from Silverton, all told.

Without the shadows of the mountains and the shady cover of trees, the heat splashed over them. Since the sun had nothing to block it, it could beat down on the men unhampered.

Culpepper, who had brought his big bear-fur coat, took it off early in the day and tied it with thongs behind his saddle. The other men—knowing that mountain nights were cold, though it was now May—had also brought heavy coats, but they, too, soon discarded them under the sun's frightful assault.

By dark, they had covered about twenty-one miles, Culpepper guessed. So when they came to a bubbling stream, they called it a night. Bear still seemed to be willing to go on, so

Culpepper was encouraged, figuring they were still on the trail. But he did not want to go stumbling around at night. There was always the chance that Ellsworth and his men were not far away.

Chapter 11

The posse pushed a little harder the next day, covered nearly twenty-five miles as best as Culpepper could figure it, and camped for the night near the confluence of Mud Creek and the Mancos River. They had turned south when Bear had brought them that way, and soon after they had begun following the Mancos River, right from its headwaters.

In the morning, Culpepper was concerned that Bear would lose the trail, since they would have to cross either the river or the creek. Since Mud Creek was far smaller, he opted to try that first, to see if Bear could pick up the scent again.

Leaving the men in camp, Culpepper rode through the muck and mire and then across the narrow, shallow creek. Bear trotted alongside Culpepper's horse. The mastiff was not happy with all the mud, but found the cool water of the creek to be fun. He splashed in the water a little until Culpepper called to him.

Culpepper dismounted and petted Bear for some moments. Feeling slightly foolish, he knelt and said, "Go find the trail again, Bear. Go on."

Bear lapped at Culpepper's face a bit, seeming unconcerned with moving right at the moment. Then he suddenly bolted toward the left. Culpepper stood, feeling some relief—until he saw Bear pounce. A moment later the mastiff was ripping a good-sized jackrabbit to shreds. "Durn stupid animal," he muttered. He waited until Bear was finished with his impromptu meal before calling him back. "You're a mess, dog," he said, still annoyed. "But I'd be some more disposed to forgivin' you this transgression was you to find that trail again."

Holding the reins to his horse, Culpepper walked southward, close to the Mancos River. Half a mile away, Bear suddenly stopped, nose testing the breeze. He whined eagerly, then barked a couple times, his deep voice resonant in the air. The dog looked at Culpepper expectantly. "Found it, did you?" Culpepper asked with a smile of relief.

Bear quivered and whined some more, eager to be off and running. Culpepper nodded and mounted his horse. "Stay here, Bear," he said. He turned and galloped back to Mud Creek. "Come on," he yelled to his men across the creek. He waved his arm, urging them to speed up.

They were ready, and within moments the men of the posse had mounted and galloped across the muddy flat creek. Culpepper turned as they neared and galloped off again. When he neared Bear, he slowed to walk, and the others followed suit. "Go on, Bear," he said firmly. "Go find them for us."

The large dark-brindle mastiff bounced off, nose working overtime. The men followed. Before long, they entered a narrow, not too deep canyon through which the Mancos River flowed. And still they pressed on.

The canyon turned slowly west some hours later, and by late afternoon, Bear was taking them up out of the canyon, until they were riding atop a huge plateau. At times it gave them a view of hundreds of miles. It was eerie, Culpepper thought, though he said nothing. It seemed as if they were on the top of the world and would ride right off it. He finally managed to shrug off the gloom.

Not so the men, who continued to follow Bear and Culpepper docilely. But some of the posse men were beginning to grumble about all the travel, the sleeping outdoors, and all the trouble. Even the miners could see little reason for spending so much time away from their jobs and families just to recover silver and money that belonged to the Anvil Mining Company.

Culpepper couldn't really blame them for feeling that way, and that night, as they were sitting around the campfire, he said, "We'll give it 'til tomorrow, boys. We don't find those scoundrels by then, we'll head on home."

The men accepted that. Culpepper wasn't sure he did. After all, it was his job to run men like Mack Ellsworth and his ilk down. He hated to give up before the job was done. He stood and walked off into the darkness, enjoying the cool temperatures and the silence. And the stars. He had always liked gazing at the heavens and wondering about the stars he saw.

Bear sat at his side. Like Culpepper, he stared heavenward. Then the mastiff let out a small, soft whine. Culpepper looked down to see Bear with his head cocked. "You hear something, Bear?" Culpepper asked quietly.

The dog shifted his head, cocking it to the other side, still intent. Culpepper shut up and listened, but he could hear nothing but the low rumble of the conversation of the posse men near the campfire. Still, the wind was blowing lightly from the west, and in a place like this, sound would carry a good long distance. He was certain that the dog had heard something, and he wondered if perhaps Ellsworth and his men were out there in the darkness somewhere.

Culpepper finally shook his head. "Come on, Bear. Time for sleepin'." They headed back to the camp.

The morning's ride was slow, but even the men seemed to be more eager today. Culpepper wondered if it was because they sensed they would find the outlaws, or if it was because they figured they'd be heading back toward Silverton the next day.

The plateau they traveled on had far more vegetation than the stark flats they had been on a couple days ago. There were forests of piñons and junipers and cedars, plus plenty of brush, most of it scrubby, but some quite large. Wildflowers were growing in a colorful profusion.

Bear ranged out ahead of the posse by a hundred yards or

more, wandering with his nose to the ground, or occasionally in the air. He stopped now and again, cocking his head, as if listening for something. The latter gave Culpepper hope that they might be able to run the outlaws down today.

They turned almost due north, passing around the end of another steep, narrow canyon, and pushed on. Just before noon, they skirted some mud ruins that held little attraction for any of the men. They spotted some more of them a few minutes later, and Bear headed toward them.

Riding a hundred fifty yards or so behind his dog, Culpepper began to feel uneasy. He touched his heels to the horse and broke into a trot. The others looked at each other in surprise, but then spurred their own horses to catch up to Culpepper.

Less than fifty yards from the ruins, a shot suddenly rang out. The bullet kicked up earth a few feet from Bear. The mastiff dodged to the side and then stood growling.

"Durn it, Bear!" Culpepper shouted. "Get your tail back here!"

Another shot came, and Luke Brown tumbled from his horse.

Culpepper dismounted. "Ride, boys! Ride!" he roared. "Back to them other ruins. Go!"

"What about you?" Reinhardt asked.

"I'll be on your tails as soon's I grab Luke. Go!"

The posse wheeled and raced off. The men hunched their backs, each waiting for a bullet to strike them.

Culpepper grabbed Brown, noting straight off that Brown was dead. He threw the body across Brown's horse. Holding Brown's horse's reins, he jumped back on his own mount's back. Lying low over his horse's neck, Culpepper slapped the reins on the animal's withers and raced off, toward the ruins. Bear ran along close behind.

Culpepper stopped inside the ruins and dismounted. He pulled Brown's body down and set it gently on the ground, out of the way. Reinhardt took the two horses and put them with the others. Three men were guarding the animals in an open space surrounded by crumbling walls, a place that apparently had been a room in some long bygone time. The rest of the men were lining the walls facing the ruins where the shots had come from.

Culpepper joined them, noting almost without looking that the walls of the old abode were stone, covered with mud, much of which had washed away in rains or was worn away in the ever-present wind. The other ruins were less than a quarter of a mile away. Like the ones sheltering Culpepper's men, they appeared to be made of the same material. They could be easily seen, since there was nothing between the two sets of ruins— nothing but open space and brush. A few scattered cedars and clumps of brush would not provide much, if any, cover. That was both good and bad. While it meant that the outlaws could not sneak up on the posse, the posse could not sneak up on the outlaws. It was a Mexican standoff, at least for the time being.

Culpepper turned and sank to the ground, sitting with his back against the wall.

Reinhardt and Maguire joined him, the former lighting up a cigarette. "I think we found those bastards, Jonas," Reinhardt said, his words accompanied by puffs of smoke.

"I'd say so," Culpepper said flatly.

"What're we gonna do, Jonas?" Maguire asked.

"That's what I'm tryin' to figure out. For now, though, John, I'd like you to keep lookout on the wall. You're the best rifle shot I know. Keep alert. One of those pukin' scoundrels shows his face, put a bullet in it for him."

Maguire shrugged and rose. He walked to his horse and pulled his rifle out of the scabbard. Then he took up his position along the wall, right where he had been sitting, his rifle lying flat on some rocks that formed the wall.

Culpepper looked at Maguire and nodded to himself. One of the reasons Culpepper had often used John Maguire as a special deputy was because of Maguire's abilities with that old .44-90 Sharps rifle. The twelve-pound Sharps with the extra-heavy barrel and the adjustable rear sight was a relic from Maguire's days as a buffalo hunter. Maguire was a slightly older man—in his forties, which to a man of Culpepper's age was slightly older. He had fought in the Civil War, and had been something of a hero, Culpepper had heard. But these days, Maguire generally led a quiet, reserved life, running a general store with his wife, Caroline, and raising four children, the oldest of whom had struck out on his own a year ago. The youngest was nine. He was a good man to have around, Culpepper thought.

As was Reinhardt. Culpepper relied on Buster Reinhardt quite a bit. Even more so than Maguire. Reinhardt was short and stocky, with a wide face and a ready smile. He was jovial much of the time, but could be as hard a man as Culpepper ever saw. He didn't like violence, though Culpepper had heard Reinhardt had made his way in life with a gun for some years. That was before he'd met Vera Carruthers, who had tamed him and made a decent husband out of him. Reinhardt now made his living selling and repairing guns—and being a special deputy for Culpepper when needed.

"You come up with any bright ideas yet, Jonas?" Reinhardt asked.

Culpepper grinned a little. "Shooting you so's you won't ask no more durn fool questions comes to mind."

Reinhardt chuckled, then grew serious. "You know we ain't got a hope in hell of takin' them boys from here, don't you?"

Culpepper nodded. He didn't figure that really needed a verbal answer.

"Then we got us only two choices—hope they come at us and that we can take 'em; or get the hell out of here and go after those bastards another day."

"I didn't come all this way to give up without a fight," Culpepper said evenly.

"We've got one dead already. And for what? Some goddamn silver and cash that belongs to Anvil Minin'? Shit, Jonas, that ain't worth riskin' our necks for."

"No, Buster. No, it's not worth it. But there's more to it than that."

"Like what?"

"Like bein' true to our word. I gave my word when I became sheriff to do this kind of thing. I don't have to like it, but I ought to do it, since I give my word. So did you and John, even if the others didn't. I swear you two rascals in every time I hire you as deputies. In doin' so, you give your word, too."

"Yep, there's that, isn't there." It was not framed as a question. "It's hell bein' an honest man, ain't it?" he said with another sudden chuckle.

"At times it is, my friend, yes."

"So, what do we do, Jonas?"

"I got an idea, I think." He paused, then nodded. "We'll start takin' a few potshots at those pukin' scoundrels for the rest of the afternoon. Just enough to keep them from chargin' our position. Then, as soon as it gets dark, me, you, and John'll sneak on over there and see if we can't encourage those maggots to surrender to the forces of good."

"You've been out in the sun too long, Jonas," Reinhardt said with a laugh.

"I have, have I?" Culpepper countered. "You gone yeller in your old age?"

"Old age?" Reinhardt snorted. "You're older'n I am by a few years."

"True," Culpepper agreed. "Well, have you turned yeller since you've up and got a wife and children?"

"Tell you the truth, Jonas," Reinhardt said with a rueful smile, "I'd rather face those goddamn outlaws over there than face Vera when she's on one of her tirades. Not that it happens too often, you understand, but when it does, goddamn if it ain't a humdinger."

Culpepper laughed a little. "So, you agree to the plan?"

"Well, if that cockamamie idea you come up with is a plan, I guess I got to go along with it."

Culpepper looked up. "How about you, John?" he asked.

Culpepper knew that Maguire had been listening to every word, even while keeping his lookout.

"Well, hell, if that knobheaded young punk there's goin' along with you, I might's well do so, too. Somebody's got to keep an eye on you two damn fools."

Chapter 12

John Maguire picked off one of the outlaws late in the afternoon. The man had gotten either brave or stupid and stood up to yell insults. Maguire let him go for about two minutes, letting the man fill himself with bravado. Then Maguire punched a hole in the man's head.

That brought forth a fusillade from the outlaws' position. Culpepper's men hunkered down where they were, and let the outlaws' bullet whine harmlessly off the stones. About the only effect all the gunfire had was to spook the horses a little, so all the men but Culpepper, Maguire, and Reinhardt went back to help the three men already there calm the animals down.

Finally the gunfire dropped off and Culpepper's men retook their position along the wall. The shadows were deepening, but the fading sun was right in their eyes. Still, they managed to make sure none of the outlaws was either fleeing or attacking.

About that time, one of the men began a fire and threw some coffee, as well as salt meat and beans, on to cook. Since they would be leaving soon, Culpepper, Reinhardt, and Maguire ate first, filling their bellies against the night's chill and the coming work.

Dark at last began to arrive in full, and Culpepper and his two special deputies prepared to leave. Each made sure his two pistols were loaded—all six chambers this time—and that their cartridge belts were full. Culpepper pulled on his great bear coat and dumped a box of .44-caliber shells in one pocket. He looked at his two companions.

Maguire and Reinhardt also had pulled on their coats, the former's of fur-lined canvas, the latter's of heavy blanket material. Both were short, coming to about halfway down the men's buttocks. Maguire tied his hat on, but Reinhardt tossed his aside.

"You boys ready?" Culpepper asked.

"Shit yes," Maguire snapped.

Reinhardt only nodded.

The three walked around the wall and began moving slowly toward the other ruins. Bear padded along silently at Culpepper's left side. It was near about pitch black, since the moon and stars had not risen yet, but Culpepper had counted on that. The inky night would hide them from the eyes of the outlaws until they were right on top of them. It might cause the three some problems because they couldn't see, but if necessary, Bear could help them get to the ruins without much trouble, despite the darkness.

They were three-quarters of the way to the ruins, Culpepper estimated, when the sound of horses running suddenly washed over them.

"Shit, goddammit," Maguire snapped angrily. "The bastards're gettin' away."

A moment later, Bear growled low in his throat, and then several shots rang out.

"I'm goin' in!" Culpepper shouted. Then, more quietly, "Come on, Bear." Culpepper drew one of his Remingtons and charged forward, the dog at his side. He moved to his left a little, in case someone had tried to pick up on his voice. Then he ran straight ahead—and straight into one of the walls of the ruins.

"Durn all to Hades and back," he muttered angrily at himself. He got up, found the pistol he had dropped, and then leaped over the wall, using one hand on it.

A bullet banged off the rocks inches from his head as soon as he landed on the ground. He dropped down to one knee. With relief, he spotted the outlaw in the low glow of the fire. He fired twice, hitting the crouching man twice in the chest. The man went down.

Bear growled fiercely and suddenly shot forward. Culpepper rolled onto his right shoulder and then rolled a few more times before coming to a stop up on one knee again moments later. By then, Bear had an outlaw's arm in his mouth and was gnawing at it while the outlaw screamed.

The outlaw was frantically trying with his left hand to pick up the gun that had fallen when Bear had latched onto his right arm. He finally managed to get it. He brought it up and clobbered the mastiff on the head. Bear yelped but did not let go of the arm.

"Bear, here!" Culpepper bellowed. "Now!"

The dog let go of the outlaw's limb, whirled, and dashed toward his master. As soon as the mastiff did that, Culpepper calmly fired twice more.

The outlaw slumped onto his knees, dropping his pistol. His arms swept around his midsection as he fell onto his face.

"Good boy," Culpepper said, patting Bear a moment. "There any more? Huh? Is there? Any more outlaws?"

The dog rushed off, and Culpepper rose slowly. Warily he approached the man he had just shot. He stuck a boot toe under the man's chest and then rolled the outlaw over. The man was still alive, but he wouldn't linger long. Culpepper knelt and quickly searched the man for weapons. He found another pistol and he shoved it into his coat pocket. He swiftly replaced the four cartridges he had expended.

Bear came trotting back, looking pleased with himself, and plunked himself down next to Culpepper. "Didn't find no others, then?" Culpepper asked, petting the animal's head again. "Come on, let's go see about that other pukin' scoundrel."

That outlaw was already stone dead. Culpepper breathed a sigh of relief, but then worry reasserted itself in his stomach.

There still could be more outlaws lurking about, but he seriously doubted it. Still, he had neither seen nor heard from either Maguire or Reinhardt since the first burst of gunfire some minutes ago.

"Buster?" he yelled, trying to keep the urgent worry out of his voice. "John? Where are you rascals?"

It was a few heartshaking minutes before Reinhardt called out, "Over here, Jonas. Outside the wall."

Reinhardt's voice hadn't sounded right to Culpepper, and he hoped his friend was not wounded. He slapped a hand down on the top of the wall and vaulted over it. Then he had to wait a moment before his eyes adjusted to the darkness once again after they had become used to the light cast by the fire.

"Bear, go find Buster," he finally said. "Come on, take me to Buster."

The dog moved off, but kept half a step ahead of Culpepper, who kept an ever-so-light hold on the dog's tail. Finally some shadows moved and he saw Reinhardt, who was crouched or kneeling. Culpepper almost tripped over Maguire's body before he knew it was there.

"Oh, sweet Jesus, no," he whispered, as he knelt alongside Maguire's still figure. His thick fingers felt around on Maguire's throat, searching for a pulse.

"He's dead, Jonas," Reinhardt said flatly. "I figure he died right off."

"That first fusillade get him?"

"Yeah. I saw him go down, and I knew he was hit just by the way he fell. I've seen it too many times before not to know that look. I threw myself down right away and popped off a couple shots of my own, but I don't think they did any good. I heard you and Bear chargin' up there, and decided I'd wait where I was, just in case. Hell, I didn't want to shoot you—or get shot by you—runnin' around in the dark there." He sighed. "Damn it, damn it, damn it," he snapped. Then he calmed himself down some. "You get any of 'em in there, Jonas?" he asked.

"Two. One's dead. The other wasn't far from it when I left him. I suppose he's crossed the divide, too, by now."

"There any more about?"

"Doubt it. I figure those pukin' scoundrels were ridin' out of here when we heard the horses. I expect they left those two just in case we tried somethin'. I suppose they would've lit out before dawn and caught up to their cronies."

"I suppose. But I don't like it, not knowin' for sure."

"Me neither. But if any of those maggots was still there, they'd've shot me down easy, considerin' I was standin' right there in the firelight."

"Yeah, you must be right." Reinhardt sighed again. John Maguire had not been his best friend or anything. They hardly even socialized outside of this work they did for Culpepper. Still, Maguire had been a good man, and Reinhardt had not minded working with him. He was sad to see his friend—for that's what he and Maguire were, friends, when all was said and done—die. "What do we do now?"

"Wait here 'til I get back," Culpepper said. He left and went back into the outlaws' camp, where he found two horses. He also found the body of the man Maguire had killed earlier in the day. He grabbed that body and tossed it across the saddle of one horse. He did the same with the first man he'd killed, using the same horse. Then he took the third body and put that on the horse, too. He usually wasn't nearly so cruel to animals, but the horse would have to walk less than a quarter of a mile with the three bodies on its back.

Culpepper led both horses out around the fallen-down side wall of the ruins and over to where Reinhardt still waited. "Put John's body up on this horse here, Buster," he said, indicating the animal with no bodies on it.

Reinhardt did so and then the two men, each leading a horse, and Bear walked slowly back toward their own camp. As they neared it, Culpepper called out, "It's Jonas and Buster comin' in."

Then they were in the camp, and the posse men were crowding around, full of questions as well as fear.

"Shut up!" Culpepper finally bellowed. "All of you." When they had quieted down, Culpepper said in an even tone, "John opened his mouth out there, and that gave away his position. Most of the outlaws took off, but they left two behind. They got John, then I got them. The third one there is the one John shot from here this afternoon. That's all there is to tell. Now leave off with all your questions."

"I got to ask one more, Sheriff," Ward Graham said tentatively.

"What's that?" Culpepper asked, fighting his temper.

"What'll we do now?"

"What do you want to do?" Culpepper countered.

"Head back to Silverton," Graham said flatly. "I don't know about the rest of these boys, but I've had enough of this shit of trackin' outlaws. Not for Anvil Minin's money. I'm sorry about Maguire's bein' dead, but I hardly knew him, and I've got no time for grievin' over him."

Culpepper rose and turned to face the men. "The rest of you boys feel the same?" No one said or did anything, so Culpepper snapped, "Have the sand to stand up and say what you feel, boys."

All the men except for Reinhardt nodded their agreement.

Reinhardt was about to berate them all when Culpepper held up his hand to stop him. "Leave them be, Buster," Culpepper said. "They're entitled to their opinions. And their feelings. These men've been away from their families for what, four, five days, maybe, and it'll be several more before we get back to Silverton. They're not like you and me, Buster. You know that as well as I do."

Reinhardt nodded. He didn't like it, but he could accept it. "So, what's next, Sheriff?" he asked.

"We leave for Durango at first light. From there we head home."

"And then?"

"And then, Buster, I'll see. If you're of a mind to join me on my next little mission, I'll be glad to have you along. But there's a heap of things got to be done first."

Reinhardt nodded again. "Anything you need me to do before I take to my bedroll, Jonas?"

"No. Thanks, Buster. Ward, you and Pepperill stand guard over the horses. Phelps and Curran, you relieve them in four hours. The rest of you'd best get some sleep. It's going to be a long day tomorrow."

Culpepper had a little trouble getting to sleep himself. Telling the wives of the two posse men who'd been slain was not going to be easy, especially Caroline Maguire. The thought of it gave him an uneasy night.

Culpepper pushed the men as hard as he dared the next day. He knew they could not make it to Durango in one day, but he wanted to make as much distance as possible then to make the run into Durango easier the next day.

Maguire's body was wrapped in a blanket and tied across his own horse. Brown's body also was blanket wrapped and tied on his horse. The three dead outlaws were tied to the horses taken from the outlaw camp—two on one horse, one on the other. The next day, the bodies were switched on those horses.

It was well past dark when Culpepper called a halt and allowed camp. The men were tired and complained some about the pace and the many hours they had ridden that day. But they didn't grouse too much. Each mile they had put behind them today was one less mile they had to go before getting to Silverton.

Four other men split the horse-guarding duties. They grumbled about that, saying that there was no need for it now as there had been the night before.

But Culpepper was taking no chances. "Just because those pukin' scoundrels rode off out of that camp last night doesn't mean they went all that far. They could be right on our tails, lookin' to get revenge for sendin' their three cronies across the divide."

That was enough to quiet the men down, though it did nothing to help the others sleep comfortably. Most kept waking throughout the night, sure they heard outlaws creeping into their camp to kill them in their bedrolls.

Chapter 13

They rode into Durango under the interested eyes of a fair portion of the town. Durango was a wild enough place at the best of times, but it was still unusual for a posse to coming riding into the city with five bodies dangling over saddles.

Culpepper stopped them in front of the office of La Plata County Sheriff Frank Hammond. Culpepper dismounted. Everyone waited on their horses as Culpepper and Bear went into the office.

"Back so soon?" Hammond asked. It seemed to Culpepper as if Hammond had not moved since the last time he'd come into the office. "Any luck?"

"We picked off three of those maggots."

"That's good news. I didn't think you'd even find 'em."

"But we lost two men from the posse."

"That's not good," Hammond agreed. "Am I the first to know?"

"Yep. Except for the people standin' outside gapin' at my men."

"Why?"

"I need your help."

"Doin' what?"

"I need your undertaker to fix up my two men."

"Go see Marshal Hernandez for that. That's his jurisdiction."

"I will. I also need your help in gettin' the reward money for those three maggots we killed."

"You're in a hell of a hurry."

"Yes I am. You should have paper on all three of them. I think their names are Buckley, Knight, and Chamberlain. I don't know how much they're worth, but I figure it's at least a couple hundred each."

"I'd say so." Hammond did not move.

"I'd be obliged if you was to find the papers on them so we can get this taken care of."

"Come on, Sheriff," Hammond said easily. "You know it ain't that easy. There's paperwork to fill out, and banks to deal with, and all that kind of shit. You leave the three bodies here. I'll get all the particulars in my own good time and send the money up to Silverton."

"You don't seem to understand, Frank," Culpepper said flatly. "We're leavin' tomorrow. And I want that reward money in my pocket when I do leave."

"Jesus, you're a money-grubbin' son of a bitch, ain't you, Jonas?" Hammond said, not asked.

Culpepper got up from his chair and reached over the desk. He grabbed Hammond's shirtfront in his big left hand and jerked Hammond forward until his face was only inches away.

"Now, you listen to me, you maggot-eatin' little puke," Culpepper said harshly. "I've got two dead men out there. One of them's a good friend of mine. I've got to go back to Silverton and tell their wives that they died doin' their duty. I ain't going to do that without some kind of money to give them to tide them over and maybe ease the pain of their losses a little."

"Well, don't get so goddamn uppity, Sheriff," Hammond said with a distinct quiver of nervousness in his voice. "I didn't realize . . . I wasn't thinkin' about that."

"It's obvious you weren't thinkin' at all, you maggot," Culpepper said, still roughly. He shoved Hammond back into his seat. "I'll go speak to Ed Hernandez about the undertakin'. But I expect you to take care of this other. I aim to be on the durn train when it pulls out tomorrow mornin'. Either I have the reward money in my pocket when I get on the train, or I'll pay you another visit. I have to do that, it won't be as pleasant as this visit. And you'd best goddamn heed what I just said, boy."

Hammond blanched. Anyone who knew Jonas Culpepper more than an hour knew that if he ever used a curse word, then he was deadly serious, and mighty angry. "Yeah, yeah, Sheriff. It'll be ready. Hell, I'll bring it over to the train myself. Sure thing."

"Make sure of it." Culpepper spun. "Come on, Bear," he said, walking out. Outside, Culpepper mounted his horse and silently led the way to Marshal Hernandez's office. His reception there was considerably more favorable than it had been in Hammond's. Culpepper quickly explained what he needed.

"I can see to that for you, Jonas," Hernandez said. "You just leave your friends with me and I'll make sure they get taken care of. I'll have them in nice coffins, waitin' for you at the train station in the morning. You can leave the outlaws, too. I'll see that they get cheap coffins and get buried over near the cemetery."

"I appreciate it, Ed," Culpepper said, feeling relieved.

Culpepper and his men were just loading their horses onto a small boxcar on the narrow-gauge train when Hammond arrived. He looked nervous, and he pulled out a wad of cash. "Seven hundred dollars," he said. "Three hundred on Chamberlain, two hundred each on Buckley and Knight." He shrugged. "The bank'd only give it to me in paper money," he said apologetically.

"That'll do," Culpepper said, as he took the cash. He stood and patiently counted it in front of Hammond, making almost a show of it. "It's all there," he finally said, stuffing the money into a pocket. "Thank you for your help, Sheriff." He turned, dismissing him.

Meanwhile, his men finished loading the horses. Moments

later, Hernandez arrived. Behind him were two hearses moving slowly, majestically. The hearses stopped and several men took one coffin out of one and carried it to another train car. That done, they did the same with the second. Then the hearses moved off again, their large black horses almost prancing.

"I hope that's satisfactory, Jonas," Hernandez said. "It was kind of a hurried job."

"It appears to be all we could ask for, Ed. How much do I owe you—or the undertaker—for it?"

"Mister Drake—he's the undertaker—said to tell you that there's no charge. He says it's to thank two brave men."

"Well, you tell Mister Drake I appreciate it considerably, Ed. And these men's families'll appreciate it, too." He and Hernandez shook hands.

"Time to get movin', Sheriff," fireman Chester Graves said. "You and your men best go aboard before Lou decides to pull out without you."

Culpepper nodded. "Well, Ed, thanks again. You ever get up to Silverton, I'll spot you a beer and a beefsteak dinner. It's the least I can do." Then Culpepper helped Bear up into the boxcar where the other men were already sitting or lying.

The whistle blew and a moment later the train jerked as it puffed into motion. Slowly it gathered speed, and before long it was chugging away at a pretty good clip.

It took only five hours for them to get to the spot where the robbery had taken place a week ago. It was cleared of all the boulders, as Culpepper had known it would be. How else would engineer Lou Barber and fireman Chester Graves have gotten to Durango? Or be ready to take another train north?

Not long after, the train puffed into Silverton and hissed to a stop. Culpepper hopped out of the boxcar first and called to Lee Bondurant, the boy who worked at the depot. He bent and spoke with the ten-year-old for a few moments, handed Lee a coin, and then the boy ran off.

"Want me to stick around a while, Jonas?" Reinhardt asked.

"Might not hurt," Culpepper said with a nod. "Get the

horses unloaded and then send the men on their way. And here." Culpepper peeled off one hundred dollars. "Divide that up among the other men."

"Sure," Reinhardt said, taking the money and jamming it in a pocket. "What about the other?" he asked, pointing to the boxcar that held the coffins.

"I just sent Lee over to get Dietrich. He ought to be here soon."

Reinhardt nodded. "I'll stick around after the others go, just in case."

"If you're really feelin' brave, you can come with me to tell Caroline Maguire and Brown's wife, what's her name?"

"Cora, I think." Reinhardt hesitated. "I'll come along. John was my friend, too. I didn't know Luke, really, but we were all in that mess together. I might as well stick it out to the end."

"Guess you are pretty brave after all," Culpepper said with a tight smile. "Or else pretty durn stupid."

"I wouldn't wager on either side of that one," Reinhardt said with a little laugh as he walked away, heading toward the boxcar in which the horses were.

Silverton was also big enough a city to have several hearses, and Culpepper stood and watched as Karl Dietrich and some of his men rode majestically down the street. The two carriages stopped, and Dietrich climbed down. He was a short, thin, dapper man, with a perpetually somber face.

"Vhere is dis coffinks?" he asked.

Culpepper pointed to the boxcar. "Treat them well, Karl," he said quietly.

Dietrich look sharply at him, then nodded. "Yah, I alvays treat dem vell."

"I suppose you do, Karl. Just take them up to your place for now. As soon as I tell the families, we can decide when to do the burying."

"I vill have de graves dug," Dietrich said, then turned away and began issuing quiet, insistent orders.

Reinhardt strolled up. Culpepper looked at him. "We'd best

get our work done with." The two walked slowly up the street. Like many of the married miners, Luke Brown lived in a shack along Eighth Street, near Reese Street.

Telling Cora Brown was difficult, though she seemed to take it well. Especially when Culpepper handed her one hundred fifty dollars. She had never seen so much money at one time. That, she knew, would keep her and the children alive for a while—long enough to find another husband. Even in a place like Silverton, where there were numerous married couples, men still outnumbered women considerably. Cora would have no trouble finding another husband, despite her slovenly dress, unattractive person, and five children. She would want another husband, too; that was a fact. A woman like Cora Brown, with five children and no discernible talent, would die soon after the reward money ran out if she didn't find another husband.

Afterward, Culpepper and Reinhardt reluctantly walked north along Reese Street, then east on Fourteenth Street. Halfway to Greene Street, on the north side of Fourteenth, was John Maguire's house. Culpepper hoped Mrs. Maguire was there; he would hate to have to tell her at the store.

She was there. Caroline Maguire knew as soon as she answered Culpepper's knock on her door. She was a tall, stately woman, with an almost regal handsomeness to her. She allowed Culpepper and Reinhardt into the house, had them sit, then poured them coffee. Finally she sat, too.

"How?" she asked. She was heartbroken, but trying hard not to show it too much.

Culpepper explained it, embellishing it a little as to Maguire's role. They settled on a burial for the next morning. Then Culpepper sat and held Caroline for a spell while she cried out some of her grief.

When she finished that—for the time being—Culpepper gave her four hundred dollars of the reward money. "I know that don't in any way make up for your loss, Caroline. But it might help tide you over. The undertaker down in Durango paid for fixin' John up, and the coffin and all. If Dietrich wants to charge for the burial, the county'll pay it. Or I will. The money's reward money, and John earned it. Not only this time, but for all those other times he's helped me." He stopped, not knowing what else to say.

Finally he rose, as did Reinhardt. "If you need anything, Caroline," Culpepper said, "anything at all, you come see me."

"Or me," Reinhardt piped in.

Caroline nodded. "Thank you, Sheriff, Mister Reinhardt. I appreciate all you've done."

Feeling absolutely miserable, Culpepper and Reinhardt stepped outside. "Here, Buster," Culpepper said, handing Reinhardt the final fifty dollars of the reward money.

"I can't take this, Sheriff," Reinhardt protested.

"Durn well you can. And you and Vera can use it, too. You were a big help out there, and you deserve it."

"But what about you? You didn't get anything out of it."

Culpepper shrugged. "There'll be other times. Go on to your wife now. She's probably pinin' away for you." He smiled easily.

Reinhardt nodded. The men went their separate ways, with Culpepper heading for his office. Cahill was there, pacing. He knew when the train had come in, and he knew two coffins had been taken off it. He had waited, though, knowing that Culpepper would come to the office as soon as he could—unless the sheriff was in one of the coffins. He had found out that wasn't true half an hour after the train had pulled in when someone who had watched the proceedings at the depot came by and reported seeing Culpepper.

"Where the hell've you been, damn it?" Cahill asked, letting his agitation show.

Culpepper slumped into his chair and rubbed a hand tiredly across his face. "Luke Brown was killed," he said, even more quietly than usual. "And so was John Maguire."

"No!" Cahill was shocked.

"Yep. I went to talk to Brown's widow first. I just come from talking to Caroline Maguire. She took it hard."

"I'm sure she did." He paused. "Damn, Jonas, that must've been hard, tellin' her."

"About the hardest durn thing I ever had to do. And I'll tell you somethin' else, Jimmy—I don't want to have to ever do it again. No, sir."

"So what happened out there? Did you get Ellsworth?"

"Nope. We popped three of those pukin' scoundrels, but they got Brown and John. We left off chasing them then and went back to Durango to see that our two men were cared for. Then we came back up here."

"What're you plannin' to do next?"

"Go back after them. After I've spent a day or two with Merry." He rose and walked out.

Chapter 14

Culpepper walked into his office two days later, feeling almost refreshed. Spending a lot of time with Merry always went a long way toward making him feel better, and she had been particularly solicitous of him once she'd heard what had happened. He had felt a little better after the first night with Merry, but then the melancholy feeling had come over him again the morning before—when he'd attended the funerals for Luke Brown and John Maguire. The former's was sparsely attended, since Wilson Pennrose would not let his miners off work to go to the burial.

Still, Merry brought him around again as they had spent all of yesterday after the early morning burials together, simply enjoying each others' company.

His fine mood evaporated in a hurry, though, when he and Bear walked into the office and saw a stranger sitting in his chair, his feet up on the desk. The man wore a badge and was smoking a fat, stinking cigar.

"Get your feet off my desk, maggot, and get out of my chair," Culpepper growled.

"I'm Deputy United States Marshal Ned Coakley," the man said, blowing out a long stream of smoke.

"I don't much care if you're the President of all these-here United States, you pukin' scoundrel. Get your feet off my desk and get your tail out of my chair."

"Or what?" Coakley sneered.

"Get him, Bear," Culpepper said quietly.

The mastiff bared his fangs and squatted back, ready to launch himself.

"Hold on there, pardner," Coakley said with an uneasy smile. "I'll get up here in just a minute."

"Down, Bear," Culpepper said. He took the few steps separating him from the desk. Then he grabbed Coakley's ankles where the spur straps cross his boots, and jerked them up. He gave a final shove, sending Coakley rump over teakettle over on his head, the chair crashing backward.

Coakley jumped up, his now-broken cigar sticking out of his fingers, making him look quite foolish. "Why, you overstuffed son of a bitch," Coakley growled, throwing away the cigar. "I'm gonna gut you, you fat . . ."

Culpepper ignored him. He simply walked around the back of the desk and righted the chair. Then he sat down and crossed his hands on his stomach. "You're not going to do a durn thing, maggot. So shut up."

Coakley's flaccid face was pasty, and his right hand moved toward a Colt revolver.

"I wouldn't do that if I was you, maggot," Culpepper said calmly.

Coakley glanced at Bear. "I'm gonna shoot that goddamn stinkin' animal of yours. Then I'm gonna shoot you . . ."

"Before you got your piece out, Bear'd have your throat. If there was anything left when he got done with you, I'd finish up for him. Now, quit threatening me. If you've got something you need to say to me, say it, then get lost."

Coakley steamed for a few moments, then grinned. His face brightened, and he didn't seem quite the crazy man he had. In fact, he looked rather handsome in a pale, sly kind of way. He wasn't too tall, but had broad shoulders and a slim waist. His hair was long and stringy, except where it curled at the ends. He wore a dark wool suit with a collared off-white shirt that had only four buttons from the top. It was closed with a string tie.

Like Culpepper, he wore two pistols high up on his hips. His hat, which he'd been wearing before Culpepper had dumped him over, had a wide, round brim with a short, flat crown. Despite the suit, he had a tough, well-used look about him.

"They told me you was a hardcase, Sheriff," Coakley said. "Guess they weren't wrong."

"Fine. Now that you're done complimentin' me, maybe you'd like to tell me the reason you're here."

"Well, Sheriff," Coakley said, "that might take a little doin'."

"It's going to take all the durn day if you don't get started on it," Culpepper said dryly.

Coakley picked up his hat, dusted it off, and set it on his head. Then he took the other chair in the room and turned its back toward the desk. He straddled it, arms folded along the top of the back. "You were supposed to deliver a prisoner to me in Durango a little while back. You never did."

"Nope."

Coakley looked annoyed. "Then I heard about the trouble you had here a week or so ago."

"The train robbery?"

"Yep." Coakley took out another cigar and struck a match.

"That durn thing going to stink as bad as the last one?" Culpepper asked.

"I expect so," Coakley said with a chuckle. "It's the same damn kind."

"You fire that foul thing up, and I'll throw it—and you—out in the street."

"You are joshin', ain't you, Sheriff?" Coakley asked, surprised. He jerked as the match singed his fingers, waved the match in the air to put it out, then dropped it in the spittoon by the desk.

"Does it look like I'm joshin', Marshal?"

"No, I guess it don't. You know," he added, as he put the cigar back into an inside coat pocket, "you are one mighty unfriendly cuss, Sheriff."

"I won't argue that point with you. But you seem to forget

that you're in my town, in my office. If you had any manners, we wouldn't be sittin' here makin' threats at each other."

"All right, Sheriff, you're right," Coakley said unctuously. "Let's call a truce, huh?"

"Fine. Now, if you've got a reason to be here, perhaps you'd like to make it known."

"Well, as I was sayin', we heard about the trouble you folks had up here, so Norm Hendershot—he's the United States marshal for Colorado—wired me in Durango to come up here and take a look-see for myself."

Culpepper nodded. "Understandable, I suppose." He paused, then shrugged. "Now that you've had your look-see, you can get out of Silverton."

"You're not the town marshal."

"True," Culpepper said agreeably. "So get out of San Juan County, which, of course, includes Silverton."

"Damn, Sheriff. I come in here ready to offer you a helpin' hand, and you go and spit in that hand of friendship."

"Hand of friendship my tail," Culpepper spat, growing angrier.

"How'd your posse do against Ellsworth's bunch?" Coakley asked with a sneer.

"Not as well as I'd like," Culpepper said flatly.

"Didn't get any of 'em, did you?"

"Three."

Coakley's eyes widened. "Didn't you bring 'em back here?"

"What for? They was dead and they were startin' to get ripe."

"But what about the reward on them?"

"It's been paid."

Coakley scratched at his straggly mustache a moment. "You know, Sheriff, when Marshal Hendershot sent me out here, he put me in charge of all of western Colorado. Left it to my care, as it were."

"So?"

"So, as the United States deputy marshal for all of western

Colorado, it only stands to reason that I should receive a portion of the reward for the slain outlaws."

Culpepper laughed, though there was little humor in the sound.

"I don't see that there's anything funny about this," Coakley said angrily.

"You mean you weren't foolin'?" Culpepper asked sarcastically.

"Damn it, me gettin' some of that reward is only right and proper. Damn right it is. Happens all the time."

"Takin'—and demandin'—bribes is against the law in San Juan County, Marshal," Culpepper growled.

"What bribe?" Coakley asked, seemingly surprised. "All I'm askin' is for what's due me."

"Due you my tail, you pukin' maggot," Culpepper snarled angrily. "You come waltzin' in here with your fancy federal badge and expect everyone to bow at your feet. No, sir, I'm afraid you're in the wrong town. If others're givin' you portions of reward money other folks've earned, then I suggest you go on back to one of those places."

"I see," Coakley said tightly, "you plan on keepin' all that reward money yourself, is that it?"

Culpepper had to wait a minute for the rush of rage to simmer down some. "Marshal," he said slowly, softly, when he thought he could be reasonable, "I come in here today and find a maggot with no manners takin' over my office. Then he threatens me, and now he insults me. While I'm a reasonable man most times, I can only be pushed so far."

"What insult?" Coakley asked. "You keepin' the reward money? Hell, all sheriffs and marshals do that. I can understand that. But with the system most of us've worked out, I should get a little share of it. Hell, twenty-five percent's all I ask."

"I couldn't give it to you even if I'd lost my reason and decided I wanted to do that."

"Why?" Coakley asked. "I thought you said you got it down in Durango."

"I did. But it's gone."

"How the hell could you blow several hundred dollars in a place like Silverton in only two days?" Coakley demanded, his voice rising in agitation.

"Didn't say I blew it. That's another insult. A third one'll get you thrown out."

"Then what happened to it?" Coakley asked sarcastically. "If you don't mind my askin'."

"Actually, I do mind you askin', durn you. But since you're going to be a burr in my tail about it, I'll tell you. I gave a small portion of the reward money to the men of the posse. I gave the bulk of it to the widows of the two men in my posse who were killed."

"I don't believe that for a goddamn minute," Coakley blurted.

"Your time's just run out, Marshal," Culpepper said, standing. He walked around the desk, grabbed a surprised Coakley by the collar of his suit coat, hauled him up, marched him to the door, opened it, and then threw Coakley out into the street.

Coakley landed with a plop in the mud. The sun was still melting the snow on most of the mountainsides around Silverton, making Silverton a muddy mess for most of the spring. Coakley stood, looking at himself in horror when he saw the glop all over his suit. "I'll get you for this, you dumb son of a bitch!" he shouted, shaking a fist at the office. He turned and stomped off angrily, which caused him to lose his footing. He plopped into the mud again, this time to the accompaniment of laughter from the people on the street.

Culpepper sat in his office wondering if he had done the right thing. He finally convinced himself that he had, more or less. He had done right in refusing to split the reward money with Coakley, but he had not done it the right way. All he had done was to create an enemy where there might've been a friend. He felt lousy about that, and considered trying to find Coakley and apologize to him—for throwing him into the street, not for anything else. Then he decided he would wait until the next day. He would see how he felt then.

Late that afternoon, one of Luke Brown's children—Culpepper didn't know which one—tentatively entered Culpepper's office.

"Afternoon, son," Culpepper said. "What can I do for you?"

"Ma says she'd like to see you, Sheriff. But only if you ain't too busy." He seemed ashamed to be asking such a thing of the important, busy county sheriff.

"I ain't doin' anything at the moment. Are you, Jimmy?"

Cahill shook his head.

"You don't think your ma'd mind Deputy Cahill comin' along, too, do you, son?" Culpepper asked.

"Nah, I don't think so."

They walked swiftly to the Brown house and were let in. "I don't know how to say this, Sheriff," Cora Brown said uncomfortably.

"Just say what you got to say, ma'am," Culpepper coaxed.

"It's about the money . . . you know, the money you gave me the other day?"

"The reward? Sure. Wasn't it enough?"

"Oh, it was more than generous, Sheriff. Yessir, it was."

"Then what's the problem, ma'am?"

"A marshal—a federal marshal—come here a little while ago and told me he had to have that money back, since there was some kind of problem about the way it had been handled."

"So you gave him the money?" Culpepper asked, furious.

Cora nodded. "I was too scared of him to say no."

"All right, ma'am, don't you worry. I'll have your money back to you in no time flat. Don't you fret."

"I don't want to cause you any trouble, Sheriff."

"No trouble at all, ma'am. Now, if you'll excuse me, Deputy Cahill and I have some business to take care of."

Cahill knew better than to say anything to Culpepper as they

110

marched down Eighth Street toward Greene Street. They turned left on Greene, heading for the saloon district a few blocks away. Culpepper's face was set in stone. But he did manage to ask, "You know where that flatulent skunk's been hangin' around?"

"Who, Coakley?"

"Yep."

"I ain't sure. But I heard either Goode's or Fatty Collins'."

They did not see him in Goode's, and no one there had seen Coakley, so Culpepper and Cahill turned for Blair Street. In minutes, they were entering Fatty Collins' place.

Chapter 15

Coakley was leaning against the bar with one foot on the brass rail. He was talking to Fatty Collins. There were few other patrons in the saloon at the moment, and those few were drinking or gambling quietly.

Culpepper marched straight up to Coakley, who was looking toward Collins, grabbed Coakley by the back of the neck, and shoved his head down toward the bar. With his other hand, Culpepper grabbed Coakley's right wrist and jerked the arm up and around behind his back, spilling the whiskey as he dropped the glass.

"What the hell . . . ?" Coakley choked out, as his nose brushed the wood bar.

"You owe Cora Brown a hundred and fifty dollars, maggot," Culpepper said harshly. "You either fork it over now, or I'll break your arm and then throw you in jail for robbin' a poor widow and her children."

"What the hell're you talkin' about, you asswipe?" Coakley mumbled into the bar.

"You know durn well what I'm talkin' about. No sooner than I told you I gave some of the reward money from those three outlaws we caught to Cora Brown, you went and took that money from her by use of threats and intimidation."

"I didn't do no such . . ."

Culpepper twisted the arm a little more, making Coakley

gasp. "It's a simple thing, Marshal," he said. "The money, now, or your arm and jail."

"All right, all right," Coakley said, pain in his voice.

Culpepper let Coakley's arm go, but kept his head down until he had pulled out both Coakley's pistols and handed them to Cahill. Then he released Coakley's head and moved back a step.

Coakley turned around, rubbing his twisted arm. His eyes blazed with hate and anger. "You're foolin' with dangerous stuff here, boy," he hissed.

"The money, maggot," Culpepper said quietly. Then he roared, "Now!"

Coakley reached into his shirt pocket and pulled out a wad of money. He carefully counted out one hundred fifty dollars and held it out.

"Add fifty for the sufferin' you caused Mrs. Brown."

Coakley glowered, then counted out fifty more and handed it all to Culpepper.

The sheriff stuffed it into a pants pocket. "You have half an hour to get out of Silverton, Marshal Coakley. I'd advise you not to return—unless your attitude improves considerably."

"You can't throw me out of town, boy," Coakley said, trying to regain a little confidence and swagger. "I'm a deputy United States marshal for this area, which gives me leave to go anywhere I damn well please and stay as long as I damn well see fit to."

"Then go somewhere else and stay as long as you want," Culpepper said reasonably. "Just get out of Silverton, you pukin' scoundrel."

"You're in big trouble, Sheriff," Coakley said tightly, anger still stamped on his face.

"I'm quakin'," Culpepper said dryly. "Half an hour. Not a minute longer." He turned, and with Bear on one side and Cahill on the other, began walking away.

"Hey," Coakley shouted, "what about my pistols?"

Culpepper stopped and looked back. "They'll be at my office. You can pick them up as you leave Silverton."

Culpepper, Cahill, and the mastiff walked slowly back up to the shabby Brown house and handed Cora Brown the money—including the extra fifty dollars. "Now, you don't give that money to anybody except when you're buyin' something," Culpepper said. "I'm going to make sure that marshal leaves Silverton. But if he should come skulkin' back here and bother you again, you tell him that I'm holdin' the money for you, or that the money's in the bank, or that you've spent it. Then get word to me." He smiled a little. "But I don't think he'll be back."

"Thank you, Sheriff," Cora said gratefully. She was confused and stunned. First she'd lost her husband, then she'd had more money than she'd ever seen at one time. But that had been snatched away from her so suddenly. And now, just as suddenly, the money—and some extra—was back. She wasn't quite sure how to react.

"You're welcome, ma'am," Culpepper said quietly. "Now, you come see me—or Deputy Cahill—if you have any trouble, you hear?"

Culpepper and Cahill went back to the office and waited.

Twenty-eight minutes after they'd left Fatty Collins' place, U.S. Deputy Marshal Ned Coakley walked into the office. He was still livid, and simply growled, "Give me my pistols."

Culpepper picked one revolver off the desk and tossed it to Coakley. Then he did the same with the second. "They're empty," he said. "You can reload them when you get out of town." He paused, tugging at his mustache as Coakley checked the pistols and then put them in his holsters.

"And," Culpepper finally continued, "to make sure you do leave Silverton, Deputy Cahill and Mister Reinhardt here"—he pointed to Buster Reinhardt, who was leaning against a wall—"will escort you for a way, just to make sure you don't have some foolish change of heart and try to return."

"Oh, I'll be back one day, Culpepper," Coakley said harshly.

"And when I come back, you're gonna sure as hell regret it."

"You come back here with that durn attitude and you'll be in more trouble than you know how to deal with. Good-bye, Marshal Coakley," Culpepper added with finality.

Cahill and Reinhardt returned late in the afternoon. "I don't trust that son of a bitch, Jonas," Cahill said. "He'll be back, sure as hell."

"I know that," Culpepper said. "But there's not a durn thing I can do about it. He wants to come back, he'll come back. I'll deal with it then. Or you will."

"What do you mean by that?" Cahill asked, eyes questioning.

"I'm headin' out in the mornin'," Culpepper said flatly. He had been planning to all along, but hadn't gotten around to saying anything about it to Cahill until now.

"After Ellsworth again?"

Culpepper nodded.

"The trail's gone cold, Jonas," Reinhardt said. "It's been a week and a half or so."

"Buster's right," Cahill added. "Besides, we've had rain twice. That'd be sure to wipe out any trail they might've left."

"That all might be true, but I'll be durned if I'm going to let Mack Ellsworth and his pukin' scoundrels run roughshod over the folks in San Juan County like they did last summer."

"I'll start gettin' some supplies and stuff, and roundin' up some men," Reinhardt said, pushing off the wall on which he'd been leaning.

"No, Buster," Culpepper said with a shake of the head. "I'll be going alone this time. Just me and Bear."

"But, Jonas, you said . . ." Reinhardt started.

"I changed my mind, Buster. I won't put any more men at risk."

"You're bound and determined to do this, ain't you?" Cahill asked.

Culpepper nodded.

"Then let us go with you," Cahill said. "Or at least me."

"No, Jimmy. I need you to stay here and keep an eye on things. I have a feelin' I'm going to be gone awhile this time, and I'm not leavin' the county without a lawman around."

"You're a pain in the ass, Jonas, you know that?" Cahill said sourly.

Reinhardt chuckled. "Better watch what you say, Jimmy," he laughed. "Or he'll be runnin' *you* out of town, too."

Despite being in a foul mood because of the trouble with Coakley, Culpepper had to smile at that. "Now, that sounds like a durn good idea." He released an exaggerated sigh. "But it wouldn't do no good."

"Why not?" Reinhardt asked, fighting back laughter.

"There's a certain June Ladimere that'd go straight out and drag him back here," Culpepper said, beginning to laugh. "And worse, she'd come after me for tossin' him out in the first place."

Cahill's face remained stoic for a few seconds. Then his sour facade cracked and finally broke completely. He joined his two friends in laughter. "You ain't far from the truth on either of those things, Jonas," he said.

"I still say you ought to ask that gal to marry you, Jimmy," Culpepper said. "She might even make an honest man of you."

"Hell, I marry June, she'll make me quit bein' your deputy. Too damned dangerous, she'd say. She's told me so already."

"Well, there's a heap of truth in that, Jimmy," Reinhardt said soberly.

"Oh, hell, I know that. But what's life without a little danger and excitement? Why in hell do you keep signin' on whenever Jonas asks you?"

"I think it's my duty," Reinhardt said stiffly.

Both Culpepper and Cahill laughed. "Like hell," Cahill said. "You do it 'cause you like to get your blood pumpin' chasin' some goddamn outlaw."

"Well," Reinhardt admitted, "I suppose there's a little truth in that." He, too, started laughing again.

"Well," Culpepper said, standing, "all this talk about marryin' and danger and such has got me thinkin' about my Merry. So I think I'll just mosey on home."

"Don't you ever get tired of . . ." Cahill asked, his face suddenly turning red.

"Hell, no," Culpepper said, the sentiment echoed by Reinhardt. Both laughed.

"Not when I have a woman like Merry as my wife," Culpepper said seriously. "Every minute with her is special."

"I'd like that feelin'," Cahill said.

"Don't you feel like that when you're with June?" Culpepper asked.

"Well, yeah, of course, but she and I, well, you know, we've never been . . . never done . . ."

"That don't matter so much before you're married, though it's nice to know before takin' the vows that you'll be compatible that way, I suppose," Culpepper said. "But if you enjoy each other's company, just like bein' with each other, then the other'll work itself out somehow."

Cahill smiled just a little. "Maybe I *will* have to give some serious thought to askin' June to marry me."

"Well," Culpepper said heading for the door, "while you're thinkin' about it, I've got some business to take care of. Come on, Bear."

Instead of going straight home, though, Culpepper went to the livery and told Art Cassidy to have his horse saddled and waiting around dawn the next day.

"You want a mule, too, Jonas?" Cassidy asked.

Culpepper nodded. "I expect I'll be gone a while this time, so I'd best be prepared. Why?"

"You get the supplies and bring them over here, I'll have the mule loaded as well as the horse saddled." He grinned. "For an extra twenty cents, I'll even bring 'em over to your house in the morning."

"Sounds fair enough," Culpepper said. "Make sure you give me twenty, thirty pounds of horse grain, too." He paid Cassidy.

Culpepper sauntered to Maguire's store, where Caroline Maguire was back at work. She seemed as cheerful as ever, but Culpepper could see in her eyes and the stiff way she moved that she was still in deep pain over the loss of her husband. Culpepper hoped she'd be able to overcome her grief eventually. Caroline was too fine a woman in all ways to not live life to the fullest.

He picked out all his supplies and made arrangements for Caroline to have them delivered to the livery later that afternoon.

Merry said nothing about his leaving again, but he could tell that she was upset about it. Culpepper wondered why. She'd never been this way before. Or if she had, he hadn't been able to tell it.

Still, she tried not to let her feelings in the matter get the better of her, and she treated him as well as ever. She knew she could not tell him she was more worried about him than usual because of the two deaths on the last posse he'd led out of Silverton. John Maguire's death had shaken her far more than she was willing to admit, and she wasn't sure why. She figured it was because Culpepper, Maguire, and Buster Reinhardt had done much work together, and they'd seemed invincible. Now one of the three was dead, the other had been wounded while trying to take Ferd Wiley to the penitentiary. And if that could happen to those two, it could also happen to her husband.

No, she could not tell him any of this. That would only make him worried about her, and that, in turn, would not allow him to keep his mind fully on the job he had to do. Because of that, his chances of getting injured or killed were sharply increased. So, by telling him, she would raise the chances of having what she feared so much come true. Better to keep her thoughts to herself, she figured. She just hoped he didn't suspect that anything was bothering her.

Culpepper slept soundly that night, but Merry could not. Naked, she rose and slipped on a nightshirt. She went into the kitchen, made herself some tea, and drank it quietly. Then she sat, unable to sleep and trying to keep from thinking about her fears too much. Two hours before dawn, she finally cast off her nightshirt again and slid back into bed with Culpepper.

She managed to sleep at last, but she was exhausted when the cocks crowed soon after, waking Culpepper. She was tempted to spurn his rough advances, but she did not. There was still the fear in her that something might happen to him on the trail, and that this might be the last time they ever made love. Still, she got little enjoyment out of it. Then, feeling listless, she got up and made breakfast.

Chapter 16

Culpepper sat at the opposite side of the boxcar from his horse and mule. He had never told anyone, but he hated the trip from Silverton to Durango—and back—on the narrow-gauge train. It hugged the cliff on one side and overlooked precipitous drops on the other far too often for him. It wasn't so much that he was afraid of heights; it was more that he had absolutely no control over the train. One loose rail somewhere could pitch him into eternity without so much as him having a howdy-do about it. At least when he was facing an outlaw he generally had some say in the outcome.

Still, taking the train meant a journey to Durango of only about five hours instead of two or three times that. And right now, time was of the essence. Since he'd decided yesterday that he'd leave this morning, he'd felt pushed to hurry, as if he'd miss something important if he didn't make the best time he could to . . . to where, was the big question. Culpepper had no idea where he was going to look for Mack Ellsworth and his gang of cutthroats. So he decided that he'd figure that out when he got to Durango. Or maybe later.

As the train neared Durango, Culpepper loaded the mule and then saddled his horse—a sturdy, patient buckskin gelding. As soon as the train came to a halt in a hissing screech of steam and brakes, Culpepper opened the boxcar door, kicked down the ramp, and rode out on the opposite side of the station. With

Bear right beside him, he crossed the tracks around the rear of the train and spotted Marshal Ed Hernandez standing nearby, watching the few people who got off the train. Culpepper stopped next to Hernandez.

"What're you doing back here, Jonas?" Hernandez asked, looking up and shading his eyes against the bright sun. "Still on Ellsworth's trail?"

Culpepper nodded. "Yep. I spent too long back in Silverton, settlin' things and seein' that my men were buried and all. I should've been back after them a couple days ago."

"Trail's probably gone cold, all right," Hernandez agreed.

"They haven't been through here, have they, Ed?"

"No. I'm kind of surprised about that, too. Maybe you and your men put a scare into him."

"I'm sure a motley crowd of townsmen and miners from Silverton really scared the pants off him," Culpepper said, only a little sarcastically.

Hernandez laughed. "Maybe he's just gone on to better hunting grounds."

"Could be, but it's more like him and his boys're gone off somewhere to have themselves a whoop-up with their ill-gotten gains. I wouldn't even be surprised if at least a few of them retired on their loot."

"Could be." Hernandez paused, looking around a moment away from the sun. "You know a U.S. marshal, Jonas?"

"Feller named Ned Coakley?"

Hernandez nodded. "That's him. He rode in late yesterday. He's been trying to throw his weight around some. You know anything about him?"

"I kicked him out of Silverton," Culpepper said flatly.

Hernandez's eyebrows raised in question.

"That pukin' scoundrel had the gall to ride into town and demand a portion of the reward money for those outlaws my posse brought in last time. And if that wasn't bad enough, when I told him I'd given most of it to the widows of the two men who died, he actually went and browbeat one widow and took the money."

Hernandez shook his head in disbelief. "I take it that's when you asked him to leave town?"

"Yep. After I got the money back, plus a little extra for the widow. Good Lord, the nerve of that maggot. I'd watch him good while he's in Durango if I was you, Ed."

"I'll do so, Jonas. Thanks. Well, good luck to you. I'll be around town here, if you need my help."

"Thanks, Ed." He turned his horse's head and, towing the mule, rode north out of Durango.

He swung west before he came to the spot where the posse had done so last time, figuring he could cut a little time off. He would head back to the ruins where the gunfight had taken place and then decide which way to go from there. He set a steady but not too stiff pace, not wanting to wear out the horse, the mule, or the mastiff.

Culpepper camped that night out in the open, on the rough hills covered with small pines. There was no water but he had enough wood for a fire. Since his canteen was low, though, he decided to have a cold camp, doing without hot food or coffee. Bear had a good time, though, chasing down rabbits and pack rats. The mastiff ate well.

He had considered going to Fort Lewis, which wasn't far away, but he decided he did not want the company. And he thought it would take him a few miles out of his way, something he didn't want.

He was on his way early in the morning. Sleeping in the open and with no fire, they had little to do in the way of breaking camp. Mostly he had to swallow some hard biscuits, a little chicken Merry had sent along with him, and a few mouthfuls of water; load the supplies on the mule; and saddle his horse.

Over the next two days, the land began to turn stark and flat, with only small humps of hills up ahead of him every now and again. Vegetation began to get sparse, and soon was limited mostly to sagebrush and some rough grass. Everything seemed to be a dull, reddish-brown color, and little was pleasing to the eye. A steady breeze blew over the countryside, enough so that it was an annoyance to Culpepper. He bore that stoically, since there was nothing he could do about it.

The increasing drabness of the scenery made it hard for Culpepper to keep his mind on the job at hand. He much preferred to think of Merry and what he and she might do when he got home again. Occasionally he thought of Jimmy Cahill and his possibly impending nuptials to June Ladimere. He even thought about U.S. Deputy Marshal Ned Coakley once in a while, hoping Coakley would not show up in Silverton again. Culpepper figured he had enough troubles without a pest of a deputy marshal bringing more with him.

The sudden lurch and frightened squeal by his mule brought him back to attention in a hurry. His renewed alertness was reinforced a moment later when he heard the crack of a rifle. Out in the distance, on one of the irregularly shaped humps of land, he saw a puff of smoke.

Culpepper glanced at the mule, which looked to be seriously hit. Culpepper cast off the rope to the mule, spun the buckskin, and rode hell for leather back the way he'd come. "Come on, Bear!" he shouted. Even as he spun the horse another bullet kicked up dirt a few feet away from him, and a steady stream of dirt puffs followed by rifle reports followed him as he rode in a zigzag pattern.

A quarter of a mile or so away, he finally pulled to a halt and turned back. No one was coming after him, and the gunfire had stopped a little bit ago, as he got out of range of whoever it was shooting at him. He dismounted and loosened his saddle a little to let his horse breathe some. Then he poured some water from his canteen into his hat and let the horse drink. Bear got a little after that, and finally Culpepper drank some himself.

That done, he took stock of his situation. The only water he now had was that left in the canteen. There were three other canteens on the mule, but that was doing him no good now. He had no food, only a little extra ammunition, and no horse grain.

"All right, you pukin' scoundrel," Culpepper muttered. "We're about to fix this." He tightened the saddle and climbed aboard. He turned south and rode that way about a mile before he swung west again. Half a mile or so later, he turned north until he was sure he was well past the point from where the gunshots had come. Then he rode east and finally south, figuring to come on the gunman from the north, which he hoped would surprise the man.

He thought he spotted the correct hillock and so he dismounted. He swiftly hobbled the horse so it wouldn't be able to stray very far, and then he started walking. He hadn't gone far when he realized he was still just a bit to the west, and that the hill he had seen before was not the right one. But momentarily he had gotten his bearings and moved cautiously on.

Suddenly he spotted a horse, and he stopped. With some reluctance, he lay down on his stomach. "You be quiet now, Bear," he whispered to the mastiff. Then he began slithering forward. Bear emulated him.

When he was within ten yards of the man still lying on the crest of the hill, Culpepper stood, eased out a pistol, and thumbed back the hammer. "Lookin' for me, maggot?" he said more than asked.

The man started, then froze.

"Put your hands where I can see them, and then roll over onto your back."

The man began doing as he was told, but halfway around, he snatched at the Winchester rifle. He didn't get far with it before Culpepper fired once, hitting him in the left shoulder. The man dropped the rifle and clutched at the wound.

"Now, ease out your pistol and toss it away, maggot," Culpepper said harshly. When the man had done so, Culpepper asked, "What's your name, you pukin' scoundrel?"

"None of your damn business," the man spat, pain in his voice.

"All right, Mister Business, what're you doin' out here, tryin' to kill me?"

"My name's Owen Fauss, ya damn fool."

"All right, Mister Fool, same question."

"You goddamn idiot," Fauss ranted on. "My name's Owen Fauss."

"All right, then, Mister Fauss, same question to you. I don't much care which one of you three answers."

"I ain't tellin' you shit, lawman," Fauss snapped.

"It might go better on you if you were to be reasonable."

"I don't have to be reasonable, god damn it, and you can't make me tell you anything."

"Would you care to wager on that?" Culpepper asked coldly.

Fauss looked into the piercing blue eyes and decided he definitely would not want to make such a bet. He licked his lips, then offered, "I'll talk to you, Sheriff, but you gotta promise to let me go after."

"You, Mister Fauss, are in no position to make demands," Culpepper said calmly. "Nor even requests. I'd suggest to you that it'd be best to talk to me and then hope I'm feelin' beneficent enough to treat you better than you deserve, maggot."

Fauss decided to talk—and hope. He might be able to get to his belly gun and shoot the sheriff. Besides, he had no reason to protect the man who hired him. "Marshal Ned Coakley sent me to drop you."

"When?" Culpepper asked, surprised.

"Yesterday. I ain't sure, but I think he saw you get off the train. He went lookin' for a man to do his dirty work for him, and he found me. I rode out here right off, passin' you in the night, as best as I can tell."

"Must've been by a good distance, or Bear would've alerted me."

"I stuck a mile or so south of your trail."

Culpepper nodded. "How much did that pukin' rascal pay you?"

"A hundred dollars. In advance."

"It wasn't enough," Culpepper said flatly.

"I suppose not."

"All right, maggot, get up and turn around." When Fauss did so, Culpepper said, "Move two steps to your left. That's away from the rifle, if you don't know your right from your left." When Fauss had done that, Culpepper picked up the rifle in his left hand. He backed up and slid the rifle into the saddle scabbard on the man's horse. He untied the reins from the picket ring and mounted Fauss's horse. "March," he ordered.

"Which way?" Fauss asked, looking over his shoulder.

Culpepper pointed with his pistol.

Dejectedly, Fauss moved slowly off toward where Culpepper had left his own horse. As he walked, he held his left shoulder with his right hand. It hurt like hellfire, but he tried to ignore it as he worked his left hand toward the belly gun without trying to move the wounded shoulder any. He was sweating hard from the pain and exertion, but he kept at it, especially when he spotted Culpepper's buckskin up ahead, and knew he had very little time.

Finally his hand touched the butt of the small Colt under his shirt. It was turned the wrong way, and he switched it to the left, so he could grab it with that hand. He would rather use his right, but to do so would let Culpepper see that arm moving suspiciously, so it had to be the left, even though bringing the pistol up with that arm would be excruciating.

At long last, he was ready, and he decided there was no time like the present, seeing as how he was less than ten feet from Culpepper's horse now. He sucked in a breath to settle himself and prepare for the pain. Then he jerked the pistol out and began whirling.

Chapter 17

Culpepper fired twice. One bullet caught Fauss in the side as he began to turn. The second punched a hole in Fauss's chest and knocked him down. With a sigh of annoyance, Culpepper stopped the horse and dismounted. Holding the reins in his hand, he walked to where Fauss lay in a small but growing puddle of blood.

Culpepper had half figured that Fauss would try something, though he had hoped Fauss would have enough sense not to. Culpepper supposed now that he should have checked Fauss over for other weapons, but he wanted to get handcuffs on Fauss, and the handcuffs were in his saddlebags. It had been a foolish thing to do, and Culpepper was angry at himself for having made the mistake.

Culpepper knelt alongside Fauss, who was still alive, though barely. "That was a durn fool thing to do, boy," he said harshly. "There was no reason for you to die like this."

"You would've killed me anyway, sooner or later."

"Not unless I had to. If you'd only . . ." Culpepper stopped, realizing Fauss was dead. With a sigh, he stood and put his Remington away. Then he hobbled Fauss's horse. Finally, he cleaned the pistol he had used. He wasn't sure it was necessary, but it gave him time to think.

Culpepper was inclined to just leave Fauss's body where it was, take the man's horse and use it to replace the pack mule and ride on. Trouble was, he was a conscientious lawman, and his conscience would not let him do that. He could take the body back to Durango, but that would waste at least a day and a half. There was one other choice—Fort Lewis—and he decided that it would have to do.

He finished cleaning his pistol, and then tossed Fauss's body across his saddle. Fauss's horse did not like it one bit, but there was little he could do, hobbled as he was. Culpepper waited him out, and finally the horse settled down. Mounting his own horse, Culpepper rode off, trailing Fauss's horse behind.

Shortly after, Culpepper came to his pack mule, which he had heard just after getting past the hill from which Fauss had done his shooting. The animal was hurt bad and still braying pitifully.

"Durn it all," Culpepper muttered. He hated using his pistol again, since he had just cleaned the weapon, but he was not about to let the mule suffer any longer. Then he remembered Fauss's Winchester.

Culpepper got the rifle and quickly shot the mule in the head. "Sorry, old feller," he said. He got the extra canteens, plus his ammunition, and loaded that on Fauss's horse. He was tempted to take everything from the mule and put it on the horse, but that would slow him down too much, and possibly kill Fauss's horse before he got to Fort Lewis.

With another sigh of annoyance, Culpepper mounted up and rode off, leaving the mule where it was. Two and a quarter hours later, he rode into Fort Lewis. Minutes afterward, he was introduced to Major Abel Watkins, the commanding officer.

"What brings you out here, Sheriff?" Watkins asked, after he and Culpepper were seated.

"Had to kill a durn outlaw a few miles on. I ain't got time to take his carcass back to Durango, so I was hopin' you might do so for me."

"That's not generally our line of work, Sheriff," Watkins said. He did not seem all that put out by the idea, though.

"I understand, Major. But I figured you probably have fairly regular runs to Durango and might not mind your men takin' along a little extra baggage."

"We can probably do that," Watkins said with a nod. "What do you want us to do with it once we get it there?"

"You might want to have someone come write this down. I'd be obliged if it wasn't forgotten."

Watkins looked at him with a question in his eyes for a few moments, then he nodded. Shortly afterward, a weary-looking first lieutenant entered the office carrying a pen, bottle of ink, and some paper.

"Go on, Sheriff," Watkins said.

"Thank you, Major." He paused, thinking a moment. "Give the body to town Marshal Ed Hernandez. Do *not* give it to county Sheriff Frank Hammond. Tell Ed to make sure that Ned Coakley knows that Fauss is dead, and who did it."

"United States Deputy Marshal Ned Coakley?" Watkins asked.

"Yep. You know him?"

"Met him once or twice. He struck me as something of an ass."

"He's a festerin' puke of a scoundrel is what he is, Major," Culpepper said flatly.

"Did he have something to do with this, Sheriff?" Watkins asked.

"He's the maggot who sent Fauss after me."

"I can arrest him and hold him for you, if you want, Sheriff."

"No, but thank you, Major. I'll deal with him in my own good time, and there's no reason for you to get mixed up in all this. Just have your men make sure Coakley knows who killed Fauss."

"Anything else?" the lieutenant asked.

Culpepper never had gotten the man's name, but he figured it didn't matter all that much. "Yes, Lieutenant. If there's any reward money on Fauss, tell Hernandez to pay for the burial out of it. Tell him to take twenty-five percent of what's left, and give the soldiers the rest to divide amongst themselves."

"Very generous, Sheriff," Watkins said honestly.

Culpepper shrugged. "It's the least I can do." He thought a few more moments. "Tell Hernandez to sell Fauss's horse, rifle, and other stuff. Tell him to keep that money and use it for something he thinks is important." He paused. "Well, Lieutenant, that's about it."

The junior officer nodded, packed up his things, and walked out.

"One more favor, if I may, Major?" Culpepper asked.

"I can't promise, but ask."

"Fauss killed the mule that was carrying my supplies. I didn't want to overload his horse, so I left the mule and most of my supplies out there. I figured the animals'll have gotten to it already, so I think I'd best re-supply while I'm here."

"That can be arranged."

"I need a mule, too."

"We have some you can choose from."

"Trouble is, Major, I don't have a whole lot of cash money on me. I was wonderin' if you could extend me some credit. San Juan County'll pay you back as soon as I get back to Silverton, which might be some weeks."

"I see no problem in any of this, Sheriff."

"I'm obliged, Major," Culpepper said humbly.

"This may sound right foolish coming from a man of my age and position, Sheriff," Watkins said with a small smile, "but I believe in the work that men like you do. After all, you lawmen're much like we soldiers are—stuck in a hostile land, fighting an enemy that at times seems to outnumber us by a fair amount, and doing it all while ill-supplied and usually miles from any help."

"I reckon we do have similar jobs at that," Culpepper said with a slow laugh. "Well, Major, if you don't mind, I think I'd better get a move on. Night comes early, as you probably well know."

"Why don't you stay here for the night, Sheriff?" Watkins

asked. "It's getting late, and by the time you get resupplied, find a mule, and maybe have a bite to eat, it'll be close to dark."

"I don't want to put anyone out, Major," Culpepper said with a shrug.

"On the contrary, Sheriff," Watkins said honestly. "It'd be a pleasure to have someone new to talk with. My officers and I are about talked out. You can bunk with some of the troops in one of the barracks, if that's suitable."

"If you don't mind Bear here hangin' around, too," Culpepper said, stroking the dog's head. "I don't go anywhere without him."

"Fine, fine. My children might get a kick out of him."

"Then I accept your generous offer," Culpepper said. He tugged at his mustache a bit, then said, "Well, if you don't mind, I'd as soon pick out my supplies and mules and such now, so I'll be all set for leaving in the morning. Then we can sit to supper." He smiled a little. "It's been since the mornin' before yesterday that I've had a hot meal."

"Cold camps are no fun, Sheriff, that's for sure. Well, I have work to do, but I'll have Captain Kelly take you around."

Culpepper had a mostly pleasant evening at the fort. After he had bought his supplies at the sutler's store and then chosen a mule, it was close to suppertime. He ate voraciously, enjoying the hot food at Watkins's quarters, and enjoying the company of Watkins's wife and three children. The youngsters, ages fourteen, eleven, and eight, were amazed—and a little frightened, at first—at Bear's size, and all three had a fine time rolling around on the floor with the giant but gentle mastiff.

In the morning, Culpepper loaded his mule in the stable alongside a small troop of soldiers preparing for the ride into Durango with Fauss's body. Then he saddled his horse and rode on out of the fort. The new mule trotted behind at the end of a rope Culpepper held, and Bear loped alongside Culpepper and his buckskin.

A couple of hours later, he arrived at the site of his dead mule. He stopped to see if he could salvage anything. The packs had been pretty well torn asunder, and the small store of supplies that was left was strewn all over. There was almost nothing usable, so Culpepper spent little time looking.

He pushed on at a good pace, and that night he camped on the Mancos River. Early the next day, he crossed the river and headed into Mancos Canyon, following the same trail he had when he and the posse were on the trail of Ellsworth's outlaws. He reached the ruins where the gun battle had taken place shortly before dark. He ignored the ruins where he and his men had holed up, instead going to the one where the outlaws had taken cover.

He unloaded the mule, then found wood and started a fire. He put food and coffee on the fire, and while it cooked he unloaded his horse. Bear raced off at one point and came back a few minutes later with a large jackrabbit clutched in his bloody jaws. Man and mastiff ate well that night.

In the morning, Culpepper loaded up and left, heading roughly northwest, the way he thought the outlaws had gone. After a few minutes, Bear seemed to get excited, and Culpepper began to think that the dog had found the scent. It might be possible, he reasoned, since there'd been no rain in the area that he knew of between the time of the gun battle and now. So he let the dog go and followed along.

He came to a creek, running pretty well, late in the day and decided to camp there. He crossed the creek in the morning, and then sat and waited patiently as Bear raced back and forth trying to pick up the trail again. Culpepper figured that it was lost, when suddenly the mastiff barked and charged off.

The land began to change some. While it was no more barren than it had been, much of the ground was covered by reddish dirt, and there were tall, spindly spires of sandstone in odd formations. The land was cut through with dozens of canyons and long, flat mesas. The air was hot and dry, with the wind bringing along a sometimes stinging blast of sand.

Bear had trouble following the trail anymore, and so it took Culpepper lots of time to explore each canyon, or to go around mesas, hills, or rock formations. Sometimes, the mastiff would pick up the trail and the going would be a little faster for a while, but eventually they would come to another canyon.

Ten days after leaving Fort Lewis, Culpepper came to a small creek that in places was barely running, if at all. Bear seemed to not be able to find the trail, but on a hunch, Culpepper began following the winding creek through rough, low hills. It was a hot journey, with the breeze bringing no relief, only new gusts of warm, seemingly dead air.

For some reason, Culpepper was certain he was on the right trail. He didn't know why, and Bear seemed not to have any trail to follow. But Culpepper was absolutely sure he was right. Not only that, he was just as certain that he was close to the outlaws.

Still, he did not want to push on too late, moving through these rugged little hills in the dark. If his hunch was right, he might just stumble into an outlaw camp, and that would certainly do no good. So he stopped and made camp.

He ate well in the morning, wanting to have a fully belly if his instincts proved true and he found the outlaws. He rode on slowly, still following the creek. A couple of hours later, he heard voices, sometimes shouting. He stopped and tied his horse and mule to a tree. Pulling his Winchester out of the scabbard, he winked at Bear. "Time to go to work, boy," he said quietly.

He edged up onto a low, scrubby hill until he was up on the crest and looked over it. Down in a little valley, between the hill Culpepper was on and one just like it fifty yards across the creek, was a cabin.

Chapter 18

As he lay there looking at the leaning, dilapidated cabin across the creek, Culpepper could not help but wonder where the wood for the place had come from. There was almost none for miles around here, and what was here came from short, stubby little trees that would never provide the planking to build a cabin. It was an intriguing question, but it didn't matter, really, so Culpepper finally put it out of his mind.

The shack was cocked to the north and looked as if it would fall over at any time. The planking, such as it was, hung loose in a few spots, and in others, poor wood was hammered on to cover up holes. There were no windows in the front, and only one door there. A small tin tube stuck out of the roof. A thin streamer of smoke curled out of the tube. Culpepper suspected they were pulling boards off the walls for firewood.

After a little, Culpepper went back down the hill and got a canteen plus some jerky and hard biscuits. He carefully carted the supplies up the hill and stretched out again. Bear sprawled beside him, lying on his side. Man and dog gnawed on jerky at times. Occasionally Culpepper would pour some water into his hat and let Bear drink.

A couple of hours into the morning, Culpepper had decided that he'd seen all the men in the cabin. There were only three that he had counted. He had wanted papers on at least two of them, so he knew these men were part of Mack Ellsworth's gang. Trouble was, Ellsworth was nowhere to be seen here. What he figured he needed to do was capture at least one of the men staying at the cabin. With luck, that man would tell him where Ellsworth and the others had gotten off to. That, of course, would not be easy.

He began to think that there would be no way out of killing at least one of the outlaws, not without risking his own neck too much. He didn't really think he could just walk on down there and tell all three outlaws they were under arrest. But if he shot one down, the other two might surrender. That was a mighty iffy proposition, though.

Culpepper pondered his limited options for several more hours, but nothing changed, and he came up with no new alternatives. Still, he did not like what he was faced with. He could ride on, skirting the cabin, but that was not really an option, as far as he was concerned. The people of San Juan County had elected him to do a job, and he would do it, no matter how difficult or onerous it might be at times.

The outlaws had been inside most of the time, only wandering outside now and then to relieve themselves or to get a breath of fresh air. Judging by the outside of the cabin, and the men inhabiting it, Culpepper figured the inside was foul of sight and smell.

Culpepper sighed, ready but unwilling to do the job he faced. Jonas Culpepper was not a bloodthirsty man, and tried as often as possible to avoid killing. When it became necessary, he could be as ruthless as anyone.

Then another idea hit him: he could wait until night and then go down to the cabin. Of course, that would put him inside a dark cabin with three outlaws, any one of whom would be not only happy, but eager, to blow his head off. It was an intriguing thought, but probably not workable. He sighed again, back to the beginning.

For another hour or so he tried to conjure up some reason to hate these men. If he could, it would make it easier to drop one or two of them in cold blood. But he couldn't. The only thing these men had done, as far as he knew, was to rob a train. They more than likely had robbed many another person or thing, and Culpepper would've bet money that they had killed before, but he had no proof of that. They weren't even the ones who had killed John Maguire, not as far as Culpepper knew. And so he couldn't work up any hate for these men.

Then he found a reason. Late in the afternoon, the door opened and a naked woman was shoved outside. She fell and lay sobbing in a heap. An outlaw followed her out, holding a hand on his face.

"Bitch!" the man snarled, as he stepped up and kicked the woman several times.

The mastiff growled low and dangerously, but Culpepper said quietly, "Hush, Bear." Culpepper brought the rifle to his shoulder and fired as soon as his sights fell on the man still kicking the woman.

The man had started to bend, and the bullet hit him in the top of the head, instead of in the chest, as Culpepper had intended. The results were the same, though. The man went down in a heap.

The woman looked up, frightened, searching for what had happened. She gasped when she saw the outlaw dying in a pool of blood.

The two other outlaws tumbled out the door of the cabin, guns in hand. They stopped just outside the shack when they saw their friend's body.

"What happened, girl?" one of them demanded. His voice came up to Culpepper clear as a bell.

"I don't know," the woman cried. "He was . . . he was . . . kicking me. Then . . . there was a shot and . . . and . . ."

"Shit," the same outlaw said. Culpepper recognized him from a handbill as Cory Powell. "Milt, go on out there and find out who shot Danny."

"And what're you gonna be . . . ?"

Culpepper put a bullet into Powell's chest. The other man bolted, racing back into the house.

"Durn," Culpepper breathed. "Miss!" he yelled. "Miss, can you hear me?"

The young woman looked around dumbly, then sort of nodded. Or so Culpepper thought.

"Come on up to the hill, Miss. Go slow."

"No," she said, her voice almost a wail.

"Miss," Culpepper called again. "Miss, I'm San Juan County Sheriff Jonas Culpepper. I can help you, but you've got to help some, too."

"No." Shame was evident in her voice.

"Miss, I expect you've been abused somethin' awful. But that don't matter to me. Nor will it matter to any decent folks. Don't you go frettin' about what's happened here. Now, ease your way up here where I can look out for you."

Seeming stunned, the woman began crawling across the rough grass and small stones, heading toward the little hill.

The cabin door cracked open, and a voice growled out, "Don't you go anywhere, you bitch."

The woman stopped, numbed from the abuse she had taken, but at the same time, Culpepper let fly seven shots from the Winchester. The bullets thudded into and through the thin door, and Milt Adler—the only man left inside, as far as Culpepper knew—screamed in pain.

Culpepper, who had not looked away from the cabin while talking with the women, still kept his eyes fixed on the shack. As he began sliding shells into the Winchester's tubular magazine, he said, "Come on ahead, Miss. Don't you worry about that pukin' scoundrel. He ain't going to bother you again."

The woman began her slow movement up the hill again, as Culpepper kept a close watch on the cabin. Every now and again, he would flick his eyes to the woman to check her progress.

Finally she reached the crest of the hill. She gasped in fright when she saw the huge mastiff.

Without looking at her, Culpepper said, "Don't you worry about Bear, Miss. He'll look out for you, not hurt you. There's a big coat tied on the back of my horse down there. Why don't you get it and use it to cover yourself? You'll be safe now."

The woman stared at the bulky sheriff a moment. Fairly certain that he would not look at her, she rose.

As the woman started down the hill, Culpepper said, "Bear, go with her."

The woman stopped, frightened anew. Then Bear walked up to her and gently licked at her hand. She almost managed a smile. With her hand on Bear's broad head, she walked down the hill.

"There's some jerky and biscuits in the packs, Miss, if you're hungry. There's a canteen, too." He paused, not sure she had heard him or was interested. "You can stay down there if you feel more comfortable. Bear'll stay with you. Or you can come back up here." He was surprised when she came up and lay down on the crest of the hill a few feet to his left. Bear was between the two.

"What's your name, Miss?" Culpepper asked, after some moments of silence.

There was a dead time, before a soft, gentle voice said, "Daisy Greenwalt."

"A pleasure to make your acquaintance, Miss Greenwalt. In case you didn't hear me before, I'm Jonas Culpepper, sheriff of San Juan County. Where're you from?"

"Durango, I suppose."

"You suppose?"

"Well . . ." Daisy hesitated. Then she shrugged and said, "I worked in one of the . . . cathouses there." She sounded fatalistic.

"That's where those boys grabbed you?"

"Yes," Daisy said, with a resigned sigh.

"They treated you some poorly, I'd say?"

"No more than a woman like me's got a right to expect."

"Don't be so hard on yourself, Miss Greenwalt. Many a good woman's come out of such a place. And even if that wasn't true, no woman deserves to be treated the way those men treated you."

"Thank you, Sheriff," Daisy said shyly. A man had never spoken to her so nicely before. She wasn't used to it. She kept quiet for a little, chewing on jerky and casting flickering glances from the cabin to Bear and Culpepper and then back. She still couldn't believe her good fortune, if that indeed was what it was. Culpepper certainly seemed a decent man. But time would tell.

"How'd you come to be here, Sheriff?" Daisy finally asked.

"Been followin' Mack Ellsworth's gang. They robbed the train between Silverton and Durango a couple weeks ago. I got a posse up right off and took out after those pukin' scoundrels, but they got away after killin' a couple men in the posse. Not before we got three of them, though. After bringin' the bodies of my friends back to Silverton and buryin' them, I headed out again. I got to where we'd had the gunfight with them, and Bear's been followin' their trail since. Then we got here."

"I'm glad you did." She did sound grateful, but also still ill at ease at being here.

"I wish it could've been a little sooner, miss." He paused. "You comfortable enough, Miss? We're liable to be here for some time yet."

"I guess I am." She shuddered. "What're we waitin' for? Why don't we just leave?"

"I aim to arrest that maggot down there, if I can."

"But why?" Daisy's voice quavered with fright.

"He's got a lot of misdeeds to answer for, includin' what they did to you. Plus I figure he can tell me where Ellsworth's holed up."

"You'll never get into that cabin."

"Maybe not. But he's got to come out sooner or later. When he does, he'll get a choice—surrender or get shot."

"Won't he try sneakin' up on us tonight?"

"Let him try. He won't get within ten yards of us before Bear lets me know. Then him and I can prepare a little surprise for that scoundrel."

Daisy was quite convinced that Culpepper was crazy, but there was nothing she could do. She did feel a lot safer with the broad-shouldered sheriff and the big mastiff. At least she was out of the clutches of those animals down there. Still, she kept casting glances at Culpepper, wondering if he, too, would turn out to be a beast. Most men she had encountered in her eighteen years were, and she saw no reason for this one to be any different. So she lay there, gnawing on jerky and sipping water, grateful for the cover provided by Culpepper's large and heavy bear-fur coat.

As darkness began to draw over the high desert, Daisy rested her head on her arms and drifted to sleep. She jerked awake every few minutes, sure that one of her captors was coming for her again. Then she would look over at the big, wet-nosed mastiff and feel comforted. Despite the many times she woke, she never saw Culpepper move from where he was. After a while, she drifted into a deeper sleep, her subconscious telling her she was safe now.

Sometime during the night, Bear growled softly. Culpepper became alert, but realized it was only a coyote beginning to nose at Powell's body. In the light of the stars and the sliver of moon, Culpepper could see two more coyotes moving warily toward the bodies of Powell and the other man. He brought the rifle up, ready to fire, to scare the scavengers off. Then he decided to let nature have its way, and he uncocked and lowered the Winchester.

"Keep alert, Bear," Culpepper whispered. He rested his head on his canteen, and told himself to wake a half-hour before dawn. Then he went to sleep.

His timing was a little off, but not too much. It was still dark, though pink was tinting the eastern sky behind him. Culpepper sat up and rubbed his face. He took a few swallows of water, then rose and stretched.

The movements woke Daisy, who sat up, her heart beating in panic.

"It's almost dawn, Miss Greenwalt. I'm going on down there to see if that last pukin' scoundrel is still alive."

"What about me?"

"You stay here. You'll be all right."

"Leave Bear with me?" Daisy asked, frightened anew.

"I need him with me. You can watch. If somethin' happens to me, get on the horse and ride like the dickens." Without waiting to hear any more protests, Culpepper said, "Come on, Bear," and headed down the hill.

Chapter 19

Culpepper stopped alongside the wall next to the cabin door. Bear was on the other side of the door. Then they waited. When he figured there was enough light to see by, Culpepper suddenly kicked the cabin door open. The move was greeted by three gunshots.

"Go," Culpepper said, nodding at Bear.

The dog raced inside and suddenly a scream was heard, but no more gunshots. Culpepper spun inside, Remington in his right hand. He found Bear straddling Milt Adler, with Adler's right wrist in his mouth.

"Back off, Bear," Culpepper said. When the mastiff reluctantly backed up and sat next to Culpepper, the sheriff aimed his pistol at Adler. "Mornin', Mister Adler. I'm San Juan County Sheriff Jonas Culpepper, and you are under arrest, maggot. Get up."

"I can't," Adler said, pointing to his leg.

The leg was bloody just above the knee, and Culpepper figured the bone was broken. "I weep for you, maggot. Now get up, you pukin' scoundrel, or I'll drag you all the way back to Silverton."

"You're a cold-hearted son of a bitch, Sheriff," Adler said.

"That I am, especially to mewlin' pukes like you who've abused a poor woman like you've done."

"Hell, Sheriff, she ain't nothin' but a strumpet."

"Even a trollop deserves some respect. Now get up."

"I need some help."

"The only help you're going to get from me is to have Bear here bite you on the tail to get you movin'."

Adler struggled to get up, but finally made it.

"Put your hands up and turn around."

It took some hopping, but Adler did so. Culpepper set his rifle down and put his Remington back into the holster. Then he searched Adler, finding nothing but a folding knife in one pocket. He took that and tossed it in a corner.

"Put your hands behind you," Culpepper ordered. When Adler did, Culpepper locked handcuffs on him, then picked up his rifle. "Outside," he said.

"Bastard," Adler muttered. He hopped around until he was facing the door. Then he moved forward, trying not to put too much weight on his leg.

Outside, Culpepper said, "Head for the horses."

Adler turned right, staggered a few yards, and stopped where three horses were tightly hobbled.

"Which one's yours?"

"The pinto."

"You want saddled or not, maggot?" Culpepper asked.

"Saddled."

Culpepper nodded. "You stand there and be nice. You try anything and Bear'll start ripping off your flesh." Culpepper swiftly saddled the pinto and then helped Adler onto it. He tied Adler's legs under the horse's belly with rope taken from inside the cabin, much as he had done with Tucker Reynolds a while back. Holding the reins to the horse, Culpepper walked up the hill, sidestepping the two bodies, sending the buzzards flapping away in squawking protest. The two corpses had been fairly well gone over by coyotes last night, and the buzzards were well on their way to finishing off the job.

A frightened-looking Daisy Greenwalt was waiting at the top of the hill. Now that the sun was up, she looked hot and decidedly uncomfortable in the heavy coat.

"You have any clothes down there in the cabin, Miss Greenwalt?" Culpepper asked.

Daisy shook her head. It was the first good look Culpepper had really had of her. Swamped by the huge coat, she looked tiny. Her long, dirty-blond hair was matted and stringy. Her face was small and well formed, with a thin, straight nose and a slightly pointed chin.

"You didn't have a dress or anything?"

"I did," Daisy said quietly. "But those . . . those animals, they cut it to shreds."

Culpepper nodded. "Those scoundrels have any extra clothes down there?"

"Maybe. I ain't sure."

"Go on down there and find out. Take Bear with you."

Daisy nodded. She took a few steps, but then stopped. "They've got a fire goin' down there. A hot meal'd do us both some good, Sheriff," she said.

Culpepper smiled. "By golly, I believe you're right, Miss Greenwalt."

"My name's Daisy, Sheriff."

Culpepper nodded. "And my name's Jonas." He paused. "Go on down there and see if you can find something to wear. Give a holler when you're ready."

Accompanied by Bear, Daisy moved down the hill toward the house. She seemed to move with more assurance, and barely noticed the two scavenger-ravaged bodies. Ten minutes later, she stepped outside the cabin and called up to Culpepper.

The sheriff looked down the hill and saw Daisy waving at him to come down. He nodded, smiling a little. Daisy was wearing a man's pants and a man's shirt. The trousers were wool, the shirt cotton, and both were far too large for her small frame.

Culpepper had loaded the mule and saddled his horse while waiting, and now walked both animals—plus Adler, on his horse—down to the cabin. He hobbled all three animals and then went inside.

"Hey, I'm hungry, too, damn it all," Adler shouted.

Culpepper stepped back through the door and glared at Adler. "You stop your hollerin', maggot, or I'll stop it for you."

Daisy was a far better cook than Culpepper would have ever thought, not that she could compare with Merry in cooking or anything else. But it was an edible meal, and a heap better than anything Culpepper would have been able to make for himself. The sheriff and the young woman ate swiftly and quietly, more interested in getting on the trail than in making polite conversation.

As Daisy began to clean up a little—not that there was much to clean up in the hovel of a cabin—Culpepper brought a plate of food out to Adler. Undoing the cuff from Adler's left hand, he pulled the right around to the front and handcuffed that to one of Adler's belt loops. He could move the right hand, but not far. It was enough to allow him to balance the tin plate in the saddle horn, and he could eat with his left hand.

When Adler had finished eating, Culpepper gave him a cup of coffee, and then allowed him to roll and light a cigarette. Then Culpepper cuffed Adler's hands behind his back again. Culpepper mounted his buckskin and Daisy mounted one of the other outlaws' horses, which Culpepper had saddled for her, and they were off.

With Daisy around, Culpepper was real careful at making sure that Adler was handcuffed almost every moment of the day and night. And when the outlaw was not on the horse, his legs were shackled. Culpepper had to get fairly inventive sometimes in the four days to San Miguel to find ways of keeping Adler chained to something fairly immovable.

They rode north the first day. The next morning they turned east, heading toward Gypsum Gap. They moved through the low gap the next afternoon, and that night set camp along Gypsum Creek, which was nearabout bone dry.

The heat was, more often than not, almost unbearable, the far expanse of sky unbroken by clouds, the landscape unmarred by shade. The nights were still rather chill, and after a full day of perspiring heavily, the three were often uncomfortable once the sun dropped. Adding to the oppressiveness of traveling out here, water was scarce as shade, if not more so.

Daisy proved to be a rather resilient young woman, despite it all, and one who was fairly inventive in making their meals as appealing as could be expected under the circumstances. By the night they camped on Gypsum Creek, she had opened up some, though Culpepper noticed that she kept a wary eye on Adler at all times. Worse, Culpepper noted that Adler rarely took his eyes off the young woman when they were in camp. Culpepper did not worry too much about Adler trying anything with Daisy. Not with Bear there to keep an eye on the young woman.

Each night, Culpepper would pump Adler for information, but the outlaw was being close-mouthed. He would say nothing about where Mack Ellsworth and the other members of the gang were, nor would he say anything about where the loot from the train robbery was. He wouldn't even so much as admit he knew Ellsworth. His reticence did nothing to endear him to Culpepper.

The night on Gypsum Creek, Culpepper was just spreading out his bedroll when Daisy came up to him. "You have a few minutes, Sheriff . . . Jonas?" she asked tentatively.

Surprised, Culpepper nodded. "Sure. Sit." They both sat on the bedroll, Culpepper uncomfortably cross-legged, Daisy with her legs folded under her. "What's wrong?" Culpepper asked, puzzled.

"Nothin's wrong so much, Jonas. It's just that I . . . I . . ." She paused while the tip of her tongue searched the perimeters of her lips.

Culpepper waited her out. He could see no reason to rush whatever it was Daisy had to say.

"Well, Jonas, dang it, I'd like to thank you for what you've done for me."

"There's no need for thanks, Miss Greenwalt. It's my job."

"Be that as it may, Jonas," Daisy said practically, "I'd still like to do something to thank you."

"Like what?" Culpepper was almost amused.

Daisy stared straight into his piercing blue eyes. "Considerin' the kind of woman I am, just what the hell do you think I mean?" she countered brazenly.

Culpepper was no longer amused. He was flustered, though, but he managed to hide it pretty well. "I'm obliged for the offer, Miss Greenwalt, but I'm afraid that's out of the question."

Daisy's eyebrows shot up in surprise. "Don't you find me appealin'?" she demanded.

"On the contrary, Miss Greenwalt, I find you highly appealing, dirty face, men's clothes, and all."

"Then why . . . ?"

"Because I'm a married man."

Daisy laughed hollowly, more than a little confused. "That's never stopped most of the men I've met. Hell, most married men come to girls like me because their wives don't . . ." She stopped, mouth making a sudden O of surprise. "Your wife is one of those who *likes* to . . . ?"

"That's none of your concern, Miss," Culpepper said, suddenly very ill at ease at the turn this conversation had taken.

"Maybe not," Daisy said with a laugh—a real laugh, full of joy as well as humor—"but if it's true, which I suspect it is, you're one lucky *hombre*, Jonas."

"I am, yes," Culpepper said with quiet dignity. "Does that surprise or shock you?"

Daisy shrugged. "Both, in some ways. I know there're women out there who like to po . . . to be intimate with men. I've just never known one—or a man fortunate enough to be married to one." She laughed a little, then saddened. "That's the kind of wife I'd be to some man," she said in a faraway voice. "If I could find a man to marry me after all I've done and"—she glanced at Adler—"all what's been done to me."

"Plenty of girls in your . . . profession wind up marryin' respectable men."

"I suppose. I've never met one who I'd want to be married to, even if he asked me," Daisy said bluntly. "Most of what I've seen're barflies and drunks, cowboys, rowdies, soldiers, and outlaws. There ain't much to pick from when you got a clientele like that."

"Maybe not," Culpepper said in reassuring tones, "but things happen in strange ways sometimes. You keep your eyes and ears open, and"—he added with a shrug—"you never can tell, something good might happen when you don't expect it."

"I think you've gone *loco*," Daisy said, chuckling, her spirits mostly restored. "You must love your wife very much."

"I do," Culpepper said, without apology. He felt no sense of shame that he loved his wife dearly, and so he didn't care who knew.

"That's unusual, too," Daisy noted. "What's her name?"

"Merriam. I call her Merry."

"What's she like?"

"A little taller than you, maybe not as full-figured. Prettiest face I ever saw, and hair that hangs all the way down to her rump when she lets it. She loves that hair, all dark brown and shiny. And so do I." He was not ashamed of his feelings for his wife, but he felt a little odd voicing them to a stranger. Particularly a female stranger.

Daisy smiled softly and warmly at Culpepper. "I'll say this, Jonas—not only are you one lucky man, she's one lucky woman to have someone like you."

"Thanks."

Daisy pushed herself up. "One last chance, Jonas," she said with a grin.

He smiled back. "I'll pass, Miss Greenwalt. But if it's any comfort to you, if my wife leaves me, I just might come look you up."

Daisy walked away, feeling a lot better about herself.

Chapter 20

They rode into the town of San Miguel shortly after noon the next day. Culpepper stopped right off and asked directions to the doctor's office—if there was a physician in town.

The town resident nodded, pointed, and said, "Go two blocks down that way. Turn right there. Halfway down that block is an alley. The entrance to Doc Parmenter's is in the alley, leadin' up to the second floor."

Culpepper touched the brim of his hat at the man and rode on. "You know, maggot," he said, as he was helping Adler down off the horse, "it never made no sense to me to have a doctor put his office on the second floor. You're going to have a devil of a time gettin' up those stairs."

"Eat shit, ya fat-ass bag of wind," Adler snarled.

"Watch your mouth, you pukin' scoundrel," Culpepper said evenly. "Or I'll break your other leg for you. You'll be real interestin' to watch tryin' to get up the stairs then."

Adler growled but said nothing as he started easing himself up the steps. He was rather pleased when he realized that Culpepper was directly behind him. All he figured he'd have to do now was to plan carefully, and then set himself just right. The small balcony at the top of the stairs was nearing, and Adler began to steel his mind. He was sure it was going to hurt, but if he did this the right way, Sheriff Jonas Culpepper would get pitched over the railing and be dashed to death on the ground.

Finally he made his move, planting his left foot on a plank step, then half turning, bringing his shoulder and bent arm around to pound Culpepper off the stairs. He hit Culpepper somewhere between chest and face. Culpepper did not move, but Adler thought he had broken his own shoulder.

"You through playin' now, maggot?" Culpepper asked calmly.

Defeated, Adler sucked in a breath through his teeth, turned, and lurched up the last two steps and then inside.

Dr. Curtis Parmenter looked up from the large medical book he was reading. Peering over his half-frame glasses, he asked, "Can I do something for you folks?"

"You Doctor Parmenter?" Culpepper asked.

"I am."

Culpepper went to the man and shook his hand. "San Juan County Sheriff Jonas Culpepper. That gimpy maggot over there is my prisoner, Milt Adler. The young lady is Miss Daisy Greenwalt. She was ill-used by Adler and some of the pukin' scoundrels he was runnin' with."

Parmenter nodded. "I take it you want the gimp's leg fixed?"

Culpepper nodded. "Soon's possible. I'd like to get back on the trail."

Parmenter shrugged. "I can have him out of here in less than an hour, if you're in a real rush. But if you have any sense, you'll listen to your friendly neighborhood doctor—spend the night in San Miguel. You look like you could use a decent night's sleep. You can lock the gimp there up in the jail. Marshal Childress is pretty accommodating."

"I suspect you're right, Doc." Culpepper sighed. "Well, get him fixed up, so's I can go make arrangements."

"No need for you to wait around, Sheriff. We'll strap the culprit to my examining table, and then I'll administer a dose of ether—that's an anesthetic."

Both Culpepper and Daisy looked at the doctor in some puzzlement.

"It'll knock him out and, depending on the dose and the frequency with which I administer it, will keep him out as long as I want."

"You ain't usin' that shit on me, you butcher," Adler snapped.

"Aha," Parmenter said, "an unwilling participant. Always one of my favorites."

Culpepper grinned, deciding that he liked the doctor. "All right, Doc," he said. "Where do you want him?"

"In here," Parmenter said, heading toward a room in the back.

"After you, maggot," Culpepper said.

"Eat shit, you . . ."

Culpepper stepped up and calmly kicked Adler's good leg out from under him. Adler fell on his seat and groaned as pain tore through his injured leg. Culpepper reached down and hauled him back up. "Now move it, you pukin' scoundrel," he said easily.

Adler shuffled and hopped into the examining room. Between Parmenter and Culpepper, it was but a few moments before Adler was lying on his back on the table, several thick leather straps holding him firmly to the table. His hands were now handcuffed in front of him, and under two of the straps.

"You go on now, Sheriff," Parmenter said. "You and the young lady. This jasper won't give me any more trouble. And take your time. Go talk to Marshal Childress, maybe have yourselves a bite to eat."

"Where's the marshal's office?" Culpepper asked. "And the livery?"

"Both on Center Street. Go out of the alley to the north, turn left, two blocks up is Center. Turn right there for the marshal's office. The livery's across the street and a little farther on."

Minutes later Culpepper and Daisy walked into the town marshal's office. A tall, lean man with a long, flowing mustache looked up at them from his work. "Somethin' I can do for you folks?" he asked. Then he spotted the star on Culpepper's shirt. "Sheriff?"

Culpepper nodded and introduced himself.

"San Miguel Marshal Stan Childress." The men shook hands.

Then Culpepper nodded toward Daisy. "And this here's Miss Daisy Greenwalt. She's from down around Alamosa way," he said easily. "She and her parents were movin' to Durango a couple weeks ago when they were set upon by Mack Ellsworth and his gang."

"Nasty bunch, those boys," Childress said flatly.

"You're acquainted with them, then?" Culpepper asked.

"Damn right . . . pardon me, Miss . . . darn right I am. But that's neither here nor there. You were saying?"

"Ellsworth and his men killed Daisy's ma and pa," Culpepper continued, ignoring Daisy's look of shocked surprise. "And they spirited the poor girl off with them. Kept her their prisoner for a couple of weeks, till I come on the small cabin where they had her. Wasn't but three of them left at that point, and they seemed like they were gettin' tired of the unfortunate miss. I ended up killin' two of them maggots."

"And the third?" Childress asked.

"That's what brought me here to your office, Marshal," Culpepper said. "He's over at Doc Parmenter's gettin' his leg fixed up from where I shot him. The Doc suggested I spend the night in town, leavin' my prisoner locked up in your jail. Doc says you're usually pretty accommodatin' that way."

"I sure try to be," Childress said with a nod. "There's precious few enough of us law dogs around these parts. If there's any help I can give to another, I'm more'n willin' to do so."

"Glad to hear it. Well, Daisy and me'll take the horses down to the livery, and then . . ." He stopped, then nodded. "There a halfway decent place to eat around here, Marshal?"

"Brickley's. Not far down the street. I can take you there, if you're of a mind."

"I think that'd be good. Me and Daisy can eat, then ride back to the doc's to bring Adler over here. Then we can bring the horses to the livery. Unless that'll harm any plans you have . . ."

"Nope. Come on, I'll take you to Brickley's."

Daisy urgently grabbed Culpepper's elbow. When he looked at her in question, she crooked a finger at him, wanting him to bend. He did, and she whispered furiously in his ear.

Culpepper nodded. "My apologies, Marshal, but I've been forgetful—or maybe just thoughtless. Whichever, Miss Greenwalt just reminded me that she's not properly clothed to eat in public. Is there a dry goods store nearby where she can get something decent to wear?"

"Sure is," Childress said. "Come on, I'll take you there."

Daisy felt considerably more relaxed when she was clad in a plain calico dress, matching bonnet, and new, simple button shoes. Then the three headed to the restaurant.

Culpepper invited Childress to eat with him and Daisy, but the marshal turned him down. "I'm still full up from lunch. I'll see you back at the office when you get back. Take your time and enjoy yourselves."

As soon as Childress had walked away, Daisy looked at Culpepper with fire in her eyes. "What the hell'd you go and tell him that story for?" she demanded.

"Watch your mouth, Missy. And order your supper."

Daisy bit her lip, but ordered. When the waiter left, she said, "Answer me, damn you."

"I told you, watch your mouth." Culpepper grinned. "Didn't you tell me last night that you'd like to marry some nice, respectable townsman somewhere and settle down to raise a family?"

"Yeah, but . . ."

"Women ain't all that populous around here, Daisy," Culpepper said practically. "A young, good-lookin', healthy woman like you shouldn't have any trouble findin' a marriageable feller hereabouts."

"But . . . but what about my past?"

"Your past? You're a young woman whose parents were killed by outlaws, a young woman who's been treated harshly by life. A woman ill-abused by the outlaws, but otherwise unsullied by man."

"You really are *loco*," Daisy said. "My real past'll be sure to come out sooner or later."

"Why? What're the chances of you marryin' a man here who's seen you down in Durango? What're the chances that a feller you marry here will ever go to Durango—and take you with him? Pretty durn small, I'd wager. And even if someone who knew you in Durango comes up here and says somethin', you just stand your ground and tell him he's full of beans; that you haven't even heard where Durango is, let alone spent time there."

Daisy looked interested, but she was scared of the idea. It was something she'd longed for for quite some time, but now that it seemed even remotely possible, she was having second thoughts. "Do you really think it could work?" she asked tensely.

Culpepper was about to answer, but closed his mouth when the waiter came along and began slapping dishes on the table. He went away but returned with more. All the while, Culpepper and Daisy kept mum.

When the waiter was finally gone for good, Daisy asked nervously, "Well, do you?"

"Do I what?" Culpepper asked innocently, as he shoveled a hunk of beefsteak into his mouth.

"Damn it!" Daisy looked around guiltily. She lowered her voice. "Darn it, Jonas, answer me."

Culpepper was about to josh her some more, but then he saw the look on Daisy's face and decided he could not be so cruel right now. "I'll put it this way, Daisy," he said quietly, "you won't know until you give it a try. If it doesn't work, you can always try something—or somewhere—else. Or, I can take you back to Durango straight off and you can go back to your old life."

Daisy almost shuddered at the thought. She suddenly grinned. "I think I'll take my chances here." The grin turned impish. "Besides, maybe that old wife of yours'll dump you and you'll come back here to marry me."

Culpepper laughed. "Old? She'd kill us both if she heard that."

Daisy grew serious again. "How'm I gonna go about all this, Jonas?" she asked, worried anew.

"Eat your supper, Missy," Culpepper said gruffly. "We'll get you set up before I ride out tomorrow."

Daisy looked at him skeptically, but the aroma of the food began to get to her, reminding her of how hungry she was. She began to eat with enthusiasm as the possibility of a new life in San Miguel filled her mind with daydreams.

After eating, they walked back to the marshal's office, mounted up, and rode to Dr. Parmenter's. Adler was groggy from the ether Parmenter had given him, and so Culpepper had to carry the outlaw down the stairs over his shoulder. He tossed Adler's limp figure across the horse, and then rode back to the jail, where Adler was lodged.

"I'll show you down to the livery," Childress said. "I feel the need for gettin' out again. To tell you the truth, Sheriff, I hate the damn . . . pardon me, Miss . . . dang paperwork worse than anything."

"You're not alone, Marshal," Culpepper said with a laugh. When they were outside and walking up the street, Culpepper said, "I was wonderin' if you might be able to give us a little more help, Marshal."

"If I can. What do you need?"

"Well, Miss Greenwalt is in a fix. As I told you before, she's got no more folks, and no place to go. I was wonderin' if you might be able to find somebody to put her up a while. Just till she gets her feet under her. I don't expect she'll have any trouble attracting suitors, but it'd be nice if somebody was to look over her for a spell, sort of make sure the suitors're respectable men."

"Well, now," Childress said slowly, "I don't expect that'd be much of a problem. I think Mister and Miz Stanton—a nice old couple I know—would be willing to let you roost there a little, Miss."

"Are they good folk?" Daisy asked, sounding perfectly innocent.

"Yes, Miss, they sure are. They run the Stanton House, the finest hotel in San Miguel. In fact we'll go on straight over there after the livery, if that's all right with you. Sheriff, you can stay there tonight."

"If it's the finest hotel in San Miguel," Culpepper said dryly, "I might not be able to afford their rates."

Childress laughed self-consciously. "Truth to tell, Sheriff, it's the *only* hotel in San Miguel. We don't get many travelers out this way."

Culpepper nodded. "That'll suit me fine."

"And, Miss Greenwalt," Childress said, once more ill at ease, "if you weren't to object too much, I'd like to be among your first suitors."

Daisy glanced at Culpepper, who was trying hard to conceal a told-you-so grin. Then she looked at Childress. "Well, Marshal," she said demurely, "I suppose that'd be all right. But I'll have to check to see that it's all right with the Stantons—if they take me in, that is."

"That's good enough for me, Miss!" Childress said. His step suddenly got a little more self-assured.

Chapter 21

It took Culpepper and Adler eight days to make it back to Silverton. After more than two days of traveling southeast, still in the arid high desert, they turned north east along Fall Creek, heading higher into a cleft between the Uncompahgre Plateau and the San Juan Mountains. The next morning they made their way through Dallas Divide, and the next day they turned southeast again, heading into the heart of the San Juans. It was a longer journey this way than if they'd kept going south and east from San Miguel, but it was less wearing on men and horses. It took more than a day to work up to the town of Red Mountain City. The next day took them through Red Mountain Pass. The day after, they rode into Silverton in the early afternoon.

Adler had given Culpepper no real trouble on the journey, for which Culpepper was at least a little grateful. The traveling in and of itself was hard even without Adler kicking up a fuss. It was bad enough that Culpepper had to do so much for Adler, what with his broken leg and all, plus the fact that Culpepper wasn't about to let him loose from the handcuffs for any extended period of time.

Culpepper rode straight to his office and the jail. He stopped outside, a little surprised that Jimmy Cahill was not there to meet him. He shrugged, figuring that Cahill was probably out on business. He eased Adler off his horse and then pushed him gently forward. "Inside," he said, "while I get the keys to the hoosegow."

Culpepper shoved the door open, then waited for Adler to hobble inside, followed by Bear. Culpepper's eyes narrowed in anger when he saw U.S. Deputy Marshal Ned Coakley sitting in Culpepper's chair, his feet up on the desk.

Coakley smiled smugly at Culpepper, and said, "Welcome back, Sheriff." Sarcasm was thick in his voice.

Culpepper stepped inside, noting the two young gun toughs with badges on their shirts. One was sitting in a chair; the other was standing in the back corner, arms folded across his chest. Bear plunked himself down not far from the two, growling slowly and steadily as he licked his floppy chops. The two deputies looked mighty nervous all of a sudden.

Culpepper was not sure he could speak, considering the rage he felt inside. He pushed Adler to the side and then strode behind his desk. Shoving Coakley's feet off the desk, Culpepper reached into a drawer and got the keys to the jail. Culpepper straightened with the ring of keys in his hand. Then he turned and shoved Adler outside. He had said nothing the whole time. Bear followed him.

Walking Adler next door to the jail, Culpepper went through the laborious process of unlocking the doors and gates and then locking them again once Adler was inside. Then he walked back into the office. "What're you doin' here, maggot?" he asked, as soon as he stepped inside. The mastiff took his old position near the two deputies.

An oily smirk eased across Coakley's thin face. "I was called here by some of the fine citizens of Silverton," he said unctuously. "Since you've been gone so long, folks figured you were bein' derelict in your duty. So I came up here and assumed the duties of San Juan County sheriff. In addition to my role as United States deputy marshal, of course. I even brung a couple deputies of my own to help me sort things out here. Lou Boxham and Neil Corcoran."

Each touched the brim of his hat when he was named. Boxham was the one sitting; Corcoran was standing.

"Mighty nice of you," Culpepper said flatly. "Who was the durn fool gave you the say-so to pull this durn stunt?"

"Not that it's any of your concern, but Wilson Pennrose was kind enough to seek my services when you run out on the good people of Silverton."

Culpepper nodded. He would see about Pennrose later. "Where's Jimmy?" he asked.

"He that stupid ass of a deputy you had?" Coakley asked.

"Where is he?" Culpepper asked tightly.

"Around somewhere. Now get out of my office, fatso, or I'll have my two boys throw you out."

Culpepper grinned, but it was not a pleasant sight to Coakley or his two companions. "Tell them to come on ahead," he said quietly. "They won't fare no better'n Owen Fauss did." He got a small jolt of satisfaction at the look of anger that passed swiftly over Coakley's face. "I got some things to do, and I might not be back here till mornin'. You and those two pukin' maggots over there," he said, pointing to the deputies, "had best be gone. Not only from my office, but from Silverton."

Coakley laughed. His two companions joined in nervously.

Culpepper turned to look at the deputies. "If you two got any brains at all, you'll ditch this pukin' scoundrel and go your own way."

"I think we'll stick around as long as Marshal Coakley wants us to," Boxham said with bravado.

Culpepper shrugged. "Don't matter none to me," he said easily. "It's your funeral." He turned and with Bear at his side, walked out. Still fuming with anger, he went to the Exchange livery to leave his horse and mule.

"Welcome back, Jonas," Art Cassidy said without much enthusiasm.

"Somethin' botherin' you, Art?" Culpepper asked, as he pulled his Winchester out of the scabbard.

"You been to your office—what was your office—yet?"

"Yep. That egg-suckin' scoundrel Coakley told me he come up here and took over my job. That misconception'll be taken care of by mornin'."

"You run out on us, Jonas," Cassidy said, almost plaintively. "Why'd you ever do that?"

"That what that skunk told you?" Culpepper demanded, fire snapping in his blue eyes.

"Him and Wilson Pennrose."

"You've known me since I arrived in Silverton, Art," Culpepper said, a little more calmly. "Do you think I'd do somethin' like that?"

"No," Cassidy said. "But when Pennrose . . ."

"I'll deal with that pukin' scoundrel, too." He paused, then asked, "Where's Jimmy been through all this?"

Cassidy suddenly looked immensely uncomfortable.

"Tell me, durn you."

"He tried to prevent Coakley from takin' over, sayin' that you'd never run out on us . . ." Cassidy said weakly.

"Nice to know I got one friend in Silverton," Culpepper said dryly. "So what happened to him?" A sudden blast of cold touched his insides, as he thought of Coakley's comment that Cahill was "around somewhere." That could as easily mean Hillside Cemetery as anything else.

"Didn't Coakley tell you?" Cassidy asked, surprised.

"Nope."

"He's in the town jail."

"The what?" Culpepper exploded. "What in Hades is he doin' there?"

Cassidy shrugged nervously. "I ain't sure. But I think Coakley cooked up some charges to hold him for a while."

"Why not in the county jail, then?"

"Don't know." He paused. "Look, Jonas, I don't know what's goin' on around here. All I know is what I see or hear."

Culpepper nodded and stuffed the Winchester back into the saddle scabbard. "Take care of my horse. I'll be back for the rifle and saddlebags after a little while." Then he and Bear strode out, heading north up Greene Street and then east on Twelfth Street. In minutes he was entering the marshal's office-jail.

Town Marshal Wes Hennessy looked up, surprise stamped on his fastidious face. "Well, howdy, Jonas," he said, not quite cheerily. "When did you . . . ?"

"Is Jimmy here?" Culpepper demanded.

"Jonas, that you out there?" Cahill called, from one of the cells in back of the office.

Culpepper glowered at Hennessy. "Release him."

"But, Sheriff," Hennessy protested, "Marshal Coakley wanted him locked up. Said there was a number of charges pending against him. And Mister Pennrose . . ."

"I don't give a good goddamn who said what to you, Wes," Culpepper growled. "You let Jimmy go now, or I swear to the Good Lord above that I'll gut-shoot you and then go let him loose myself."

One look at Culpepper's face let Hennessy know the county sheriff was deadly serious. He jumped up, grabbing his keys. He almost ran to the cells and unlocked the one housing Jimmy Cahill.

"My pistols, you putrefyin' son of a bitch," Cahill snapped at Hennessy.

The marshal gave Cahill's his gunbelt and pistols, then sank into his chair. "I'm confused by all this, Jonas," he said weakly.

"Well, when I get it straightened out, I'll come explain it to you," Culpepper said harshly.

Culpepper, Cahill, and Bear left. As they were walking up the street, Culpepper said, "What's happened here, Jimmy?"

"You know anything?"

Culpepper nodded. "I stopped at the office to get the keys to lock up a prisoner. Coakley and two other maggots were there. Coakley said he took over since I'd been derelict in my duties as county sheriff. Art Cassidy said he had you locked up in the town jail. That's why I went over there. That's about all I know."

"There's not much more to know," Cahill said. "I was up in Charlottesville to run down a gambler who wound up stabbin' one of the girls of the line—Long-Tooth Annie—and then run off. He didn't want to come back here and pulled a gun on me, so I had to plant him. When I got back, Coakley was at the office and told me he had taken over. I objected, of course, and he arrested me for gettin' in the way of a marshal's sworn duty. He and his two friends disarmed me and marched me over to Hennessy's."

"Why?"

"I asked that myself. Coakley said the county jail was plumb full up—a sign of the good job he was doin'."

"I just put my prisoner in there. He's alone."

"Damn," Cahill snapped. "He's sure got the wool pulled over everyone's eyes. You know, Jonas, I don't think Hennessy really knows what went on with all this. I think he's been duped just like most everyone else."

They were at the livery stable, and Culpepper gathered up his rifle and saddlebags. Then he and Cahill, with Bear, left again.

"I'm going to straighten this all out tomorrow," Culpepper said. "But for tonight, I want some of Merry's cooking—and her company. If I were you, I'd lie low for a bit. That scoundrel Coakley sees you walkin' around town, there's no tellin' what he might do."

"I ain't afraid of him," Cahill said stubbornly.

"Then you're an idiot," Culpepper said flatly. "You know what kind of man he is, and what he's capable of. A man like him wouldn't think twice about back-shootin' someone. He even sent out a man to ambush me on the trial."

"I take it he didn't hit you."

"Nope. Killed my mule, but I got him."

"When did this happen?" Cahill asked.

"Day after I left here, I suppose. Yep, that was it. Why?"

"It was only four days later that Coakley and his two asswipe partners showed up. You take the body back to Durango?"

"No. Took it to Fort Lewis, though, and had them bring it to Durango, with a warning from me."

"Then he took a day or two to recruit those two he brought with him, and make arrangements to get up here by train. That was when I was in Charlottesville. It still doesn't make all that much sense, though. How could he just waltz on in here and take over—with Wilson Pennrose's acceptance?"

Culpepper shrugged. "I have no idea, but I figure a talk with Pennrose'll clear at least some of it up. Has Coakley tried anything much since he's been here?"

"Nah, not too much. Locked up a few men here and there, from what I heard. Seems almost like he was waitin' for somethin'."

"He probably was." When Cahill looked at him in puzzlement, Culpepper said, "Me." He stopped and looked at Cahill. "Remember what I said. Lie low tonight. I'll come get you sometime tomorrow."

"Don't you go after those bastards by yourself, Jonas," Cahill warned. "I owe them boys, and I don't want to see you gettin' killed tryin' to take on all three of 'em."

Culpepper nodded absentmindedly. He turned toward the house, his mind awhirl with all he'd learned today and with the trouble he was having in puzzling it out. A few minutes later, he was home and Merry was warm and hungry in his arms, and he mostly forgot about Ned Coakley and all the others.

They had a quick tumble in the bed, lusting for each other. Then came a leisurely supper of pork chops and potatoes. After dessert of apple cobbler, Culpepper shaved and then took a bath—with Merry's willing help. And finally, they were in bed, straining for each other again.

Afterward, Merry told Culpepper what she knew of what had gone on in Silverton since he had left. He acknowledged that he knew some of it, though he did not let on he knew as much as he did. He did not want to make her worry any more than she already did.

She tried to question Culpepper then, but he was reluctant

to tell her anything. He simply told her, "Trust me, Merry. I'll straighten everything out. You needn't worry about it."

"But I can't help frettin' about it," she countered.

"Maybe I can help you keep it out of your mind a little," he said with an impish grin. He pulled her toward and then on top of him.

Chapter 22

When Culpepper walked into his office the next morning, Coakley and his two minions looked as if they had not moved from yesterday. Coakley still sat behind the desk with his feet up on it. A smirk distorted his face. Lou Boxham was sitting in the other chair, grinning vacuously. His hair was blond almost to being white. Neil Corcoran, who was again standing in the corner, chewed a matchstick. He was serious, and Culpepper considered him the far more dangerous of the two deputies.

"Well, fatso," Coakley said with a sneer, "seems we're still here. You aim to do somethin' about it?"

"Maybe later," Culpepper said easily. "Right now I just need to get some papers out of my desk drawer there." He moved to the desk, as if reaching for something. Suddenly he drew back his meaty right fist and slammed Coakley a good shot on the side of the head. Coakley crashed off the side of the chair and hit the floor.

"Holy shit!" Boxham snapped in surprise. He started to come up out of his chair.

Culpepper slapped his palms on the desktop and vaulted over the desk, the soles of his boots landing in Boxham's chest. Boxham fell back into the chair with such force that it went over backward, dumping him on the floor.

As soon as he had seen Culpepper hit Coakley, Corcoran went for his pistol. But Bear jumped into him and clamped viselike jaws on the deputy's arm. Corcoran yowled once and dropped his revolver. He tried getting his other pistol with his left hand, but the mastiff was jerking him back and forth.

Heading for Corcoran, Culpepper stomped on Boxham's right arm, breaking it. Then he said, "Back, Bear." When the dog moved away from Corcoran, Culpepper grabbed the shaken deputy and jerked him forward. He swiftly latched onto the back of Corcoran's shirt high and low and then ran him forward until Corcoran's face slammed into the log wall. Corcoran slumped to the floor with a soft moan.

Culpepper whirled, looking for Coakley. The marshal was just getting up. He seemed groggy as his hand absently searched for a pistol. Culpepper grabbed him by the shirtfront and yanked him forward. Without a word, Culpepper lifted Coakley and then pitched him through the glass window and out into the street.

"God damn it, Jonas," Cahill's voice came in from the street through the hole where the window had been, "you said I'd get a crack at 'em."

Culpepper stepped up to the window. "Just come in here and get the keys to the jail," he said pleasantly. "Then help me cart their festerin' carcasses over there."

In ten minutes it was done, with Coakley, Boxham, and Corcoran relieved of their weapons and all in one cell. The only other occupant of the jail was Adler, who had the other cell to himself.

Outside, Culpepper ignored the gathered crowd. "Go get somebody to fix the window, Jimmy. And send Doc McQuiston to look at those three pukes."

"Where're you gonna be?"

"I think I'm going to go have a little chat with Mister Pennrose."

"I'd rather go with you."

"Go where?" Buster Reinhardt asked, as he walked up.

"To talk with Pennrose," Cahill said.

"You need somethin' done here, Jonas?" Reinhardt asked. "I can help out."

"If you go get someone to fix the window and get Doc McQuiston, Jimmy can come along with me. That might keep him from mewlin' some."

"Will do. Glad to have you back, Jonas."

"Glad to be back—I think."

Culpepper and Cahill headed up toward the Anvil Mining Company offices. No one tried to stop them as they headed straight toward the boardroom at back. Culpepper opened the door and stepped inside. Cahill followed and closed the door.

"To what do we owe this honor, Sheriff?" Pennrose asked sourly. He was not surprised to see Culpepper. He'd heard the sheriff was back in Silverton. Indeed, he had even thought of leaving Silverton on some "urgent business" to miss the call he expected from Culpepper. But he'd decided against it.

"Oh, I think you're a smart enough man to figure that out, Pennrose," Culpepper said dryly.

"Yes, I am," Pennrose said with a nod. "So, Sheriff, speak your piece and then leave."

"Why'd you call that pukin' scoundrel up here to take over my job?" Culpepper asked harshly. He stood with feet wide apart, arms folded on his big chest.

"I didn't call him here," Pennrose said, now surprised.

"You didn't, eh? Coakley says you did."

"That's a damn bald-faced lie, Jonas," Pennrose said vehemently. "I got a note from him, delivered by one of those two gunmen he has with him, sayin' that you had come through Durango, gotten drunk, and in your besotted condition mentioned how you were never going back to Silverton again. That you'd set your sights on California."

"And you believed that pile of hogwash?" Culpepper asked, incredulous. "Knowin' how I feel about Merry? And knowin' the kind of man I am—a man devoted to his duty?"

Pennrose shrugged. "This came from a United States deputy

marshal," Pennrose said without apology. "I even went so far as to send a wire to the La Plata County sheriff."

"Hammond? He ain't got the brains the Good Lord give a rock."

Pennrose shrugged again. "He confirmed the story, so I wired Coakley and told him to come on up and take your place. I must admit, I was rather surprised last night when I heard you had returned. Still, Marshal Coakley does seem to have a better handle on things."

"Marshal Coakley is sitting in the San Juan County Jail at this very moment. So are the two pukin' maggots he had with him."

"Why?" Pennrose asked, surprised again.

"For one, he threw Jimmy here in jail for no good reason other than tryin' to stop his takeover. For another, he sent a man out to shoot me down outside of Durango."

"Oh, come now, Sheriff," Pennrose said skeptically. "A federal marshal sending out a hired man to kill a county sheriff? That's preposterous."

"Not for a man of Coakley's ilk. You don't believe me, check with Major Abel Watkins, down at Fort Lewis. You can also check with Durango Marshal Ed Hernandez. The skunk who came after me was named Owen Fauss. He said Coakley paid him a hundred in advance for the job. I found five double eagles on him."

Pennrose sat in thought. He was beginning to think he had seriously misjudged things here, and all because he didn't think Culpepper was properly respectful to him. Now there could be a world of trouble. "What're you planning to do, Sheriff?" he asked finally.

"Head out after Ellsworth's gang again. I hear tell the Denver and Rio Grande's raised the reward money."

Pennrose nodded. "So has Anvil Mining."

"With that much of a reward, there's a better chance that I can find the pukin' scoundrels, since people'll be more willin' to talk." He sighed. "It's also going to bring out the bounty hunters and such."

"When're you planning to leave?"

"Tomorrow. Day after, maybe."

"And what're you going to do with Marshal Coakley and his two cronies?"

"Leave them settin' right where they're at. I'll deal with those three maggots when I get back."

Pennrose tried not to show his relief. He nodded. "I'm sorry for the trouble I inadvertently caused you, Sheriff," he said unctuously. "If I'd only known . . ." He held up his hands as if indicating he was helpless in the matter.

"It's over and done with now," Culpepper said flatly. "But it'd go better for everyone if you'd keep your nose out of business that doesn't concern you." Culpepper turned and left, Cahill and Bear following him.

"You know, Jonas," Cahill said as they hit the street, "I ain't so sure I trust Pennrose. Not after this."

"Me neither, but there's not a whole lot we can do about it. But it's one of the reasons I'm leavin' you in charge when I ride off again."

Cahill began to protest, but Culpepper cut him off. "There's too many scoundrels around here these days, Jimmy. I need somebody I can trust to watch my back while I'm gone. Even more important, I need someone to watch over Merry. And . . ."

Cahill suddenly grinned widely. "In all the excitement of late, Jonas, I never did tell you—I proposed to June while you were gone. Before Coakley arrested me."

"Well I'll be dogged, boy. When're the nuptials?"

"We thought we'd like to get hitched on Independence Day."

"A good choice," Culpepper said with a nod and a smile. Then he grew serious again. "You think you'll be able to keep your mind on the jobs at hand?"

"Damn right I can," Cahill growled.

"Good. I want you in Silverton all the time. Somethin' happens elsewhere in the county, you send Buster or somebody else you think you can trust."

"All right, Jonas. But I still'd rather be with you out there. Christ, there's no tellin' how many men Ellsworth's got with him."

"I'll be all right. Don't you fret." Culpepper smiled a little. "Unless maybe you're afraid of stayin' here on your own, after Wes locked you up and all."

"Shit," Cahill snapped. He calmed himself down, knowing that Culpepper was only joking with him. "What're you gonna do the rest of the day, Jonas?"

"I got some durn paperwork to finish up. Then I want to talk to Adler."

"You think he'll tell you anything? You said he was powerful reluctant to do so while you two were on the trail."

"He was that. But maybe bein' locked up'll change his mind some. If not, I ain't lost much."

With more than a little reluctance, Culpepper headed to the office and sat to his paperwork. As annoying and as time consuming as it might be, it had to be done, and letting it set till the last minute wouldn't make it any easier.

He went home for a leisurely lunch with Merry and then headed for the jail with Bear at his side. He unlocked the doors, until he and the mastiff were in Adler's cell. He ignored the annoying comments from Coakley and his two men in the adjoining cell. Boxham sported a fresh splint on his one arm.

"What do you want here, Sheriff?" Adler asked in unfriendly tones.

"See if you've changed your mind about talkin' to me," Culpepper said, leaning back against the bars.

"Fat goddamn chance."

"It might go some easier on you if you was to cooperate a little, maggot. I might even be willin' to talk to Judge Pfeiffer at your trial. A good word from me might be enough to save your scrawny neck from the hangman's noose."

Adler was about to retort, but stopped himself. Instead, he thought about it. If Culpepper was true to his word—and he had shown every indication so far that he was that kind of man—and he could keep Adler from being sentenced to death, he would be much better off. Even if he had a long prison term, he'd get out someday. And there was always the chance that he could escape and make his way back to Ellsworth and the others to get his share of the loot. But he couldn't tell too much. No, that would never do.

"You promise you'll say a good word for me?" he asked.

"Yep—if you give me any information that's helpful. You're gonna stay in the jail here till I get back from wherever it is I go chasin' Ellsworth. Your information turns out to be hogwash, I'll be more than willin' to stand in Judge Pfeiffer's courtroom and watch him sentence you to hang. And, seein' as how I usually act as hangman, I'll look forward to stretchin' your neck."

Adler believed him. "There's not too much I can tell you, Sheriff," he said smoothly. "Mack Ellsworth don't take nobody into his confidence, except maybe Hugh McLeod."

Culpepper nodded. He knew that McLeod was about the only man Ellsworth trusted.

"After robbin' the train, we went south. Just before we got to Durango, Ellsworth sent me, Cody, and Pete Brolin to Durango, to pick up some supplies. We also grabbed that little whore you saved then, and rode on after the others. After that fight we had with you near those ruins, we headed north. We spent a couple days at the cabin, then split up. Me and my two pals gave Ellsworth a few bucks for the whore and stayed at the cabin. Mack, Hugh, and a few of the others rode on. Northwest, I think. The rest of the boys went in all different directions."

Culpepper waited until the sound of the train pulling into the station not far away had faded. Then he asked, "What about the loot?"

"What about it?"

"You split it up?"

"Not yet. We're supposed to get together in a . . . a few months to divvy it up."

Culpepper nodded. "Ellsworth still have it?"

"I ain't sure," Adler said with a shrug. He licked his lips. "Mack . . . well, Mack said he and the boys with him were gonna bury it somewhere over near the border of Utah Territory. Only four of 'em was gonna know where it was."

"Where're you supposed to meet?"

"A little town called Westville, over on West Creek, near where it enters the Dolores River. It's out in the goddamn middle of no-goddamn-where. Why'n hell anybody'd ever try settlin' in such a place is beyond me."

Culpepper nodded absently. He figured Adler was lying at least about some of it, but there was no way of telling what and how much until he checked it out. Without another word, he unlocked his way out of the cells and headed back to his office.

Chapter 23

Culpepper walked into the office and stopped dead in his tracks. Next to him, Bear looked at the man behind the desk, and then up at his master. He whined plaintively and his tail wagged tentatively, since he was confused.

Standing next to the repaired window, Jimmy Cahill grinned at Culpepper. "Goddamn, it ain't bad enough I got to put up with one of you. Now I got to deal with two of you." He paused a second. "I do believe you know this feller, don't you, Jonas?"

Culpepper's face split in a wide grin as he headed toward his brother, who rose from the chair to greet Culpepper. The two men hugged a little and slapped each other heartily on the back.

Cahill looked at them. The resemblance was uncanny, though now that he saw the two of them together, Cahill could see some differences. Jody Culpepper was about two inches taller than Jonas, but about twenty pounds lighter, and a few years younger. Jody was clean-shaven, but they each had a mane of fiery red hair. And the same piercing blue eyes.

"When did you get here, Jody?" Jonas asked after their greeting.

"Come in on the train just a few minutes ago."

"What're you doin' here?"

"Sorry to see me?" Jody countered.

"Didn't say that," Jonas said a little gruffly. "It's just unexpected, and I don't know as if I'll have much time for visiting and such."

"Trouble?"

"Always is," Jonas acknowledged. "This's worse than usual, though."

Jody nodded. "I couldn't stand my boss no more," he said with a grin. "He kept treadin' on my good nature, so a couple weeks ago I cleaned his plow for him and walked out. Since I didn't have anyplace in particular to go, I thought I'd come out here and see how things were. Thought maybe I'd get me a job." He paused. "I didn't mean to get in your way."

Jonas grinned. "You ain't in the way. It's just that I'll be gone for a spell. On the trail of some outlaws."

"Tell me about it," Jody said with a gleam in his eye.

Seeing that glint of excitement, Cahill found another difference between the brothers. He would wager a month's pay that Jody was a hell of a lot wilder than Jonas was.

"Later," Jonas said. "Come on, let's get you over to the house."

"Merry's well?" Jody asked.

"She is." Jonas looked at Cahill. "Can you keep an eye on things, Jimmy?"

"Sure, Jonas. You and your brother go on. Anything major comes up, I'll send someone for you."

The Culpepper brothers walked swiftly to Jonas's house, Jody carrying his cloth valise. Bear bounced along, round and round the two men, still trying to figure out what was going on here.

"Merry!" Jonas called as he opened the door. "Merry, come look who's here."

A little worried, Merry came out of the bedroom where she had been sewing. Her face brightened when she saw her brother-in-law. "Jody," she said happily. She hugged him and kissed him on the cheek. "What brings you to Silverton?"

"Lookin' for work," Jody said blandly.

"Are you hungry?"

"Sure am. I ain't had anything since a foul breakfast down in Durango."

"Well, sit. Sit," Merry said. "Jonas, take his bag and put it away. Don't just stand there."

"Yes'm," Jonas said, not meekly at all, as he took the valise and set it against the wall, out of the way.

"Still henpecked, I see," Jody said with a laugh.

"She can't help it," Jonas said with a straight face. "She's just naturally bossy."

"Oh, you stop it now, Jonas!" Merry said in mock anger. Then she and her husband laughed.

Merry served Jody. Jonas was satisfied with coffee, since he had eaten not long ago. After Jody was done, though, Merry figured that the two men wanted to talk, so she took up her sewing again and went into the bedroom.

"So, Jonas, tell me," Jody said, "what's all the big trouble?" Before Jonas could begin explaining, though, Jody asked, "You got any whiskey, Jonas? Merry's coffee's good and all, but I need somethin' a little stronger to cut the dust."

Jonas got the bottle he kept in one of the cabinets and poured a mugful for his brother and himself. Jody lifted his cup in a salute, and Jonas returned the gesture. "Glad to see you, little brother," Jonas said.

"Same here."

Each took a healthy swallow, and then Jonas told the tale of the train robbery and his hunt for Mack Ellsworth and his gang.

"And now you're goin' back out after them, Jonas?"

Jonas nodded.

"How many men you got in your posse?" Jody asked idly.

"Just me."

"You're going out there alone?" Jody asked incredulously. "Are you crazy?"

"Yes," Merry said from the bedroom. She had not been able to resist.

"Be quiet in there, woman," Jonas said quietly. "There ain't too many men I can trust of late, Jody," he said. "Jimmy Cahill's one. There's another man in town, named Buster Reinhardt. That's about it."

"You havin' that much trouble in Silverton?"

"Not really. There's a number of men I can trust with information and such, but not too many I can trust to stand back-to-back with me when the goin' gets rough. I've got to leave Jimmy here to watch over things. Buster'd come if I asked him, but I've put him in danger enough times already. He . . . he was wounded a while back, and then another man I could trust—John Maguire—was killed while we were chasin' Ellsworth."

"Well, by God, I know where you can find another man you can trust," Jody said. "When do we leave?"

"I can't ask you to go ridin' out there with me, Jody," Jonas said with a half-smile.

"You ain't askin'. I'm offerin'."

"It's liable to be plenty dangerous."

"Life's dangerous."

Jonas thought about that a little. His brother had a wild streak in him, but Jonas could trust him implicitly. He didn't know if Jody had ever killed a man, but he was as good with his fists as anyone he'd ever seen. Jody was a good shot, too, though again Jonas didn't know if his brother had ever fired at a target that was shooting back. Still, it would be nice having someone he could rely on with him. Especially if he found the outlaws and arrested a bunch of them. The trip back to Silverton would be a whole lot easier with two of them.

Jonas nodded. "I'll swear you in at the office later. That way you'll get paid for this. We're leavin' first thing in the mornin'. You got a horse and saddle?"

"Nope."

"Guns?"

"An old pistol in my bag. That's all, though. I don't usually carry one." He did not sound apologetic.

Jonas nodded. "We'll get you outfitted this afternoon, too. You sure you want to do this?"

"Yessir." Jody Culpepper had always looked up to his older brother, even when he had surpassed Jonas in height by the two inches or so, and he'd always wanted Jonas to think the best of him. Jonas had helped him considerably when they were younger, and Jody saw this as a chance to repay his brother some.

Jonas nodded again. "All right, you rascal, let's go." He polished off his whiskey and rose. "We'll be back after a little, Merry," he called. When his wife stepped out of the bedroom, he added, "I'm going to take Jody over and get him a horse and other such things as he'll need on our trip."

Merry nodded. "You be careful," she said. It was the only sign of her worry.

The two men and the dog walked to the Exchange livery. "My brother Jody," Jonas said. "Jody, Art Cassidy. Jody needs a good horse, plus saddle."

Cassidy nodded. "Go on out back to the corral. Pick out whatever beast you want. That light bay mare's still there. She seems a good one. I'll rustle up what I got in the way of saddles while you're out back."

It did not take long for Jody and Jonas to decide that the light bay mare was indeed the best of the lot. She was big for a mare, and looked stout and strong, with good teeth and no obvious physical flaws. The two went back into the stable and told Cassidy they would take the horse.

Cassidy nodded. "I ain't got but three saddles for sale," he said apologetically. "Over there on the wall of the first stall. Take your pick."

"How much is this gonna cost me?" Jody asked.

"I got to get ninety-five for the horse. Give me a hundred ten and you can have your pick of those three saddles, plus whatever other tack you need."

Jody looked skeptical, but Jonas grinned. "Make it one twenty-five—and bill the county."

"Damn, Jonas, I was afraid you were gonna say that," Cassidy said with a rueful grin. "I'm still waitin' for the county to pay me for that mule you took last time."

"I'll talk to Pennrose before I leave," he said seriously. "There's no reason a man should have to wait weeks to get the money due him."

"I'd be obliged, Jonas. You know I don't like to complain, but . . ."

"No need to apologize, Art. A man sells something or does something for which he expects to get paid, he should get his money, not have to go beggin' for it. Come on, Jody, let's go look over those saddles."

One of the saddles was a little less worn than the other two, though all three had seen considerable hard use. Jody pointed it out to Cassidy, but then said he wanted the saddle scabbard from one of the others. Cassidy nodded and made the change.

"We'll need the bay and my buckskin saddled first thing in the mornin'. We'll be back later with supplies. You can load the mule, too, if you're of a mind."

Cassidy nodded.

The two Culpeppers walked up to the Anvil Mining Company headquarters, Culpepper explaining along the way that Wilson Pennrose was head of the company and head of the County Board, making him the power both in Silverton and in San Juan County. They walked straight into the boardroom.

"These constant interruptions are getting to be a real annoyance, Jonas," Pennrose said haughtily.

Jonas shrugged. "My heart weeps for you, Pennrose," he said.

"Who's he?" Pennrose asked, pointing to Jody.

"My brother Jody."

"What can I do for you this time, Sheriff?" Pennrose finally asked, after staring for some moments at Jody, who stared calmly back at him.

"Art Cassidy says he ain't been paid for the mule and such I used last time I went out after Ellsworth."

"So?"

"So, the county's supposed to pay him. A man can't work for nothin'."

"He'll get his money. He always does."

"He'll have it before dark or I'll come callin' on you before I ride out at dawn tomorrow," Jonas said, a warning in his voice.

Pennrose glared for a few moments, then nodded. "It must've been overlooked the last time the County Board met," he said blandly.

"I can understand that," Jonas said, letting Pennrose know in no uncertain terms that he knew Pennrose was lying. "I also want Cassidy paid the one twenty-five for the horse, saddle, and tack for my new deputy here." He indicated his brother.

"You're going out after Ellsworth again tomorrow?" Pennrose asked stonily.

"Yep."

"Well, I hope you get him this time, Sheriff," Pennrose said sarcastically.

"You want to be such a smartass, Mister," Jody said harshly, "why don't you get off you fancified ass and go with us? Since nobody else in town's got any balls, Jonas has to do most of this himself."

Pennrose looked like he was about to burst. He said nothing.

"Just what I figured," Jody said with a sneer. "Another loud-mouthed chickenshit. Come on, Jonas, let's get out of here before I puke."

Outside, Jody looked anxiously at his brother. He thought Jonas might be furious with him for his outspokenness. But Jonas could no longer hold back the guffaws that had been fighting for release. Jody joined him in laughing.

They went to Maguire's general store then, where Jody picked out two good pistols—.45-caliber Colts—a holster, a bowie knife, and a Winchester. Then Jonas ordered what supplies he would need and made arrangements to have them taken to Cassidy.

Finally, just before going back to the house, Jonas took Jody to the office, where he told to Cahill what was going on, and swore in Jody as a special county deputy sheriff.

Chapter 24

San Miguel looked the same as it did when Jonas Culpepper had come through the town almost two weeks earlier. Accompanied by his brother and Bear, he could make much better time than he had when he was alone and dragging along a handcuffed prisoner. They made the trip in three and a half days, riding virtually from sunup to sundown.

Though they hadn't seen each other in more than four years, Jonas and Jody Culpepper did not feel a great need to gab constantly. They rode quietly more often than not, sometimes side by side, sometimes in single file. When they stopped, each man went about the duties of making camp without fuss or argument. It was the same in the morning, when they broke camp.

Jody had come to view his brother with more respect than ever, watching how he moved, how he acted. Before they rode out of Silverton, Jonas had made sure that Wilson Pennrose had brought the liveryman, Art Cassidy, the money owed him.

"Sure did, Sheriff," Cassidy said with a grin. He flashed a wad of paper money. "Mister Pennrose himself come by last night, just before I was ready to close up for the night. Paid me for your brother's horse and all, too."

It had impressed Jody considerably that his brother would remember to check on that, despite all the other things he had to do and to worry about. Jody was also impressed by Jonas's competence and sureness on the trail. Jonas moved with effortless grace, or so it seemed to Jody, a surprise in a man as bulky as Jonas Culpepper.

Jody Culpepper was a man more inclined to chatter idly at times, but he kept his silence mostly because he was feeling a little inferior to his brother. That and the fact that Jonas was prone to traveling in silence.

It was shortly after noon when the two men and the huge dog walked into San Miguel.

"Dusty goddamn little place, ain't it," Jody commented as he slapped some reddish dust off his shirt.

"Yep." Jonas stopped in front of the town marshal's office and dismounted.

Marshal Stan Childress was sitting inside, an open bottle of whiskey on his desk, a full glass in his right hand. He looked a little drunk.

"You remember me, Marshal?" Jonas asked.

"Sure I do," Childress said, his words slurred some. "The great goddamn sheriff of San Juan County. What're you doin' back here?"

"Still lookin' for Ellsworth and his men. You see any of them around here of late?"

"Hell no, I ain't seen 'em. Have you?"

Jonas stepped up and slapped the glass out of Childress's hand. The glass clattered on the floor, leaving a trail of droplets in the dust covering the wood. "You're a durn disgrace, maggot," Jonas said.

"Go to hell, you son of a bitch," Childress snapped.

Jonas shook his head. "Where's Daisy?"

"How the hell should I know?"

In disgust, Jonas led the way out.

"Who's Daisy?" Jody asked, when the Culpeppers were outside and mounting their horses.

"She's that girl I was tellin' you about. The one who was grabbed up by the outlaws."

"Why're lookin' for her?"

"See how's she doin'," Jonas said with a shrug. "I sort of feel responsible for her."

"No other reason?" his brother asked pointedly.

"Like what?"

"Like maybe you're gettin' tired of Merry and're lookin' around for someone else."

"You weren't my brother, Jody," Jonas said harshly, "I'd knock you crown over tail feathers for such a stupid statement."

Jody grinned a little. "Just makin' sure," he offered.

"Well, don't do it again." Jonas stopped at the Stanton Hotel. He, his brother, and the mastiff went inside.

"Sheriff Culpepper!" Sarah Stanton said with a wide smile. "It's good to see you again." She turned to face the room behind her and called, "Silas! Silas Stanton, you come on out here now and see who's come callin'."

Silas Stanton pushed through the old blanket that covered the doorway between the lobby of their small hotel and their kitchen behind it. He, too, smiled when he spotted Jonas. He shook hands with the sheriff. "And this must be your brother, yes?" he asked.

Jonas nodded. "Jody, Silas Stanton and his wife, Sarah. Folks, this is my brother Jody."

"What brings you back to San Miguel, Sheriff?" Stanton asked when the greetings were done.

"Thought I'd check up on Daisy, see how she was gettin' along. Also thought I might be able to pick up some information."

"About Mack Ellsworth?"

Jonas nodded. "You seen or heard anything about him?"

"Not really," Stanton said with a shake of the head. "Except . . ."

"Well, out with it, Silas."

"Well, there's some bounty men in town. They've been askin' a heap of questions about Ellsworth."

"What kind of questions?"

"Where he might be hidin' out and such. That sort of thing.

It's what you'd expect such men to ask, but there seems to be more to it." He paused. "It's almost as if they know somethin' about him and were tryin' to get the last bit of the puzzle."

"Know what about him?"

"I ain't sure, mind you, Sheriff," Stanton said, "but there's talk goin' around that Ellsworth and his men buried the loot from that train robbery."

"You hear where?"

"Somewhere near the Utah Territory line is all I've heard."

Jonas nodded. "I've heard the same. Durn, that's all I need, a bunch of bounty hunters stickin' their noses into this business."

"A few of 'em're stayin' here, Sheriff," Stanton said apologetically.

Jonas nodded. "I'd expect that, since it's the best place in town." He grinned a little. "I'll see about it later. You got a room left to accommodate me and Jody?"

"Sure do. Only one left, but it's the best." He smiled. "How long're you two plannin' to stay?"

Jonas shrugged. "Probably not more than a night or two. I want to get back on the trail. But this'll give the horses a chance to rest up, and let me poke around to see what I can learn." He paused. "Well, now that business is done with, how's Daisy?"

Stanton suddenly looked a little concerned. "In general, she's just fine, but . . ."

"But what?" Jonas asked harshly. "Somebody givin' her a rough time?"

"Sort of."

"Who?"

Stanton was not sure he should answer, but then he decided he could trust Jonas Culpepper as much as anyone. "Marshal Childress."

"What's he done? Last time I was here, he was polite as he could be, askin' if he could come courtin' Daisy." The thought of the half-drunk town marshal sitting in the office flashed through his mind.

"He did come 'round courtin' her for a few days. Then one day he showed up drunk and smacked her around some."

Jonas suddenly felt a coldness coating his insides. He figured that Childress had somehow found out where Daisy had come from and what she was there.

"It turns out," Stanton continued, "that he didn't much care for her at all. He just figured that since she was held captive by them outlaws for a while, she might know where they buried their loot."

Jonas was relieved to hear that.

"She kept tellin' him she didn't know anything, but he didn't believe her. So he was in a saloon drinkin' when it got the better of him and he come over here and started knockin' her around. He left after she managed to grab his pistol and threaten him with it."

Jonas nodded. That would explain Childress's surliness minutes ago in his office. "Daisy in her room now?" he asked.

"That she is, Sheriff," Sarah interjected. "She'll be plumb delighted to see you, I'd say. You go on up there now and call on her."

Jonas smiled and headed for the second floor. Bear bounded up the stairs ahead of him, seemingly eager. Jody was right on his brother's heels.

When the Culpeppers got to the door, Bear was sitting there, tail wagging like crazy, soft little whines erupting from the short, fierce muzzle. Jonas knocked on the door.

A moment later came a faint, "Who's there?"

"Jonas Culpepper." He grinned at the door. "And Bear."

The door flew open to a happy Daisy Greenwalt. Bear could hardly contain his excitement as Daisy bent and rubbed his head behind both floppy ears and let the mastiff lap at her face a little. Finally she looked up and smiled at Jonas. "It's good to see you, Sheriff," she said almost breathlessly.

"Sheriff?" Jonas said with a laugh.

"You know what I mean," Daisy said. "Come in, you and . . ." She cast a telling look at Jody.

Jonas made introductions as he and his brother went inside and sat. Before they could really get into talking again, Sarah Stanton knocked and entered when Daisy opened the door. The older woman was carrying a tray on which sat a coffeepot, three crockery mugs, a small bowl of sugar, and plates of tiny sandwiches and cookies. She set the tray down on the room's only real table. "Enjoy yourselves," she said, as she bustled out.

As Daisy served him and his brother, Jonas took a good look at her. She was dressed like a proper young lady, in a high-necked, long-sleeved calico dress—a different one from the last time Jonas had seen her—that hugged her figure. Her hair was done up in some sort of bun, with a few hairs straying out, and she was scrubbed clean. She wore some sort of perfume or toilet water with an appealing scent. She looked and smelled fine, Jonas thought.

Jody was of the same opinion as he watched Daisy with eagle eyes. Had Jonas not told him what a hard time she'd been through, he'd never have been able to tell by looking at her now. She was positively delightful looking to him.

Finally Daisy sat, too.

"I hear Marshal Childress has been givin' you a hard time," Jonas said.

"Oh, darn," she snapped, "I told Mister Stanton not to say anything about that."

"He hurt you any?" Jody asked, surprising everyone.

"No," Daisy said, flustered, looking askance at him. She had liked Sheriff Culpepper more than a little, but she knew he was married. But here was a copy of him, and one that might not be married. She allowed herself to hope a little.

"Good thing," Jody growled softly.

"You have any other callers?" Jonas asked.

"No, not really. At first, I think anyone else who might've been interested in such a thing was put off by the marshal's comin' around. It's only been two days since I told Childress I didn't ever want to see him again, so there's really been no time for others to come around."

"You all right otherwise?"

"Oh, yes," Daisy said enthusiastically. "Mister and Mrs. Stanton're the nicest people. It's like . . . well, it's like a real home with them, almost." She looked a little embarrassed.

"That's good, Daisy. You're lookin' like this place agrees with you. In fact, you're lookin' mighty durn good."

"Better'n good," Jody added, in a voice so low that Daisy and Jonas were not sure if he'd really said anything at all.

Daisy flushed at the compliments.

Jonas stood. "Well, Daisy, we've got to see to the horses and such. We'll be stayin' at least tonight, maybe a little longer. We can talk more later. Come on, Jody."

The brother continued to sit. "I'd just as soon stay here a few minutes, if Miss Daisy don't mind," Jody said seriously to his brother, but he was looking at Daisy.

Jonas stared at Jody a moment, eyebrows raised. Then he, too, looked at Daisy. *Good Lord,* he thought, *they're smitten with each other.* "Well, Daisy?" he asked.

"I'd like that, Sheriff."

Jody finally looked up at his brother. "You can leave my horse and the mule. I'll take care of them later." He did not want Jonas to think he was a slacker.

"I'll get them."

"I'll make it up another time."

"You're durn right you will," Jonas said with a laugh. "Well, then, I'll be on my way." He stabbed his brother with a stare from his piercing blue eyes. "You mind your manners around this young lady, boy."

"Yessir," Jody said, still seriously.

Shaking his head, Jonas headed out the door and down the stairs. Bear had looked a little confused, undecided whether to go with his master or stay with the woman. But loyalty won out, and he trotted alongside Jonas.

Chapter 25

It was well past dark when Jody entered the room he was to share with his brother. Jonas looked at him and gave him a grin. It was returned. Jody sat down and pulled off his boots.

"You seem taken with Daisy, little brother," Jonas said quietly.

"She seems to be a girl to be taken with," Jody said without apology.

"I suppose she is." Jonas paused before deciding to continue. "But you don't know the whole story about her, Jody."

"I don't?" Jody leaned back in the chair and wiggled his toes in his socks.

"No," Jonas said flatly.

"Then tell me." He still did not seem concerned.

Jonas rose and pulled a pint bottle of whiskey out of his saddlebags. He found two glasses and poured some whiskey into each and set them on the table. Then he put the bottle away and sat again. He sipped a little whiskey. "I lied about how she got to be with the outlaws. She wasn't on the trail with her parents, nor did the outlaws attack the wagons she was with."

"Then what happened?" Jody asked evenly.

"I hate to say this, little brother, but Daisy worked in a fancy house in Durango—that's where the outlaws got her. They spirited her away true enough, but she weren't exactly innocent when they did so. Not by a long shot."

"I never thought I'd see my older brother, a man I've looked up to and trusted my whole life, stoop so low."

"Think what you want, Jody. It's the God's truth."

"Then what about that other story?"

"I started tellin' that here so Daisy'd have a fresh start."

"Sounds like a crock of shit to me, Jonas. If you wanted her to yourself, you should've told me earlier. Now that I'm taken with her, I ain't about to let her go just for you."

"I've nearabout killed men for such insults," Jonas said in flat, deadly tones.

"Touchy bastard, ain't you," Jody said more than asked. "Supposin' it is true—which I ain't sayin' it is. What's your problem with it?"

"Didn't say I had a problem with it. All I was doin' was makin' sure you knew what you were gettin' into. Now that you know, if you're still smitten with her, so be it."

"You really mean that, don't you, brother?"

"Of course I do."

Suddenly Jody laughed. "She told me already. Earlier tonight, while we were over in her room."

"And you gave me such a hard time, you fractious little snot," Jonas said, only a little heatedly.

"Just wanted to see if you were on the up and up."

"Good Lord, but if you ain't enough to try a man's patience," Jonas said with a laugh. "So you really are taken with her?"

"Yessir. And I think she returns it." Jody paused, watching the light reflect through his glass as he twirled it in one hand. "I ain't ever felt like this about a woman before, Jonas. And as strongly as I have felt about some women, ain't a one of 'em come over me this fast." He paused again, a little embarrassed. "I aim to come back for her, Jonas," he said almost defiantly.

Jonas raised his glass in something of a salute. "Here's to you both, boy," he said, and downed the drink.

Jody smiled and then swallowed his whiskey. "It don't bother you none what she did before?" he asked suddenly.

Jonas shrugged. "Why should it matter to me?" he countered. "I ain't the one smitten with her. Does it bother you?"

"Not too much. But," he admitted, "if I think about it more than a little, it does some."

"It's not somethin' easily gotten over," Jonas said, "knowin' what she used to do. But it ain't the worst thing in the whole wide world." He stood. "Well, it's time for this ol' boy to be asleep. I'll flip you for the bed."

"You take it. If we stay tomorrow night, too, I'll take it then."

"Fair enough."

Jody grinned. "I'd be obliged if we was to stay tomorrow night."

Jonas nodded, but did not return the smile. Instead, he said seriously, "We got important business, Jody. If that keeps us here another night, or another week, you can call on Daisy all you want. But our work's more important than your courtin'."

"I'm sorry, Jonas," Jody said, abashed. "I didn't mean . . ."

"I know you didn't mean anything by it, little brother. But you're still new to the sheriffin' business, and might not be used to the calls it makes on a body. Daisy's a good woman. She'll understand when I drag you away from her."

Jody nodded. "Just as long as you drag me back here."

"Sooner or later, little brother. Sooner or later."

Jody spent as much time with Daisy the next day as he thought he could get away with, letting Jonas wander the streets and saloons of San Miguel in an attempt to pick up any kind of information that might be useful in finding Mack Ellsworth and his gang.

The Culpeppers went together in the morning, but by noon, Jonas was aggravated and frustrated by the futility of their search. After lunch, he told Jody to go call on Daisy. Jody needed no special invitation.

Watching his brother walk away, Jonas smiled. In some ways it was good having his brother along to watch his back, but right at the moment, Jonas figured he'd be better off prodding people for information by himself. Two large, hard-looking, fiery-maned lawmen were enough to intimidate a good many men.

He did learn somewhere during the day that he was being followed. He counted four at one point. All had the tough, vicious look of bounty hunters. Culpepper was a little concerned about it at first, but after a short while he realized the bounty hunters were not about to do anything. Not until he—and therefore, they, too—learned something of value. Once he figured that out, he pretty much ignored them.

Still, by late afternoon he was again frustrated at the lack of information, and having the four men following him increased his irritation.

Deciding to have some fun with them, he went into the Deuces saloon, and walked straight out the back door. From there he headed to the Lucky Buck saloon, where he had a beer in peace. He sat at the back of the room, waiting. It took the four bounty hunters twenty-two minutes to catch up with him there.

But Culpepper was tired and hungry and annoyed, so he left soon afterward. He met Jody and Daisy for supper in Brickley's hash house. Afterward the brothers escorted Daisy to her room. She was not happy about it, but she knew that Jonas needed his brother for a while, and she owed Jonas Culpepper far too much to put up a fuss where business was concerned.

The brothers stood just outside Stanton's and talked a little, with Jonas bringing Jody up to date—and laying a plan to perhaps keep the bounty hunters off Jonas's trail for a while.

Ten minutes later, Jonas went to the Lucky Buck and ordered another beer. When he spotted the four bounty hunters, he sauntered outside and turned up the street. Just across the alley next to the saloon, he stopped in the space where the doors of a hardware store were set back from the front wall of the building a little. He leaned back against the wall of the building and waited, watching back the way he had come.

A few minutes later the bounty hunters came out of the Lucky Buck. They hesitated a moment before turning up the street rather than down it. As they stepped up onto the boardwalk past the alley, Culpepper moved out from his spot in front of the store.

"Evenin', boys," he said.

"Sheriff," one of them said politely.

"You boys've been followin' my tail all day, and I must admit to y'all that I'm just a wee bit weary of it."

"I don't know what you're talkin' about, Sheriff," the same one said with a look of innocence.

"You boys ain't that durn stupid, and neither am I." He paused. "What're your names, boys?"

"I ain't gonna tell you jack shit," the same man replied in harsh tones. He looked at Bear when the mastiff growled. "And you tell that goddamn mangy dog of yours to keep his yap shut."

"Calm down, Bear," Culpepper said quietly, with a small smirk. "You bite one of these pukin' scoundrels and you'll probably get poisoned."

"Very funny, you big, stupid bastard. Now you're in our way. Move, or . . ."

"Or what, asshole?" Jody asked with a sneer. He stepped out from the shadows of the alley behind the bounty hunters. "Now, the sheriff asked you punks a question. Answer it."

The man who had spoken cranked his head around and glared at Jody, who stood with a pistol in hand. The bounty hunter looked back at Jonas. "My name's Carl Jaegger." He pointed to each of the men as he named them. "Adam Cole, Dave Eberhardt, and Danny Hillman."

"You're bounty hunters, yes?" Jonas asked.

"Yeah," Jaegger snapped. "What of it?"

"I don't like bounty hunters. Especially pukin' maggots who're a pain in my tail feathers. You want to collect the bounty on Mack Ellsworth's head, you go find out where he is and what he's done with the loot. Don't expect me to find out for you. Next time I see you followin' me, I'm going to kill one or all of you. It don't make any difference to me. You boys got that?"

"Yeah," Jaegger growled. The others nodded sullenly.

"Good," Jonas said easily. "Now, go find yourselves somewhere else to be. Somewhere well away from me."

The scowling bounty hunters shuffled away, backs stiff with anger. Jody stepped up onto the boardwalk with his brother. "Those walkin' pukes're gonna be trouble," Jonas said, as he and Jody watched the four striding off.

"We could fix that," Jody said flatly.

Jonas smiled a little, but there was no humor in it; only sadness. "They ain't done anything wrong, little brother." He turned a questioning stare on Jody. "You ever killed anyone?" he asked bluntly.

"Once," Jody answered honestly. "I didn't feel so good about it for a while, but that feelin's long gone."

"I hope so," Jonas said, turning his head again to watch the bounty hunters, "for as sure as the sun comes up in the east of a mornin', we're going to have to kill us some men before this venture's over."

"Don't be so damn gloomy," Jody said glumly.

Jonas shook off a little of the darkness that had settled on him. "Good idea. How's about a beer?"

"Now you're talkin'. Where? The Lucky Buck?"

"Good Lord, no," Jonas said with a forced laugh. "That place is a dump. The Deuces ain't much better, but it's the best place in town."

"Lead on, then, big brother."

Before long they were leaning against the bar in the Deuces, each with a beer in front of him. The Deuces didn't have a very ornate back bar, but the one there did have a large mirror which allowed the Culpeppers to keep an eye on the door as well as the entire inside of the saloon. From the small spread of food, the brothers had laden their plates with hard-cooked eggs and two kinds of cheeses. They nibbled as they drank, one set of eyes always on the mirror.

"You learn anything today, Jonas?" Jody asked.

"Nothin' that'd help find Ellsworth."

"Damn. Somebody's got to know some—"

"There you are, you stinkin' son of a bitch!" Marshal Childress roared as he staggered into the saloon.

The Culpeppers turned and leaned back against the bar so they faced Childress. "You have a problem, Marshal?" Jonas asked.

"Yeah, god damn it. But not with you, you stinkin' shit sheriff. With him." He pointed a slightly shaking finger at Jody.

"What's your beef with me, mister?" Jody asked calmly, though his voice was hard.

"I want you to leave Daisy alone, goddammit."

"*She* don't," Jody said flatly.

"I don't care. I had first claim on her, and by Christ, I'm gonna keep that claim. I'll be damned if the likes of you is gonna waltz into San Miguel and start makin' nice with that bitch and pumpin' for information. What she knows is mine to learn, you son of a bitch."

Jonas suddenly flipped an egg at Childress. It plopped on the marshal's chest and then fell on the floor. It did no damage, but it made Childress shut up.

"Dumb maggot," Jonas muttered. "Another couple of words out of him and the whole town'd know what's going on."

"I do believe it's time for us to escort the good marshal out of here, don't you think, Jonas?"

"Indeed, little brother." Jonas looked at Childress. "Seems you've had a wee bit too much to drink for one night, Marshal," he said smoothly. "I think it's about time you slept it off. Me and Jody here'll take you back to your place. Make sure you don't fall down and break a limb or somethin' on the streets."

"That'd be a shame," Jody agreed.

"You ain't takin' me nowhere, you bastards. I'm gonna . . ."

Jonas stepped up and slapped a hand across Childress's mouth. Then he and Jody each grabbed an arm and hauled the marshal out of the saloon.

Chapter 26

The Culpepper brothers came awake at the same time, roused from sleep by a loud crash, Bear's sudden growling and then a stream of hoarse shouting. The two looked at each other, shrugged, and came up fast, grabbing for their guns. Together the brothers raced for the door, where Bear was already waiting, low growls still coming from his brawny throat.

Since Jonas had been sleeping in the chair this night, he was mostly dressed—with pants and boots, and the shirt part of his long underwear. Jody, on the other hand, was in red longhandles and socks. Both had swiftly wrapped their gunbelts around them on their race to the door.

Jonas flung the door open and Jody raced out right behind Bear. The noise in the hallway was louder, and Jody knew right off it was coming from Daisy's room. Other people in the hotel were standing in their doorways, looking out in wonder, and some in fear.

Jody smashed through the door into Daisy's room and became enraged when he caught sight of Marshal Stan Childress lying half atop Daisy, trying to strangle the life out of her. The San Miguel lawman was shouting obscenity-laced orders at Daisy to tell him where the outlaws were holed up.

Jody tossed his pistol down, and with a roar, latched onto Childress. Almost lifting the lawman off his feet, Jody swung and threw the marshal away as he had his revolver.

Childress hit the wall with a bang and fell. Bear pounced on him first, and Jody growled in anger. "Get the hell away from him, dog," Jody snapped. He looked at his brother. "God damn it, Jonas, get that dog off him," he shouted.

"Bear!" Jonas commanded. "Here, boy!"

The mastiff backed away from Childress reluctantly, and Jody surged in, pounding the marshal unmercifully.

Jonas stood leaning against the doorjamb, pistol dangling loosely from his right fist. The Stantons and several other residents of the hotel crowded up behind him, trying to see inside.

Somehow Childress managed to get to his feet. He reeled around, swinging a fist. It hit Jody on the jaw, but had no effect, and Jody slammed him back against the wall and pounded on Childress's face for a while.

Finally Jody grabbed Childress's shirtfront, jerked him forward, and spun him around. Away from the wall, the marshal had no support, and when Jody pasted him one in the face, Childress staggered backward toward the door.

"You folks'd best get out of the way," Jonas warned, as he and Bear moved from the doorway, where the door was barely held up by one hinge.

Moments later, Childress came stumbling out, still backward, and he fell. Jody was right behind him. "Son of a bitch," Jody muttered, "I'll show you, damn it all." He pulled Childress up and hammered him some more, driving him backward down the hallway. Everyone else followed, watching, sometimes wincing.

"Shouldn't you stop him, Sheriff?" Silas Stanton asked.

"Can't see why I should," Jonas commented.

"But your brother might kill him." Stanton didn't seem all that concerned.

"Well," Jonas said slowly, "I suppose he could. But to my thinkin', that ain't such a bad thing."

"Perhaps you're right, Sheriff," Stanton said quietly.

Jody pitched Childress down the stairs. The marshal went

with so much momentum that he bounced a few times and almost ended up against the door.

Stanton suddenly burst forward, shoving past Jody on the stairs. At the bottom, he yanked open the front door. "I ain't gonna replace another door for you, Mister Culpepper," he muttered.

Jody sort of nodded at Stanton, and kicked Childress in the ribs as the marshal tried to get up. The kick rolled Childress just out the door. Jody stalked forward, pulled Childress up by the hair, and then pounded him a good shot in the face.

Childress wobbled backward and fell in a clump off the edge of the boardwalk onto the street. Jody followed him out. Once more he kicked Childress, this time in the face.

"Don't you ever come near Daisy again, you son of a bitch," Jody snarled, pointing a finger at the downed marshal. "Or I'll kill you sure as anything." He turned and began walking slowly toward the hotel, rubbing his knuckles. He began to feel a little foolish, attired as he was in nothing more than long underwear, a pistol belt, and socks.

Everyone else who had been watching at the door of Daisy's room had come downstairs and outside. They had watched with something approaching awe. They were still staring in fascination.

Childress groaned in the street and managed to roll over onto his back. Then he half sat up. He got the loop off the hammer of his pistol and drew the pistol in shaky hands.

Daisy, standing on the boardwalk in her nightdress, gasped and pointed.

As Jody began to turn back toward Childress, his brother stepped forward, pistol in hand. "Don't, Childress," he warned.

But the marshal would not—or could not—hear him, and Jonas fired. The single shot hit Childress in the chest and knocked him back to the ground. He lay there gasping.

The Culpeppers walked to Childress and looked down. The marshal had died in the few seconds it had taken them to get there. Jonas turned and walked to the boardwalk. "There an undertaker in San Miguel, Mister Stanton?" he asked.

Stanton nodded. "Mister Wallace. I'll get him."

"Please do." He looked at the hotel residents. "All right, folks, go on back to bed. I'll see to what needs doin' here. Go on, now." He turned to his brother. "Take Daisy on upstairs, Jody. Bring her to our room. Let her have the bed. You can stand watch."

"What about you, Jonas?" Daisy asked.

"Once I get done here, I'll go to your room. I can prop the door up enough to keep unwanted eyes out."

"But supposed someone wants to cause you some trouble?"

"Bear'll be there, Daisy. He'll warn me if someone comes around. Now, go on upstairs with Jody."

Finally Jonas was alone in the street, alone except for Childress's body—and Bear, of course. Before long, though, a grumbling, rumpled little man in a frayed robe over his nightdress came growling up in the wake of Silas Stanton.

"Why don't you kill people in the daytime, Sheriff?" he asked, as he knelt over Childress's body.

"Just to make it inconvenient for you," Culpepper said dryly.

"I think you did," Wallace said.

"Enough of this nonsense, Reuben. Just cart the corpse out of here so we can all go back to bed," Stanton said.

"Yeah, yeah," Wallace said, rising. "You stay and watch while I get some help."

"Just don't take all goddamn night."

It seemed like it was several hours, but it was probably no more than fifteen or twenty minutes before Wallace returned with two strapping young men who unceremoniously hauled the body up and toted it away.

When Wallace and his helpers were gone, Culpepper asked, "What're the good people of San Miguel going to do for a marshal?"

"We'll figure somethin' out, Sheriff. But . . ."

"I know," Culpepper said with a sigh. "You want me to stick

around and play town marshal for a few days until you can find a new man to replace Childress."

"Well, yes. I hate to impose on you, Sheriff, but . . ."

"It's all right, Silas. But I'm tellin' you here and now, I'm not stickin' around more than two, three days, tops."

"We should have someone by then." The two turned and headed toward the hotel.

"What gives you the right to make such decisions, anyway?"

Stanton grinned. "I'm the mayor of San Miguel," he said proudly.

"I'll be durned," Culpepper laughed. He stopped at the bottom of the stairs. Sarah Stanton waited just behind the screen to the Stantons' quarters out back. "Well, goodnight, Silas. Mrs. Stanton."

"Goodnight, Jonas," Stanton said. "And thank you."

"For what?" Culpepper asked a little tensely. "For killin' a man? There's no thanks in such deeds."

"That's true many times—and for many men. But you didn't kill a man just for the hell of it. You saved a young girl's life, when it comes down to it. And you saved your brother's life, too."

"I suppose that's so. But I still don't have to like it any." He smiled weakly and began climbing the stairs. Culpepper propped Daisy's door up as best he could, took off his gunbelt, and lay down on the bed. It took him a little while to get to sleep, though.

In the morning, Daisy looked the most refreshed of the three, though she had a slightly haunted look in her deep blue eyes. Jody was tired but otherwise chipper; Jonas was grumpy.

"Come on, Jonas," Jody said with a grin as the Culpeppers and Daisy were eating breakfast, "cheer up some."

"Bah. It ain't you was drafted to nursemaid San Miguel till the good folks hereabout get themselves a new marshal."

"You didn't say anything about that," Jody said with a laugh.

"Never had a chance. But I only give them a couple days to get it done."

"You know, Jonas," Jody said, punctuating his words with his fork, "I could act as marshal here, if you want to get on the trail."

Jonas noticed that Daisy perked up at that. "That what you want, little brother?"

"I didn't say that. In fact, I think it'd be a plumb foolish idea to let you go wanderin' around out in the wilds alone, lookin' for outlaws and stolen loot. I just thought I'd mention it in case you'd prefer it that way."

"Thanks for the offer, Jody, but I think it'd be best if we stuck together—both in San Miguel, and out there in the wilds. There's no tellin' what kind of characters we'll run into in either place."

After breakfast, Jonas had Jody and Daisy go off together, while he went to Childress's office and looked things over. He didn't really expect to have to do a lot while he was the town's acting marshal, but one could never tell. He wanted to make sure he knew where things were just in case trouble started.

Done with that, and tired of sitting around, Culpepper strolled around town, poking his head into the bars and shops. He was a little surprised when nearly everyone greeted him with a polite, sometimes even cheery, hello. The bounty hunters he had accosted earlier the night before gave him a wide berth, though they always seemed to be just where he was going. Most other folks kept their distance from him, too, which made him wonder. Until he realized nearly all of them were scared to death of Bear. Despite his puggish, droopy-jowled face, the huge mastiff was rather terrifying to anyone who didn't know him, Culpepper supposed. Over the next few days, though, Culpepper and Bear made friends with many of the children in San Miguel. They delighted in playing with the big dog, who was as gentle as could be with the youngsters.

By the time Culpepper went back to his room that evening, Stanton had had Daisy's door repaired. Jonas could see on his brother's face that Jody wanted to stay with Daisy to protect her, if nothing more. Jonas suspected it was more, and he could understand that. "You'd best stay in Daisy's room tonight, Jody," he said when they were at supper. "You never can tell but what Childress had a friend or two—certainly no more than that—who might be foolish enough to come tryin' to bother her. And then there's those durn bounty hunters."

"You think that'd be all right, Jonas?" Jody asked seriously. He wanted that very much, but there was Daisy's reputation to be thought of. That's all she would need was rumors about her behavior. "I mean, you know, won't people talk about Daisy?"

"They might—if they was to know about it. You keep quiet, and come back to our room just before dawn. Nobody'll be the wiser."

Both Jody and Daisy beamed brightly.

The two Culpeppers—and Bear—rode out of San Miguel three days after Jonas had killed Marshal Stan Childress. Jody was more quiet than usual, and cast frequent glances behind him, longing for Daisy. He had fallen for her hard, and was heartbroken at this separation.

His looks back, though, served another purpose. In doing so, he noticed that the mastiff quite frequently would stop and sit, looking toward the town and whining or growling a little. Jody figured the dog missed Daisy and somehow felt protective of her. Then he began to realize that the dog was checking for someone or something behind them. Near noon he rode up alongside his brother.

"I think we're bein' followed, Jonas," he said.

Jonas nodded. "Have been since we left San Miguel. I ain't positive, you understand, but I'd wager a year's pay that it's those four durn bounty hunters."

"What do you think they want?"

"I suspect they figure we learned something back in town, and they're plannin' to follow us 'til they can find out what it is. Once they do that, they'll kill us. Or so I figure they'll be thinkin'."

"You gonna let them follow along like this?"

"For a time, little brother. For a time."

Chapter 27

Jonas Culpepper allowed the bounty hunters to follow him and his brother all that day and all the following day as the two Culpeppers rode northwest. But on the third day, he turned them more westerly, into a small valley between two low, long lines of hills. About midday, they crossed a riverbed that actually had some water flowing through it. There wasn't much, but it was far more than in all the dry watercourses they had seen out here.

Just across the muddy creek was a haven of colorful rocks piled atop each other over an area maybe twenty yards long by forty deep. Small clumps of brush provided some cover, but little in the way of shade. Jonas and his brother pulled into the rocks and tied their horses and mule to a fair-sized juniper, the only tree of any consequence that the Culpeppers could see. Rifles in hand, the two men climbed up onto the rocks. Bear hopped from boulder to boulder nearby. Then they settled in to wait.

Less than half an hour later, the four bounty hunters hove into view. Jonas let them get almost to the muddy depression that was the ford of the creek. Then he fired his rifle once, putting a bullet into the ground in front of Carl Jaegger's horse. They all stopped fast. Adam Cole, who was leading a supply-laden mule, had trouble with the fractious animal.

"This is San Juan County Sheriff Jonas Culpepper," he

shouted. "You boys been on my tail plenty long enough. You got warned about it once in San Miguel. This here's your second warnin'. Turn back now and keep away from me. There won't be a third warnin'."

"You can't stop us from tryin' to find Mack Ellsworth and collectin' the reward on him," Jaegger said with bravado.

"That's a fact. But I can stop you from tryin' to crawl up my tail while I find him for you. Now get goin' or get dead."

Jaegger and his companions sat there a few moments, as if mulling over their choices. Then Jaegger turned his horse. He had enough sense to know there were no alternatives. The others followed suit, but as they began to ride away, Danny Hillman spun in his saddle, tearing out his pistol. He emptied the weapon in the direction of the rocks.

The Culpeppers simply kept their heads down until Hillman was done. Then Jonas fired once with the Winchester, hitting Hillman in the chest. Hillman was knocked backward, but a good grip on the reins and his feet in the stirrups kept him from falling. At least at first. When he started to tumble off the horse, Dave Eberhardt managed to catch him.

The bounty hunters galloped off, wanting to get out of range of the Culpeppers' rifles as quickly as possible.

"You think they'll turn back, Jonas?" Jody asked.

"I doubt it. But maybe they won't be right on our tails any more."

"What're you fixin' to do?"

Jonas shrugged. "I vote for stayin' here for the night. That'll give us a chance to rest a little, and give the animals a breather. There's a little wood around and water. Besides, if those bounty hunters decide to start followin' us again, we'll be well defended here and can put a stop to their foolishness right off."

Jody nodded. "Sounds good to me. You keep a watch for those assholes. I'll try'n find what firewood there is."

The rest of the day was quiet, and the Culpeppers saw nothing more of the bounty hunters. In the morning, they rode northeast, following the course of the creek, heading for a small gap in the low line of hills. In early afternoon they were through the gap and turned northwest.

A mile on, gunfire suddenly erupted from a small grassy ridge to their left. Jody grunted and weaved in the saddle. Jonas glanced at his brother and saw blood on the upper back of his shirt. He then looked toward the ridge and saw the three remaining bounty hunters racing toward them, firing on the run. The two looks had taken little more than a few seconds.

"Ride, Jody! Ride."

"No! I . . ."

"Just ride, durn it!"

Jody nodded and spurred his horse, racing off, towing the big mule behind him.

"Go with him, Bear," Culpepper said, as he slid out of the saddle, Winchester in hand. When the mastiff did not move, Jonas muttered, "Durn dog."

Holding the reins to his horse tightly in his left hand, Culpepper brought the Winchester to his shoulder. He fired six times, hastily, yet smoothly.

Jaegger and Adam Cole were knocked off their horses, but Dave Eberhardt remained steadfastly upright in the saddle despite the red stain spreading across his shirtfront.

Culpepper considered firing at Eberhardt again, but decided he did not need to waste the ammunition. Eberhardt had dropped his pistol and was too concerned about staying in the saddle to be able to draw the rifle from the saddle scabbard.

Just before horse and rider reached Culpepper, Bear raced out, barking and growling fiercely. Eberhardt's horse reared in sudden fright at this strange apparition. Eberhardt fell backward off the horse, and then was stomped on several times by the animal, which was still rearing and dropping, whinnying in fright. Finally the horse galloped off, stirrups flapping madly.

"Good work, Bear," Culpepper said, as he walked over to

check on Eberhardt. The bounty hunter was dead, with a red frothiness coating his lips. Culpepper wondered how the man had ridden as far as he had with two bullets in him, at least one of them through a lung.

Culpepper jammed his Winchester into the saddle scabbard and mounted his buckskin horse. He glanced back over his shoulder and saw that Jody was riding swiftly toward him. Culpepper breathed a sigh of relief. He had been certain that Jody was bad hurt when he saw the blood. Culpepper clucked at his horse and trotted over to Cole and Jaegger. They, too, were dead. Culpepper was a little surprised to see that Cole had died of a broken neck, gotten when he had fallen off his horse.

Culpepper mounted up again and trotted over the ridge. He found the bounty hunters' mule hobbled with a short length of rope. Culpepper cut the hobble and brought the mule back to where Jody and Bear were waiting a few feet from Eberhardt's corpse.

"How're you doin', Jody?" Jonas asked, hoping his voice did not convey his suddenly renewed worry.

"Fine and dandy," Jody answered with a grin. "I was lucky. The bullet just slid across the back of my shoulder. It's more blood and sting than serious."

"We'd best get it cleaned out soon, though, before it festers up on you."

Jody nodded. "Good idea. But I figure it can wait till we make camp for the night." He pointed and then winced as pain struck him in the shoulder a little. "That their mule?"

"Yep. You never can tell, they might have somethin' usable in their supplies."

"You aimin' to bury those boys?"

"Nope," Jonas said flatly.

"Damn good thing, too, big brother," Jody said with a growl. "Them bastards aren't worth bein' consigned to the ground."

"That's a fact. You sure you're going to be all right with that shoulder?"

Jody nodded. "It's painin' me some, but not too bad. Let's just get going."

That night in camp, Jonas brought out his small kit of medical supplies. There wasn't much in it—a bottle of laudanum, some herbs for poultices, and two kinds of cathartic. Jonas cleaned Jody's wound with water from Mesa Creek, which had almost no flow, but had water stagnating behind rocks here and there. Then he made up a poultice and slathered it on the wound. He found a fine new shirt in the bounty hunters' packs and he sliced it into bandages with his bowie knife. Then he bandaged his brother.

The camp was in a low spot along Mesa Creek. A couple of cottonwoods rose tall from near the creek bed, and there were junipers and a few box elders scattered around the area. The trees provided enough wood for a small fire, for which the Culpeppers were grateful. After a day such as they'd had, there was little more disheartening than a cold camp.

The wind had sprung up, though the brothers felt little of it in their sheltered little camp. But the temperature dropped and thunder rumbled off in the distance. Jonas figured they'd have rain before the night was through.

He was right, but there actually was precious little rain. There was a lot more blowing dust than precipitation, and even that was gone by morning.

Jody awoke a little stiff from his wound, and he grumped around the camp about it.

"Good Lord, Jody," Culpepper finally said, "I was going to offer you the chance to stay here another day or so to let you heal a little, but I ain't going to make the offer if all you're going to do is growl at me the whole durn day."

"I ain't going to hold you up for no damn stupid little wound. You want to press on, we'll leave. Don't try to blame stayin' here on me when it's you who needs the rest, you old bastard."

"It's no wonder you never found some gal to marry you,

boy," Jonas said tightly. "You're such a pain in the tail feathers that no woman could stand you." Then he grinned. "You want to stay here another day or not?"

"Nah. Hell, like you said, Jonas, all I'm going to do is grouse and make a nuisance of myself. I'll be all right."

Jonas nodded. He refreshed the poultice and bandages, then made his brother sit while he loaded both mules and saddled their two horses. All the while, Jody sat there issuing profane directions as to how he wanted everything done. He laughed frequently as he saw Jonas's ire begin to rise.

Jonas, for his part, ignored the pestering as best he could. He knew what Jody was doing, and he was determined not to play into his brother's hands, if he could help it. Still, the constant drone was wearing on him. Finally he turned and said, "Bear, get him!"

The mastiff looked at Jonas in question for a moment, then pulled back on his haunches a little. His hackles rose and he emitted soft, dangerous-sounding growls. He edged toward Jody, his teeth bared ferociously.

"You and him're jokin' here, ain't you, Jonas?" Jody asked nervously as he watched the dog. "He ain't really going to attack me, now, is he?"

"He ain't attacked nobody in a couple days," Jonas said offhandedly. "Not since you were smackin' the bejeebers out of Marshal Childress back in San Miguel. Bear gets mighty edgy when he ain't allowed to attack for some time. So there's no tellin' if he's serious or not."

Bear was within three feet of Jody now, still growing and looked mighty fierce.

"All right, you old bastard, I'll shut up," Jody said suddenly. "Just call him off!"

"Bear!" Jonas said sharply. "Face!"

The mastiff suddenly pounced, landing on Jody's chest, forcing a worried screech from the man's lips. Then Bear was slobbering all over Jody's face, while Jody squiggled wildly until he realized what Bear was doing.

"All right, Bear," Jody finally said. "You've made your point. Now get off me, you big galoot."

Jonas laughed and called Bear. The mastiff bounced happily over to his master, who petted him. "Good boy," Jonas repeated.

"I'm going to get you for that, you son of a bitch," Jody said, grinning ruefully. "Damn, that was a nasty prank to pull on a feller."

"I thought it was quite funny myself," Jonas said with a chuckle.

"I didn't say it wasn't funny," Jody said, laughing. "I just said it was a nasty prank to pull on your own dear brother."

The humor died in the next few weeks as the fruitless searching led them nowhere. They had finally found the town of Westville—where the outlaw Milt Adler had said Ellsworth had planned to divvy up the loot. Westville turned out to be a ghost town, with no sign that anyone had been there anytime in the recent past.

Culpepper had stood there, watching a tumbleweed blowing across the deserted street and wondering what to do now. He was no longer certain that Adler had told him the truth. Westville was not the kind of place a flamboyant outlaw like Mack Ellsworth would hole up, since there were no women, whiskey, or amenities of any kind. On the other hand, it was such a remote, deserted place that few people would think to look here for loot, buried or otherwise.

They stayed at Westville that night, and in the morning, they began following the Dolores River as it headed vaguely northwest. Somewhere in the next few days, Jonas thought they had crossed into Utah Territory, but he was not sure.

The land they traveled was a vast wasteland. A massive peak could be seen to the southwest, and a smaller ridge of mountains to the northeast. Except for that, the land was flat, barren and offered almost nothing in the way of relief from the heat.

The only saving grace was that the Dolores had water in it, and there were sporadic clumps of trees along the riverbank.

When they reached the Colorado River two weeks after their run-in with the bounty hunters, they turned northeast, following that large, swiftly flowing river.

Chapter 28

Eight days later they rode wearily into Grand Junction. They spent two days there, asking questions of whomever they could. They learned that Ellsworth had been seen there, but that had been several weeks ago, and no one knew where he was now.

Angry, frustrated, and disgusted, the Culpeppers resupplied there and then headed southeast along the Gunnison River through a long, flat valley. They rode slowly, still trying to find some clue as to where Ellsworth and his men might be. They would ride away from the riverbank now and again, looking for clues, but they found nothing.

Jody began to worry about his brother. Jonas seemed to be obsessed with finding Ellsworth. If he wasn't, he would've been able to see that they had no hope whatsoever of finding any clues out here in the middle of nowhere.

They stopped at each of the infrequent towns they came to and asked questions, but got no information that was of any use to them. Jonas grew more quiet than usual, and more withdrawn.

A little more than a month after they had left Silverton, they were sitting in a cold, rained-on camp they had made just after they had crossed the Gunnison River.

"Maybe we'd best get back, Jonas," Jody said softly. "Merry'll be worried sick about you."

"She's been alone before."

"Probably not this long. We're not doin' any goddamn good out here, Jonas. You should damn well know that. All we're doin' is spittin' into the wind. Look, Ellsworth is an outlaw through and through. Even I can see that, and I don't know anything about him other than what I've heard since I've been with you. He's not going to give that up just because he hit the big one once. That'll only goad him on, make him want an even bigger jackpot. He might take some time off to enjoy his loot, but he'll try somethin' else again sooner or later. And I'd wager all I own that it'll be close to Silverton, or maybe Durango—the train again. Or a bank. You know that as well as anyone."

"Yeah. So?"

"When he makes his move, you and I'll chase his ass down right from the start."

Jonas nodded. He knew that everything Jody had said was true, but he didn't like it any. Still, he missed his wife considerably more than he would admit to anyone, even his brother. He wanted to eat her cooking instead of the slop he and Jody prepared for themselves. He wanted to feel her smooth, soft skin under his hard hands; wanted to see the lust for him burning deep in her soft brown eyes; wanted to know the taste of her lips on his.

"You're right, Jody," he finally said firmly. "We'll push on for Silverton in the mornin'."

They moved much more quickly after that. Now that Jonas had made up his mind, he was eager to get back to Silverton. Thoughts of Merry were with him almost constantly, driving him on. Thoughts of finding Ellsworth faded with each mile they put behind him. He would get Ellsworth, he had no doubt of that. Sooner or later, he would get Ellsworth and see the outlaw hang.

The Culpeppers still stopped at each town they came to—Olathe, Montrose, Colona—but not for very long. Jonas would introduce himself to the town marshal and ask if Ellsworth had caused trouble or even been seen in the area. The answer was always negative, and Jonas would leave. Depending on the time of day, he and his brother would find quarters in town for the night, or resupply and then ride on.

They stopped—reluctantly—several times a day to loosen their saddles and let the horses breathe a few minutes before moving on again. They did not stop for a midday meal; instead, they would make one of their rest stops and grab some beef jerky and hard biscuits from their packs and eat while they were riding again. Their night camps were small and quickly made. Breakfast was a gobbled affair in the predawn darkness.

Six days after making their decision to press on home, they came to yet another small town, one with the unlikely name of Horsefly, named after the nearby peak. Jonas had been there numerous times, since it was not too far north of the San Juan County border. Jonas called on Marshal Sean Dowling and learned nothing more than he had at any of the other towns he and Jody had stopped at.

Since it was late, the Culpeppers got a room in a small boarding house for the night. They ate an almost decent meal and hit their beds early.

They were on the trail just as dawn was cracking. But little more than a mile out of Horsefly, still heading southeast, Jody called for Jonas to stop.

Jonas did, looking back in concern, and even with a touch of anger. Now that he was within a few days of Silverton, he wanted to push on and get home.

"I aim on going that way, Jonas," Jody said firmly, pointing southwest.

It took Jonas a moment to realize why. Then he nodded. Jody wanted to see Daisy, again, and Jonas could not fault him for that. The younger Culpepper had mentioned Daisy frequently on their travels, but other than some vague references to going back to see her one day, Jody had not said what he planned to do about her. Until now.

"You know the way?" Jonas asked. He was surprised when Jody nodded.

"I asked in Horsefly," Jody said. "I didn't know how you might take to the idea of headin' the other way."

Jonas smiled a little. "It's the right thing," he said. "Any other reason than a woman, though, would've put me out some. But I know what it's like to have a woman get to you deep inside. I'm still taken that way with Merry, and I miss her somethin' awful when I'm on the trail like this."

"You don't show it."

Jonas shrugged. "It's not somethin' a man likes to make public. But thoughts of her are with me all the time." He paused, looking around at the towering peaks that he would be entering as soon as he got back on the trail. "You figured out what you're going to do about Daisy?"

"Marry her," Jody said flatly, almost as if in defiance. Or maybe as a challenge.

"I figured that. When and where? And then what're you going to do with yourself?"

"You might not believe this," Jody said with a laugh, "But I've given this considerable thought since I met her, and . . ."

"Do tell," Jonas interjected.

"Well, I have," Jody said seriously, then laughed. "I'll decide when I get to her in San Miguel. I can marry her there, and then bring her to Silverton to live—and so I can work with you when needed. Or I can bring her to Silverton and then marry her."

"Which way do you want it?"

Jody shrugged. "It ain't so much a matter of the way I want it, Jonas. It's more what she wants."

Jonas laughed. "Spoken like an already married man."

"You have any preference in this?" Jody asked, ignoring the friendly jibe.

"Me?" Jonas asked, more than a little surprised. "Why should I have a preference?"

"Well, you might be thinkin' of bein' in the weddin' party. And Merry, too. After all, you was the one saved Daisy from those outlaws. And she looks up to you. So do I."

"Well," Jonas said, a little embarrassed, "if you was to ask me—me and Merry—to be at your nuptials, I'd be honored, and that's a fact. But Daisy might be more comfortable gettin' married with the Stantons present instead of me."

"I'd had that thought. It's why I hedged when I told you my plans."

Jonas nodded. "Whichever way she wants it is all right with me, Jody. I won't be put out any if she'd rather have the Stantons standin' by for the nuptials than me."

"Thanks, Jonas," Jody said, holding out his hand. "For everything."

Jonas clasped Jody's hand. "Wasn't so much, little brother. You watch yourself on the trail." He paused. "I think San Miguel's got a telegraph. Send me a wire tellin' me what your plans are. If Daisy wants to get married there, I don't think Merry'd object to the journey."

"That'd cover it all," Jody said thoughtfully. "I'll mention it to Daisy." He suddenly grinned. "But maybe she won't be able to wait that long before she's got to have me."

"Listen to this foolishment," Jonas said with a laugh. "Good Lord, he thinks he's got somethin' every woman wants. Hah! You'll learn better." He paused. "Now, give me the rope to my old mule. You can take the other with you. I'd not want you ridin' back into your lady love's life half starved."

They went their separate ways, then, Jody heading southwest toward the Dallas Divide, the San Miguel River, and the town of San Miguel; Jonas going southeast toward Red Mountain, the town of the same name, and finally, Silverton.

Culpepper made it back to Silverton in two days of hard riding, pulling into the town an hour or two before dark. As he rode down the mountain road toward the town, he had an uneasy feeling. He took side streets to avoid the busier parts of Silverton. He finally reached the alley that would bring him to his office and the county jail. The uneasy feeling grew as he moved along, though he saw nothing that looked wrong. People still moved about the streets, a few even called out greetings to him, which he returned perfunctorily.

He stopped outside his office and dismounted. He looked around as he tied his horse to the hitching rail next to one that looked familiar, but he couldn't place it. Something didn't seem right, though there was nothing he could put his finger on. With Bear at his side, he walked into the office and stopped.

Buster Reinhardt was sitting at Culpepper's desk, writing. He looked up when he heard the door. His face was grayish with fatigue, and a haunted look spread over it when he saw Culpepper. "Jonas," he said with relief—and fear.

"What're you doin' here, Buster?" Culpepper asked, a cold feeling growing in the pit of his stomach. It wasn't that he disliked Reinhardt; quite the contrary. But seeing Reinhardt just reinforced the worry he had had since riding into town.

"I'm . . . I'm . . ."

"Where's Jimmy?" Culpepper demanded, concern growing.

"He's . . ." Reinhardt paused and sighed, shaking his head. "He's dead, Jonas."

"But how . . . ?"

"Let's go up to Anvil Mining's headquarters," Reinhardt said firmly, rising from his chair.

"Why?" Culpepper's voice was as cold as a Silverton January.

"Because," Reinhardt said cryptically. He tried to smile and almost accomplished it. "Please, Jonas. Don't give me a hard time on this. Just do as I ask."

"I don't like this, Buster," Culpepper said harshly. "Not one bit."

"You're gonna like it even less when you hear the full tellin' of it," Reinhardt said in a nervous voice.

Culpepper said nothing. He just turned, stomped outside, and mounted his buckskin. Reinhardt got on a horse standing next to Culpepper's. The ride was only a few minutes, and then the two, with Bear, entered the Anvil Mining Company headquarters. The clerks had gone for the day, and Culpepper and

Reinhardt went straight through the empty office to the boardroom and then inside without knocking.

Wilson Pennrose's face fell when he saw Culpepper. But he regained his composure right away. He stood and came toward Culpepper, hand outstretched, a solemn look on his face. "Welcome back, Sheriff," Pennrose said flatly.

"What the hell's going on here?" Culpepper demanded, ignoring Pennrose's hand.

Pennrose dropped his arm. He turned. "Out," he ordered the other principals of the company.

Without argument, they all filed out the door.

"Sit, Sheriff," Pennrose said. He went to a sideboard and filled a large glass with fine Scotch whiskey and set it down in front of a chair. Culpepper had remained standing. "Please," Pennrose said, indicating the chair with a wave of his hand.

Culpepper sat and glowered at Pennrose. The mining executive poured himself a drink and then took his accustomed chair at the head of the table. Reinhardt also got himself a drink, but he remained standing, near the door into the outer office.

"All right, Pennrose," Culpepper said harshly, "I'm sittin'. All Buster's told me is that Jimmy Cahill's dead and that he wanted you to help explain. So I'm here. Now explain."

Chapter 29

"All of what I'm about to tell you is my fault, Jonas," Pennrose said quietly. "If there's any blame to be laid here, it should rest on my head."

Culpepper nodded. "Fine, now that you've proclaimed yourself a durn martyr, get on with the tellin'."

Pennrose gulped some whiskey. "Just one more thing, Jonas. I want you to let me finish telling it before you do anything. Will you do that?"

Culpepper swigged a mouthful of whiskey, then nodded.

"I went to the county jail several times to talk to Marshal Coakley."

"About what?"

"About Ellsworth, of course. I thought that since he was a deputy U.S. marshal and all, he might have a better chance of trackin' Ellsworth down than you did. The power of the federal government and all that." Pennrose smiled wanly.

"So?"

"So," Pennrose said with a sigh, "about two weeks after you left, I let Coakley and his two friends go."

"You did what?" Culpepper asked.

The question surprised Pennrose. The executive wasn't surprised by what Culpepper had asked, but by the *way* in which it was asked. Pennrose had expected Culpepper to explode, not ask the question in that low, heart-chilling way he had at times.

"Yes, I let them go."

"Jimmy never would've allowed that," Culpepper said coldly. It had already dawned on him that this was how Cahill had died.

"He didn't," Pennrose said flatly. "I had Judge Pfeiffer write out a court order telling him to free Coakley and the others. Jimmy didn't buy it, so I went back the next day with a half-dozen of my toughest miners, all of them armed. We got the drop on Jimmy and made him hand over the keys."

"And he resisted and one of your boys killed him. Is that it?" Culpepper demanded, slapping a hand on the table with a loud report.

"Oh, no," Pennrose said, almost horrified at the very thought. "No, he gave up the keys readily enough. Especially when I told him that I was accepting all responsibility for Coakley's release."

Pennrose paused, looking as if he was in pain. "Oh, God, I was such a fool," he wailed. He took a few moments to get control of himself. "Coakley promised me that he'd go to Durango and get up a posse. He'd leave from there and not stop until he had Ellsworth and all his men."

"You believed that malarkey?" Culpepper said, somewhat amazed.

Pennrose nodded sadly. He suddenly looked old and worn. Once again he had to bring himself into control. "I figured the reward the company and the railroad were offering would be enough to keep him on the straight and narrow. That's neither here nor there now. I let the three of them go. Then Coakley asked to have the other prisoner released, too."

"Milt Adler?" Culpepper asked.

"Yes," Pennrose said tightly. "I asked why, and Coakley said he overheard you questioning Adler . . ."

"Wasn't hard, since I wasn't tryin' to hide anything at the time," Culpepper said dryly.

"Anyway, Coakley said that Adler told you Ellsworth and his men had buried the loot near the Utah Territory border. Coakley said that he'd be able to get more answers out of Adler than you did."

"And I suppose he said it with a sneer?"

Pennrose nodded and gulped down the rest of his whiskey. "It made sense at the time. After all, Adler had been one of Ellsworth's men, so I agreed and set him free, too." He sighed, and nodded his thanks when Reinhardt set another glass of whiskey down in front of him.

"They took what supplies they wanted from Mrs. Maguire's store—the company paid her for them," he added hastily. "Then they rode out, heading south. I thought that was the last we'd see of them until they came back to Silverton to collect the reward."

"But it wasn't, was it?" Culpepper asked sourly.

"No, Sheriff, it most certainly was not." Pennrose sipped a bit. "They came back a week and a half ago. Coakley had gone to Durango and gotten a posse up, all right—eight gun toughs hired from Durango, Denver, Alamosa, Albuquerque—wherever he could hire them. They rode back into Silverton like an invading army. They practically took over Fatty Collins's place for a couple days, then looted Mrs. Maguire's store. The company reimbursed her for that, too."

"Jimmy challenged them, didn't he?" Culpepper said in a dull voice. "Tried to arrest them?"

"No," Pennrose said with a faint smile. "He just kept an eye on them to make sure they didn't cause any real trouble. He told me, though, that since I had been kind enough to accept responsibility for Coakley and his men when I released them, they were now my problem. I tried to talk to Coakley a couple of times, but he wasn't listening."

"Then what happened?"

"Coakley told me one night that he and his men were heading out the next day, going after Ellsworth. I had no reason to doubt them."

Seeing the look on Pennrose's face, and the sloppy gulp of

221

whiskey the executive took, Culpepper knew the worst part was coming up. He just wanted to get it over with.

Pennrose glanced at Reinhardt. "Did you tell him?"

Reinhardt shook his head. "Only about Jimmy."

"Tell me what?" Culpepper demanded, not liking this at all.

"Coakley . . . he . . . Coakley . . ."

"Jonas," Reinhardt said from his place at the door behind Culpepper, "Merriam's gone. Taken by Coakley."

Culpepper sat perfectly still for some seconds. Then he roared something unintelligible and bolted up from his chair, hands heading for Pennrose's throat.

Pennrose sat there, face frightened, but otherwise calm. But Reinhardt charged forward and grappled with Culpepper, trying to tear the tough sheriff's hands from Pennrose's neck. All the while he was shouting at Culpepper to stop.

Bear got into the act, bouncing around and barking, threatening Reinhardt with bared teeth and harsh growls.

Culpepper proved to be too strong for Reinhardt, and finally Reinhardt stepped back, pulled a pistol, and whacked Culpepper on the head with it, trying not to do so too hard.

Culpepper groaned and released Pennrose. He turned enraged eyes on Reinhardt, who stepped back a few paces and leveled the revolver at Culpepper. "Sit your ass down, Jonas, and let Pennrose finish his tale. You gave your word that you'd do that."

"Yes, you did," Pennrose squawked through his injured throat. "And I'd appreciate it if you kept your word. If, after I've had my say, you still want to kill me, I won't stop you."

Culpepper glared from Pennrose to Reinhardt. Then he rubbed his head, sat down, and gulped down the whiskey. "Finish," he ordered.

Bear went back to lying on the floor next to Culpepper's chair.

Pennrose took another drink, then coughed several times. When he spoke again, his voice was almost normal. "Nobody knows why he went to grab Mrs. Culpepper," he said. "But he did. I understand you had asked Jimmy to watch over your wife while you were gone." It was something of a question.

Culpepper nodded curtly.

"Somehow, he got wind that Coakley was heading there, or something. But he raced to your house. Him and Wes Hennessy."

"Marshal Hennessy?" Culpepper asked, incredulous.

Pennrose nodded and then offered a wan smile. "You weren't the only one who thought Wes was a useless piece of manhood. I don't know what possessed him, or why he went after Coakley when they grabbed your wife. But he did." Pennrose shook his head in sadness. "Both of them were killed."

"Shit," Culpepper breathed, the harsh, flat obscenity revealing the depth of his anger. "Then what happened?" he asked.

"Coakley and his men rode off, taking Mrs. Culpepper with them. When Mister Reinhardt heard what had happened, he came to me and asked—no, he damn well demanded—that he be deputized, either as a county deputy sheriff, or as a deputy town marshal. Then he wanted to lead a posse out after those outlaws."

"But you couldn't bring yourself to allow that, could you?" Culpepper said bitterly.

"That's not true. I *did* deputize him—as a deputy county sheriff—but I wouldn't let Mister Reinhardt lead the posse."

"Was there a posse at all?" Culpepper asked harshly.

Pennrose nodded. "Mostly miners."

"Who was in charge of it?" Culpepper demanded. "One of Hennessy's useless deputies?"

"Mister Pennrose led it, Jonas," Reinhardt said quietly.

Culpepper continued to stare at Pennrose, not sure he believed it. Then he nodded. "Trying to regain my good graces, is that it?" he asked roughly.

"I deserve that," Pennrose said. "And it's even true to some extent. I feel terrible about all this, Sheriff. I don't know if you can understand how deeply horrified I am at all that's occurred because I was such a damned idiot. I can never make up all that has happened. I can't bring Jimmy or Wes back. I thought I could get your wife back, so I led out a posse after Coakley. Yes, I was doing it to make me look better to you and everyone else in town. But I was also doing it because of deep regret. I don't expect you to understand that, or to forgive me, but it is the truth. I wish I could've done more."

"You've done plenty," Culpepper said unmercifully.

"I suppose I deserved that, too, Sheriff," Pennrose said in a small voice. "But there is one small piece of good news in all this."

"Oh?" Culpepper asked, surprised.

"We—the posse, that is—did catch up with Coakley. Unfortunately, we were unable to spirit Mrs. Culpepper away from them. We lost two men, but we killed one of the outlaws. And we captured another. He was wounded, but alive."

Culpepper's interest perked up considerably. "He's still alive?"

"Yep," Reinhardt said. "He's over in your own goddamn jail."

Culpepper grabbed his hat and slapped it on. He shoved himself up. "I'm going to talk to that pukin' scoundrel. You two want to come?"

"I'm goin'," Reinhardt declared.

"You, Pennrose?" Culpepper asked.

"Yes," Pennrose said tentatively. "Yes, by God, I think I will." He suddenly sounded stronger, more sure of himself. Almost back to his own arrogant self.

The three men and the dog walked outside. Culpepper mounted his horse, as did Reinhardt. "Come on, Mister Pennrose," Reinhardt said, holding out a hand. Pennrose looked at the appendage blankly for a moment. Then nodded, took the hand, and let Reinhardt help pull him up behind him on the horse.

They rode to the jail and went inside, working through the series of locks. "You know, Jonas," Reinhardt said, as he undid the last of the locks, "this is a pain in the ass. We need to get rid of at least half these goddamn locks."

"Later," Culpepper growled, in no mood for humor. Finally he was in the cell with the outlaw. "What's your name, maggot?" he asked. When the outlaw did not answer right off, Culpepper grabbed him by the throat with one hand, hauled him up, and slammed the back of his head against the bars. "I ain't of a mind to play games here, you pukin' maggot. You either answer my questions, or I'll grind you into the floor. Now, what's your name?"

"His name's . . ."

"Let him tell me, durn it!" Culpepper roared.

"Lonnie Oates!" the man shouted. Sweat glistened off his pale, round face.

"Good. Now, where's Coakley going?"

"I don't know." Then, when Culpepper squeezed his throat a little more, he added, "Wait."

Culpepper eased the pressure. "You won't get any more chances, maggot," he said quietly.

"I'm not exactly sure," Oates said, when Culpepper had let go of his throat. "He hired me and most of the rest of the boys down in Durango. He had two men with him. Well, three, actually, but one of 'em wasn't one of us, if you know what I mean."

"Were their names Lou Boxham, Neil Corcoran, and Milt Adler?" Culpepper asked.

"Yeah," Oates said in surprise. "How'd you know?"

"It doesn't matter. Just talk."

"Coakley beat the shit out of that Adler fella to get him to talk. Adler was one of Mack Ellsworth's gang, from what I heard."

"Did Adler tell Coakley anything?"

Oates nodded. "You mind if I smoke?"

"Not as long as you keep on talkin'."

Oates rolled a cigarette and fired it up. "Since I was a new man with Coakley—though I knew him a little back in Den-

225

ver—he didn't tell me too much, but I gather that Ellsworth buried the loot from that train robbery a while back. I heard he also robbed a bank in Grand Junction a couple weeks ago. That loot was supposed to be buried, too."

"I know all this. What I don't know is where he's buried the loot, and when they're all going to get together to divvy it up."

"Adler said it was in a place a little southwest of Grand Junction. There's some area up there supposed to be very odd, with wind-twisted trees and all. I've never been up that way. They're supposed to get together right around the time fall arrives."

Culpepper nodded. "What happened to Adler?"

"Coakley killed him." Oates sounded quite nervous. "Beat him to death."

Culpepper nodded again. "You're lucky to have gotten away from him, maggot," he said.

Chapter 30

"I'm leavin' as soon as I can get some supplies," Culpepper said, as he stopped outside the jail.

"I'm ready," Reinhardt said.

"No, Buster," Culpepper said quietly. "You're needed here. And I can travel much better on my own."

"But . . ."

"No arguin', Buster," Culpepper snapped. "I've made up my mind."

"What can I do to help?" Pennrose asked.

"Still tryin' to get in my good graces for all the trouble you've caused me, you pukin' rascal?" Culpepper said harshly.

"That was uncalled for," Pennrose said stiffly.

Culpepper shrugged, unconcerned about Pennrose's feelings. "If you really want to help, go to Maguire's and get me enough supplies to last me a couple of weeks and have someone load them on my mule there." He pointed to the hitching rail in front of the office, where the mule was still standing, lazily munching on the sparse grass. "Caroline Maguire'll know pretty much what I need. And pay for them, of course."

"That all?" Pennrose asked.

"I suppose. Come back to the office here when you're done with that." When Pennrose had hurried off on foot, Culpepper said, "Buster, come with me." He quickly went to the office, sat at his desk, found paper and a pencil. Then he wrote a few moments. "What I need you to do right now is go to the telegraph office and have Steve wire this to my brother in San Miguel, over in Montrose County."

"I was wonderin' where he was," Reinhardt said, as he took the piece of paper. "In the rush of everything, and in the pain of tellin' it, I never did get a chance to ask. What's he doin' in San Miguel, if you don't mind my askin', Jonas?"

"I don't mind. He found himself a woman there he's thinkin' of marryin'. So he went back to try to talk her into bein' foolish enough to tie the knot with him." A thought suddenly came over him, and he saddened anew. "How's June Ladimere?" he asked.

"She took Jimmy's death hard," Reinhardt said glumly. "She's still in mournin', of course, seein' as how's it's only been a week and a half since he was killed."

"You been watchin' over her any?"

Reinhardt shrugged. "A little."

"Vera givin' you a hard time about it?"

"Nah. I just ain't got the time." He smiled weakly. "I've been pretty busy lately."

Culpepper nodded. "It's a pity, durn it all. She and Jimmy would've made a fine couple." Culpepper sighed. "All right, Buster, go on and get that wire sent."

Reinhardt looked down at the piece of paper. The writing simply said: *"Jody. There's been big trouble in Silverton. Stay in San Miguel. I'll be there in a couple days. Jonas."* Reinhardt looked at Culpepper. "What're you gonna be doin' while I'm off on these chores?" he asked.

"Go shave and put on some fresh clothes. I've been wearin' these since I left. Then I suppose I'll go to Moldovan's for some food."

"It'll be dark by then, Jonas. You ought not to be leavin' in the dark."

"There'll be enough moonlight for me to see where I'm going," Culpepper said flatly. "I'll be going over Red Mountain

Pass. I could make that trip blindfolded. Night ain't going to make a difference."

"I think you're a damn fool, Jonas," Reinhardt said. Then he shrugged. "But there ain't no talkin' to you about it. I'll go send this wire. Anything else you need me to do?"

"Take my horse and mule over to Cassidy's. Have him check the mule over good to make sure he's got no sore spots. Have him tend both animals, then grain them and water them good."

"Yessir. I'll meet you over at Moldovan's."

"Buster," Culpepper called, when Reinhardt was halfway out the door. The young man turned back. "Thanks. I'm obliged for all you've done."

"I wish it could've been more." Then he left.

"Come on, Bear," Culpepper said, standing. He plodded to his house, feeling Merry's loss severely when he was near to the small place and remembered that Merry wouldn't be waiting at the door for him.

The house was cold and musty smelling from not having been used in a week and a half. Culpepper lit a lantern and then got a fire going in the stove. He found some old salt beef and cut off enough chunks to feed Bear pretty well. After eating, the mastiff stretched out near the stove and fell asleep. Every once in a while, he would make a high-pitched sounds as his jowly lips flapped when he dreamed of chasing some plump jackrabbits.

Culpepper heated some water, which he used to scrub up with as best as he could. Then he reheated it and used it to scrape off the thick red fur on his cheeks. Then he changed into fresh clothes. "All right, Bear," he said quietly, "you've had enough of a nap. Come on." They walked to Moldovan's restaurant.

The place was only half full, for which Culpepper was grateful. He ignored the looks that the few customers gave him, as well as the quiet whispers and finger pointing. He ordered from Eleni Moldovan, who touched his shoulder in sympathy. He nodded and patted the hand.

Eleni made sure Culpepper had heaping portions of chicken, potatoes, beans, and bread, as well as coffee. Culpepper nodded in thanks and dug in. Eleni had also brought a plate with old meat scraps and a bone and set it on the floor for Bear. The mastiff went to eating with as much gusto as Culpepper had.

Culpepper was about halfway through his meal when Reinhardt and Pennrose came in and sat at his table.

"Everything's done and ready," Reinhardt said, as he took the coffee cup Eleni handed him. He filled the cup. "Art's going to wait till you're ready to go. Then he'll load the mule and saddle your horse."

"He ain't complained about stayin' so late?" Culpepper asked around a mouthful of chicken and biscuit. He didn't really care, but he figured he ought to make some kind of conversation.

"Not when he's gettin' what Mister Pennrose is payin' him."

Culpepper nodded. "All the supplies there already?"

Reinhardt nodded. "I still think you're a damn fool for leavin' now, Jonas. Wait till mornin'. You'll be fresh, and the animals'd be fresh."

"I know all that," Culpepper said swallowing. "And you know why I'm leavin' now. Those pukin' skunks've got a week-and-a-half lead on me. I've got to make as much time as I can to catch up to them."

Reinhardt nodded. "Yeah, I know."

"You should take a posse with you, Sheriff," Pennrose said.

"That wouldn't do me much good. Look what happened to the last one."

"We'll have more men this time. Better men."

"Face it, Pennrose," Culpepper said evenly, "they'd still be miners and townsmen, and as such'd most likely get themselves killed. I don't want that on my conscience."

"But . . ."

"I admire your desire to help, Pennrose," Culpepper said, "and maybe someday I'll even forgive you for all the grief you've caused me and others. But for right now, I think you'd be best keepin' your own counsel for the most part."

Pennrose nodded, afraid now to say anything at all.

Culpepper finished eating a few minutes later, and then settled back with a final cup of coffee.

"Well," Reinhardt said, setting his cup down, "I better go tell Art to start loadin' up that mule."

"Let Pennrose do it," Culpepper said pointedly. "I need to talk to you a few minutes."

Looking like he had just swallowed a four-day-dead skunk, Pennrose nodded. He stood and left, back stiff.

"I don't reckon you're too awful popular with Mister Pennrose right now, Jonas," Reinhardt said with a grin.

"It works the other way, too, Buster," Culpepper said.

Reinhardt nodded. "Well, what'd you want to talk to me about, Jonas?"

"Nothin' much," Culpepper responded. "I just wanted to knock old Pennrose down a notch or two more. He's lorded it over durn near everyone in Silverton since he's been here. A little humility'll be good for him."

"He's really tried to do all he could since . . . well, since Coakley rode out."

"I expect he has. He should've done more, though. Well, actually, he shouldn't have started all this troublesome mess. Durn! If he'd only kept his nose out of other folks' business, none of this would've . . ." He stopped and sucked in a breath, irritated at himself for getting carried away.

"He thought he was doin' right then, too, Jonas."

"You takin' his side now, Buster?" Culpepper asked harshly.

"Nope. Just statin' what's true. There was nothin' in all this for Pennrose. No benefit in it for him—or for Anvil Mining—by settin' Coakley and those others free. The only thing he could've gotten out of this was to have Coakley catch Ellsworth."

"I suppose that's a fact, Buster. But because of his durn fool action, a friend of mine is dead, and my wife's been carried off by a bunch of pukin' maggots worse than the durned outlaws they was supposed to catch."

"Well, you're right," Reinhardt countered. "But I ain't so sure that treatin' Pennrose poorly just to rub his nose in the dirt is gonna accomplish anything. For you, or for him."

"Durn it, Buster," Culpepper said sourly, "you have an annoying habit of speakin' the facts." He tried to smile but couldn't. His thoughts were on Merry, and what abuse she was probably undergoing at the hands of Coakley and his men. He finished his coffee and stood. "Well, I'd best be on my way." The renewed thoughts of Merry had instilled in him a sense of urgency. Or maybe it was just a desire to get on with what had to be done. He didn't know which, nor did he care.

"I'll walk with you down to the livery, if you don't mind, Jonas."

"I'd be obliged for the company."

As the two men walked down the street, Culpepper said, "Keep a good watch on the town while I'm gone, Buster. Anybody the likes of Ellsworth—or Coakley—comes along, you shoot the maggot down right off."

"I'll do so."

"And don't rely on nobody but yourself. You start relyin' on others, and you'll end up in a pot of trouble."

"Hell, Jonas, you're relyin' on me."

"I suppose I am at that. Well, then, don't rely on too many folks, especially ones you don't know too well or can't trust."

They were at the livery now. The stable was lit by several lanterns, and Cassidy was just tightening the saddle on Culpepper's buckskin. The mule stood nearby, still munching on some oats, packs tied down and covered with waterproofed canvas. Pennrose was standing straight, arms folded across his chest, watching.

"All set, Sheriff," Cassidy said, patting the horse on the neck. "This old gelding's lookin' pretty good for what he's been through lately."

"Think he'll hold up under some more rough handling?"

"I do." He paused. "I can let you have another mule, if you want, to pack more supplies. Or I can let you have another horse, as a spare."

"Thanks for the offer, Art," Culpepper said, as he pulled himself into the saddle, "but I don't think either one'll be necessary, and havin' extra animals along'd just slow me down." He reached down and shook hands with Cassidy, and then Reinhardt. He touched his hat brim in Pennrose's direction. Then he was riding out of the stable, Bear pacing the horse.

Culpepper made the trip to San Miguel in just over three days, going without sleep for the entire journey. He ate all his meals in the saddle, and stopped only for short periods to relieve himself and to give the horse and the mule a little rest.

He was bone tired when he finally rode into town. He stopped in front of the Stanton House and sat there weaving, half asleep, in the saddle.

A shout of "Jonas!" startled him into wakefulness. He opened bleary, reddened eyes. "Jody," he said softly. He saw Daisy right behind his brother, standing between Silas and Sarah Stanton, but he was falling off the horse by then and did not even greet them.

Jody Culpepper caught his brother and then eased him the rest of the way out of the saddle. He managed to get Jonas up and over his shoulder. "Watch the animals, Daisy," he said as he carted his brother up the stairs, and into his room and deposited him on the bed as softly as he could. Then he went back downstairs and took Jonas's horse and mule to the livery and had them cared for.

After going back to the hotel, he and Daisy sat up throughout the day and intermittently through the night, until Jonas awoke twelve hours after he had ridden into town. He came awake slowly, trying to remember where he was.

"About time you got up, big brother," Jody said, rubbing his eyes. "You hungry?"

"Yep. What time is it?"

Jody checked his pocketwatch. "Four in the morning."

"When did I get here?" he asked sheepishly.

"Somewhere about three, four, maybe a little later. Yesterday afternoon. You were asleep on your horse."

"You get my wire?"

"Yep."

"Good. Let me tell you about . . ."

"After you've eaten. Whatever it is, no matter how bad—and I gather it's real bad—it can wait till then."

Chapter 31

Jonas could not wait until he had breakfast. As soon as Daisy had returned from asking Sarah Stanton to bring some food upstairs for everyone, Jonas began talking. It took only a few minutes for him to explain what had happened.

When Jonas had finished, Jody stood. His face was hard. "I'll get the horses and mules ready," he said harshly. "You eat. As soon as all that's done, we'll hit the trail."

Jonas nodded, but glanced at Daisy. The young woman was gazing at Jody with fierce resolution etched on her face. "What can I do?" she asked.

"Stay here with Jonas," Jody said. "If he thinks of anything else needs doin', you can either do it, get me, or find someone else to do it."

Daisy nodded. She owed so much to these two men. One had saved her life, and the other had won her heart. She was afraid for both brothers. They were going out against probably impossible odds. It was doubtful they would even be able to find the men they would be chasing, which was a mixed blessing as far as Daisy was concerned. If they did not find the lawman-turned-outlaw, the Culpeppers would be safe, but Jonas's wife would never be found. If, on the other hand, they did find Coakley and the others, they would be terribly outnumbered, and thus in serious danger. She knew she could not keep from worry, but she was determined that she would not let the Culpeppers see it.

Jody opened the door, startling Sarah, who was trying to juggle a tray of food while getting ready to knock. "Sorry, Miz Stanton." Jody took the tray from the woman and brought it inside.

Sarah followed him inside. "You'll be leaving soon, the two of you?" she asked. She didn't know what was wrong, only that there was serious trouble.

"Yes," Jody said.

"Then you need some food, too. You sit down, I'll be back in a few minutes."

"No, ma'am," Jody said firmly. "There's a heap of work to be done before we can leave, and it needs to be done now."

"She's right, Jody," Daisy said. "You need to eat. You go on about your chores. Miz Stanton, make him up a tray. I'll take it to him over at the stables, and then help there."

"No, you stay here, in case . . ."

"No, Jody," Daisy said. "I can't do no one any good here. If Jonas needs somethin', Mister and Miz Stanton're here to help. Besides, I've loaded a mule and saddled horses before. The more help you get, the quicker you and Jonas can get on the trail. Now you go on. I'll be over to help you directly."

It was still dark less than half an hour later, when the Culpepper brothers rode out of San Miguel. They headed northwest, up the valley, between a line of low hills on the southwest and the Uncompahgre Plateau on the northeast. They pushed pretty hard, but tried to temper their desire to move ahead as fast as possible. It would do them no good to find Coakley and his men and then be too exhausted to take them on.

They still managed to reach the town of Westville in three days instead of the usual four. They edged up onto it slowly, since Bear was showing signs of agitation. A quarter of a mile or so away, they heard noises. They could not determine exactly what the sounds were, but they knew they could only be made by men.

The Culpeppers stopped and went behind a short, squat hill, where they staked their horses and mules.

"Well, big brother, what do we do?" Jody asked.

Jonas wanted to just ride into Westville and do whatever it was that was necessary, but there were some serious problems with that. If those in the ghost town were not the ones the Culpeppers were chasing, some innocent people might get hurt. If either Coakley's bunch or Ellsworth's were in Westville, they could be riding to their deaths without being able to accomplish anything.

"I think we'll wait till nightfall. Then I'll mosey on over there and snoop around."

"You'll do that?" Jody asked.

"Yep. You'll stay here and keep watch on the animals."

"Why don't you stay here with the animals?" Jody asked, trying to keep the petulance out of his voice.

"Several reasons. For one, I'm the sheriff; you're only the deputy. For another, I'm older. But those're just small reasons. For the main one, I've got to ask you this: Do you know the men we're lookin' for?"

"Well, no, but I know Merry."

"Supposin' it's not Coakley? Supposin' it's Ellsworth?"

"That would be a problem, wouldn't it?" Jody commented, feeling like a fool to need to have such a thing explained to him. "All right, so you'll go in there. Then what?"

Jonas shrugged. "Depends on what—and who—I find there."

It was several hours to sunset, so the Culpeppers dozed, trying to make up some of the sleep they'd been shortchanged on the journey so far. Finally they roused themselves and ate a cold supper. Even though they were still a quarter-mile or so from the town, and behind a hill, neither wanted to be detected because of their fire by someone wandering around outside the town. Or coming to the town.

Finally Jonas stood. "It's about time," he said, looking up at the spreading darkness. "Come on, Bear," he said quietly, as he stepped off to go around the hill.

As it had since about halfway here from San Miguel, the trail followed the southwestern bank of the Dolores River. As the trail entered the "town," it petered out when it hit the only street in Westville, which was at right angles to the river. A quarter-mile or so across the flats from the hill behind which the Culpeppers had taken shelter were two houses fronting the street. Two other houses were across the street. The only other house was set back from the street, twenty or thirty yards up the river.

Culpepper wondered again as he walked toward the town what had ever possessed people to try to populate this godforsaken place. He supposed some folks were traveling through here—probably lost—and one of their wagons had broken down. Seeing the river, they most likely assumed they could irrigate and raise crops here. But this land was not conducive to farming anything. They probably had learned that fast enough, and—if they were mighty lucky to have survived a winter with little or no food and all the cold and snow—gotten out as fast as they could. If that was true, it must have been interesting, since it looked like the houses had used a considerable amount of wood from wagons, along with the reddish adobe.

Culpepper shrugged off these thoughts as he neared the houses. They were of no concern to him. He stopped a moment and listened. He patted the mastiff's head while he did so. Then he whispered, "You'd best be quiet, dog, or we might find us in deep trouble." Then he was walking again, softly and slowly.

He came up on the nearest house from the back, since the front was facing the street. He could see no light coming from chinks in the wood and adobe, but he continued moving warily along the one side, heading toward the street. He neither saw nor heard anything.

He stopped at the corner of the house and peered around it,

up the street. The other house seemed to be equally deserted, as did the two across the street from him. Still, he could hear voices, and now he could smell woodsmoke.

He moved around the corner to the front of the house, sticking close to the wall. The front door was a gaping maw, but it was evident even in the dark that no one had been through the portal in a long time, what with the cobwebs and the dust caught in them glinting dully in the pale silver moonlight.

Still wary, Culpepper moved swiftly to the next house and checked it. That one showed no more recent use than the other. Brazenly he walked across the street, hoping that if the outlaws were indeed here, that they had not placed a guard on one of the roofs. Those two houses had not been used recently, either.

"Well, Bear," he muttered into the night sky, "reckon that whoever's here is over by yonder house set apart from the others." He headed in that direction, moving slowly and stopping frequently. If anyone was on the lookout, he hoped to blend into the shadows, such as they were.

As he drew nearer to the house, the sounds increased, and the mastiff seemed to catch a scent that made him dance in agitation—or eagerness; Culpepper could not be sure in the darkness. He moved closer to the wall of the house—a side wall, he learned; the front faced the river a few yards away. The river was not running very fast, or it would have obscured the sounds from the house.

Just as he was inching around the front corner, someone almost walked into him. Culpepper did not even think—his hands shot out, grabbed the man's throat, and squeezed. At the same time, he slammed the man's head against the adobe and wood wall. The man slumped, held up only by Culpepper's strength.

Culpepper eased the man onto the ground. With swift assurance, he pulled out the bandanna he carried in his pocket. He used it to tie the man's hands. He pulled the other bandanna from around his neck and gagged the man with it. The man seemed only semiconscious anyway, so Culpepper figured he had a little time before the man began to recover.

As he worked, Culpepper looked the man over. He was not familiar, but the lean hawkishness of his face, the twin Colts he wore, and his fancy long suit coat and string tie identified him as a gunman, as far as Culpepper was concerned. If the man turned out to be innocent, Culpepper would apologize to him, but right now he didn't much care how badly hurt the man was.

Culpepper removed the man's Colt pistols and tossed them toward the river. Then he stood and poked his nose around the corner of the building. He found that there was no door on this house, either; just a gaping doorway. The noise and laughter were much louder and clearer now. And he could hear Coakley's hoarse voice among them. He spun and went around back.

Behind the house was a corral. Rickety posts of wood brought from who knows where kept in a dozen horses and four mules. The animals shuffled uncomfortably as Culpepper and Bear walked around the corral to the other side of the house. In the side wall, near the back, was another doorway. It was dark, but the sounds came through it quite clearly.

Culpepper stepped just inside. He drew a pistol and held it at arm's length down his leg, thumb on the hammer. Then he eased inside. He could tell from the way his tail whipped furiously back and forth that Bear was even more excited, but the mastiff made no sounds.

Culpepper peered around an inside doorjamb and saw three men. One was Ned Coakley. Culpepper itched to just put a bullet in the rogue lawman's head here and now. He fought the feeling, though, since that would only lead to his death. And Merry's, too—if she were still alive.

Regaining his control, he backed through the room and then was outside again. He walked down the side wall of the house, peering through cracks, but he could see little. Finally he sighed and turned back. He went back around the corral to the other side of the house. His prisoner was there, but was standing and showing other signs of alertness.

Culpepper walked up to the man and hammered him a shot in the kidneys. The man's midsection jumped out with the impact, and he sank to his knees. Culpepper knelt and whispered into his ear. "You and me're goin' for a little walk, you pukin' skunk. You give me any trouble and that little pop I just gave you will seem like a love tap. That clear?"

The man nodded.

"Good." Culpepper rose and pulled the man with him. He turned the man and shoved him. "Walk." Before long, he was nearing the hill and called out softly, "Jody, we're comin' in." He waited tensely for the few moments before his brother's voice told him to come ahead.

Jonas tied the prisoner's hands and feet with rope and then shoved him down. He knelt in front of the man. "I've got neither time nor patience to fool with you, maggot," he said harshly. "You'll answer my questions, and make no move—includin' shoutin'—to cause trouble, or you will die in considerable pain. You be helpful, you might come out of this with no more pain that you've had already. That clear?"

The man nodded, and Jonas removed the gag.

"What's your name? And how'd you get hooked up with Coakley?"

"Greg Riddell. He hired me down in Durango," Riddell said without hesitation. He owed no allegiance to Ned Coakley other than the services for which Coakley paid. And Coakley was not paying him to be tortured.

Culpepper nodded. "How many men's he got in the house?"

"Seven. No, wait, six, now that I'm out here."

"The woman?"

"She's there." Riddell licked his lips, nervous, since he figured that the woman meant something to this broad-shouldered, flaming-haired lawman. "She's . . . all right."

"Where is she?"

"The house's got four rooms, two in front, two in back, with a hallway down the center from the front door. The woman's in the front room on your left as you go in."

"Coakley and the rest of the men?"

Riddell shrugged. "They could be anywhere in the house. Coakley's sort of taken over the other front room, which is somethin' of a kitchen. But he doesn't always stay there. The rest of the men sleep wherever they're at. And they sometimes go into the room with . . . the woman."

Culpepper nodded again, his face tight with anger.

Chapter 32

"Well, Jonas, what're we waitin' for?" Jody asked. "Let's go down there and get Merry out."

"No," Jonas said through a constricted throat. There was nothing he wanted to do more, especially knowing that she was being abused and would continued to be degraded as long as she was with Coakley and the others. But it was foolish. "No," he repeated. "There's too much risk involved. Too much of a chance of you or I shootin' each other in the dark. Or worse, shootin' Merry. No, it'll have to be dawn."

Jody nodded, accepting the wisdom of it, and sympathizing with what his brother was going through. "What about him?" he asked, pointing to Riddell. "Won't they miss him down there after a spell?"

Jonas shrugged. "Maybe. But if they do, there's a good enough chance they'll think he fell in the river or something. These boys don't have any loyalty."

"Sad but true," Riddell said softly.

Jonas nodded and pulled out the gag again. "I got to do this, boy," he said.

"I understand," Riddell said with a nod.

The Culpeppers sat back, munching on jerky and stale bread, and sipping from their canteens. For each bite of jerky that Jonas ate, he gave a bigger piece to Bear. The mastiff did not seem to mind the leathery dried meat. Each brother wished he had some hot coffee even more than a hot meal, but each knew that was not possible.

After their meal, such as it was, the men dozed, as did the dog. Riddell decided to see if he could slither away, but Bear roused right up and growled once at him. Riddell froze, shrugged when he saw Jonas looking at him, and then decided he might as well sleep, too.

Twenty-five minutes before dawn, Culpepper rose and stretched. He splashed a little water from his canteen into his hands and then rubbed them over his face. He kicked Jody lightly on the boot. "Time to go, little brother," he said softly.

Jonas felt lousy from not having slept well. Visions of evil men attacking Merry made it difficult to sleep. With sleep-blurred, angry eyes he looked at Riddell. "Was the woman debased?" he asked in a rage-clotted voice.

Riddell nodded tentatively, suddenly worried.

"You take part?"

Riddell nodded again, and tried to speak around the gag, to plead for mercy, but all he could manage were unintelligible sounds.

"I can fix it so you don't ever do that to another woman," Culpepper said. He pulled the big bowie knife from his belt and ran a thumb along the side of the blade. "How would that suit you?"

Riddell's head swung furiously back and forth.

"It's either that, or I kill you here and now," Culpepper said. The edge of rage in his voice had not lessened an iota.

Riddell nodded glumly. If he was going to die, he'd rather have it be quick and sure, rather than be emasculated and left to die in a pool of blood where his manhood had been.

Jonas knelt. "You took up with the wrong fellers this time, you puke-suckin' maggot," he said, in a voice that would have sent chills up the back of the Grim Reaper himself. Then he grabbed Riddell's hair, jerked his head back, and whipped the bowie's blade across Riddell's throat. He ignored the spurts of blood that splattered his shirt.

When Riddell had quit jerking, Culpepper wiped his blade on the man's pants, then stood and slid the knife away. "You ready?" he asked, looking at his brother.

Jody nodded grimly. He didn't think he could ever be as cold-hearted as he had just seen his brother be. He had never seen that side of Jonas before, and it chilled him to the bone. But he vowed silently that he would not let Jonas down. He would do whatever needed doing, no matter how nasty or cold-blooded it might be.

"Your shoulder all right?" Jonas asked.

Jody looked blank for a moment, then remembered the gunshot wound. It had been a few weeks, and he had already pretty much forgotten about it. Only an occasional twinge made him think of it on occasion. "Just fine, Jonas. It won't slow me any."

Jonas nodded.

In the darkness, the Culpeppers plodded across the muddy trickle of West Creek and then walked toward the house. Bear trotted just ahead of them. As they walked, Culpepper quickly told Jody what he wanted him to do and where to be in the house.

When they came up to the side of the house, Jody broke off and went around the corral to the doorway in the opposite side wall near the back. Culpepper went along the front wall and flattened himself back against it right next to the door. Bear sat on the other side of the door. And they waited.

Dawn was not long in coming, and this was the most dangerous time, Jonas figured. The men inside were beginning to get up, and they would be heading outside sooner or later to take care of personal business. More noises of waking men drifted out the open doorway.

Jonas drew both Remingtons and eased the hammers back. "Stay here, Bear. Stay here," he whispered. Then he bellowed, "Now!" He swung inside, firing twice through the doorway to the room to his right, but he moved into the room at his left. He saw Merry, her two hands tied together and then tied to the iron bedstead. She was wrapped in a thin blanket. He thought something about her looked wrong, but he had no time to place it.

Ferd Wiley was trying to push the blanket aside, but was having a hard time of it, since Merry had it clamped between her thighs. He slapped Merry with his left hand, snarling, "Hold still, damn it, bitch." Neither the two gunshots nor the shout had disturbed him. He was concentrating on trying to have his way with the woman again, and figured it was just some of his companions cutting up. Then a voice got his attention.

"That's enough of that shit, you puke-eatin' maggot," Jonas said, his voice raspy.

Wiley half turned, his face feral and frightened. "You!" he breathed. He fell onto his seat on the floor, trying to say something.

Culpepper shot him. Then he walked to where Wiley lay, still alive. Culpepper looked down at him in contempt. "I thought you once told me you weren't much of a violent man, nor one to whomp on the defenseless," he said.

"I lied," Wiley gasped. He tried to sneer but couldn't.

"Too bad." Culpepper shot him in the face. Jamming his pistols away, Culpepper headed for the bed, where he began untying Merry. As he did, he heard gunfire from the back of the house, and he hoped Jody was all right. He was almost through when something punched him a terrible blow to the back. Culpepper groaned and fell forward. But he immediately pushed himself up and began to spin, drawing one of his Remingtons as he did. He saw Lou Boxham in the doorway, still wearing his cast, ready to fire again.

Boxham fired, but hit only a wall. Culpepper used the final shot in his pistol. The bullet ripped into Boxham's forehead. Boxham was slammed back up against the doorjamb, and then sank to the floor, dead.

"Durn," Culpepper muttered as he fell. He heard more gunshots, and a woman's scream. And he felt something warm and wet licking his face. "Silly dog," he muttered as the blackness swept over him.

When he heard his brother shout, Jody Culpepper charged into the dark back room. It was empty, as they had figured it would be, but he saw both doorways and he nervously moved across the room toward the hallway. He heard two gunshots, then another one moments later. By then he was in the hallway, just entering the other back room.

Two men were just pulling on their gunbelts. "Shit!" one of them shouted when he saw Culpepper. He tried getting a pistol out.

Culpepper fired three times at the man, knocking him against a bed in the corner. The man fell on the bed. By then the other outlaw had gotten a pistol out and fired twice. One bullet clunked into the wall near Culpepper's head. The other tugged at his shirt.

"Son of a bitch," Jody snapped, as he fired off the three remaining shells in his pistol. He hit the man, but he wasn't sure how many times, or if any of the bullets had been fatal. He swiftly ejected the spent shells and began jamming new ones home, trying to keep an eye on the two men in the room.

He heard a sound behind him, and he began turning, still trying to get his pistol loaded. A bullet punched him in the chest, and another hit him in the throat. He twirled away and down, hands scrabbling futilely to stop the blood gushing from his neck. As the blackness drew over him, he saw a man with a badge on his chest standing in the other back room. He had a smoking pistol in hand. He was dimly aware of someone stepping over him from inside the room, and he figured it was the second man he had shot. *Must've not done too good a job, you dumb bastard*, he thought to himself. *Sorry that I've failed you, Jonas.*

Ned Coakley waited only moments after hearing the first two shots. He wanted to know what was going on. Then he saw a blur charge into the room across the hall. "That son of a bitch," he muttered, knowing it was Jonas Culpepper from the mane of red hair under the hat. He wondered how many other men Culpepper had with him.

"Get in there and get that bastard," he snapped to Boxham.

"Damn," Coakley swore, when he saw a figure moving across the door to the back room. He figured now there was a posse waiting for them outside. All he figured to do now was to get away. When Boxham had eased out of the room, Coakley noticed that Neil Corcoran, the only other man in the room with him, had already gone into the back room directly behind this one. A faint "I'll get us horses" drifted back to him from Corcoran. Gunfire broke out from the back of the house.

Coakley dashed into the back room and glanced across the hall. He saw a man who looked much like Sheriff Jonas Culpepper trying to reload his pistol. "I'll fix your ass," he mumbled. He drew his pistol and fired twice, noting with satisfaction that the man he had shot was certainly dead, even if he didn't yet know it.

Coakley almost shot one of his own men when he saw movement in the other room. At the last moment, he realized it was Barney Strickland, one of the men he had recruited in Durango. Strickland looked to be pretty badly wounded, but he was mobile. "Move it, Barney," Coakley spat at the man. "We ain't got all day."

Strickland nodded and continued shuffling forward. He seemed as if he were afraid that any faster movement would cause pieces of him to break loose and fall to the floor.

Coakley chafed at Strickland's slow pace, and was about to leave him when he figured that he might need every gun he had, wounded or not, if they had a bigger fight on their hands outside. So he waited impatiently, taking Strickland's arm and trying to hurry him along.

An impatient—and thoroughly frightened—Corcoran was waiting just outside the door. He was on a horse that had no saddle but did have a bit and bridle. He held the reins to four other similarly equipped horses. "That it?" he asked fearfully.

"I think so," Coakley said, as he helped Strickland onto a horse. "That damned sheriff went into the front room with the woman. I'm sure he got that weasel Wiley. I figured he got Lou, too, since Lou ain't out here." He leapt onto his own horse. "But it don't matter now. Ride!" He viciously lashed the horse.

Merry Culpepper furiously worked at freeing herself from the last of the ropes that had held her to the bed almost all the time since they had gotten to this godforsaken town a week ago. She was in a panic. Jonas looked so forlorn lying there with his life's blood draining out of him. She had to get free to help him. She just had to!

Bear was lying next to Jonas, whimpering as he licked the sheriff's face, trying to rouse him. His master had never slept like this before, and it was disquieting. From time to time he looked up at Merry, his soft brown eyes pleading for her to come and do something about this unusual situation.

Finally Merry got free. Holding the blanket around her, she raced to Jonas and rolled him over onto his belly so she could check the wound in his back. The bleeding had slowed a little, but was still coming out much too fast. Using Jonas's knife, she sliced her blanket up some. Making a thick, soft pad of one piece, she placed that directly over the wound. She cut a strip of blanket, lay it across the bandage, and then managed to roll him over again. She tied the quilt tightly against his chest.

Sweating and frightened beyond all belief, she stood. Jody was here somewhere, she figured. He just had to be. Then a chill trickled down her spine as she had the thought that perhaps he, too, was injured.

Tentatively, she edged out of the room into the hallway. She peeked in the opposite room, but saw nothing. She went up the hallway to the room at back—and found Jody's lifeless body sprawled in the back room, a half-loaded pistol near his hand.

Merry sank to the floor and began to sob, her shoulders

shaking with the despair that seemed as much a part of her as her heart and lungs and blood.

She didn't know how long she sat there like that, but she suddenly became aware of Bear. The mastiff was licking her face and whining. She patted the dog's massive head. "But what can I do, Bear?" she asked. "I'm alone and I can't do anything for Jonas."

Bear backed off a step or two and barked at her. He pawed the floor, and barked some more.

Merry wondered what had gotten into the mastiff. Then she smiled. She wiped away her tears as she rose. "You're right, Bear. Jonas'd never give up on me. I can't give up on him. I can save him. I can." She went to check on her husband.

Chapter 33

Culpepper was still breathing, and the blood seemed to have stopped flowing. Merry wished there was something she could do for him, but she didn't know what, other than trying to get the bullet out, and she had neither the ability nor the resources to be able to do that. She knew that the best—and really only—thing she could do for her husband would be to get him to Silverton. Or someplace else, if there were any towns between here and there. Coakley and his men had not stopped at any town on the way out here, but that didn't mean there weren't any.

She rose, still looking down lovingly at her suffering husband. There was one thing she had to do before she could leave— bury Jody. She could not allow her brother-in-law's body to lie there in the open, subject to the whims and depredations of every scavenger that happened along.

First, though, she needed some clothes. She could do nothing while trying to keep the blanket around her. The outlaws had no extra clothes that she knew of, which meant she would have to take something off the dead. *At least I still have my shoes,* she thought, as she walked up the hallway with dread.

The only one of the outlaws even remotely close to her size was Wiley. She was revolted by the thought of wearing any of his things. Then she realized she felt that way about all of them.

Wiley's shirtfront was soaked with blood, so she decided not to take it. His pants might fit her, though. Trying not to look at the flat, dead face with the powder-burn–encircled hole where Wiley's right eye had been, Merry undid Wiley's gunbelt, then unbuttoned his pants. She pulled off the outlaw's boots. Then she tossed aside her blanket and began tugging Wiley's pants down. Turning away from the body, she reluctantly pulled the trousers on, but was relieved when she was finished. The pants were snug at the waist and hips, but the length was just about right. She did not need a belt.

She turned and looked at Wiley's corpse with more self-assurance. She thought he looked awfully small, naked as he was from the waist down, and so sickly white. In a sudden fit of rage, she kicked the body in the crotch as hard as she could, getting a fleeting feeling of pleasure.

It was easier for Merry to take Boxham's shirt. The garment was only splattered with blood in a few places.

With a sudden sense of purpose, Merry searched the house until she found a shovel. She hurried outside and found a spot near the river where the dirt was soft and she began to dig, flinging dirt furiously. She could not keep up the pace for more than ten or fifteen minutes, though, and by then she was puffing and blowing, and covered in sweat and dirt. She almost began crying again, feeling just about useless. But she fought that off and went back to digging, much more slowly this time.

Merry soon decided that a shallow grave would have to do, much as she might like to do better. Precious time was wasting away, time that meant everything to her husband's life. With each recurrence of that thought, she would dig faster.

Finally she had a hole more than six feet long, almost three wide, but only two deep. She stuck the shovel into the dirt mound beside the grave, then walked to the house, wiping her raw and aching palms on her pants.

She checked on Jonas again on the way into the house, and noticed no change in him. Bear was still watching over his master.

When she got to Jody's body, she sighed, knowing this was

not going to be easy. She bent, grabbed Jody under the arms and began pulling him. It was difficult work, since she was trying to drag almost two hundred pounds of dead weight. She jerked the corpse along inch by inch, sputtering with the effort. Eight feet from where she started, she stopped.

"Bear," she called in a strained voice. "Come here, Bear." When the mastiff trotted up, she patted him. "Where're the horses, boy?" she asked. "Where's Jonas's horse? Can you take me there?"

Bear cocked his head from side to side, as if trying to understand. Then, with a bob of the great head, he spun and ran outside. Merry hurried after him. Outside, she saw that the mastiff had stopped and was looking toward the house. When she came into view, Bear trotted off again. The dog stopped now and again, looking back to make sure Merry was following.

Merry finally got around the hill and found the two horses and two mules still staked out there. And the body, which she tried not to look at. She didn't know how Bear had understood her, or even if the dog really did. All she cared about was that she had found the horses and mules. She now had transportation and supplies. Merry petted and praised the mastiff. Then she undid the picket stakes and climbed onto Jonas's horse. She trotted to the house, towing the other horse and the two mules.

At the house, she dismounted and tied the animals off. Then she got a rope, went in, and tied it under Jody's arms, wrapping the other end around the saddle horn of Jonas's buckskin. Steeling herself about the indignities she was about to inflict on her brother-in-law's body, she took the reins of the horse and led it toward the grave. The rope tightened and then dragged Jody down the hallway and outside. Bear bounced around nearby as if directing the operation.

It took a little maneuvering, but she finally got Jody into the grave. Breathing heavily, Merry undid the rope and swiftly began covering Jody over with dirt. She would not allow herself to cry with the grief she felt; she just worked woodenly.

When she was done, she allowed herself some coffee, which

was hot on the stove in the house, and a few pieces of jerky and biscuit as she contemplated what needed to be done. The hardest work yet lay ahead for her—how to get Jonas back to Silverton, or anywhere else where he could get medical attention. Her immediate problem was how to carry him away from here. She could not lift him onto a horse, not when he was nearly double her own weight.

She took her time with her sparse meal, since she had not come up with a solution. Eventually, though, she had to get moving. The longer she delayed, the worse off it might be for Culpepper. She was about to give up in despair when the thought of dragging Jody to the grave came over again, as it had regularly since she had done it. She figured it was guilt, but suddenly she began to look at it in a different light.

"Hang on, Jonas," she whispered, as she got up and raced around the house. She found one of the doors from the back of the house lying outside. It was weathered and faded, but still mostly intact. She dragged it into the front room opposite where Culpepper lay. The stove was still hot. She got Culpepper's knife and one of the outlaws' pistols, which she unloaded. She put the knife into the fire and waited impatiently as it heated up. Then she jammed the hot blade into the wood of the door and twisted it around. Smoke curled as the blade burned into the wood. Merry grabbed the pistol and hammered the butt of the knife.

She had to do that several times, but she finally had a rough hole perhaps an inch in diameter in the wood. Merry went through the process again opposite the other hole.

Almost pleased with her handiwork, she set the knife down and dragged the door into the room and put it lengthwise next to Culpepper. Steeling herself, she went to Wiley's body and jerked his gunbelt free. She put it around her own middle, feeling a little odd, but yet somehow comforted. Then she got Culpepper's knife and slid it into the belt so she would have it handy. With a shrug, knowing it was necessary, she got some beans and bacon and put them on the stove to cook.

She took the old mattress from the bed and put it on the door. She got her rope and cut off several lengths. She threaded an end of one piece through the hole in the door and knotted it. Then she did the same with another piece of rope in the other hole. Last, she put three pieces of rope under the door, ends lying straight out from each side.

Then she worked Culpepper's body onto the mattress on the door, trying not to jostle him too much. He groaned a couple of times, and seemed to fidget once, but otherwise was oblivious. Then she knotted the ropes under the door around Culpepper to keep him in place.

When she had her husband on the door, Merry sat back a few minutes, breathing hard. Her arms and legs trembled some from the unaccustomed exertion, but she would not let that slow her down.

Merry went outside and unloaded Jody's mule, tossing the supplies off as she hurried. She left the pack saddle on the animal, though. Then she backed the mule inside and as far into the room as she could get it. She tied the ends of the ropes that were through the holes in the door to the pack saddle. There was plenty of extra rope dangling down. Once again, it took some maneuvering, but she finally managed to get Culpepper outside, where she had more working room.

She was tempted to just drag Culpepper along as he was, since that was easiest, but she decided the ride would be too rough on him. She had to get his body up a little, at least. With a smile, she picketed the mule. Then she got Culpepper's buckskin and backed it up near to the mule.

Merry unknotted the ropes from the pack saddle, and then tied them to the saddle horn on the buckskin, making sure each ran over the top of the pack saddle. "You make that mule stay where he is, Bear," she ordered, having no idea if the dog would understand, or if he could do the job even if he did.

It took some effort, as well as a heap of straining and shouting on Merry's part, but it finally worked. Using the pack saddle as a lever, she had managed to lift the door—the litter, as she now saw it—off the ground about two feet, at least on the side where Culpepper's head was.

The next part was a little tricky, too. Merry untied one of the ropes on the saddle horn and, making sure the litter did not tilt, she eventually got it tied to the pack saddle again. She rolled up the excess and hung it over one of the crossbars of the pack saddle. Doing the same procedure with the other rope was a little easier.

Breathing a sigh of relief, Merry went in and ate her bacon and beans, and drank some coffee. The food bolstered her and she felt a little better as she walked outside. "You ready to go, Bear?" she asked. "Huh? You're going to have to show me the way, you know."

She unhobbled Jody's bay mare and the one mule still laden with supplies. Finally she unhobbled the other mule. Merry climbed on Culpepper's buckskin, took the rope to the mule with Culpepper's inert form, and pulled out, praying that either the other horse and especially the other mule—the one with the supplies—would follow her, or that Bear would make them follow.

As she rode, following the huge mastiff as he trotted out a little head of her, Merry also prayed that she would get somewhere in time to save Culpepper.

Three days later, Merry rode into a small town. Bear had led her here, and she was grateful. She did not know how much longer she could go on. She had slept hardly at all, and most of what sleep she had gotten was in the saddle. She was weaving from exhaustion and felt like death itself.

Merry was dimly aware of people stopping to stare at her as she let the buckskin pick its way down the street. An older man hurried out of a building and stopped the horse. He was accompanied by two women, one older and pleasant-looking, the other young and quite attractive.

Questions filtered through to her at least, but she ignored them. "Where am I?" she asked.

"San Miguel," Silas Stanton said. "My God, Missy, what's happened here?"

Merry again countered with a question. "There a doctor in town?"

"Yes," Stanton answered. "We'll fetch him, but what happened?"

"Shut up, Silas, and go fetch Doctor Parmenter," Sarah commanded. "Can't you see this poor girl's done in? And Sheriff Culpepper looks half dead. Go. Go on, get."

Stanton nodded and hurried off. Two men came to Sarah's aid as she eased Merry down from the horse. "Take her up to room six," she ordered the men.

As the men started to go, Daisy stopped them. "Please, Miss," she pleaded, "where's Jody? I got to know." Tears welled up in her eyes.

"Dead," Merry whispered, overcome with grief. "Dead. He was . . ."

"Enough," Sarah barked. "Upstairs with her, boys." She turned to the crowd. "Some of you other boys come over here and get Sheriff Culpepper upstairs, too. Come, hurry."

Stanton returned with Dr. Parmenter just as three men were carting Culpepper carefully upstairs. The two men hurried after them. Sarah put her arm around Daisy's shoulders and slowly walked with the weeping young woman up into the room.

Parmenter checked Culpepper over first, cut into his back, and pulled out the bullet. Then he sewed him up and bandaged the wound.

"He going to live, Doc?" Stanton asked as Parmenter stepped back from Culpepper, wiping his hands on a cloth.

Parmenter shrugged. "Hard to say right now. He's lost a heap of blood, and it looks like this happened three, four days ago, to judge by the wound. It doesn't seem there's any infection yet, but I can't be sure with such things. He's a big, strapping fellow, and that'll help him."

Parmenter turned and went across the room. "Now," he said, "let's see how this young lady is."

"I'm fine," Merry whispered. She had fought off sleep all this time by waiting to hear what the physician had to say about Culpepper. Her anxiety helped her.

"Yes, ma'am, you're just fine," Parmenter said. "You won't mind if I take a look, though, would you?"

"No, sir. Just as long as Jonas is all right."

"He's as good now as he can be." Parmenter began checking Merry. As he did, he asked, "What's your relationship to Sheriff Culpepper?"

"I'm his wife."

"He told me his wife was the most beautiful woman in Silverton. I didn't believe him until now," Parmenter said, lying with ease. He knew Culpepper, but had never really spoken much to him, and certainly not about such personal matters. But since the last part of the statement was undoubtedly true, he didn't figure the lie was all that bad a thing.

Merry flushed a little, but was close to tears. *Wait'll Jonas wakes up and sees my hair,* she thought. *He won't think that no more.* Then she fell asleep.

Chapter 34

Merry slept for a solid sixteen hours, and when she awoke, it was in a panic. She thought then that everything had just been a dream—a horrible, dark vision from the depths of hell. Then she turned her head and saw Culpepper lying on the bed across the room, and she knew it was all real.

Merry spun on her buttocks, swinging her feet out of the bed and onto the floor. She sat up, vestiges of sleep still clinging to her. It took her a few moments to remember where she was and the details of how she'd gotten here. Despair swept over her anew, threatening to choke the life out of her. One great sob burst from her lips before she managed to gain control of herself. Culpepper still needed her help, she told herself firmly, and she would do everything she possibly could to see that he recovered. Maybe when this was all over he wouldn't want her anymore, she knew, and she could understand that, considering what had been done to her. Merry had a lot of confidence in the kind of man he was. There was no reason to think he'd cast her off. But that thought was ever present in her now.

She stood and looked down at herself. Her clothes were filthy and tattered. She spotted a mirror and went to it, grimacing when she saw her hair. Where it once had been her crowning glory, a sleek, brown mass that tumbled down to her buttocks, it was now barely shoulder length and choppy. She shuddered when she remembered Ned Coakley coming at her with the knife back in that festering hellhole of a cabin. She had thought at first that the marshal-gone-bad was going to kill her, but he had grinned evilly and grabbed her long hair. Then he'd begun hacking at it with the knife, laughing maniacally, while his men added to the sickening cacophony. Her heart had sunk, then, and she'd felt almost as bad as she had the first time the filthy outlaws had taken her. The hair had been a symbol to her. As long as she had it, she felt like her old self, no matter what else happened to her. But the butchering of her dark silken tresses was an outward sign of the abuse she had suffered as a woman. It was there for all to see.

Merry shuddered again and turned away from the mirror. She went to Culpepper's side and bent over him. He was still breathing strong and steadily, but his skin had an unnatural luster and was coated with a sheen of sweat. She wiped the perspiration from his face with the edge of the blanket, fighting off the tears and despair that in so short a time had seemed to become a part of her.

The door opened, and she spun, a little surprised, since Bear had not indicated that anyone was coming.

Sarah Stanton entered quietly, looking toward Merry's bed. When she saw it was empty, she looked around the room. Spotting Merry, Sarah smiled warmly and said, "You're finally up, child. We were getting worried about you."

Merry managed to work up a small smile. "You're the woman who helped me, aren't you?" she asked.

"Yes, child." Sarah came into the room. "I'm Sarah Stanton. My husband and I own this hotel." She put her arm around Merry's shoulders and looked down at Culpepper. "He's still alive," she whispered. "And while he is, there's always hope. Now come, child," she urged, tugging Merry's shoulders. "You'll need to eat."

"I am hungry," Merry admitted.

"Well, come on, we'll go to my kitchen and take care of that."

Merry jerked free of Sarah's grasp. "No," she said insistently, "I want to stay here."

Sarah nodded and smiled. "Of course, child. I'm not trying to force you into anything."

Merry smiled weakly. "I'm sorry, Miz Stanton," she said. "I don't mean to be troublesome."

"Of course you don't, child. And . . ."

"Please, Miz Stanton, my name is Merriam. I'd like for you to use it. Or Merry, if you prefer."

A small look of annoyance crossed Sarah's face, but she shook it off. This young woman had every right to want her to use her name. She also had been through a lot; that much was obvious. "Of course, chi . . . Merry. Now, what do you want to eat? Or should I just make something and bring it up?"

"Whatever you make'll be all right by me." She tried to smile but couldn't accomplish it. "Just make sure it's hot and there's plenty of it."

Sarah nodded and left. She stopped in the hall, thinking. Then she walked to Daisy's room. "That poor girl's been through an awful lot, Daisy," Sarah said. "And I'm worried about leaving her alone, now that she's up and about. Why don't you go over there and sit with her?"

"All right," Daisy said, with a distinct lack of enthusiasm. She had her own demons to wrestle with, and didn't really want to nursemaid someone else. Then she realized that Merry had probably had a worse time than she had at the hands of the outlaws, considering that Merry was a wife, not a whore, when she was taken.

"Don't let on that I don't want her in there alone," Sarah said. "If she asks, tell her you wanted to check on her—and Sheriff Culpepper."

Daisy nodded and smiled. "Especially since the last part's true."

"He don't look good," Sarah said with a frown. "I wouldn't expect too much if I was you."

Moments later, Daisy knocked on Merry's door and then

poked her head inside. "Mind if I come in?" she asked pleasantly.

"No, please do," Merry said from where she was sitting on the bed.

Daisy entered and petted Bear fondly for a few moments. Then she got a chair and pulled it up close to Merry's bed.

The two sat in silence for a little, neither knowing what to say. Finally, though, Merry asked, "How do you know Jody? You did ask about him right as I got here, didn't you?"

Daisy nodded. "Yep, I asked." She took some moments, biting her lower lip to keep from bursting into tears. "Jody and me were gonna get married," she managed to choke out.

Merry's eyes filled with water. "No!" she gasped. "That can't be."

"It's true," Daisy said, still fighting off the tears.

"But how . . . ? I didn't know . . ."

"How could you not know?" Daisy countered. "Sheriff Culpepper knew when he went back to Silverton the last . . ." She paused. Then, "Oh, my God, that was when you was taken away by Coakley and the others, wasn't it?"

"It must've been," Merry agreed, wiping away the tears. "Tell me what happened to you."

"Did Jonas . . . Sheriff Culpepper . . . tell you anything about me?" Daisy asked hesitantly.

Merry thought about it a moment. "You're the girl Jonas rescued from those outlaws, aren't you?"

"Yep. From Ellsworth and his men." She paused, nervous again. "He tell you anything else about me?"

"No. But I figured you had yourself a mighty bad time," Merry said sympathetically. "Judgin' by what I went through." She shivered involuntarily.

"Nothin' else?"

"No, not really. Only that he brought you to some little town—this one, I know now—and left you to try to find a new life."

"That he did. He even lied for me, makin' me out a better person that I am."

"Oh, no, he wouldn't need to do that," Merry protested.

"Yes, he would," Daisy said. She lowered her eyes in shame. "You see, Miz Culpepper, I . . . I wasn't exactly innocent of men before I was taken off by Ellsworth's men."

"You were married before?" Merry asked, surprised.

"No. No." Daisy shook her head, her loose hair swinging back and forth, obscuring the pinkness of her face. "I . . . I . . . worked in a . . . I was a . . ." She stopped and drew in a long breath and then eased it out. She brought her face up until she was looking straight at Merry. "I worked in a fancy house."

Merry was shocked and sat silently, trying to comprehend that this young woman, as pert and pretty as any Merry had ever seen, and just as demure, had been a prostitute. "I don't believe you," she finally said.

"It's true, though," Daisy said almost defiantly.

Merry was revolted, but then she thought about what she had suffered at the hands of Coakley and his men. Daisy had undergone the same at the hand of Ellsworth's outlaw gang. That she had made money by selling her body to whatever man wanted it didn't seem to matter much all of a sudden. They were kindred spirits, and Merry decided that Daisy must've had a good reason—and probably a heartbreaking one—for having entered the profession she had. And even if she didn't, Daisy certainly had changed since she'd been Ellsworth's prisoner. If she had planned to marry Jody, she must've been making a new life for herself. Unless Jody didn't know.

"Well, Miz Culpepper," Daisy said, rising, "I'm sorry to've imposed on you. I can see you want me to go, so I'll . . ."

Merry reached out and grabbed one of Daisy's hands. "You sit right back down here, Miss . . . Miss what?"

"Greenwalt."

Merry tugged a little on Daisy's hand. "Well, you just sit right back down here, Miss Greenwalt. Us girls got some talkin' to do."

"You sure?" Daisy asked uncertainly.

"Yes." Merry licked her lips. "I got one thing to ask first, though. I just got to know—did Jody know about you . . . your past?"

Daisy nodded.

Merry seemed relieved. "Sit. Please, Daisy." When Daisy had done so, Merry said, "Now, tell me the rest."

"There's not much to tell. When Sheriff Culpepper and Jody come through here that one time, me and Jody met. I'd never felt like that about any man before. He said he felt the same about me. I told him about my . . . well, you now, just so that he'd know and couldn't hold it against me later if he found out. You sure you want to hear all this?" she suddenly asked.

"Yep."

"Jody come back a few weeks later and asked me to be his wife. He said Sheriff Culpepper . . ."

"You're a friend, Daisy, you can call him Jonas."

Daisy smiled a little. "He said Jonas had gone back to Silverton, and that him and I were gonna go there just as soon as I was ready and get married there. We were making arrangements to leave when Jody got a wire from Jonas tellin' him to stay put. He rode in a couple days later, near done in. He told me and Jody that you'd been taken by Coakley. They rode out the next day. That's the last time I . . . I . . . saw . . ." Daisy began to weep, her shoulders shivering.

Merry moved closer to Daisy and patted her leg. She didn't know what to say. She wanted to tell Daisy that everything would be all right, but it wouldn't, and they both knew it.

Finally Daisy's tears dribbled to a halt. "I'm a mess," she said, nose stuffed from crying. She found a rag and blew her nose, but it didn't make her feel any better.

"You ain't half as bad a mess as I am," Merry said sourly. She ran her fingers through her hair.

"Your hair looks fine," Daisy said.

Merry got up and went to Culpepper's saddlebags, which someone had stuck in a corner of the room. She dug in them for a bit, until she found what she wanted. She turned and held the photograph out toward Daisy. "That's what it looked like before Coakley cut . . . hacked . . ." She bit back tears and anger.

Daisy took the photograph and looked at it, then back to Merry. "The bastards," she said flatly.

Merry looked shocked for a minute, then giggled, then laughed outright. Daisy laughed, too, and they suddenly hugged each other in newfound friendship and sympathy.

Merry was just putting the photograph away when Sarah came in with a tray of food. She placed it on the bed and left again, but returned in moments with another tray. Once more she left, and came back with a chair. She sat.

Merry shrugged and began eating. Sarah poured coffee for all three of them and she and Daisy sipped at it while Merry ate.

"You know what happened to me now," Daisy said. "Why don't you tell Sarah and me what happened to you?"

Merry did while still eating. "There's not too much to tell. Coakley was raisin' Cain in Silverton, and Jonas's deputy, Jimmy Cahill, was watchin' over me as best he could. He got word that Coakley was comin' for me and he hurried to the house, minutes before they got there. Eight of them hit the house, and Jimmy . . . Jimmy . . . tried . . ." Merry stopped eating and talking so that she could cry. She felt so forlorn.

Finally she composed herself again and went on. "Jimmy didn't have much of a chance. He got one or two before he went down and Coakley grabbed me. Outside, Marshal Hennessy got another one before Coakley's men gunned him down, too. Then we were racin' out of town. A few days later we got to Westville, I think they called that little place, where Coakley and his men . . ." She stopped from shame this time.

"It's all right, child . . . Merry," Sarah said quietly. "It weren't your fault, no matter what some folks might have to say about it."

Merry nodded, and brushed away some tears. "Then Jonas and Jody—and Bear, too—found me. I don't know how many they killed, but I counted four. I figure the other three got away. Jonas was shot right in front of my eyes. When I finally got free and went to look for something to use to help him, I . . . I found Jody. He . . ."

"Don't say no more," Daisy said with a cracking voice.

Merry nodded, joining her new friend in crying.

Sarah sat there wishing more than anything that she could help these two fine young women. But there was nothing she could do. They would have to get over their pain in their own way and time.

Merry finally thought she could continue. "I managed, somehow, to get Jody buried, then build that crude litter and get Jonas on it. Then I rode straight here, with Bear showin' me the way."

"Jonas would've never made it without you," Sarah said firmly. "And speaking of such things," she added, "I ain't sayin' bad things of Doc Parmenter, but I don't think he's as good a physician as you'll find in Silverton. I'd suggest we try to get Jonas to Silverton somehow."

Merry thought about that a bit, then nodded. "There's a wire in town?" When Sarah nodded, Merry said, "Take me to it, Miz Stanton."

Chapter 35

Culpepper awoke slowly, groggily. He was afraid to move. The last thing he could remember was the searing heat of the ball as it smashed into him and burrowed deep into his back. He figured he was dead, but then figured that there shouldn't be this much pain. And he didn't think his own bedroom would be in heaven. Or in hell, either, for that matter. That posed another problem. He was in his own room, of that much he was sure. How he'd gotten here from far-off Westville was perplexing. Then he realized that Jody must have gotten him here.

With extreme care, Culpepper moved his head a little, toward the right. Everything seemed to be in its usual place. He turned to the other side, and decided he was either in hell or having a nightmare. Merry—his beautiful Merry—was dozing in a chair. But her hair was a ragged, short mop, instead of the flowing cascade of beauty. Then it filtered back to him: he had seen that when he had burst into the room where Merry had been kept prisoner. There had been no time to ask about it then, of course, and then he was shot.

Bear came over and licked happily at Culpepper's face, tail going a mile a minute. The dog's excitement made Merry suddenly pop awake. She saw him and her eyes widened. "Jonas?" she asked in a whisper, pushing up from the chair.

Culpepper tried to speak but was having a lot of trouble, since his mouth was so dry. "Water," he managed to croak.

Without saying anything, Merry helped Culpepper up until he was propped against the headboard of the bed. Then, hands trembling, she poured some water from the pitcher to a glass and helped him drink it down.

"How's that?" she asked, when he had indicated he was finished.

"Better." Culpepper breathed deep and winced as pain stabbed into his back.

"You had us worried," Merry said, the fact evident in her voice and on her face.

"I suppose I did," Culpepper agreed, nodding a little. "How long I been out?"

"Near on two weeks now."

"That long, eh? Things're calm?"

Merry nodded, trying to keep herself from crying again. Having Culpepper come awake like this was almost too much to have hoped for. It seemed unreal now that it had happened.

"Where's Jody? I want to talk to him."

"He's dead, Jonas," Merry whispered, taking one of Culpepper's hands in hers.

Culpepper's face clouded with grief and anger. "What happened?"

"You sure you want to hear this now?"

"Yes." The word was flat and ugly.

Merry explained it, up until she got him to San Miguel. When she was done, Culpepper looked at her with new respect and compassion in his eyes. She had done all that for him, and while she was in such dire straits herself. "You are somethin'," he whispered. Then he looked perplexed amid his sadness. "But how'd I get here?"

"Miz Stanton thought the doctorin' here in Silverton'd be better than in San Miguel, so I arranged to get you back here."

"Not alone?"

"No, I had help."

"Who? How?"

"I wired Mister Pennrose."

"What'n the world for?" Culpepper asked, growing a touch angry.

"You're the sheriff of San Juan County. He's the head of the County Board. I figured he owed you. If I was wrong, he'd've told me, and I'd've made other plans. But he wired back and told me to sit right where I was, that he'd have some men come help."

"Did he?"

"He sure did. A few days later, a hundred of his men, all heavily armed, arrived in San Miguel with two wagons. He even came himself. The next mornin', with you and me in one wagon, and Daisy and Mister and Miz Stanton in . . ."

"Daisy and the Stantons're here?"

"Yep. They're your friends and wanted to see you get well. We got here a couple of days ago. They've been here most of the time. Right now they're off gettin' somethin' to eat at Moldovan's—Mister Pennrose is payin'."

"Well, I'll be durned," Culpepper said. Then he smiled a little. "You're the best damn thing could ever happen to a man."

"You don't hate me?" she asked, fear icily gripping her heart.

"Why would I hate you?" he asked, surprised.

"Because of what those animals did to me."

Culpepper shrugged, and winced with the pain again. "That wasn't any of your doin'. You didn't have no say in the matter." If he thought about it a little, he might get disgusted with her, but he would not allow himself to do that. She had undergone too much because of him; done too much for him. He'd be damned before he turned her out now.

"And this?" Merry asked, touching her hair.

"They do that to you, too?"

She nodded nervously.

"It'll grow back." Culpepper smiled at her. He was enraged at what they had done to her, at all the forms of abuse they had heaped on her. But he didn't want her to see that yet.

"I'll be a hundred years old before it grows back as long as it was."

"And I'll measure each and every week of that time, too," he said.

"You sure, Jonas? I'll understand if you . . ."

Culpepper placed a thick finger against her soft lips. "Enough, Merry. I'm tired and painin' too much to argue with you. I love you, and that's all there is to it. You're stuck with me, and there ain't no use in you fightin' it."

Merry wept with joy then, loving him more now than she ever had. And her heart felt big enough with pride to burst.

Culpepper let her go on for a bit, then whispered for her to stop. When she sat back, he asked, suddenly feeling some urgency, "How many bodies of Coakley and his men did you find in that cabin?"

"Four. Wiley, that one who shot you, one in the back room, where I found Jody, and one by your horses."

"That means three got away?"

Merry nodded.

"Durn."

"What's wrong?" Merry asked, suddenly worried.

"Coakley'll not forget this, and he'll not forget who did it to him. He'll be comin' for me if he thinks I'm alive, or for you if he figures I'm dead. He'll be here as soon as he recruits more men. That could be anytime now. We've got to get you—and Daisy and the Stantons—out of here as soon as possible."

"No, Jonas," Merry said firmly. "You've got to rest and get better."

"But . . ."

"Listen to me, my love," Merry insisted. "We're safe and protected here. Mister Pennrose has two dozen armed men around the house at all times. He has more stationed over at the office with Buster. And he's got several dozen more at his beck and call, if Coakley shows up."

Culpepper looked at her skeptically.

"We'll be all right. Now, are you hungry?"

"Yep."

"Doctor McQuiston said that if you came awake . . ."

"If?" Culpepper asked, laughing, but instantly regretting it as pain bounced around his back and chest.

"Yes, if," Merry said firmly. "Anyway, since you did, he said I can give you some soup. That sound all right?"

"I'd rather have me a giant-sized beefsteak."

"Well, you'll have soup and like it."

"Yes'm."

Culpepper made excellent progress in the following weeks, enough to astound Dr. McQuiston, who soon quit coming around.

"There's nothing more I can do for you, Jonas," he pronounced. "You have your friends here to help you. Now it's just a matter of getting your weight and strength back."

And he did, more swiftly than any of them—except perhaps Merry—would've thought possible. After two weeks, he was up and around, doing little jobs, walking through town, eating heartily. He grew annoyed with people always wanting to do things for him, and it became an effort to tell them pleasantly that he was quite capable of doing for himself. He wanted to roar at them.

Underlying his annoyance at his friends, and underlying the pain that lingered in his wound, was a festering, all-abiding hatred for Ned Coakley and anyone who dealt with him. His hate was strong enough to cover men like Mack Ellsworth, too, since if Ellsworth had not raided the train in Culpepper's jurisdiction, Jody would still be alive, and Merry would never have been debased by Coakley's men.

He quietly, steadily nursed the hatred, keeping it a strong but not overwhelming passion deep down inside. He wanted it fully ripe and ready to burst when the proper time came. He tried to keep it hidden from the others, and he figured he succeeded with all but Merry. Neither he nor she said anything about it, but he could tell in her soft brown eyes that she knew what was inside of him—and what it would take to exorcise it.

Sixteen days after he had awakened for the first time since being wounded, he turned to Merry in the night, reaching hungrily for her.

"You sure, Jonas?" she asked, fright and worry in her voice.

"Yep." He paused. "I've got to find out if I've got the strength again," he said softly. Her muscles remained tight, and he cursed himself. *Of course,* he thought. *After what she went through with Coakley and the others, she doesn't want anything to do with me or any other man no more. How could I have been so blind or stupid as not to realize that before?*

Culpepper rolled onto his back again, his head on the pillow. "I'm sorry, Merry," he said quietly, cursing himself silently. "I never thought about you, and what those men had done, and how it must make you feel. I'll leave you alone." He flung a forearm over his eyes and tried to calm himself enough to be able to sleep.

Next to him, Merry wept quietly. Coakley's men had robbed far more from her than she'd realized at the time. Until now, she had avoided thinking about what those animals had done to her. It had been relatively easy as she'd concentrated on helping Culpepper recover from his wound. Now that he was well on his way to doing so, it was natural that his mind would turn toward the intimate pleasures of his wife. And she had failed him. She wanted more than anything to just kill herself, thus freeing Culpepper to find a willing and deserving woman for his affections. But she could not bring herself to do that. Nor could she simply turn to him and tell him to go find another woman. And worst of all, she could not turn to him and offer herself to him the way she once had.

Culpepper was in a sour, worried mood the next day, and he left the house early. Merry, who was in no better humor, watched through the window as he slowly shuffled up the street. She wept in remorse at her inability to be a wife, in pain as she saw Culpepper take his still-labored steps, looking as if he had turned old overnight, in regret for what had been taken from her, and thus from her husband.

She choked off her tears and tried to clear away their traces when she saw Daisy and the Stantons coming. She could not hide the fact that she had been crying, though, and Daisy swiftly took her into the bedroom, sat her down, and asked sharply, "What's botherin' you now?"

Merry was reluctant to say anything, but after Daisy badgered her for a while, she finally spoke.

Daisy nodded, understanding. "You might want me to sympathize with you, Merry," she said. "Maybe even tell you that everything'll be all right. But it won't be all right if you don't let it."

"Huh?" Merry was confused.

"It's you who've got to get over what happened. From everything you've said, Jonas ain't bothered by it. Most men would've thrown you out as soon as they found out you'd been had by others. It wouldn't matter that you didn't ask for it or that you couldn't do anything to prevent it. They would've just sent you packin'. But Jonas wouldn't do that. No. He accepted what happened and showed that he still loves you enough to overlook it."

Daisy paused for a breather. She smiled crookedly. "Because of what I used to be and because I was so grateful for Jonas rescuin' me, I offered myself to him as a reward," she said, ignoring it when Merry flinched. "You know what he said to me? He turned me down flat. He said he had a wife at home that was as much woman as he ever could want."

"But how can I forget what those . . . those animals did to me?" Merry asked, her voice cracking with fear and self-loathing.

"You can't. But you can keep it from destroyin' your life."

"But how?" Merry almost wailed.

"I don't know," Daisy said fiercely. She liked Merry quite a lot, and wanted to help her, but there was little she could really do. "I just know I got over my past in a very short time, and I ain't no better than you. If I could do it, then, by God, you can, too." She stalked out then, leaving Merry to suffer in solitude.

Merry could do nothing that night, nor the one after, but the one after that, she turned to Culpepper in bed. "Jonas," she said softly, running a palm along his broad back, trying to avoid the bandage that still covered his wound. "Jonas, are you awake?" She was almost shivering with fear and worry.

"Yep," he said, not moving.

"Come to me, Jonas." Her fear was reflected in her quivering voice.

"No, Merry," he said. He was not bitter, just heartbroken. And enraged, not at his wife, but at those who stole his wife's lovingness. "It's all right, though."

"No, it's not. Now, turn around here and take me," she ordered. Her voice softened a little. "Please, Jonas, I need you to do that. For my self-respect, and for our marriage."

Culpepper turned to face her. "You sure?" he asked, gazing into her hurting eyes.

"More than anything." She fought to keep all her muscles from tightening as he ran his hands gently along her body. She kept her eyes open, locked onto his face, even when they kissed, just so that she could always remember he was the one who was with her, so she could see the love on his face.

She decided later—much later—that she could love her husband freely once again. And it came as a great relief to her. She would never forget what those men did to her, how dirty they had made her feel. But she could put those men, and the things they had done, out of her mind, separate them from her husband and his loving caresses. She wrapped herself around Culpepper, sighed, and fell asleep.

Chapter 36

Culpepper rode out of Silverton in the darkness. Bear trotted alongside, seemingly happy to be on the trail once more. It was close to the autumnal equinox, and at Silverton's nine-thousand-foot altitude, it was cold, so Culpepper wore his long, heavy bear-fur coat. No one looking at him these days could tell that he had been on death's door a little more than a month ago.

Only three days ago he had gone to see Wilson Pennrose for the first time since he'd gotten back to Silverton. He did not like being beholden to anyone, particularly to someone he was not all that fond of. But he had to offer his thanks to Pennrose. He might like to think that he could have recovered on his own, but he was not sure of that. So he swallowed his pride and made the now-long walk to Pennrose's office.

Pennrose was alone in the boardroom, much to Culpepper's relief. The sheriff figured after a moment that someone must have told Pennrose he was headed in this direction and Pennrose told the others to leave. It was a nice gesture, since if Pennrose had been planning to gloat, he'd have wanted to do it in front of the others.

Pennrose rose, smiling widely, and came forward, hand outstretched. "Sheriff," he said, with seemingly real pleasure in his voice.

"Mister Pennrose," Culpepper said, shaking his hand.

"Sit, sit," Pennrose said, waving to a chair. "Would you like a drink? Or has Doctor McQuiston put that out of limits for you?"

"If you don't mind, I'd as soon stand. I've been on my tail quite long enough to suit me. And, by God, I would like a drink. It's been a time. The doc ain't said anything about it, but if he was to object, I'd be forced to arrest him on charges of interferin' with a lawman in the sworn pursuit of his duties."

Pennrose laughed, poured Culpepper a drink, and handed it to him. He got one for himself and then he stood next to his chair. "What can I do for you, Sheriff?"

"First, you can have a seat. Just because I'm standin' doesn't mean you have to." When Pennrose had smiled and sat, Culpepper said, "I don't quite know how to express my gratitude for all you done for me and my wife, Mister Pennrose. You went far beyond what was called for."

Pennrose flushed, then smiled. "You might think, Sheriff, that I did it to get some hold over you, or to have you in my debt. But I swear on my dear departed mother's grave that such is not the case. For too damn long I treated you too lightly; got caught up in my own self-importance. But when those bastards—ones I'd let out of jail—did what they did to you and Mrs. Culpepper, I became something of a changed man, Sheriff. I helped as much as I did since it was I who was in your debt, but had been too damned stupid to realize it. I hope you can forgive me."

Culpepper was dumbfounded, and didn't quite know what to say. He was a little suspicious that Pennrose was trying to play him for a fool, though he had no idea what purpose that would serve. It was just so hard to believe that Pennrose was speaking the truth. "Well, I'd say we're about even now, Mister Pennrose," he finally allowed.

"Call me Wilson, please. And I'm not sure we're even yet. After all, there're still those outlaws to catch. Both gangs—Coakley's and Ellsworth's."

"To tell you the truth, Wilson, Ellsworth's gang doesn't mean a durn thing to me now. I come across them, I'll arrest them, or kill them. But right now I'm not lookin' for them. I want Coakley and his bunch, after what they did to my brother and to Merry."

"But they were the start of all this," Pennrose protested.

"I know that well enough. I'll eventually get to Ellsworth and his men. After I take care of Coakley."

Pennrose nodded, knowing it would do no good to argue. "When are you leaving?"

"Three, four days, I suppose."

"Good. I'll have a posse ready. Fifty men, do you think?"

"I don't want your posse, Wilson. This is a job I aim to do myself."

"Don't be a fool, Jonas."

Culpepper shrugged.

"I have plenty of men at my command."

"I know you do, but your men have no stake in this."

"Please reconsider, Jonas. Good Lord, man, I don't want you getting killed when we've just got you back among the living. And if you won't think of yourself, think of your wife, and your friends, who'll miss you if you get yourself killed in some foolhardy adventure."

Culpepper was silent for a little, then nodded reluctantly. "All right, Wilson. But only twenty-five men. Fifty'd be far too many to manage on the trail."

"Excellent. Now, when do you want to leave?"

"Today's Monday, right?" When Pennrose nodded, Culpepper said, "Friday mornin'. We'll meet up over near Maguire's store. Dawn."

"Very good." Pennrose actually seemed pleased. "Now, is there anything I can do for you beforehand, Sheriff?"

Culpepper though a moment, then nodded. "I'd be obliged if you had some men escort Mister and Miz Stanton back to San Miguel."

"Tell them to let me know whenever they want to leave. Or you come tell me."

Culpepper nodded again.

"And you can take the guards off the house."

"You sure?" When Culpepper nodded, Pennrose said, "All right."

Culpepper swallowed his drink in one gulp, enjoying its smooth ride down his throat. "Well, Wilson, I'd best be on my way. Once again, thanks for all you've done."

It wasn't until Tuesday night, though, that Culpepper explained his plan to Merry. She was not happy with it, though she knew it must be. And she agreed not to say anything to anyone about it. On Wednesday, he told Cassidy what was going on. He also saw Pennrose on Wednesday and nodded when Pennrose asked if plans were still all set.

Two hours before dawn on Thursday, Culpepper and Merry finally broke their loving embrace and rose from the bed. Culpepper ate a swift, hearty breakfast. He was just finishing when Bear's floppy face broke into a snarl. A moment later there was a knock at the door. Culpepper answered it.

"Everything's set, Jonas," Art Cassidy said. "Your horse and mule are around back. The mule's got plenty of supplies, and I made sure you had a good measure of extra cartridges."

"I appreciate it, Art," Culpepper said.

"It was nothin'. But I'll tell you one thing—I'm movin' out of Silverton if you get yourself killed. I ain't about to face your wife."

"I'll be all right, Art." He handed the man a twenty-dollar gold piece. "See you soon."

"I sure as hell hope so." He grinned crookedly. "Pennrose's gonna shit when he finds out about this."

"I know." Culpepper was inclined to believe that Pennrose had changed, but he still couldn't fully trust him.

Ten minutes later, Culpepper kissed Merry goodbye and swung into the saddle. He headed toward the low spot in the surrounding mountains that would eventually lead him to Red Mountain City, Ouray, and Horsefly. From there he would continue heading up the narrow valley northwest, through

Montrose, Olathe, and Delta. He had no idea where Coakley was, but he figured Grand Junction was a good place to start looking for him. If Greg Riddell, the outlaw he had questioned in Westville, was telling the truth, the money Ellsworth's gang had robbed from the train was buried someplace southwest of Grand Junction. Coakley had to know about it, and likely would be heading for there, since autumn was about to start. Coakley could recruit some gunmen in Grand Junction, and then wait for Ellsworth to arrive, hoping to follow the outlaw to the buried loot.

Culpepper pushed himself and the animals a little. He had little time, if his theory was correct, to get to Grand Junction. He also wanted to test himself a little, to see if he had regained most of his strength and stamina. By late on the second day of traveling, he came to Horsefly, and decided to spend the night there.

He had just finished unsaddling his horse at the livery stable when Marshal Sean Dowling found him.

"I heard you had ridden into town," Dowling said. "There's someone here you might have an interest in."

"I'm in no mood for guessin' games," Culpepper said tiredly.

"Hugh McLeod's in town."

"Where is he?" Culpepper asked, his face suddenly tight with anger. McLeod was Mack Ellsworth's right-hand man, and while Culpepper was less interested in Ellsworth than in Coakley, finding one of Ellsworth's men could lead to finding Coakley.

"The Wild Horse," Dowling said, mentioning the name of one of the saloons.

"Why ain't he in jail?"

"He ain't done anything in Horsefly that's broke the law. And I ain't paid enough to go around catchin' folks wanted by the county sheriff or by a goddamn U.S. marshal, neither."

"Big durn help you are." Culpepper's opinion of Dowling plunged. "You'd best go on back to your office while me and

Bear take care of business over at the Wild Horse." He shoved past Dowling and headed down the street toward the saloon.

He eased inside quietly and took a look around. He spotted McLeod and another man whose name he could not remember but whose face was on a wanted poster back in Silverton. They were sitting at a table near the back.

Culpepper eased a pistol out and began walking toward the two outlaws, his revolver held at arm's length along his right leg. As he neared the table, McLeod looked up, saw the star on Culpepper's shirt under the coat, and went for his Colt.

Culpepper shot him in the chest. By then, the other man had managed to get his revolver out, though not enough to use it. Culpepper drilled him twice—in the throat and in the forehead. He slumped sideways to the floor, blood splattering the boots of a man sitting at another table.

Culpepper kicked the table out of the way and grabbed a fistful of McLeod's bloody shirt and pulled him up a little. McLeod was living, but hanging on only by a thread. "Listen to me, you festerin' maggot," Culpepper growled. "A pukin' scoundrel of a federal marshal gone bad named Coakley knows about Ellsworth's plan to bury the loot, and he'll get it for sure, unless I can get to Coakley first. I got my own reasons for wantin' Coakley, so I ain't doin' this out of any love of you and your skunk friend Ellsworth."

McLeod knew he was dying and figured he had nothing to lose by speaking. His breath rattled around in his chest as he spoke, but he managed to get all the words out. "Southwest of Grand Junction," he gasped. "Monument Canyon. Up on a high rocky ridge, like part of a small mountain range, a few miles in, there's a real twisted-up tree, all bent around itself from the wind. Ten paces west of the tree."

"That's the first decent thing you've ever done, I'd wager, maggot," Culpepper said icily. He shoved McLeod back down, pulled the outlaw's Colt out, emptied it, and then tossed the revolver away. He dropped his own six-gun into his holster, then reached into McLeod's shirt pocket and found a small wad of bills. He peeled off twenty-five dollars, which he held in his left hand. He shoved the rest of the money into his pocket.

Culpepper turned and spotted Marshal Dowling standing by the door. He strode that way, people getting out of the way of the mean-looking sheriff and the even meaner-looking mastiff. Culpepper dropped the money on the floor at Dowling's feet. "That'll cover their burials," he snapped.

Culpepper hit the trail hard the next day, and within a week was in Grand Junction. The morning after, he headed southwest, going for Monument Canyon. It took two days of careful looking around before he thought he spotted the place McLeod had mentioned. He stopped and tied his horse off to a small juniper and then worked his way up to a flat on the ridge. Then he spotted his quarry.

Culpepper stopped behind a rock next to another bent and twisted cedar and petted Bear. Coakley was there, as was Neil Corcoran and another of Coakley's men who had been at the cabin in Westville. Ellsworth and another outlaw also were there, which surprised Culpepper. But by the way they were sitting comfortably and chatting with each other, the five evidently had thrown in together to split the money. Or else they had been in cahoots all along. Right now, Culpepper didn't much care.

"This is San Juan County Sheriff Jonas Culpepper," he shouted. "I'm orderin' all of you to surrender and submit peaceably."

All five outlaws went for their guns. Culpepper ducked behind his rock and began firing in return. In the midst of the gunfire, he spotted Ellsworth trying to maneuver around the great twisted tree so he could come up behind Culpepper. "Go get him, Bear," Culpepper said, pointing to Ellsworth. "Now!" he said, as he opened fire with his rifle, snapping off shots as fast as he could work the lever to give the mastiff some covering fire.

Culpepper heard screams as Bear attacked Ellsworth. Soon the screams ended and there was silence from that area. Culpepper risked a glance that way and saw that the huge, floppy-eared mastiff was moving toward Corcoran.

Culpepper hurriedly reloaded his rifle, watching the dog charge Corcoran, latching onto the man's gun arm. Corcoran screeched and kicked out, but he was no match for the almost two-hundred-pound dog.

Ellsworth's outlaw friend suddenly popped up from behind a rock, firing like mad in Culpepper's direction. Culpepper ducked as lead flew around his haven, whining off the rock or chunking heavily into the small cedar. Then he heard a single shot from a different direction, followed by a high-pitched yelp from Bear.

He stuck his head over the rock and saw Bear lying there near Corcoran. The dog was not moving.

"How're them apples, you son of a bitch?" Coakley bellowed with a hoarse, angry laugh. "I shot that precious goddamn mutt of yours."

Culpepper set his rifle down and pulled his two pistols. In a rage at all the grief Coakley had caused him, he stood up in one flowing motion. "Son of a bitch bastards!" he roared, as he began walking forward, firing as he went. Bullets took down the outlaw from Ellsworth's gang, as well as the other man of Coakley's, the one he did not know. He even put a couple of bullets into Corcoran, who was still moving, even though Bear had done some damage to the man before being shot down by Coakley.

Coakley had dropped behind cover again, but now he came out into the open. He grinned as he brought his rifle up. "Now it's your turn, you son of a bitch," he crowed. He fired, and his face fell when the hammer simply clicked.

"Dumb, pukin' maggot," Culpepper sneered, as he dropped his pistols into the holsters. He pulled off the big bear coat and dropped it as he stalked toward Coakley. He wanted to get at Coakley with his bare hands.

Coakley spun and began to flee, trying to reload his rifle unsuccessfully as he did so.

"Go on and run, you putrefyin' skunk," Culpepper called. "There ain't no place you can run that I can't find you."

Coakley stopped, dropped the rifle, and turned. "I am pure sick of your shit, you two-bit lawman. Come on at me, you overstuffed piece of shit, and I'll finish the job that Lou couldn't back at that cabin."

Culpepper had not slowed his approach, and he was closing in on Coakley fast. The lawman-gone-bad suddenly charged. The two met hard, and stood each other straight up. Culpepper found he didn't have nearly as much strength as he used to, but his rage gave him a power Coakley could not match.

Culpepper flung Coakley down finally, and then dropped down on him with one knee landing on Coakley's chest. Coakley groaned as he heard bones crack. Culpepper stood and hauled Coakley up with him by the shirt. He threw Coakley into the twisted tree and kicked the lawman as he fell.

Once more Culpepper dragged Coakley up, and then began pounding his head against the tree trunk, until it was a bloody, broken mess. Culpepper finally let the body fall. He stood there with chest heaving as the wind whipped and whistled around him.

With sunken heart, Culpepper turned and walked to Bear. The great mastiff was dead. He went to where the outlaws had dug up the loot, grabbed the shovel, and enlarged the hole considerably before walking back to Bear. He bent and managed to lift the huge dog and carry him the few feet to the hole and placed him in it. Then he covered the animal with dirt. As he patted the dirt down, he muttered, "Goodbye, old friend."

Culpepper barged into Pennrose's boardroom and dropped the heavy box on the table, ignoring the look of anger on Pennrose's face.

"Where've you been?" Pennrose demanded. "Why'd you slip out on your own?"

Culpepper ignored the questions. Instead, he said tightly, "Your money. Coakley's dead. So's Ellsworth." He turned and left, heading for home, and his wife.

ERNEST HAYCOX
IS THE KING OF THE WEST!

Over twenty-five million copies of Ernest Haycox's rip-roaring western adventures have been sold worldwide! For the very finest in straight-shooting western excitement, look for the Pinnacle brand!

RIDERS WEST (17-123-1, $2.95)
by Ernest Haycox
Neel St. Cloud's army of professional gunslicks were fixing to turn Dan Bellew's peaceful town into an outlaw strip. With one blazing gun against a hundred, Bellew found himself fighting for his valley's life — and for his own!

MAN IN THE SADDLE (17-124-X, $2.95)
by Ernest Haycox
The combine drove Owen Merritt from his land, branding him a coward and a killer while forcing him into hiding. But they had made one drastic, fatal mistake: they had forgotten to kill him!

SADDLE AND RIDE (17-085-5, $2.95)
by Ernest Haycox
Clay Morgan had hated cattleman Ben Herendeen since boyhood. Now, with all of Morgan's friends either riding with Big Ben and his murderous vigilantes or running from them, Clay was fixing to put an end to the lifelong blood feud — one way or the other!

"MOVES STEADILY, RELENTLESSLY FORWARD WITH GRIM POWER."
— THE NEW YORK TIMES

Available wherever paperbacks are sold, or order direct from the Publisher. Send cover price plus 50¢ per copy for mailing and handling to Pinnacle Books, Dept 4440, 475 Park Avenue South, New York, N.Y. 10016. Residents of New York and Tennessee must include sales tax. DO NOT SEND CASH. For a free Zebra/Pinnacle catalog please write to the above address.

FOR THE BEST OF THE WEST, SADDLE UP WITH PINNACLE AND JACK CUMMINGS . . .

DEAD MAN'S MEDAL	(664-0, $3.50/$4.50)
THE DESERTER TROOP	(715-9, $3.50/$4.50)
ESCAPE FROM YUMA	(697-7, $3.50/$4.50)
ONCE A LEGEND	(650-0, $3.50/$4.50)
REBELS WEST	(525-3, $3.50/$4.50)
THE ROUGH RIDER	(481-8, $3.50/$4.50)
THE SURROGATE GUN	(607-1, $3.50/$4.50)
TIGER BUTTE	(583-0, $3.50/$4.50)

Available wherever paperbacks are sold, or order direct from the Publisher. Send cover price plus 50¢ per copy for mailing and handling to Pinnacle Books, Dept 4440, 475 Park Avenue South, New York, N.Y. 10016. Residents of New York and Tennessee must include sales tax. DO NOT SEND CASH. For a free Zebra/Pinnacle catalog please write to the above address.

DANGER, SUSPENSE, INTRIGUE ...
THE NOVELS OF

NOEL HYND

FALSE FLAGS	(2918-7, $4.50/$5.50)
THE KHRUSHCHEV OBJECTIVE	(2297-2, $4.50/$5.50)
REVENGE	(2529-7, $3.95/$4.95)
THE SANDLER INQUIRY	(3070-3, $4.50/$5.50)
TRUMAN'S SPY	(3309-5, $4.95/$5.95)

Available wherever paperbacks are sold, or order direct from the Publisher. Send cover price plus 50¢ per copy for mailing and handling to Zebra Books, Dept. 4440, 475 Park Avenue South, New York, N.Y. 10016. Residents of New York and Tennessee must include sales tax. DO NOT SEND CASH. For a free Zebra/ Pinnacle catalog please write to the above address.

FOLLOW THE SEVENTH CARRIER

TRIAL OF THE SEVENTH CARRIER (3213, $3.95)
The enemies of freedom are on the verge of dominating the world with oil blackmail and the threat of poison gas attack. *Yonaga*'s officers lay desperate plans to strike back. Leading a ragtag fleet of revamped destroyers and a single antique WWII submarine, the great carrier must charge into a sea of blood and death in what becomes the greatest trial of the Seventh Carrier.

REVENGE OF THE SEVENTH CARRIER (3631, $3.99)
With the help of an American carrier, *Yonaga* sails vast distances to launch a desperate surprise attack on the enemy's poison gas works. But a spy is at work. The enemy seems to know too much and a bloody battle is fought. Filled with murderous rage, *Yonaga*'s officers exact a terrible revenge.

ORDEAL OF THE SEVENTH CARRIER (3932, $3.99)
Even as the Libyan madman calls for peaceful negotiations, an Arab battle group steams toward the shores of Japan. With good men from all over the world flocking to her colors, *Yonaga* prepares to give battle. The two forces clash off the island of Iwo Jima where it is carrier against carrier in a duel to the death—and *Yonaga*, sustaining severe damage, endures its bloodiest ordeal in the fight for freedom's cause.

*

Other Zebra Books by Peter Albano

THE YOUNG DRAGONS (3904, $4.99)
It is June 25, 1944. American forces attack the island of Saipan. Two young fighting men on opposite sides, Michael Carpelli and Takeo Nakamura, meet in the flaming hell of battle that will inevitably bring them face-to-face in a final fight to the death. Here is the epic battle that decided the war against Japan as told by a man who was there.

MAKE THE CONNECTION

WITH

Z-TALK
Online

Come talk to your favorite authors and get the inside scoop on everything that's going on in the world of publishing, from the only online service that's designed exclusively for the publishing industry.

With Z-Talk Online Information Service, the most innovative and exciting computer bulletin board around, you can:

- ♥ CHAT "LIVE" WITH AUTHORS, FELLOW READERS, AND OTHER MEMBERS OF THE PUBLISHING COMMUNITY.
- ♥ FIND OUT ABOUT UPCOMING TITLES BEFORE THEY'RE RELEASED.
- ♥ DOWNLOAD THOUSANDS OF FILES AND GAMES.
- ♥ READ REVIEWS OF ROMANCE TITLES.
- ♥ HAVE UNLIMITED USE OF E-MAIL.
- ♥ POST MESSAGES ON OUR DOZENS OF TOPIC BOARDS.

All it takes is a computer and a modem to get online with Z-Talk. Set your modem to 8/N/1, and dial 212-545-1120. If you need help, call the System Operator, at 212-889-2299, ext. 260. There's a two week free trial period. After that, annual membership is only $60.00.

See you online!

KENSINGTON PUBLISHING CORP.